An innocent Beauty. A fearsome Beast. A dangerous passion.

Mystery and speculation surround "the Dark Prince," a sorcerer who dwells in a kingdom cursed by endless winter. Though shunned by all, Prince Stellan secretly crusades against a zombie plague unleashed by his tyrannical father against the Five Lands. But only an alliance with Aldebaran will provide the support he needs to eradicate the plague once and for all

Clarysa, daughter of the Aldebaran king, struggles under the weight of her role as princess. She yearns for adventure, but her father prefers to keep his youngest daughter safe within the palace walls. During one of her rare sanctioned trips beyond the walls of the castle, Clarysa comes face to face with the answer to her prayers.

She's heard the tales of Stellan's dangerous nature. She knows a romance with him is forbidden. But one smoldering glance draws her deep into a world of dark magic and sensuous rapture.

Books by Heather Massey

Lord of Snow and Ice

Published by Kensington Publishing Corporation

Lord of Snow and Ice

Heather Massey

LYRICAL PRESS
Kensington Publishing Corp.
www.kensingtonbooks.com

I dedicate this book to my wonderful husband, a man who never ceases to amaze me.

Acknowledgements

A hearty thanks to the Lyrical Press team for being so enthusiastic about my story. In particular I'd like to thank my editor, Dianne B., for her detailed and instructive editorial insight.

Author Foreword

"Beauty and the Beast" is truly a story for the ages. Its themes will resonate with fans no matter the time period. For me, Disney's 1991 animated film version deftly captures the elements that make this classic tale so wonderful.

But even more incredible is the film preceding it by 45 years, Jean Cocteau's La Belle et la Bete. Cocteau's 1946 black and white interpretation of the traditional fairy tale is packed with atmosphere, danger, and fantasy.

Disney's Beauty and the Beast bears a striking resemblance to Jean Cocteau's film, including a fearsome beast, a magic-filled castle, and enchanted objects. That kind of homage tells you something about the power of Cocteau's work. In fact, I recommend you drop everything (well, after reading this book!) and watch La Belle et la Bete if you haven't already done so. It'll be the ultimate "Beauty and the Beast" feather in your cap.

Lord of Snow and Ice is my ode to "Beauty and the Beast." This revisionist fairy tale both inverts and subverts "Beauty and the Beast" while also featuring many of the familiar elements you've come to enjoy in such a story. During the course of this particular adventure, you'll encounter magic, danger, forbidden romance, and erotic thrills.

So don your coat, hat, scarf, and gloves because you're about to enter the mystical, wintry realm of the Lord of Snow and Ice.

Chapter 1

As Prince Stellan bent to quench his thirst in the cold waters of the Elysian River, he didn't know which sight shocked him more: the beautiful young woman who lay on the far side of the grassy riverbank, or her unabashed nakedness.

A rush of adrenaline coursed through his tired limbs as blind instinct seized control. Bereft of cover, he dropped into a crouch, keenly aware that his lean, black-clad figure left him dangerously exposed against the surrounding grasslands. He knew well his reputation as "the Dark Prince." If he were caught wandering outside of his icy realm, the consequences would be severe.

Pain shot through his back, the result of a twelve-hour patrol that had knotted his muscles with vicious glee. He ignored it, allowing his wind-parched eyes to fully drink in the vision.

Who was this woman? Why was she here? Such a sight was scarcer than plump, ready game in his desolate world--a realization that only caused his hungry body to ache for more. His ragged, desperate breaths hammered in his ears. A trickle of sweat tortured his right cheek. He didn't dare make a move to wipe it, lest he cause the fawn across the river to bolt. She was no doubt beyond hearing range, but he couldn't take the chance.

Stellan sank even lower. His raging heart pounded louder and louder. Were her eyes open or closed? Difficult to tell from this distance. As a hunter, he knew subterfuge was paramount in these situations. He inched forward. Beside him, his great black stallion lowered its head and drank noisily. Stellan's head spun. He'd almost forgotten about his companion. *Sorry, my friend, but I require your absence.*

Stellan whirled upward and led the horse back to a copse of trees. Here, it was completely hidden. He tethered the animal and attached a feed bag to its head. Now Stellan could observe at his leisure, for he had to learn more about the mystery woman intruding upon his secret resting spot.

At least, he had thought it secret. Stellan emerged from the trees with a quiet, measured gait. The woman came into his view once more, prompting shivers to course through his body. Springtime had wrought more than just copious greenery and sumptuous blossoms. As befitted the large, wealthy kingdom, Aldebaran's countryside was bursting with life. This woman was no exception. She looked like a nymph birthed from velvety petals.

A thin, shallow tributary meandering along Aldebaran's eastern border, the Elysian now brimmed with liquid silver from the melted snow of Falcon Heights. As Stellan crept closer to its edge, he coaxed a bit of saliva down his shriveled throat. A stir of any kind could mean his death. Among the local kingdoms, his reputation for odd, secretive behaviors was hardly one to engender much trust, if any at all.

Furthermore, in this very moment, Stellan was demonstrating that he didn't care about earning any.

Folk thought him oblivious, but they thought wrong. He heard the rumors, the gossip, the lies. They called him savage, bloodthirsty, and a lunatic, among other less congenial terms. Whatever the appellation, it was always spat forth with bile and scorn, underscored by fear.

He couldn't help his wry smile, for he did nothing to dispel the hearsay. Resentment had hardened his heart as surely as bitter cold induced frostbite. What did he care? Let them think he was a sorcerer of ill repute, of delirium. Let them think he culled his servants from the ranks of the undead, lining the halls of his decrepit castle and summoned forth when the macabre appetites of his kind possessed him.

Then he abruptly sobered. Some of the tales had origins in truth. A pang of regret surfaced, but he ground out the feeling as one would an ember. No matter. He could hardly do much about it right now.

Besides, he had a more pressing concern at the moment. Should the woman glance up in just the right way, she would espy him through the sparse wall of brown-tipped reeds. They swayed in a gentle breeze, enough to block his view with maddening precision. Of all the places in Aldebaran, why had she chosen *this* one? Then again, most would certainly question *his* presence in Aldebaran. If she recognized him, he'd be hunted until captured, perhaps even killed. In the Five Lands, a sorcerer--even one of royal blood such as he--was no better than the lowest beast.

Parting the reeds, he gazed around in all directions. A cream-colored mare grazed on verdant grass a mere stone's throw from her mistress. Stellan frowned. There must be a lady's maid or husband nearby. *Surely this woman wasn't so foolish as to frolic alone in a remote area!* Aldebaran was protected by regular patrols of the army's finest, but dangers hovered at the edges, constantly searching for entry at the weakest points.

Dungeon Forest, from which he had recently emerged, was also known to harbor certain…things as well, abominations to all life. The woman risked much in visiting this area by herself. He would have to exercise extreme diligence on her behalf. But there was more to it than that. Despite the potential threats, she intrigued him. He stayed to hungrily ingest every vibrant, exciting detail.

She lay on her back, one arm stretched above her head. The other rested across her stomach. *Such an invitation!* With a heated blush, Stellan fantasized about slipping his hand into her small one as he draped his tall frame upon her. The sight of the blond, glossy hair surrounding her face stirred unfamiliar feelings within him. Ensconced beneath the drab, overcast skies of a snow-laden kingdom he often loathed calling home, Stellan was not accustomed to such brightness.

Skin reminiscent of goldenrod wrapped her petite frame. It betrayed many such hours soaking up fresh air. Casting an eye toward the midmorning sun, he decided it paled in comparison to her beauty. Now thoroughly entranced, he greedily continued his appraisal. Pleasant, unblemished features marked her as royalty. There were other telltale signs as well. Only a member of a royal family would spend time so frivolously. The rich, lustrous sheen of her clothing was another giveaway. The fabric formed a deep puddle on the grass next to her.

Then there were her tantalizing and very full breasts.

The sorcerer stared, drawn to the forbidden nature of the sight. He had only seen one other pair of breasts, ones belonging to his adoptive mother as she nursed her infant son years ago. These before him now were of a different class entirely--exuberantly plump and firm. Pink tips jutted toward the sky, the perfect size for a man's mouth. Stellan gripped the soft earth beneath him, squeezing it between an ever-tightening fist as he struggled to maintain control.

The woman was easily half a day's ride from the nearest village. What purpose brought her here other than a sunbath? He had thought this stretch of riverbank to be little traveled by Aldebaran's citizens, if at all. Needing stealth and seclusion, he came to the spot periodically for respite during patrols. Years earlier he had even built a covered trench here for supplies.

Food. Clothing. Medicinal herbs. But mostly for weapons--weapons rife with deadly, magickal properties. Stellan had learned about them from another outcast, an apothecary, but he rarely made contact with him lest he endanger the man's cover.

The trench was invisible to the naked eye. But if someone like this young waif decided to go searching for pebbles or flowers or whatever females yearned to collect... Stellan grimaced. It would not do for common folk to tamper with them. Not at all. The weapons were for one purpose, and one purpose only: extinction of the abominations.

He had depended on this area remaining deserted. Obviously, that was not the case now. With a quiet sigh, he realized he would have to relocate. Though the woman's presence indicated a definite intrusion, it was one Stellan found he didn't mind so very much. The feeling both surprised and troubled him.

Movement roused him from his thoughts. The living painting stretched her arms back and rolled lazily over to one side, facing away from him. This left him with a clear view of her ripened bottom, a curvaceous peach ready to satisfy his hunger. He wanted to burst from his hiding place and claim her. Then he'd steal her away to the darkness from whence he came.

But Stellan made no such move. He'd given up on the idea of a lover long ago.

Like a barbed, relentless torture device, exile had eroded vital parts of both his mind and temperament. It was sapping at his humanity despite his sworn mission to protect the Five Lands from the nameless blight. He couldn't escape the loss no matter how many hours he spent diverting time with his ancient pipe organ, seeking solace that withered away with each passing note. Stellan sighed. Then another beguiling sight beckoned him.

The woman's legs... She was rubbing them together. The golden thighs alone promised untold pleasures far into the night. Stellan wiped the sweat from his eyes. *Damn this temptation!* What was he thinking, anyway? He had another patrol ahead of him and a long, cold trek home once he left the fertile lands of Aldebaran. The woman was proving a dangerous distraction.

And yet, he couldn't look away.

Now she had rolled back, apparently restless in her sleep. This action provided him with a view of not only her breasts, but also the seductive curve of her belly--and her sex. It glowed as temptingly as her hair.

The lush tableau prompted such wild fantasies that Stellan had to bite down hard on the inside of his cheek. Either that or release a loud moan of primitive longing. Though resigned to a lifetime of bachelorhood, he still had needs. This woman, with her wanton display of rapturous, unaffected beauty, wasn't making his solitude any easier to bear. Neither would she appreciate his intrusion, if he made his presence known. So why was he prolonging the torture?

As his conscience waged a debate about his inappropriate advantage, a swift, hard rush of heat caused a stirring and lengthening between his thighs. The prostrate position into which he had flung himself grew increasingly unmanageable. He ached for much softer, wetter comfort than the unyielding ground. Even though his mind didn't know quite what it wanted, his body definitely did.

Above, a few light, fluffy clouds cavorted with the sun. The blue sky seemed particularly vivid today. But it wasn't the golden orb's shameless heat or the breathtaking panorama of distant, white-capped mountains making his blood thrash and boil with arousal.

As anguish tempered overzealous attraction, Stellan clenched his teeth. Truly, why was he entertaining such boyish daydreams? He had left those behind even at the age of fifteen, the year of his banishment. Thanks to his purported "family," he had neither time nor inclination for romantic relationships. His sister's betrayal still burned hot in his soul. Up until that point, he had thought he and his twin were inseparable. Impregnable. One mind, one soul, and one heart. Together, they would have ruled a powerful, mystical kingdom. But in a single hour, Stellan had destroyed everything. The Black Mage may as well have killed his son, "the traitor," than forced him into the depths of that cursed region--an endless hell of frozen horrors deep in the heart of the Five Lands.

Painful memories surfaced with their usual vigor. *I only did what was just, and for my action I was rewarded with nothing but ruin.* Inside, locked away in the deepest pit of his being, a sense of abandonment gnawed with sharp, voracious fangs. Sexual relations merely scratched the surface of the closeness he craved. But he was far too damaged to be of value to anyone. Far too bitter.

Because of all these factors, the woman who lay in peaceful repose would never want him. The knowledge that she--or any woman--could never be his sent a sharp lance of pain into his heart. She would sooner toss lye into his face than to look at him. Seeing one so enchanting was a stark reminder of his barren life, one made all the more egregious by the chilly wastes blanketing his kingdom. Even when the sun shone feverishly everywhere else, brutal winter storms draped his habitat with veils of ice.

Despite his woes, he wanted to sweep his fingers across her flawless skin, delight her with provocative touches. Her parted lips begged for capture, for feasting, and Stellan was one to deliver. He felt sure of it. The thought of one of her breasts in his mouth was almost enough to soothe his dry throat, especially as he also imagined burying a hand between the folds of her sex. By now, under a hot, steamy sun, it must have been dripping.

Ah! Stop it! Stellan shut his eyes fast against a tide of raging libido. He willed his dark part to take over, the part that hated, seething with anger. He could know neither pleasure nor comfort, nor beauty or love. A crusade such as his couldn't be swept aside for mere indulgences of the flesh or the heart. Much work lay ahead, and he ought to be planning a clean escape. He had to exercise better control. His conscience demanded nothing less.

But when he opened his eyes, there was movement again. *One more look, then. One more to last me the rest of my life.* Stellan angled forward, breathing hard. He was now at the water's edge. Dragonflies and gnats buzzed about his dampened black locks, but he didn't care. He hoped the woman would turn onto her stomach so he might catch a glimpse of her bottom again. The anticipation made such a tightness of his leggings that they threatened to tear. Heavens but he wanted to drink every drop of her!

Then he frowned. It wasn't the woman who was moving.

Stellan rose a few inches and gazed around. He studied the river, the woods, and the long stretches of grass. In the end, he found nothing untoward. Perhaps in the heat of his fixation he had let his imagination run wild. All the more reason he should depart. He had just begun to edge back from the river when a blur of movement passed across his vision.

He narrowed his eyes. There it was, near the woods! Something had moved the tall grass bordering the trees on the opposite side. Tufts of greenery jerked back and forth. At first, it seemed random, as though the victim of impish field mice. But the longer he watched, the more quickly a pattern emerged. Every muscle tensed, turning to stone as he poised for the worst. Surely one of *them* wouldn't be so brazen as to travel this far?

He glimpsed a patch of brown. Could it be a swarm of rodents? Or perhaps an earth tremor loomed, threatening a cave-in. A large swath of grass shifted unnaturally, disproving his suppositions. Stellan wiped sweat from his forehead. What was causing the mysterious movement?

Then his scalp tingled, and not because of sexual arousal. Squatting, he parted the reeds. Though his eyes could not yet discern the type of animal coursing through the grass, other senses, evolved among his kind for generations, had different means of analyzing this new development. Magick was present, and one of the most hostile sorts in existence. The creature began to emerge more clearly. Its mottled-brown hide stretched far back into the woods even as it pushed forward toward the river. Stellan could both sense the enormous size and see the disturbance it created among the flora. As though revolted, the trees and grass seemed to flatten themselves away from it. This undulating menace was not indigenous to Aldebaran, of that much he was certain.

Stellan rose. The new vantage point revealed startling details. Before him was a huge slithering entity, not quite a snake, but not exactly a lizard, either. With its misshapen legs and crooked, gangly protrusions, it reminded him of a centipede, albeit the largest he had ever seen. The image was too fantastic to describe, even for the tallest of tales.

A chill passed through him. He'd been so busy studying the pulsing quagmire of flesh that he'd momentarily failed to gauge its purpose.

The creature was heading straight toward the woman.

Cursing, he leaped forward--and then fell. Snarling, he glanced down. Ropy weeds latched fast to his black boots as if trying to yank him underwater and drown him like the merfolk of legend. But only one thought dominated his mind: save the woman.

To accomplish that goal, he needed supplies from his saddlebag. With a violent kick, he freed himself and lunged toward the trees concealing his horse. It seemed too great a distance to cover. But cover it he must, or feel his soul burn eternally for failing.

Once at the horse's side, Stellan wrenched the bag free. After affixing a coil of rope to his right shoulder, he ran back toward the river. He gulped in great breaths, pumping his legs past their limits. At this point, it didn't matter if the woman saw him.

Words spilled from his lips, syllables of ancient tongues summoning forces from phantasmagorical realms. With a final, guttural inflection, Stellan flew across the river, the tips of his boots skimming the water's surface. At the far bank, he jumped nimbly over a boulder and ran up the slope.

A putrid smell washed over him. The sickening scent suggested a mountain of deer carcasses dripping with rancid fat in the summer's hot sun. He covered his nose and mouth with a gloved hand. But now, at least, he knew his adversary.

As so often was the case, the whole encounter made him ill--physically ill, but also emotionally. This foul creature had no right to invade such healthy, wholesome land. Furthermore, it represented all he held in contempt about his own kind. Yet the ignorance of Aldebaran's citizens troubled him only slightly less. *Fools, all of them!*

Before he could catch his breath, the creature reared at least ten feet into the air. A lolling, cactus-like appendage formed some kind of antennae. Too many bristly, clicking pincers to count made a madcap of its head. Undoubtedly they were poisonous. Its red-slashed hide leaked sallow-colored pus, sloughing off in random bursts. Globs of it now littered the surrounding grass. Slowly, the grotesque brute began swaying back and forth, acting as though time was its slave to abuse with impunity.

Why, and for what purpose? Any further philosophizing on the vagaries of nature would have to wait, however. Its heinous existence strengthened his resolve to conquer and abolish it. Were he any other man, Stellan might simply have whisked the woman away to safety, where no doubt a kiss of gratitude would be his to claim. Perhaps more. But he wasn't just any other man. Indeed, some would say he wasn't a man at all.

A hungry thought blasted his mind. The alien craving was ancient and primitive and greedy--*feed.*

Stellan debated whether he should call out to the woman. Did slumber have such a stranglehold on her senses? How could she be so heedless? But in his heart he knew she could not have known the danger. She was an innocent person simply enjoying nature's bounty. Over the years, Stellan had done his job almost too well, but as of late his fortune had been changing. This awful development was proof enough of that. Nevertheless, for whatever reason, the woman was clearly unaware of the hoary predator.

The creature stopped swaying. Stellan caught a flash of bright red. A protrusion he hadn't noticed before now extended from the creature's maw. Long. Vein-ridden. Thick. Stellan shaded his eyes against the bright sun as the appendage lengthened. Alien sensations invaded his mind once again. Rape and devour, devour and rape--in no particular order. The intent was all too clear--the creature meant to ravage the woman as fully as it knew how.

Stellan's features contorted with disgust, but then a wave of shame coursed through him. Ripe memories of rampant lust echoed in his mind. He'd just had a brush with his own animalistic tendencies. Was he any different than the beast before him? The woman deserved far better regard than he had given.

He had to act now. If he failed, then his only task would be to rip open the beast's body to free nothing but a dead woman.

The creature was drawing its abominable length into a lopsided, uneven coil even as its upper body targeted the woman. The dangling rod of flesh stretched before it like a herald.

No! Stellan rushed toward it. He lashed his rope around the centipede's head. He'd force it away from the woman and into the woods. There, hidden from prying eyes, he'd destroy it.

That was the plan, anyway.

Stellan pulled hard—and crashed to the ground. Sharp stones dug into his back. He gritted his teeth against the pain. He dug his ankles into the ground and pulled again. The rope grew taut. His feet carved deep grooves in the soft earth, yet the creature moved only a few hand-lengths.

It's useless. This damnable thing is too strong! He would have to kill it first.

Stellan lashed the rope to a nearby tree. He rummaged in his satchel for the needles with bulbous gray tips. Moving quickly, he inserted them into the creature's flesh. Then he retreated to a safe distance.

The monstrosity twitched. *So hungry,* came the thought, followed by a questing probe. It turned around, seeking the source of disturbance. Then Stellan's neutralizer began coursing through its body, infusing it with a searing, thaumaturgic fire. Its primitive mind broadcast an onslaught of excruciating pain.

But it didn't die.

Damn! Distracted by convulsions, at least the creature would be easier to wrangle. Stellan untied the rope.

The creature's talon-studded tail shot toward him. A gust ruffled Stellan's hair as he dodged it. His only chance for control would be to tie the thing into a great knot of rope and sinewy body. Stellan leaped back, his gaze never straying from the unearthly chimera. He tossed an additional loop of rope around the creature's upper body. Would it be enough?

It whipped around to face him. Multiple pincers along its midsection began clicking. The undulating mass slithered forward, coiling, tightening, mandibles stretched wide.

The centipede lunged, aiming for his head. Stellan pulled hard on the rope and shifted to his right. Sharp mandibles clamped upon a nearby tree.

Stellan drew a small dagger from its sheath. With a quick downward stab he made a deep puncture in the scaly hide. Dark green ichor swelled from the point of contact. The creature shrieked and released its hold on the tree.

The dense blanket of pines harbored deep shadows--all the better for two dark forces to clash. Stellan redoubled his efforts at pulling the creature after him.

But the bedeviled vermin grew shrewder with each passing second. Even as it fought off Stellan, another part of it somehow kept slithering back toward the woman.

"Wake up!" he shouted at her while dodging the creature's jabs. "*Wake up!* Get away before you're killed, woman! There's danger here, *danger*!"

On and on he roared. Soon he noticed the place where she had lain was nothing more than flattened grass. But he didn't dare allow himself relief until he saw her leaving or he killed the creature, whichever came first.

With a great heave, he coerced the sprawling, twisted mass farther into the woods. Pine needles scratched his face and for a few alarming moments the low hanging branches obscured his vision. All he could hear was the creature's ominous chorus of clicks and hisses.

His opponent thrashed violently. Stellan sensed its rage and frustration. The rope began slipping through his hands. He desperately held the last few lengths, but it was precious little leverage. As he grasped for new ideas he witnessed an unexpected sight--the woman stood at the edge of the woods. She was tugging her dress onto her shoulders and peering among the trees. What in the name of the heavens was she doing? Why wasn't she running away?

"Hello? Who's there?" She cupped her mouth. "Who's in there?" she said loudly.

Annoyance burned a frown upon his face as he sidestepped one of the creature's darting pincers. She was calling out a *greeting*? Madness!

"Run away, you fool," he shouted back. "Run and don't stop!"

Still, she hesitated. This was growing tedious. Stellan couldn't contain a venomous beast and indulge a curious sprite at the same time. He uttered an incantation--a basic one, but all he could spare at the moment. A small yellow flare appeared. Narrowing his eyes, he sent it hurtling through the woods. The impact ignited a branch by her shoulder. After one look at the consuming flame, she turned and bolted. Stellan knew the expression of shock and fear etched upon her face would haunt him in nightmares forever.

Regardless, he had a task to complete. Now that the woman was no longer a liability, Stellan could prepare his final attack. He focused his mind, drawing the eldritch energy about him. The surrounding air crackled with black discharge as he unsheathed his weapon of last resort.

He raised the roughly soldered metal tube and aimed it at the creature. Propelled by magick, three nut-sized pellets shot forth. Within seconds they unleashed their power, incinerating the beast without mercy. Stellan moved upwind of the foul stench, watching in silent vigil as the obsidian fires consumed first the rotten hide and then melted its internal organs. By the end, neither pincer nor protuberance was left unburned.

As the flames withered down into a messy lattice of ashes, remorse filled him. Despite his shield of bitterness, he missed the woman already. He lamented the fact that he'd not even had the courage to introduce himself, or ask her name. A heavy heart dragged behind as he gathered his belongings and returned to his horse.

While his steed drank its fill at the river, Stellan consumed a meal of dried meat. He intended to patrol for a few more hours and would venture deeper into Aldebaran territory than usual given his recent encounter with that abomination. Once full, he emptied the trench of its contents and filled the gaping hole with dirt. His steed faced an arduous journey with the extra weight, but better a little muscle strain than discovery of a certain sorcerer's intentions. He quickly bathed to remove the sweat and grime from his body.

Once mounted, Stellan guided his horse northeast. He did not look back. Instead, he rode on, a dour, black streak against the vivid landscape. Resolve burned in him, more than any day during his untold years of crusading. The woman symbolized everything good and pure in the lands, everything worth saving from the vile ambitions of his clan. Even though Stellan could never know the beauty's name, be with her, or see her again, he vowed to protect her.

Stellan knew he would continue protecting her--silent, invisible, and beyond her knowledge, until the day he died.

Chapter 2

Duke Lionel of Belleressort led the charge of seven riders and their horses across the northern hunting grounds of Aldebaran. Rumbling hooves announced their presence as they streaked across the valley. Panicked rabbits sprinted for their burrows. A sea of multicolored birds took flight in all directions.

With a collective determination they advanced, leaping and lunging after their elusive prey. The intended target was a white stag, one of only seven thought to be left in the world. It was a magnificent beast built of solid muscle and a flowing mane white as winter's first snow. The animal sprang through a sea of tall grass, all of which magically parted before its slender legs struck even a single blade. It was all Lionel and his men could do to keep up, for the stag moved so fast it left a stream of blue radiance trailing in its wake.

Nevertheless, Lionel rode on, undaunted. They had been chasing it for an hour, and with good reason. For as anyone worth his salt in basic necromancy knew, the essence culled from such an animal's tail alone could extend one's life many a year--perhaps even decades.

Now this *is a hunt*! *Give us your best, oh mighty beast, for soon I shall have you stabled and tamed in the bit of my golden bridle.* Lionel broke into a broad smile as he thought about this animal in his stables-- oh, how it would drive the others mad with envy! They should gnash their teeth bitterly and curse his name behind his back as gardens of young ladies swooned before him. Ah, yes, this would certainly be a day long remembered.

As the thunder continued across the verdant dale, he savored the sharp, woody scent of the wind as it whistled past his ears and snapped through his regal coiffure's honey-blond locks. Therefore he missed the telltale signs of gullies and other obstacles pockmarking the uncivilized ground.

The duke's horse swerved without warning to avoid a particularly nasty patch of brambles.

Lionel tightened his grip on the reins. *Heh.* True, perhaps he should be far more consumed with the path ahead than with his dashing good looks. His favorite cousin was bound to agree, seeing as how she was always ready with a witty chastisement--or two, or three--about his grandiosity and inflated ego.

But then, what was the point of worrying when a rider like him looked this marvelous? *Forgive me, Clarysa, but I am too far gone!* Lionel's smile widened. What tales minstrels would weave of this day! What legends would spring from it!

He thought back to the comely young woman he had met at the ball the night before. He could barely recall her name, but he remembered the gorgeous red tresses that had spilled across her creamy white bosom so enticingly. She'd spotted him from across the room, and he her. No doubt she had been staring at him with those smoldering cobalt eyes for simply the longest time. What would she say upon catching wind of this adventure? What a sight he would make for her today, his red cape arched gracefully in the air, his broad chest a veritable shield against the elements. Yes, incomparably impressive! He would have to visit the young wench soon and tell her all about it.

The laws of reality arrested Lionel's fantasy. His horse vaulted over a muddy hole. The movement jerked him forward as the sound of nearby hooves crashed against his ears. First left, then right. Lionel quickly glanced about him to get his bearings. The gaining horse belonged to Prince Edward, his cousin and heir to the Aldebaran throne. Edward's dark features were clustered in a resolute expression. He clearly meant to overtake Lionel at any cost.

Not this time, you bugger. Lionel's ego still bore scars from the last few hunts when Edward had soundly trumped him.

"You ride like my sisters!" Edward shouted. A smug look plastered his face as he whipped past Lionel.

Lionel kicked his horse into a gallop. Neck and neck, the two riders pulled ahead of the others. The edge of another forest surfaced in the horizon, but they did not slow. He found himself distracted; the competition now involved who was the better rider with the faster horse. The stag was forgotten, banished from his mind. Only besting his cousin remained in the forefront of his recently bruised ego. He spurred his steed forward in a mad dash toward the trees ahead, right at the spot the stag had dove into moments earlier.

Faster and faster his horse sped. The wind tore about his ears, as if shrieking his success. Lionel rode parallel alongside Edward and then passed ahead with ease. To this victory, he said nothing, for Lionel felt he was not one to rub the proverbial salt in another's wounds. Instead, he simply threw back his head and laughed.

Edward tossed off some other quip, which Lionel supposed was meant to goad him, but the wind snapped up the words in its powerful jaws and swallowed them. Even the very elements about them seemed to favor the fair-haired one of Belleressort. *And now for the real test.* Lionel glanced ahead at the maze of tangled growth. *Let's see you beat me now! I'll have that stag in my stable yet.*

Before he could relish his victory further, an anguished screech rendered all else mute.

Lionel brought his horse up too quickly and it reared. Edward, advancing rapidly behind him, banked sharply in avoidance. The other riders slowed and grouped around them haphazardly.

"What in high blazes was *that*?" cried Edward.

Lionel cursed, fighting to regain control of his spooked steed. "It came from the woods ahead," he announced through gritted teeth. "Confound it, horse! Stop flouncing about like a skittish cat!" His agitated tone did little to assuage the frightened animal beneath him.

The men stared ahead into the enveloping darkness of branch and leaf, their mouths agape. "Something must have happened to the stag," said one finally.

"Probably a wolf," added another. "Or a mountain lion."

A weighted silence poured from the forest. Lionel peered toward the edge. His breathing sounded unnaturally loud, as did the panting of his companions. When he spoke, his words came out flat in the still air. "No mountain lion could capture that stag." He looked solemnly at his cousin.

"Maybe the scream was a tactic to scare us off," said Edward. His voice, too, lacked normal resonance.

Then Lionel realized what was missing--every single ambient sound. *How bizarre.* "Well, should we enter here," he said, gesturing to the uneven path before them, "or split up and--wait, did you hear that?" His right hand immediately shot up, a signal for absolute silence.

The sound of splintering tree limbs cracked the air.

Then again.

And again.

A heavy thumping sound soon followed. Edward motioned for the men to regroup. Without hesitation, they formed a line. Shallow ruts developed as the horses, nostrils flaring, dug into the grass with their hooves. Some of the trees shook, scattering their leaves like flies in a maelstrom. Then...nothing.

Lionel waited with his men, hardly daring to breathe. Finally...

He blew out a breath. "Oh, it's nothing but an earth tremor. Let's continue, shall we?"

Edward threw up his hands. "It wouldn't kill you to wait another minute."

"Perhaps for you, but *my* minutes are very precious." Lionel urged his horse forward at a trot, but it took some doing as the animal didn't share his confidence.

He had just reached the shadow of the nearest branch when a particularly loud *crunch* shattered the air about him. A tremendous growl followed. Low at first--guttural. This was followed by mile-deep intonations, the bass of which seemed to shake the very earth around him. Lionel stiffened. As his horse eased slowly back, he did not move to stop it.

He made a quarter turn, attempting to keep one eye on the forest. "I... think we may have something here."

A colossal, bloated creature advanced from between two trunks. It rose up on two massive chunks of hind legs. Viscid slabs of flesh ringed them from hips to paws. Bits of leaves and twigs clung to darkened flesh that perhaps once had sprouted fur. Oozing red sores as wide as a man's chest spotted the creature, which was now moving considerably faster as it neared the clearing.

Lionel's gloved hand flew to his face. A preposterously foul odor preceded the animal. It smelled worse than a sop barrel. Worse even than the entrails of a freshly slaughtered animal. Lionel wondered where he had encountered the scent before. Then he remembered.

It smelled like death.

But despite the unmistakable odor and loathsome hide, the creature lived. Its mucus-coated eyes fixated on Lionel and his horse.

"Run, Lionel!" urged one of his men.

Lionel risked a quick look back. His companions stared at the monster with a mixture of fascination and disgust--here was a creature unknown to any of them. But Lionel only allowed his horse to retreat several feet. *Such an abomination*, he thought. *An animal this horrid* must *be destroyed*. With slow urgency, he drew his sword.

"Steady," he whispered. But the horse, an intelligent creature now convinced more than ever who had the better sense, inched timidly back.

The hideous beast growled again. Its putrid breath washed over Lionel like a wet, suffocating blanket. The animal's heavy jowls flopped back and forth while a blackened snout peeled back to reveal what was left of its large white fangs.

With a snarl, it attacked.

Lionel roared and hoisted his sword, but he was too late. Lumbering forward, the beast raised one of its filthy paws and swiped away, knocking him from his horse. The ground rushed toward him at a ridiculous velocity. He bounced upon landing and heard a sickening *pop* as his right arm bore the full force of the impact. Intense pain racked his body within moments.

The earth shook beneath him. Raising his head, he watched in a daze as the beast singled him out and began to accelerate.

"Bloody sword, where are you?" he mumbled. Consciousness threatened to slip away. Vaguely, he heard Edward shouting something and was aware the men were regrouping. Did they mean to save him? "You'll never make it in time," he said hoarsely. "Just get away!"

The air about the beast began to sing. Arrows filled the sky, but it was all for naught, ineffectual. Shooting the creature seemed much like shooting into a pile of mud. The arrows merely glanced off, or hung loosely in the beast's thick hide. The creature might as well have wandered into a cluster of windborne dandelion seed. Rocks and other sharp objects launched from slingshots were none the better. Nothing slowed its advance, nothing.

Lionel groaned. The bloated monster seemed intent on plunging its decomposing gums into his neck for sure. He tried to crawl away, but his arm had lost all motivation to cooperate. He thought back to the red-haired wench. She'd believed him to be "quite striking--breathtakingly so." Was this to be his epitaph?

Then seemingly out of nowhere, another rider appeared, dark as shadow. Lionel watched groggily while a black horse leaped into the gap between him and the monstrous beast. The mystery rider drew and fired a number of arrows in quick succession, succeeding in piercing the hide in several places where Lionel's men had not. The creature halted, bellowing out its pain and swatting clumsily at the points of contact.

Astride his horse, the stranger glanced over his shoulder at Lionel. His head was ringed with the hazy aura of the afternoon sun, and the effect obscured his features. "Now would be a good time to run," he urged.

Even through the fog of pain, Lionel discerned the confident, resonant tone of the man's voice. *Who in the Five Lands are you?* A bout of snarls and barks erupted on his right. Lionel stared in amazement as a large white wolf joined the fray, its face twisted into a menacing grimace. Fur stood on end as it slowly circled the mutant animal like some sort of perimeter guard.

Calmly, as if it would be a sin to rush, the mystery man pulled an object from a well-worn sack and affixed it to an arrow tip. He raised his bow, then fired. The arrow landed in the center of the creature's gaping maw.

The animal stopped. It advanced toward the stranger a few feet and then stopped again. Confusion plagued its movements. The monstrosity began to sway. Its angry wail ripped through the air, one filled with the haunted, choking gasps of a being meeting its mortality. Lionel watched in fascination as the creature cascaded to the ground in one stinking, sordid heap.

The beast that smelled like death was no more.

Three sets of eager hands clutched at Lionel and dragged him back a good twenty feet from the spectacle. But the show was not over, and he watched in avid interest.

Nudging his horse forward, the mystery man approached the corpse and dismounted. He withdrew more items from the sack and knelt. A long black cape shrouded his actions, but he obviously had further intentions with the carcass.

Some of the men shifted closer, appearing curious. But they were ordered back not only with the rider's fierce glare, but the bared fangs of the white wolf.

Edward knelt by Lionel, brushing back sweaty locks of his thick, brown hair. "I don't like the looks of him," he muttered.

Lionel shushed him with a hand.

A crackling sound punctured the silence, and the smell of sulfur wafted through the immediate area. The corpse burst into flames, but not with the warm yellow light of a hunting lodge fire. Tinged with green, this one seemed to burn inwardly, as if burrowing into the creature's flesh. The pyre assaulted the men's nostrils with a suffocating smell as it burned.

Lionel had to see more. "Help me sit!"

Edward obliged. Lionel tossed back his cape and inspected his injured arm. It hung in his lap at rather an odd angle. He also felt weak. *Whatever you do, be a man and don't faint. Most definitely do* not *faint!* The pain gnawed at him, the likes of which he had never experienced before in his twenty-two years. How long would he have to bear the horrid anguish?

None of his companions were proper healers. And the ride home would take hours. Lionel sucked in his breath hard, as if stiffening his insides would offset the pulsing throbs. *Do...not...faint!* His eyes begin to involuntarily close. Darkness drank his soul.

Then, something changed. He experienced a presence like no other. Lionel opened his eyes. When next he glanced up, it was into the face of the stranger.

The man knelt and reached toward Lionel's arm, but Edward intervened and pushed him back roughly. "No one touches the duke without permission!"

The two men glared at one another. Edward slowly reached for his hunting knife, secured by his side. This movement did not go unnoticed by the stranger, whose eyes gleamed with preternatural menace. In the background, the wolf steeled itself with a low, treacherous growl.

"No!" Lionel exclaimed. "We'll have none of that!" He admonished his cousin with a look and declared, "I'm the one in excruciating pain here, so humor me." Reluctantly, Edward backed off. Lionel gave a quick nod, inviting the stranger in for a closer examination.

The man laid gentle fingers upon his twisted limb and then sprinted to his horse for more items from another sack. He returned and began to administer aid at once.

Lionel studied him openly as he worked, but he seemed oblivious to the attention. The pale stranger was handsome, in a raggedy sort of way. He was tall and muscular, but somewhat thin. Glossy, raven black hair shorn into uneven locks framed an angular face with high cheekbones and lips set in a determined line. Exquisitely etched brows lined emerald green eyes. Their lashes were thick and dark, but not overly pronounced.

Lionel made particular note of his clothes. Every last stitch screamed black, but the careworn material looked faded. By the number of visible loose threads, this was either the man's preferred outfit, or his only one. One detail in particular caught his attention over everything else--an embroidered, multicolored patch covering one elbow. *Good heavens! Does he seriously think that's acceptable fashion?* But the outfit's classic tailoring hinted of something noble, something...regal?

As the stranger set his shoulder back in place, Lionel was literally snapped out of his reverie. "Ouch! You might have warned me," he told him, attempting a graceful smile through gritted teeth. Lionel swore he saw the hint of a smile in return, but it disappeared as quickly as the thought itself had come. Perhaps he was mistaken. The stranger did not seem one to often part with a grin.

Lionel was quite the opposite though, for soon he felt better--much, *much* better. The man had rubbed some kind of ointment into his skin. It soothed the pain completely away. *What healing skill is this? I must know more about this man.* After his arm rested in a makeshift sling, Lionel spoke. "Well, friend, may I know the name of my hero and savior?"

The stranger glanced uncertainly to one side, and then resumed packing his belongings. Wordlessly he stood, and his cape flicked smartly behind him as he walked to his horse.

"Oh, but I must know!" Lionel rushed to his feet, ignoring Edward's glare of disapproval. Arriving breathlessly at the stranger's side, he reached out his good arm and thrust his hand into the stranger's for the firmest handshake he could manage. "A good…no, a *great* deed such as yours will be acknowledged as loudly as I can shout and as far as I can ride." He flashed his most charming grin, and continued to shake the stranger's hand. To his delight, the man clasped his in return. "You must join us for the evening repast. It's the least I can offer in return for your services, Sir…ah…?" Lionel cocked a brow and continued to pump his hand, waiting for a response.

"Stellan," said the stranger.

Lionel interpreted his averted gaze for shyness. *I would feel shy too, if I had a patch on my elbow.* "Well, Stellan, what brings you to the hunting fields of Aldebaran?" He leaned in conspiratorially, sweeping his lips into a half grin. "Something tells me you're not from around here."

"How very astute," Stellan responded in a low voice. He busied himself with securing his pack.

Lionel laughed. "And my reputation precedes me! Come, my kin and friends will feed and warm you." He stared reproachfully as Stellan began to mount his horse. "You'll pain me greatly if you leave now. You could have simply minded your own business, but instead saved my pitiful neck from that godforsaken hellion. One does not forget such a deed. I will be tortured until the end of my days if you don't allow me to grant you even a single drop of gratitude."

Stellan regarded him with lips parted in surprise. He searched Lionel's face for a long moment, ignoring the other men who had gathered around. His guarded mien dissolved ever so slightly, like an icicle being kissed with day's first sunlight. "All right," he said, releasing his grip on the reins.

"Splendid!" Lionel swiveled his head to and fro. "Well, what are you all standing around for? Stellan's hungry, I'm hungry, an adventure comes to a close--now to feast!"

* * * *

During the evening meal, as dusk surrendered to night, Lionel fixed his gaze on his new companion by the light of a blazing fire. He had never seen an appetite so voracious or seemingly bottomless. Stellan consumed the food with candid gusto. Long, slender fingers swept each morsel up in a graceful arc to his mouth. Nary a crumb made its way to either his lap or the ground. *It's as if he hasn't eaten in days.* Lionel dumped another half platter of roasted meat and root vegetables onto Stellan's plate and poured wine to overflowing in his goblet.

They sat slightly apart from the others. Lionel was fully aware Edward occasionally shot a suspicious glance in their direction from the other fire. Lionel acted as if he hadn't noticed. *Cousin, will you ever stop being so desperate for control? I'm not one of your sisters.*

He sipped from his own drink while waiting for Stellan's gorging to abate. Twenty minutes or so passed before he saw an opening to speak. "So, my friend," Lionel began, "where do you hail from?"

A sliver of meat flapped from Stellan's fingers as he gestured west. "Beyond the plain."

Lionel maintained a polite expression. A gentle coaxing was in order. This man represented a world of mystery, and he was determined to uncover every last clue. "I see. But *where* beyond the plain?"

Stellan eyed him over his goblet's rim, and then swallowed heartily. "This is good wine."

Lionel chuckled. "Agreed. But again I put the question to you--*where* beyond the plain? Regardless of what you may have heard, I don't bite." A curious eyebrow arched upward.

Stellan's answer was in the form of a noncommittal expression. He was obviously weighing his options. Finally, he answered. "You know of Dungeon Forest?"

"Of course." Lionel had heard the legendary tales of the dark place since childhood.

"It separates my home from Aldebaran. I hail from Vandeborg Castle."

"Ahh," Lionel said, leaning forward. Intrigue made his heart beat faster. "Can it be... You are *the* Dark Prince? We've heard so much about you for years, but quite frankly I didn't know if you truly existed. Amazing! Strange tales are whispered about you, my friend, not to mention your wintry kingdom."

Stellan paused midchew, then shrugged.

"Nevertheless, it's an honor to meet you."

Stellan nodded and then resumed eating.

"So tell me about that, er, the mons--"

"A moment, Lionel, if you please!" The voice cutting him short belonged to Edward, who gripped him tightly by the uninjured arm and pulled him up.

"Uh, yes, hmm...pardon me," he muttered, confused at the sudden interruption. Edward dragged him out of their guest's earshot.

"I wouldn't advise you to get too friendly with that...with him," Edward stated, his features locked in a troll-like scowl.

Lionel arched a well-manicured brow. Whenever Edward bandied about phrases such as "wouldn't advise" it was actually code for "This is an order." Lionel, however, was no servant. "Really? On what grounds?"

Edward's gaze darted to their guest, who was still feasting away. His furrowed countenance left no doubt as to how he felt about their visitor. "How do we know the rascal did not guide that monstrosity here?"

Lionel snorted. "Ha! That's ludicrous and you know it." He swept back a lock of hair from his face. "I had just begun an interrogation when you so hastily interrupted. Did you know he lives in Vandeborg Castle? Stellan is the very Dark Prince himself. Remember when Old Man Griffin used to tell us stories about him? 'A magician with powers most macabre!' And to think, you used to doubt his existence as a child." Lionel grinned. "I seem to recall how you once wagered a full week's chores against ever laying eyes upon him. Well there he is!" He stroked his chin. "I fear my larder has grown frightfully dusty of late. Do you think you can start on it tomorrow?"

Edward gave Lionel a rough shake. "This isn't a game. Think, man! Why is he here? His behavior is suspicious. Don't forget--he's trespassing on the King's lands. My father will *not* be pleased."

Lionel flashed his eyes. "Is that how you plan on reporting this to the King? That he's hunting on--oh, dare I say it?--on *hunting* grounds?"

"Rubbish! The beast was cursed. This ruffian is not hunting for pleasure. I say we arrest him now and transport--ack...*what?*"

Lionel had gripped Edward's collar with his good fist. He drew him closer until they were nose to nose. "You will do nothing of the sort. This 'ruffian' saved my life, and probably the whole lot of us." He gave his cousin a flabbergasted look. "And you want to *arrest* him for it?" Lionel shook his head. "That's bad politics...very bad politics." He sneered as his competitive streak reared to life again. "Let's see how many of the men support you on this."

Edward pried open Lionel's grip and took a step back. "Fine," he retorted. "Play with your little friend if you must. But I'll be watching his

Heather Massey

every move, and if he trespasses again, he's mine!" With a final warning look, Edward stalked back to his seat.

"Not if I invite him first," Lionel called after him.

Edward shot back his most withering glance, but Lionel merely laughed. Straightening his tunic, he resumed his seat next to Stellan.

"He doesn't have to like me, you know."

Lionel wasn't surprised Stellan had so accurately discerned the topic of their conversation. He waved a dismissive hand. "Edward may be the King's son and heir, but he can also be incredibly boorish and shortsighted. Don't worry about him."

"I wasn't."

"That makes two of us." A yawn seized Lionel as the day's events suddenly took their toll upon his tired body. He clapped Stellan's shoulder and regarded him kindly. "I fear exhaustion claims me. Here we must part. Once again, I am incredibly grateful for your help today. I am in your debt, and I always repay what I owe."

Stellan put down his empty goblet. "It was nothing."

"So says you. Listen, we hunt here the last two days of every month. I invite you to join us whenever you wish as my guest." Lionel then leaned in with a smile and added, "And as my friend."

Stellan nodded in thanks. "You should get some rest." As he stood, his horse emerged from the surrounding darkness. The steed's flowing dark mane whipped about burning blue eyes. Lionel stood in awe of its gargantuan size as Stellan deftly mounted it.

The Dark Prince turned to Lionel with a thoughtful look. "One other thing, mind what you hunt. A scourge is upon the game you seek, and it's quickly spreading." After delivering his warning, Stellan whispered something into his horse's ear. Then rider and horse took off--faster than candlelight snuffed out in a cold winter's wind.

Lionel, perplexed, now stood alone with his thoughts. *"Scourge?" Now what exactly did he mean by that?*

Chapter 3

"Thanks for inviting me." Sarcasm dripped in torrents from the woman's statement and seemed to slide down Lionel's bedroom walls only to congeal onto the floor below.

Lionel started; he hadn't realized anyone was in his room. He pulled aside the nearest blue velvet curtain. Late afternoon sunlight rippled across the interior, revealing a petite figure propped against the matching brocade pillows on his bed. She wore a shimmering gold gown, but her mood didn't match the luxurious fabric. Her arms were crossed and she stared petulantly up at the ceiling.

"Fancy meeting you here, Clarysa."

"You know why I'm here," she growled.

Lionel smirked. "Well, fair Princess, like I explained before, you can't come along on every expedition. It's for men only. We do a lot of, you know, manly things and such." He tossed his cape onto the bed and opened his mahogany wardrobe.

Clarysa scrambled into a sitting position. "But you promised! You said not the next time, but the one after."

Lionel studied the wardrobe's contents. "I did not."

"Fibber!"

He swept his good arm into a dramatically wide arc, as though a performance artist. "And so it shall be! You'll accompany us...the following expedition after the next."

Clarysa's eyes narrowed. "That's exactly what you've been saying for the past five outings! I--what happened to your arm?"

Lionel had removed his vest and was struggling with the buttons of his shirt. "An attack. A wicked creature appeared, the horse spooked, and I fell...confounded...Johann!" he said, summoning his valet. "In my bedchamber, if you please!" Lionel sat on the bed and began to remove his boots.

Clarysa tugged at his sleeve. "What kind of creature? Did you kill it? Is it here?"

He eyed his cousin, an audacious woman of nineteen years. Vivid hazel eyes stared back, voyeuristic and eager. "It's kind of involved. Do you really want to hear it?"

Clarysa slapped him playfully on his uninjured shoulder. "Of course! What else do I have to amuse me around this incredibly boring place? Yet more lessons in etiquette and stitching?" Clarysa beat the goose-down mattress with rapid fists. "Ugh!"

Lionel grinned and then glanced toward the door. Johann had arrived. "Oh, there you are. Help me off with this shirt, will you? And then heat some water for a bath, please."

"Yes, Your Grace."

While Johann attended to the bath, Lionel chatted away, regaling his cousin with the tale of his most recent adventure. After he finished, a stoic Clarysa shook her head slowly.

Lionel shot her a bewildered look. His cousin was obviously a glutton for excitement. But hadn't he delivered enough tonight? "What's wrong?"

"I don't believe you."

"You think I dislocated my arm while eating breakfast? Do I look like someone who needs that much attention?"

"To answer your questions, no, and yes. But what I meant to say is about this 'Prince Stellan.' I'm sure you made that part of it up only to tease me."

Lionel snorted. "Cousin, I have better things to do with my time than conjure up whimsical fairytales."

"Nonsense. You have plenty of time to do all sorts of things and you know it."

Lionel smiled. She had him there for sure. "Yes, I suppose you're right. But I spoke truthfully. Many of the stories we heard about the Snowflake Kingdom while growing up may turn out to be true." Lionel cocked his head. "Heh. Oddly fascinating isn't it?"

Clarysa nodded. "So what's he like?"

"I just told you!"

"Tell me again!"

"Excuse me, Your Grace, but your bath is ready." Johann stood patiently by the door.

Lionel stood. "Thank you. That will be all for now. As for you," he said, glancing at his cousin, "I'll tell you about him again at supper. You are staying the night, aren't you?" Clarysa nodded. "Splendid. Now be off with you."

Her shoulders drooped while she offered Lionel a supplicant look.

"Shoo," he said, motioning her out the door.

Clarysa dragged herself toward the exit as if trudging through quicksand. But then she whirled at the door and blew Lionel a kiss. "Hope you feel better," she said before closing the door firmly.

* * * *

Clarysa stepped into the brightly lit hallway. Servants nodded as they passed, some carrying linens, others tending to small children or other errands. Supper lay a good hour away, but she felt not so much hungry as bored. She ambled down a wide, curving stair to the next level, swinging her arms and humming a tune sung by a minstrel who had visited the castle earlier in the day.

Though her uncle's estate was smaller in scale than the King's, she had more freedom here. Or at least she had the illusion of such. Not that she couldn't go about as she pleased, but there were certain...restraints. Then guilt about her resentment made her sigh. She didn't crave more wealth or privilege--simply something different.

Clarysa ducked into the Hall of Tapestries. Elegant glass lanterns illuminated the giant woven canvases spaced regularly along the walls. They featured a kaleidoscope of tales, including historic battles and legendary quests. Vivid colors of every hue greeted the visitors who came from all over the Five Lands to see them. But as evening approached, the hall stood silent.

She veered to one side and ran fingers along each tapestry as she walked. The creations had taken years to complete, and so demanded careful preservation. Clarysa shook her head, knowing she would never have such patience. She had a restless energy, always, her body thrumming like an instrument in constant play.

How one could ever find the patience to devote months, or even years in some cases, to constructing a glorified rug was simply beyond her understanding. Without a doubt, she admired those who possessed the quality, but the thought made her heart sink. She wished she had something of equal measure to offer her people. *Well even if I did, I'm sure I wouldn't be allowed to use it.* So being denied endeavors such as politics or agriculture, she channeled her energy elsewhere.

She liked animals and books and physical activity of any sort. Horse riding thrilled her, and she wondered if it weren't too late for a quick ride before supper. The best part of her visit had been the day before when she'd spent the morning scrambling over rocks and sunbathing by the Elysian River. The trip had been wonderful until that strange calamity had sent her scurrying back home. Insatiably curious, upon her return she had promptly ordered a contingent of guards to investigate. Perhaps they would locate the strange man who had so urgently warned her. Against what, she hadn't been able to determine, for the interior of the woods had been very dark.

But the guards had found nothing except an area of burned earth deep in the woods. In their estimation, it was an accident born of a careless vagrant. Clarysa knew otherwise, but kept her silence. *It figures. The moment anything exciting starts to happen, Fate conspires to bury it.*

Nearing one of the lanterns, she bent to inspect the set of scratches on her knees. Regardless of the adventure that wasn't meant to be, the river had been bursting with bright stones and odd-shaped fish and slimy weeds. She'd had to experience them all. The scratches still stung, but they made her feel alive. That was much more than she could say for this dreary place. She briefly traced a few old scars.

Unbidden, her older sisters' scolding voices penetrated her thoughts. *"How could you let your skin get so marked up? It's unbecoming, especially for a princess. Why can't you sit still? Have you been kidnapped and a boy put in your place? Good heavens, stop wrestling with that dog! You're an embarrassment to the monarchy."*

Clarysa let her skirts drop. Her life was dull and sheltered, and she hated it.

Sometimes she hated herself more for having such ungrateful thoughts. Undoubtedly there were thousands of folk who would gladly trade their downtrodden lives for her privileged one. What was wrong with her, anyway? Why couldn't she accept the inevitable?

Thank goodness for Lionel. He understood her need for thrills. Perhaps this was because the same adventure-craving blood pumped as hotly in his veins as it did in hers. He could always be counted on for some fun. Unlike Edward. Now there was someone best avoided at festivals, if he even bothered to show up at all. She loved her brother, but he was so caught up in the politics of the royal court she couldn't relate to him at all.

True there were a few ladies, mostly kin, with whom Clarysa could spend time when a longing for those distinctly female diversions took hold. Her cousin Mirabelle on her mother's side shared Clarysa's interest in books about dragons and fairies and faraway lands. Occasionally they'd weave flower garlands while spinning tales for each other, ones that often slipped into territory deemed too mischievous for "innocent" maidens.

LORD OF SNOW AND ICE

But the others were often close-minded and vapid. They would only titter politely whenever she proposed recreation beyond the castle walls. And her sisters, well, "peculiar" would not be too strong a word for their view of her. Surely she had been adopted into the family. She couldn't have possibly been birthed by the same mother as those creatures. Clarysa sighed heavily. She envied Lionel and his freedom. He could ride wherever he wanted, see whomever he pleased. She frowned. Her mother the Queen had been hinting recently of marriage in earnest, probably because her next oldest sister would be wedded three months hence. Unfortunately, the suitors who came calling often revealed irritating narcissistic traits within the first five minutes. The cads among them skipped talking altogether in favor of groping. Regardless, Clarysa feared none would truly want or love her given her overactive nature. She had spent so much time with Lionel and his entourage that they treated her more like a sister than a potential lover, so no luck there.

There must be a more exciting life than her current one, but how would she find it? *Where* would she find it? Clarysa frowned. She didn't begrudge her lofty station in life, she...

No. She did. Yes. But only when it was boring. Which was daily. Hourly.

And as she aged the trappings of royalty became like a noose around her neck. A silken noose replete with gold perhaps, but a noose nonetheless. Nothing scared her more than to wind up as an elegant tapestry on the wall--beautiful, yet lifeless.

"Life is what you make of it," one of her tutors had once said.

Yes, but for royalty? For whom every outfit, every lesson, even every glance seemed predestined? Still, she wanted to believe. She wanted to believe her mind would not be left to waste. Out there, somewhere, there might even be a man who would find her zeal for the fantastic refreshing instead of tiresome. *Knowing my luck, he's probably living in somebody else's lifetime.*

Clarysa turned to depart the hall, giving one last glance at the tapestries and the tales they wove. "My life is what I choose to make of it," she whispered. Her glance fell upon a brave knight shown brandishing his sword in victory over his opponent. "My life, no one else's." With renewed determination, she turned on a heel and left to ready for dinner.

There, at least, she would find adventure, if only in a tale.

Chapter 4

Two months later

Squatting flush against a tree trunk veiled in age-old bracken, Stellan watched his prey with a measured stare. His discipline was absolute--neither a muscle moved, nor a hair shifted. He'd been in the same position for an hour, and he greatly appreciated the cool air dampening his scent. Now, at last, patience had finally rewarded him.

A mountain lion crept along the carpet of leaves. The animal had wandered down into the valley, only a stone's throw away from Aldebaran's border.

Or rather, it *used* to be a mountain lion.

Its plaintive cries drifted through the air as though a newborn cub. Stellan had tracked it for a mile now. At first the beast had sounded feral and mighty as it wandered, casting about its glowering mien if even so much as an insect crossed its path. Stellan understood well its mood swings, for a strange transformation had overcome its body. The pitiful creature strained for an escape, one that would regretfully never come.

Slinking out into a clearing, the creature dragged hind legs that had become hairless and bloated, far out of proportion to the compact musculature of its torso. The mottled black skin jiggled like a full drinking sack. A constant twitch plagued its left ear. The feline trailed a brownish, gooey discharge, of which Stellan had already collected a sample.

Now was the time to act and put the animal out of its misery.

The lion had finally slowed down to where Stellan could try his experiment. Days earlier he had crafted a special dart, one filled with a potion he hoped would not only kill the diseased animal, but also disintegrate it entirely. The ingredients were not easy to come by, and their synthesis had been highly complex. However, if this worked, those long, hard hours would be more than acceptable. This alternative held far more appeal than a fire, which could lead to discovery. He eagerly awaited the results.

Stellan crept forward; the beast could not outrun him now. Yet caution would still be prudent, for the mutated animal could turn against him at any moment. He had one chance and one chance only to make this work. Slowly, he removed a glass vial from his side pouch. He poured its contents into a small dart. At the sound, the mountain lion's head turned to him, a silent wail behind its eyes. Affixing the dart to a small mechanical launcher, Stellan slowly took aim.

"I really wouldn't do that if I were you."

Stellan whipped around. Four sinister horsemen stood before him. The mountain lion uttered a weak snarl and then slumped to the ground. Stellan hid the launcher in the folds of his cape. It was too late. His window had closed. Through gritted teeth, he spoke. "What do you want, Alucard?"

The lead rider was an older man with platinum-gray hair. Neatly combed, it fell to his shoulders. Haughty features like those of an eagle looked down upon Stellan with amusement.

"How devastating." He raised a hand to his chest in mock grief. "I would have thought your words would be kinder for your estranged uncle. I've missed you, boy." Alucard's harsh tone belied his words. He signaled, and the other men grouped their horses around Stellan, blocking him from the beleaguered animal.

Alucard inched his own steed closer. Stellan felt like slicing daggers through his uncle's patronizing expression. He envisioned the blood soaring out into a hundred rainbow-like arcs. No, make that two hundred. He deliberately locked his face into a stone-hard expression, a frequent habit because he often felt so angry. The unexpected visit from his kinsfolk only stoked his ire more. *You will get nothing from me,* he thought.

Alucard assumed a bored look. "What we *want* is what doesn't belong to *you*." He gestured lazily to his men.

Stellan watched as the other riders unfolded a sturdy wooden cage. They proceeded to load the mountain lion into it, being quite careful to avoid its abnormal parts.

Stellan tried to hide his confusion. Why were they collecting it? "That doesn't belong to anybody," he said, jutting his chin up in defiance. "It's merely a sick wild animal."

"Wrong!" Alucard lunged forward and hit Stellan across the cheek. His next statement sounded more like a hiss. "It belongs to the Black Mage. And he's livid about your continued interference."

Heather Massey

The blow stung, but Stellan had endured worse. *Breathe. Breathe, and don't say a word.* Though prudence might save his life, he couldn't resist a retaliatory barb. "Aren't you rather close to Leopold's kingdom? I hear Aldebaran swordsmen enjoy smiting barbaric warlocks like you."

Alucard glowered, but he refused to take the bait. "Our business takes us wherever His Highness desires." His gaze took on a distant look. "Aldebaran and its guileless yet hateful citizens will soon acquaint themselves with the true meaning of fear." His eyes closed as if in rapture. "The storm is gathering."

The new development made Stellan suspicious. "Enough riddles. What do you mean?"

An ominous smile fell over Alucard's face, one masking answers Stellan desperately wanted to uncover. *Why have you been following me? Why now, after so many years of silence?*

"We're finished here," said one of the men.

Alucard nodded slowly and regarded his nephew with a stern expression. "If we find you interfering like this again, it will mean your life. I don't care who your father is. Oh, and here." He reached into a pocket and withdrew a small gray sack. It landed at Stellan's feet and something metallic clinked inside. "Something for your trouble." Alucard snickered. "I know times have been rough."

Stellan remained still, sullen and resolute, avoiding their gazes.

In the background, he heard one of the men whisper, "Look at the fool! He's waiting for us to leave so he can pick up the money." Raucous laughter followed.

The men hooked the cage to one of the horses and signaled the animals to ride. A few jeers floated back in the air, followed by even more riotous laughter. Eventually, it faded. All around him, the wood creatures resumed their light chatter. They too seemed to take great delight in the impoverished man before them. Stellan rammed a fist against the nearest tree. *Damn you all, then!*

His scalp tingled. Looking around, he spotted a hooded figure astride a horse many yards distant, peeking at him from among the trees. The rider wore a lavender cape--a woman's raiment. His wary gaze followed her for a few moments, but he quickly tired of the game.

"Be gone, sister," he muttered. He watched until she, too, retreated.

Then, and only then, did he pick up the bag of coins. It wasn't much, but despite Alucard's arrogant ways, his uncle was right--he did need the money. His food stores were hideously low. Even his scullery maid had complained there was only a finite number of ways one could cook potatoes, and no doubt she had tried them all numerous times over the past few months.

But what else could he do? There were more important issues at stake here than receiving a full-course meal every night.

Stellan pondered the recent encounter as he walked to his horse. Alucard had just threatened his life. How serious was he? Stellan's ties with his blood relatives had been estranged, to put it mildly, since that dread event so long ago.

But his uncle had never openly threatened him with death before. And what did his parting words mean? Aldebaran and fear, along with something about a gathering storm? Surely his "kin"--how the word left a sour taste in his mouth--would not be foolish enough to wage war on Aldebaran. They would be slaughtered, having neither the numbers nor strategy to face down King Leopold's military might. Alucard knew this fact, otherwise he would have led an attack long ago.

Stellan shook his head. The sorcerers of the Western Wastes had a long history of infighting. They would never successfully unite. He had learned one thing from the confrontation with his uncle, though, gaining confirmation of a suspicion he'd harbored for years now.

Their Pestilence was spreading.

"Pestilence" was his name for the virulent plague that had sickened the mountain lion, along with numerous other beasts of the forest. This included, he now knew, the bear that had attacked Lionel. It also explained the monstrosity at the Elysian River. To his knowledge, only animals had been infected so far, but how long would it remain that way? How susceptible were people? Alucard's newfound confidence about the whole thing didn't sit well with him at all.

Stellan came to an uneasy realization--he may have to forego isolation and make formal contact with King Leopold to warn him of the danger. How much assistance should he offer? After all, the affected creatures tended to hide in dark and isolated places such as Dungeon Forest. But recently the tide had shifted. Aldebaran royalty had been exposed. What, he wondered, had Lionel and the others reported to the King? Stellan frowned. Everything, most likely, down to his wolf's furry tail.

If Stellan himself reported these new developments, would the King believe him? Would he even allow Stellan to enter his halls? But most importantly, should Stellan even care about Aldebaran considering the kingdom's long-standing prejudice and hatred of those who practiced the Arts? Questions, so many questions.

He smiled wryly while mounting his horse. *I'm sure they would think it some kind of trick or blackmail scheme. You're a rascal, a fiend--even by the standards of your own clan.* No, it probably wasn't worth the effort.

These thoughts rebounded in his head, but instead of heading home, Stellan made for his neighbor's border. Perhaps his brush with the mystery woman at the Elysian River had something to do with it. Perhaps not. Nevertheless, sunset was hours away. He still had time for another patrol. Stellan spurred on his stallion and bolted out of the forest.

* * * *

An upsurge of land overlooked the large meadow, one of many in Aldebaran's hunting ground. It swelled high into the air like a wave perpetually cresting and offered an excellent vantage point of the surrounding area. As luck--or Stellan's careful planning--would have it, he came to this hill on the last day of the month.

He gazed upon the spot where Lionel had been attacked two months earlier. Usually he would keep to the borders of his own land while scouting for Pestilence victims, but occasionally he slipped past Aldebaran's perimeter guards. It was a necessary risk, because one too many times during the past year had found him tracking infected animals across its lines--creatures that knew no borders. Most he had destroyed, but a few had escaped, disappearing into the lush lands or populated areas where he could not follow.

Stellan feared such failures would come back to haunt him. *So many people live there!*

Staring out across the plain, he idly watched several horsemen crisscross the ground in an attempt to corner a pack of angry boars. A few already lay pierced with arrows, awaiting a fire to blacken their hides and tease out the succulent juices.

Stellan's mouth watered. These Aldebaran royalty certainly knew how to feast. But how long until they became aware of his presence? He withdrew an arrow and cocked it against his bow. His keen eyes narrowed as he aimed for the center of the pack.

Fwip! The bow twanged pleasantly as he released the arrow. It soared straight down to the meadow, carried aloft even faster by the southeast wind. Stellan watched in satisfaction as one of the larger boars suddenly reared up and fell back.

That did the trick. A number of confused riders below turned about to scan the surrounding land. They then turned in unison to the hilltop. No doubt, he had been spotted. One of them broke away, galloping toward Stellan's vantage point. A second rider soon followed, then a third.

Stellan waited patiently for their arrival. Hooves pounded closer and closer. A blond mane of hair appeared over the crest, followed by a rider clothed in maroon and green hunting gear.

"Well met, my friend!" Lionel reared his horse a few feet shy of Stellan's mount. The animals greeted each other with snorts and stamping hooves. "I was wondering when we would see you again." The duke flexed his biceps, a wide grin plastered on his face. "See here, my arm is just like new!" Then he reached out to clasp Stellan's arm.

Stellan noted his companions, however, were not as jovial. *Hm, I wonder why.* Edward nodded curtly, letting his scowl speak for him. The third rider watched him guardedly.

Stellan bowed his head courteously to each in return however, and then gave Lionel his full attention. "I fear this call isn't entirely social. I've come to warn you of something, Lionel. We need to talk. Now."

Lionel's grin faltered. "Of course! But not over an empty stomach. Why even the very thought is abominable! Come finish the hunt with us, and then you can speak of your warning."

Stellan hesitated, and then nodded. A few more minutes could hardly make any difference, and the thought of another hearty meal did sound enticing. It was settled then. He let them think Edward's cutting glance had gone unnoticed as he followed the men down to the meadow.

Despise me if you must, but my news could very well change the course of your lives.

* * * *

Shortly after sunset, the hunters sat around a great fire. Most of them clustered about Stellan and Lionel. Two of the swine had been cooked and eaten, and now curls of pungent smoke rose from assorted pipes. A moment of silence greeted the sorcerer after he shared what he thought they should know about the growing threat of Pestilence. Alucard's interest in the matter would remain secret for the time being.

Lionel rubbed his chin thoughtfully. "So you're saying it's mostly wild animals that have been infected. You're not aware of any domestics being at risk?"

Stellan shrugged. "That depends on how much contact there's been between the two. If you haven't had any reports from your farmers, then count yourselves lucky. I'm only saying the risk is there."

Lionel nodded. "Well, the monstrosity that nearly killed me should be enough to convince anybody."

"I don't think that's quite the case," Edward said.

Lionel cocked his head. "Oh, you don't, eh?"

Stellan looked at the other men gathered around him. Each held Edward's doubting gaze. "Aldebaran has been fortunate," he murmured. "Pestilence has stalked my land for many years and has made its way north into Falcon Heights. If more forceful measures aren't taken soon, the good citizens of your kingdom could become exposed." He paused for a moment, measuring his next words for maximum effect. "There's absolutely no cure--other than death."

Edward snorted. "And I suppose you have the defense we require hidden up your warlock's sleeve--for a price! Did I guess correctly, Sir Swindler?"

"*Cousin!*" Lionel hissed. "He's trying to help us. How dare you insult him!"

"That's only *your* opinion," Edward said. He looked at Stellan. "Have I insulted you?"

Stellan shook his head. He'd heard much worse.

"There, you see?" Edward sniffed. "I'm only being cautious. I'm sure Prince Stellan would understand our misgivings. His family is hardly… reputable."

Stellan eased himself into a standing position. "I'm just a messenger," he told the group. "What you do with the information is none of my concern. If you wish to sign a death warrant, so be it." He lifted a hand in a farewell gesture. "Thanks again for the meal."

Stellan had almost reached his horse when someone grabbed his arm. He whirled around, simultaneously withdrawing a ready knife.

"It's only me!" Lionel said with a nervous laugh. "You're not really a people person, are you?"

Stellan sheathed his blade. "Not really."

"Well, listen," Lionel continued. "I have just the cure! One of the King's daughters is getting married a month hence, at sundown on the twenty-seventh day. Guests will be plentiful, and everyone's been dying to learn about my heroic rescuer. If you want, I can try and get you an audience with the King, my uncle. I'm sure he'd be most interested in your findings."

Stellan mounted his horse. He glanced over a few yards to Edward, who fumed darkly behind his cousin. Clearly, he had overheard the invitation. He looked down into Lionel's expectant face. "I don't know. Somehow I don't sense my message--or myself, for that matter--being very welcome there."

"Oh, nonsense, it'll be fun!" Lionel cuffed him playfully. "I guarantee the most beautiful selection of ladies you've ever laid eyes on. Luscious... and looking."

Stellan nearly gave in to a smile at the exaggeratedly fervent expression on the Duke's face. Then he glanced at Edward once again, and the good feeling faded. "You're very kind, Lionel, but I still don't believe it to be a sound idea. Good night."

Before Lionel could protest, he galloped away. He dove deeply into the night and made for home.

While navigating a path through Dungeon Forest, he ruminated about the day's events. What was surely worse than the Pestilence threat he had encountered was the Pestilence threat *unseen*. How many more victims lurked in the shadows, watching and waiting to attack? How many more suffered violent mutations of form and mind, and how many yet would there be? More importantly, what hand did Alucard play in all of it?

"Aldebaran and its guileless, yet hateful citizens will soon acquaint themselves with the meaning of fear."

A cold wave of morbid dread plucked at his nerves. It grew heavy and more pronounced, like the frozen precipitation that hallmarked the entrance to his kingdom. At the far side of Dungeon Forest, Stellan drew his cape about him tightly. He wound a dark, thick scarf around his head, revealing only his eyes, and plunged ahead. As usual, snow coated both him and his horse within minutes. No matter how many times he went through this, it was impossible to adjust. Only minutes ago Stellan had been perspiring against the heat and long ride; now an invasive chill had wormed its way down to his very bones.

He pulled his cape even tighter about him and sped onward. After a while, he stopped to cover his horse with a blanket, for even it could not withstand unguarded against the bitter cold for long. Stellan glanced skyward. A deep breath told him it was only a snowfall, not another storm. Good. He'd make decent time.

Stellan began to feel more secure, but also angrier. Over the years, his clan had mostly left him alone, save for a spy or two. But Alucard's appearance made him suspect the game had changed. Either they wanted something from him, or they wanted to dispose of him.

He wondered if he should attempt a magickal barrier, but given his lack of training, such a defensive maneuver would be mere child's play for the likes of his uncle. No, it was best to forget the whole idea. However, he still couldn't shake the feeling that something now threatened his solitary life. If so, this would be a change he both feared and welcomed simultaneously.

The thought prompted him to spur his steed on faster as they traversed the snowy plains. Only he and his animal companions knew the blighted terrain so well they could navigate it without the aid of torch or marker. His thoughts drifted to Lionel's invitation. It was tempting. If he attended the wedding and spoke with Leopold, perhaps he'd gain entrance to Aldebaran for further exploration. How else would one such as himself obtain an audience with the King? But with the hope of contact came the risk of discovery, of derision, of rejection.

There *was* one positive note in favor of attending. Nothing would goad Alucard and his father more than him taking up with his virtuous neighbor, especially one whose citizens were so virulent in their blind prejudice against warlocks. Stellan still bristled at the thought, but how could he possibly measure his pride against the potential death of thousands?

Long ago, he had made himself a pledge to protect the Five Lands from Pestilence after learning how easily familial ties could be severed. The pledge tortured him because it went against everything he had been taught as a child--for he had not been taught to care.

Yet somehow he did. Stellan was sure that path would lead to his undoing, but neither could he stop from taking it.

Well, he thought. *There it is, then... The answer.* Stellan wasted no time upon his return to Vandeborg. After stabling his horse for a hard-earned rest, he sought out the one person in his kingdom who possessed the knowledge to help him succeed in his new mission. Finding his scullery maid at work by the kitchen hearth, he strode up to her with a newfound urgency.

"Teach me how to dance," Stellan commanded.

Chapter 5

The sun's rays warmed Stellan's face as he regarded the festooned entrance of Aldebaran's royal castle. Why, then, did he feel so cold? The answer came swiftly. Even though his intention was to help, it was unlikely the King and his people would agree.

Stellan slumped in his saddle. He had originally planned to enter the castle as unassuming as possible, but now the notion seemed unrealistic. There were guests everywhere. Even the youngest among them would instantly recognize him as an outsider. No doubt his arrival would spark the stern looks and bitter whispers for which he had, regrettably, grown accustomed.

Beneath him, his horse pawed the earth uneasily. Even the animal sensed his agitation. Stellan patted the stallion's strong neck. *You and me both, friend. You and me both.*

It was now or never. Stellan urged his horse onward. The sounds of music and laughter filled his ears as he passed through the open gate. He marveled at the total contrast between this scene and his usual cold, desolate surroundings.

Freshly picked lavender flowers lined the nearby Maypole as laughing children skirted to and fro. They sang songs unfamiliar to Stellan's ears, for these were tunes of family and mirth. Roasted duck, vegetables and fruit of all sorts flowed over mile-long tables adorned with silken cloth; minstrels played instruments from far away lands; people dressed in the finest regalia… It all seemed too much to take in at once.

Stellan risked a glance about him as he rode. A spreading sea of disapproval withered the faces of passersby as he calmly slid by them. Their reactions did little to disprove his initial theories about the place. He stopped and dismounted, unsure how to proceed.

"Stellan! Bravo, my good man, you made it!"

He turned around to find Lionel striding toward him. The duke was dressed in colorful, magnificent evening attire befitting his jubilant personality. Stellan braced himself for a comment about his own outfit, a somber sea of ebony from top to bottom, but none came.

Lionel clapped him on the back several times as a wide grin split from ear to ear. "Come with me! I'll get you some wine, and then there's a whole gaggle of young ladies in the corner there who anxiously await the tale of how we met. Off with your cloak. The valet will see to it and stable your horse. There we go!"

With a flourish of his arm, Lionel led Stellan into the pre-ceremony soiree. Everything in sight befitted a royal wedding. The great hall was ablaze with bright lights at every turn. Intricately woven garlands of flowers and ribbons stretched overhead from wall to wall. Countless tables overflowed with savory appetizers and wines. Troubadours wandered about playing jaunty tunes, winking and smiling at the guests who mingled about. Stellan followed Lionel dutifully through the maze of bodies. He had never heard so much laughter in his entire life. It put him on edge.

At the far end of the room, he caught a glimpse of the King and Queen. Sparkling crowns and richly embroidered clothing distinguished them both. They were greeting a multitude of guests. Stellan immediately started forward, badly wanting a word alone with His Majesty Leopold, but Lionel grabbed his arm and proceeded to drag him in the opposite direction. Stellan's mood darkened considerably. This proposed meeting with the King was why he had endured the long journey. This and this alone. Nothing else.

He turned back. But as he stepped toward the King, someone--probably a servant--pushed a glass of wine into his hand. The Duke of Belleressort promptly began to parade him before a seemingly endless cascade of faces and names, while his deeds on the hunting grounds were recounted repeatedly and at length.

Lionel, charming though he was, proved to be an unreliable host. For a while, Stellan waited patiently during each time his attention wandered to a pretty face or long-unseen friend. Some of Lionel's companions from the hunt joined him for a time, and the tale of Lionel's rescue was described to other guests yet again. But then they, too, disappeared back into the sea of unfamiliar faces.

When not accompanied by Lionel or his hunting comrades, Stellan's gaze was met with sneers or apprehensive stares. Edward especially seemed to make a point of conspicuously watching him. Even worse, by the time Stellan made his way to the King's location, he discovered the monarch had disappeared. Regrettably, his meeting would have to wait. Perhaps he could speak with Leopold after the ceremony.

Unused to large crowds--or any crowd--Stellan soon drifted away from the other guests. His compulsion to isolate himself was a habit well refined, and so he found himself heading outside to walk through one of the adjacent gardens. Dusk was beginning to creep round the edges of the horizon. An explosion of deep red and orange hues ignited the western skies. The warm, invigorating air differed markedly from the sterile environs of his castle.

White, pink and magenta flowers of various types and sizes brimmed with fragrant scents. Stellan discovered a bench flanking the outer garden wall. It faced a large fountain and so he sat, idly watching the bubbling liquid squirt from the stone horn of a stone fairy. A footman passed by to light lanterns and candles scattered about the grounds. He acknowledged Stellan with a nod and then left.

Even in a room swelled with people, Stellan had never felt so alone. What was he doing there? He appreciated Lionel's gesture, but these people clearly didn't fancy him. *Can't say I fancy them so much either.* And his mission was close to failing. How could he arrange a meeting with Leopold undetected? He rubbed his forehead in frustration.

A loud splintering sound erupted to his right. An intruder? Stellan leaped up, throwing back his cape and drawing his sword. *He must have hurdled over the wall.* A muttered curse confirmed Stellan's suspicion. Nearby bushes shook violently as the intruder fought to extricate himself.

"Who dares infiltrate the King's garden?" Stellan intoned, his voice ringing out in the clear night air.

The bushes stopped moving. A muffled voice spoke. "I beg your pardon?"

"Come forth!" Stellan raised his sword.

A limb thrust free of the confining branches. Stellan grabbed hold of the arm none to gently and pulled. As the figure emerged, he discovered he was clutching the arm of a young woman. Dressed in a boy's riding outfit, her long hair was littered with twigs and leaves. His brow furrowed in confusion.

Then the lantern light hit her. Stellan stared at her in shock, utterly convinced the bottom had dropped out of his stomach.

The memories rushed back, more vivid and enthralling than memories had a right to be. Here, in his grasp, so close he could feel her sweet breath upon his face, was the woman from the Elysian River. The woman who...

Naked. He had seen her *naked.*

Breasts, belly, sex, thighs--all flashed in his mind like rapidly tumbling snowflakes; he couldn't help it. Nor could he halt the advance of a telltale thickening. Thank the gods of fortune for his cape, for it masked his swift, hard excitement. She had only to say a word, or give a knowing glance, and he would do everything in his power to satisfy her. The garden offered plenty of soft places and privacy. He could please her for hours.

Nonsense! Stellan struggled to contain these alien emotions. Anger, hate, fear--those he understood quite well. But desire? Affection? He had foresworn them long ago, or so he'd thought. Besides, he didn't even know the woman. Why was he so damn infatuated? He more than anyone knew the deception beauty was capable of concealing. But being with her now only left him craving more. Especially since she wasn't screaming with terror at the sight of him. His mouth went dry. Gods, what should he say?

The woman was staring back at him with an equal measure of surprise. "Uh, thank you for the assistance, kind sir. You're here for the wedding, aren't you?" She spit out some dirt and barely waited for his nod. "I'm awfully late! Just had a quick horse ride. If anyone finds out, they'll have my head! Has the ceremony started yet?"

Stellan slowly lowered his weapon. "No," he said hoarsely. "It hasn't." He cleared his throat. "Who are you?"

The young woman chuckled. "Oh, where are my manners? They must've become lodged in that bush! I'm Clarysa. I'm supposed to be in the wedding party." She turned her head toward the hall, for music now filled the air. "Heavens! I'd better go and change. Umm…" She looked down at his hand, still attached to her right arm.

Stellan reluctantly let go.

"Thanks! Anyway, be a dear and don't whisper a word about this to anyone--especially the King. Agreed?"

"I, uhh…as you wish." Stellan watched as she sprinted away into the shadows. "Clarysa," he whispered after she was gone. Now the dazzling beauty had also revealed intriguing glimpses of her personality, not to mention a proclivity for secrets. Might there be more awaiting him?

She is decidedly…spirited.

Perhaps attending the wedding would be a strategic move in more ways than one. He strode back inside to rejoin the festivities. A long-dormant need chipped away at his heart, transforming it into something less than a cynical hunk of ice. He would never, ever admit it, however--least of all to himself.

* * * *

The wedding was an elaborate, overstated affair, as weddings for a princess were apt to be. Stellan had declined Lionel's invitation to sit up front. Instead, he stood and watched from afar, in the back of the great hall. There he was safely ensconced in shadow and behind the hundreds of prying, piercing eyes that otherwise would no doubt be boring into his back the entire time.

Conversely, the celebratory meal that followed felt excruciatingly awkward. Stellan was assigned a seat beside Lionel, but the other guests at the table pointedly ignored him. He braved the banal chatter surrounding him as best he could. Useless tales of fortunes doubled, fine stallions bred and visits to expensive, exotic lands blasted him from every angle. For once, he couldn't possibly finish the meal before him fast enough.

Afterward, Lionel took him to an upper balcony, and for a while it was only the two of them. This arrangement was far more palatable. The tension eased from Stellan's shoulders.

The Duke stole this opportunity to smoke from his slender pipe. He asked what Stellan thought about the celebration below, and laughed when Stellan shared his candidly cynical observations.

"Yes, the preening and posturing are quite stupid at times, I'll give you that," he conceded. "Most of these people have never met an ostentatious affair they didn't like."

Stellan's next grin turned sly. "Not including you, of course."

Lionel winked. "I taught them everything I know."

As they shared a laugh, the music swelled again. The celebratory dance would be starting soon. Stellan experienced an inexplicable urge to seek out Clarysa, but his first priority was an audience with the King. Lionel, however, had other plans. The duke peered over the balcony as if looking for someone. "Ah," he said, "follow me. There's someone I want you to meet."

They returned to the ground level, Stellan trailing him with a low sigh. The tables and chairs had been cleared away, replaced with an expanse of powdered and perfumed bodies. Lionel guided him forward with one hand, and then with the other reached out and tapped the bare shoulder of a young woman with golden hair. She turned around. As her gaze locked onto Stellan's face, she blanched in surprise.

"Prince Stellan of Vandeborg, may I introduce my cousin, the spirited and inquisitive Princess Clarysa, youngest daughter of King Leopold and Queen Arietta."

Stellan gave a low whistle even as he shuddered inwardly. "The King's daughter!"

She seemed not to notice, for her head swiveled back to Lionel. "You mean this is the one...the man who saved you?"

Lionel nodded, beaming.

Turning back to Stellan, Clarysa grasped folds of her skirt in each hand and suddenly dropped into a deep curtsy with head bowed. "You have my undying thanks, Sir, for your valorous deed. On behalf of the royal court of Aldebaran, I welcome you to our humble celebration! You honor us with your presence."

Stellan felt his eyebrows clash. He stole a glance at Lionel, who hid a bemused smile behind one hand. "Princess, that's...thank you...you're very kind." Clarysa continued to hold her deferential pose. Time inched by as if a snail. When she didn't respond, he shot Lionel a look that silently screamed, *What am I supposed to do* now?

This time it was Lionel to the rescue. "Yes, yes, get up, please. You're making an absolute scene!" He clucked half-scoldingly as he reached down and helped her stand. "Anyway, I've got to run. Someone else... uh, is expecting me." Lionel grinned impishly and disappeared through the crowd.

Stellan found himself alone with Clarysa. He eyed her, not sure what to expect.

She folded her hands daintily before her. "You must think me a fool, stumbling about like a jester in the garden bushes."

Stellan shook his head, not trusting his mouth to speak. He didn't know quite what to make of her--fully clothed or not--aside from the fact he had never encountered such an ambrosial dish full of sweet smells and delicate flavors. Her appearance was a far cry from the boyish figure that had stumbled over the wall.

Shades of Lionel's handsome features were woven into hers. Stellan would have thought them twins if he hadn't been told they were cousins. Clarysa bore the same golden skin, elegant nose, and perfectly formed cheekbones. Her lips sparkled with the kiss of fresh-morning dew. Suddenly, an unrelenting thirst grabbed hold of him.

His gaze traveled upward. She had fastened her wavy hair with two straight, sapphire-encrusted pins. Several ringlets eschewed their confines, tokens of hasty grooming. Stellan imagined exactly what he could do with those pins--namely, replace them with his hands as he plunged them into her mass of thick, glossy locks. From there it would be ridiculously easy to angle back her head to receive his kiss.

Then he devoured the rich blue material of her gown. It was a simple, modest piece made all the more attractive by the lacey fabric around her neck. And the rest of her figure was decidedly...unboyish. Supple and generous of curve, it threatened to melt away all of Stellan's inhibitions. The deep valley between her full breasts particularly enthralled him. Not wishing to betray his interest, he glanced sharply away.

They continued to stand there, but now an awkward silence developed. Then stark reality intruded. Around them, couples enjoined as the court musicians plucked at cords and beat their drums. Music swelled, and Stellan watched in horror as bodies promenaded around them, their pastel dresses and frilly white collars closing in on all sides. To his annoyance, he also intercepted a scornful glance or two. Then Clarysa placed a hand on his arm.

"Would you--" she began.

"Yes?" *Please don't ask me to dance.*

"--like to walk in the garden?"

Stellan paused as a wave of uncertainty passing over him. *Does she mean by myself?*

"I mean, I'm not much one for dancing. But if you'd like to stay, I'm sure my cousin Mirabelle would--"

"No, no," he blurted out. "The garden...it sounds perfect." He extended an elbow and enjoyed the light touch of her fingertips as her hand encircled it.

"You're too kind," she murmured.

They stepped gingerly through the crowd of merrymaking guests.

"Whew!" Clarysa exclaimed once they had passed through the archway leading outside. "These events can be so stressful. But I'm sure one such as yourself is quite used to it." Stepping ahead, she stretched her arms high into the air, and then swung them frivolously by her side as she walked.

Amused, Stellan followed her, but he still felt somewhat wary. He looked over his shoulder, half expecting someone to accost him for keeping the company of the King's daughter.

"Come on," she called back. "I'll show you my favorite place!"

He dutifully obeyed, but remained quiet as she escorted him along a path marked with polished stones. The sounds of the party faded away as they ventured deeper into the garden. Crickets sang a cheery lullaby. Stellan fixed his gaze ahead, not quite sharing their enthusiasm. As they walked, he noticed the princess kept stealing glances at him. After several more minutes of this, he cleared his throat. "Is there something you'd like to ask me, Princess Clarysa?"

She giggled into her hand. "Well, first I'd ask you to call me Clarysa." She giggled again.

Normally, he would have found such girlish behavior irritating. Meaning, had he ever been around any girls. But she had an infectious quality. Nevertheless, he maintained his guard. "Well, then, *Clarysa*, what do you have on your mind that begs escaping?"

"Lionel tells me you hail from the Western Wastes."

"True."

"And you live near Dungeon Forest!"

"Also true."

"And…you're one of those sorcerers."

Those sorcerers. Stellan paused, wondering where this was leading. "Yes. I am."

Clarysa's voice became deeper, bolder. "You practice magick."

"Yes."

"Well, is that all you can say?"

"No, it isn't." He narrowed his eyes. Old suspicions began to surface, suspicions that warned against discussing such matters with those unacquainted with the Black Arts. "What's your point?" His voice had an edge, but he didn't care.

Clarysa, however, seemed oblivious. Suddenly she moved forward and pressed closer to him. To his dismay, he discovered he enjoyed the feeling very much. Stellan glanced down.

"Show me!" she whispered, a hungry look saturating her features. "I've never met anyone who can perform magick, at least not the real kind. Is it quite difficult?"

Stellan slowed his pace, but said nothing. *What is she driving at?*

"I know why you're hesitant. You think me like the others, but I'm not."

He walked ahead, picking up speed.

"I won't tell a soul, if that's what you're worried about."

He shot her a dubious look.

Clarysa raised a hand. "I swear on my father's life I won't!"

Stellan came to an abrupt decision, followed by an abrupt halt. He glanced about, then swiftly turned and dove into a grove of flowering dogwood trees. The soft rustling of her dress reached his ears. *You're a brave woman, following around a bastard sorcerer like me in the dead of night. Well, here is your reward!*

Spinning around, Stellan caught her hand in a flash of movement. Clarysa yelped, but did not back away. Grasping her wrist, he forced her hand palm up. He began to concentrate intensely. With his fingers, he traced a symbol across her palm and muttered an incantation. The red light flickering in his pupils were reflected in hers.

Clarysa gasped. "What is--"

"Quiet!"

A small glowing orb materialized above her palm. Soon, it coalesced into a shimmering, translucent rose. Stellan watched the princess watch the illusion, its soft light enhancing the beauty of her face. After a moment or so it faded away, as soundlessly as it had come.

The grove reverted to its former state of semidarkness. Stellan heard Clarysa's heavy breathing, and then he realized he was breathing just as hard. Whether it was from the effort it took to perform the spell, or something else, he wasn't sure.

"Do it again!"

Stellan dropped her hand. "No." He headed out from the grove.

"Oh, but wait!" Clarysa clutched his arm. "I'm sorry. I was being selfish." She searched his face. "You're panting. Are you tired?"

Stellan halted. "Not particularly, no. But magick can be strenuous, yes, in ways you can't even begin to imagine." He sensed the impression he had made by the widening of her eyes and the visible shudder that ran through her. For some reason, it gave him a thrill.

A bench lay ahead of them once they reached the path. Clarysa sat down, and patted the spot next to her. Stellan looked around, thoroughly ill at ease. He really should have been trying to arrange his meeting with the King.

"Would you rather go back to the party?" she asked.

Stellan shook his head and sat down. In the middle of a wedding celebration, it was unlikely he'd gain the King's undivided attention.

Clarysa folded her hands demurely on her lap. But she regarded him with a bold and even gaze. "What's the most powerful spell you've ever done?"

Stellan looked at her sharply, and he was suddenly reminded of how different the two of them were. "Only children, charlatans or the ignorant refer to the Arts as 'spells,' and I hardly think my past actions are any of your concern."

A crestfallen expression passed over her features. "Begging your pardon, sir. I was only curious."

Frustrated, Stellan glanced away. He debated how long he should stay. Perhaps he should storm back into the castle and demand to see the King immediately. After all, it *was* for the benefit of Aldebaran. Related thoughts boiled in his brain, but then a light sniffling sound broke his concentration. Stellan gave the princess a sidelong glance.

"What's wrong with you?" he asked, unable to keep the hard edge out of his voice.

Clarysa rubbed her nose briefly. "Nothing. What makes you ask such a question?"

"No, I just…" Stellan paused. How could a man and a woman spending time together be so damn confusing?

"You just what?"

He opened his mouth to answer, only to slowly close it, thinking the better of his proposed response. "Oh, forget it."

An awkward pause followed, suspended by the rhythmic chant of cicadas. A very *long* pause.

Clarysa cleared her throat. "I'm sorry I was nosy about your spells… or magick… Whatever you prefer. You see, well, it's so exciting! And I don't get much of that around here."

Stellan looked at her in surprise. He made a sweeping gesture. "What's all of this, then? You live in the richest kingdom of the Five Lands. Surely you can find something exciting to do, or travel somewhere interesting?"

Clarysa snorted. "If you're a man, yes." She propped her chin in her hands. "Oh, I must sound like a spoiled brat. But riches aren't everything, you know."

Stellan said nothing.

"I want a *life*! I want to be challenged! I want something to make me think so hard my head will burst!"

Stellan chuckled despite himself. "So, you don't care for all this fancy celebration? Or for music, or dancing?" He began to think his hasty yet arduous lessons had gone to waste.

Clarysa shrugged. "I like it well enough, I guess. But I haven't found anybody I'd like to do it with."

"So you're saying it's overrated."

"Yes, exactly."

Stellan nodded in response to her appreciative expression. Another moment of silence passed.

Clarysa cleared her throat. "Would you like to dance?"

"Yes." The word was up and out of his mouth before he realized it. His stomach tightened. *Now why on earth did you have to go and agree to do* that? He searched his mind for any reason, any excuse, to untangle himself, but it would be extremely rude. Besides, he was here, after all, to try and make a good impression. If he endured this one dance, maybe Clarysa would facilitate a meeting with her father.

Or maybe he'd ruin everything. It wouldn't be the first time. Stellan followed her to the great hall, dragging his feet and feeling very sorry for himself.

* * * *

The hall was far too crowded for his taste. Upon reaching the edge of the dance floor, Stellan hung back. The ever-present thought warning him against such risks gnawed its way across his mind. But Clarysa turned to face him and playfully grabbed his hand. With a fetching glance, she forcefully drew him onto the floor.

At first, he could barely bring himself to look into her face, one upturned and full of expectation. His limbs felt rigid and gangly, and his feet stomped about as if made of stone. He came close to calling the whole affair off. But Clarysa took his arm and placed it snugly about her waist. One hand landed daintily on a shoulder, and the other slipped into his barely outstretched arm. She stood about a head shorter than he, but it seemed a perfect fit. Clarysa nudged him to start moving.

The plan didn't proceed as smoothly as it should have. They became entangled in each other's feet as Stellan tried to imitate the moves of the other dancers. His three quick lessons before the trip were proving to be insufficient.

Clarysa giggled. "Unconventional is a good start." But her expression turned to one of concern as she looked up at him. "What's wrong?"

Stellan leaned toward her ear. The aromatic smell of her skin briefly distracted him, and he paused to quell a stirring ache. This soon melted into a vat of embarrassment. "I...don't know this dance."

"Which ones do you know?"

"Only one, actually. 'Wind in the Willow.'"

Clarysa smiled. "I know that one! It's certainly an old...a classic." She glanced at the musicians. "But we'll need a different tune."

She raced away, leaving Stellan to awkwardly dodge a number of gyrating bodies. The music came to an abrupt halt, prompting disgruntled murmurs and numerous glares in his direction. He wished he could conjure a shrinking incantation from his magickal repertoire.

Clarysa rushed back, red-faced and breathless. "Here we go, then!" She pushed herself into his arms as the music resumed.

It was a grand, uplifting piece conveyed by gentle strings and modest horns. The couples drifted into a wide circle, spinning in place while each pair took turns in the middle showing off elaborate moves. Sometimes two couples or more pivoted about, chasing each other across the floor with laughs and challenges to whirl faster, harder. Clarysa had indicated her intention to step into the circle early on, but Stellan held her back. Not because he didn't know the steps, but because he hadn't expected the format to draw so much attention to individual pairs. He was content to remain on the sidelines.

But Clarysa foiled him. She yanked him toward the center, her petite figure belying such strength. Stellan gaped and nearly tripped. Thankfully, she steadied him as he bumped into her.

She shot him a wicked grin. "Let's show them how it's done!"

Stellan nodded. Her tone, her manner, her looks... They somehow empowered him. Tightening his grip, he swept her hard across the wide space. A rousing crescendo matched his mood.

Surprisingly, she kept up. They whipped about the floor and scattered the other couples with their enthusiasm. It was as if they had danced together a hundred times, so in tune they were with each other's movements. Clarysa laughed and laughed. The music swelled into a thunderous wave of notes.

Stellan even forgot about the onlookers. Everything was a blur except for the lithesome woman in his arms. *A woman...in my arms*. He wondered at the strangeness of it all. Then he had an idea. It would be subtle, a little extra something to enhance the splendor of the dance and top off her evening. After having seen her nude, he wanted her to experience something exciting in return.

Ever so quietly, Stellan began to speak, the words of a charm issuing from between barely parted lips. As the words faded and the magick built, he swept Clarysa into a brisk spin.

But in his excitement he miscalculated. What started as a slight lift into the air became a soaring, head-turning ascent. Stellan and his partner twirled around as if birds in flight, gliding a solid six or seven feet into the air. Clarysa clung to him tightly, though she needn't have worried, for the magick made it seem as though their feet were still on solid ground. He risked a look into her face and for a moment lost himself in her flushed, exquisite features.

After they drifted back to the floor, however, it was another story entirely. The music had come to an abrupt end as even the musicians became slack-jawed at the spectacle he had created. Clarysa smiled and encouraged him to keep dancing, but the faces behind her were awash with scowls and horrified looks. Caught up in the moment, he had forgotten exactly where he was and the expectations for his behavior. Not to mention *who* he was. *Idiot! What were you thinking?* Now he'd ruined any chance of meeting with King Leopold.

Stellan's voice sounded tight as he spoke. "I...I should go now. Pleasure meeting you. Give Lionel my regards."

He turned and strode quickly from the hall, ignoring her loud protests and avoiding the icy, fearful stares of the other guests. He hailed a stable attendant and asked for his steed. When it arrived, Stellan mounted, swiping the reins from the attendant in a mad rush. Flustered and dejected, he galloped away from Aldebaran as fast as his horse could travel.

Chapter 6

Katherine stoked the fire with more wood, attempting to produce a rolling boil in her kettle. The second wave of cabbage she and her husband Mathias had planted in the early spring was now rewarding them with thick, bountiful heads, the best she had seen in the past three years. She placed three on her chopping block and began to strip the outer leaves of one. This would make a fine meal tonight, no doubt.

Nearby, baby Andrew began to wail. Katherine looked plaintively back at the doorway of the child's room. Her heart told her to check on him, but her head believed it would be best to attend to the thin strips of meat now rapidly frying on the stove. "Mathias? Can you please see what your son has gotten himself into?" The water was boiling; the meat looked ready. She dared not leave this delicacy to be burned beyond all recognition, especially seeing how rare it was for the family to have meat these days. "Mathias? My hands are tied at the moment!"

No answer.

Katherine carefully lowered the now-cut cabbage down into the steaming water. Her husband was a good man, she had to admit. He never hurt her, nor drank away their meager savings, but sometimes…at least once a month…she would've liked to see his head out of the clouds and concentrating on what he was doing at the moment.

"Land's sake, never mind! I'll check myself." As Katherine turned, she failed to recognize that the sounds of her child, so acutely wailing moments before, had suddenly stopped. No, all thoughts of this fled her mind as she encountered the half-man half-monster before her. It was a shambling mockery of a being, one faintly resembling her husband. But was it really him?

The strange creature leaped toward her. A scream broke from the depths of her lungs--only to never see the light of day. The air began to fill with smoke from the unattended meat left burning.

* * * *

Midnight neared.

Seated in Vandeborg's highest tower room, Stellan played his pipe organ. He pressed down upon keys that resembled the stained, cracked teeth of a village beggar. When he had first discovered the room, he'd found fragile, wrinkled music sheets in the pipe organ's storage rack. The tunes predated him by at least a hundred years. Over time, he'd taught himself the pieces, having to squint and guess at smudged or faded notes.

Modest in size, the organ boasted six-foot metallic pipes and mahogany casework. Like the rest of the castle, it had fallen into heart-breaking disrepair. But other than forage for sustenance and ward off the cold, Stellan had nothing better to do in those early years than to fix it--so he had.

The room itself, large enough for the organ, the musician's bench, and a small fire grate, was always bitterly cold no matter how much wood burned. Stellan's fingerless gloves provided some warmth while allowing him freedom of movement. He loved the music dearly and played it so loudly the melodies often spread throughout the darkened castle halls. Over the years, many a sorrowful refrain delivered welcome respite from the eternal loneliness of his life. The organ was his pride and joy, and he spent hours keeping it well-oiled and maintained.

Stellan thought about the wedding party, the music a backdrop to his musings. Some parts of that evening he could have done without, particularly the stuffy and pretentious Aldebaran royalty. He smiled wryly, wondering what the wedding guests at Leopold's court would think about his music, so troubled and mournful. Would Clarysa like it? She seemed so much the opposite, full of sunlight and happiness. After the stunt he had pulled, would she ever be allowed to see him again? Stellan frowned. Most likely the answer would be "no."

"My oh my, why so gloomy tonight?"

Startled, Stellan slammed his hands down at the sound of the voice. Pipes choked and sputtered as the music died off. He shot a look toward the entrance. A tall, shapely woman in an ebony dress filled the frame.

"What do you want?" he asked with a measured stare. "And who let you in?"

A slow smile curled her lips as she glided forward. She unclasped her lavender cape and slipped the hood from her head. Lustrous black hair emerged. She gracefully smoothed it back, though no grooming was needed. The scent of jasmine preceded her.

Emerald eyes gleaming, she leaned an elbow on the organ's edge. "Is that how you're going to greet your loving sister?" She spoke in a low, sultry voice. "I've come a long way, and with diligent furtiveness. There's no need to blame your poor servants. After all, we both know I have my ways."

Stellan resumed playing. "And may I ask what suddenly brings you back into my life...after what? Four years? Five? How long has it been, Sada? But don't think I didn't appreciate all the help." He pounded harder on the keys.

"*Tsk*," she murmured. "You don't have to be so cranky." Sada rested her chin in her hand. "Hmmm...that's a marvelous tune. What's it called?"

His muscles tensed. "I know you didn't come all this way to ask me the name of a song. Quit playing games and state your business."

From the corner of his eye, he noticed her crestfallen expression. Once upon a time, he might have been fooled by her theatrics. Now, however, he viewed her every move with suspicion.

"Maybe I *have* come just to see you. Did you ever think of that? No?" She stepped over to the fire and stretched out her hands to its feeble warmth. "Stellan, I've come to warn you."

As if you care about me anymore. Ignoring the heaviness in his chest, he continued playing, and said nothing.

"You need to end this little crusade of yours. Father's becoming very upset, and so are the others."

"Alucard, you mean."

"Precisely. They've worked hard on this project, and your efforts are obstructing them. I'd be devastated if anything were to happen to you."

Stellan barked out a laugh. Again he slammed his fingers down upon the brittle keys. "Naturally, you'd do everything within your power to prevent it. The effortlessness with which you speak from both sides of your mouth is simply astounding. You truly are a master enchantress!"

Sada turned a steely gaze on him. Her right hand balled into a tight fist. "All right. I tried being nice, now I'm going to order you. Stop hunting the experiments, Brother! They exist for a purpose, and any countermeasures on your part can only be construed as traitorous to your own people!" She left the fire and kneeled at his feet. Her heavy sigh lingered in the air. "Why are you so against everyone? Against *me*? I'm on your side whether you believe it or not." She lowered her voice to a whisper. "You may be the Mage's son and heir, but don't underestimate his ambition."

Stellan hit the keys with barely contained fury. *And neither should he underestimate mine.*

"Will you stop that awful music for one moment, please?" Sada's voice turned sharp. "Take a look about you--a good, long look! This bare-bones existence is destroying you, and it doesn't have to be this way."

She rested a hand on his arm. Did she mean to comfort him? Stellan jerked away from her touch, but a small, hidden part of him regretted the loss of contact. Sada used to be more than a sister--she'd been his closest friend.

Undaunted, she continued speaking. "Think about it--when the project succeeds, we'll be mighty again. Invincible." Her gaze softened. "Come back with me, and beg forgiveness from the family."

"And destroy my integrity in the process?" Stellan began playing a melancholic tune. "You claim to care for me. How could you demand such a sacrifice?"

Sada shook her head. "Allow me to offer another perspective. If we return together as a united front, we'll be so much more powerful. No one ever has to hurt you again or force a wedge between us. You and I will pretend to go along with their plan. When the time is ripe, we'll seize the throne. Think about the possibilities!" She shivered. "And we'll use other methods of control. Truth be told, I never did care for those monstrosities. The treatment makes them terribly ugly, and they stink."

Stellan turned on her, his face twisted with anger. "Then why did you allow them to continue when it was within your power to oppose them? Father and Alucard's mad call for revenge was a mistake from the beginning and you know it. It was misguided, moronic, and poorly executed. And I've spent the past fifteen years trying to clean up His Royal Highness's ugly, stinking mess. Tell them they can both shove it all up their pompous asses."

Sada's laughter tinkled pleasantly throughout the room. "Such a colorful way with words! Is that what you learned from these servants of yours?"

Stellan sighed. "I don't see how you can overlook what Father has done to us."

"Well *I* don't understand your reluctance to overthrow him directly. Have you forgotten the importance of ambition?"

He cut her a sharp look. "Will that be all now?"

"Actually, no. There is one other concern." She stood and spent a few moments straightening her dress.

Stellan clenched his teeth. "*Well?*"

"Everyone knows about your little tryst, I'm afraid."

"My little what?" Despite his flippant denial, he tensed inside. Had she or Alucard caught him watching Clarysa at the river? No--it was impossible! He'd been extremely careful.

She crossed her arms. "You know exactly what and who I mean." She smirked. "I heard you took her on quite a flight the other evening."

Damn! They had sent a spy to the wedding. He kept himself as rigid as stone. "I didn't have a little...tryst. I didn't have anything." Stellan pounded more loudly. Notes bludgeoned the air. "You heard wrong."

Sada laughed. "Of course. Keep at her, if you want. It'll be our little secret." She swooped in to murmur in his ear. "But remember, dearest, if it becomes anything more, I'll be forced to take action."

Stellan hunched lower over the keyboard and bared his teeth. "Leave me alone."

"As you wish." She departed as silently as she had entered.

Dark images of his family's past flashed through Stellan's mind. Noisome, malignant images that tore into his heart. Deeply troubled, he earned his reputation as the Dark Prince once more by playing long and hard into the night.

Chapter 7

Clarysa turned the pages of her book one by one. She had given up on actually reading it hours ago because her mind relentlessly wandered. Placing it aside, she gazed across the meadow. The hunting party, now swelled to double its usual number, had arrived midmorning. Men and horses spotted the field, both beast and human enjoying a light snack and games before the hunting began. The bright sun nestled against a clear blue sky.

Clarysa sat on a colorful woven blanket at the wood's edge, a cup of tea by her side. This was her second time in two months joining the hunt, much to Lionel's amusement and over Edward's strenuous objections. But Father had arbitrated, and she was allowed to come. The reason for her presence was hardly a secret. The men knew the answer lay in a certain sorcerer prince named Stellan.

They were right, of course.

Clarysa sighed, for there was no guarantee he would come. He hadn't showed the month prior, but it wasn't a surprise considering the stunt he had pulled at the wedding. The memory never failed to bring a smile to her face. What an exhilarating experience! She regretted it had ended so quickly.

After he left, Clarysa had wandered the castle halls as if in a stupor. Sleep came only at dawn, and brought passionate dreams of one dark, handsome prince. Who could have known her destiny lay with a dark, mysterious sorcerer? At least, that's what she hoped. Since she wouldn't be allowed to visit Vandeborg to see him, she did the next best thing.

But the waiting had been interminable. And when Stellan had failed to make an appearance at the last hunt, the intervening days until the next were unbearable. Clarysa could deal with her sisters' teasing and Edward's staid lecturing about appropriate behavior. But to never see

Stellan again...well, that was unacceptable. She would have to stir up another plan if today were no different.

She stood and adjusted her dress. It was meant for show only as she would not be hunting herself. Her father had laid down that condition quite clearly. Clarysa had chosen a formfitting jade piece with a plunging neckline and flowing skirt--green to herald the burgeoning summer season, and plunging to herald the Dark Prince's arrival. Clarysa giggled at the thought.

This particular dress flattered her figure. Prior to the wedding, the effect it had on others hadn't mattered to her. But now she only wanted one man's attention.

If he even came.

She left her reading spot and sauntered around. One of the cooks handed her a crisp vegetable pastry. Clarysa thanked him and idly munched. But her stomach felt jumpy with anticipation, and so she tossed the other half to the ground as she wandered.

With a sigh, she figured she might as well join in a game to distract herself. She aimed for Lionel's group, which was currently engrossed in a darts competition.

Within moments the earth began to shake as hooves thundered behind her. Someone racing, perhaps? Clarysa turned around, and barely had time to jump out of the way of a rider and horse bearing directly toward her. A mighty black stallion roared past. The force of its gallop caused her hair and skirt to flutter wildly. Clarysa shivered as excitement pumped through her veins.

It was him--at last! She ran forward. A smile blossomed upon her face as a giddy thought formed. He must have read her mind using his mysterious magick and finally made the long journey to visit her.

The men crowded around as he dismounted, a sure sign of their enthusiasm. Lionel was the first to greet him. Clarysa pushed her way through the press of strong male bodies, eager to be the second.

At first, Stellan's back was to her. The men plied him with questions about Pestilence. Had he encountered any more victims? Were any people infected? Which kinds of weapons were the most effective against it?

Having a priority of a different sort, Clarysa gestured madly for Lionel's attention. Ignoring his companions, he guided Stellan around to face her. "Of course, you remember my cousin, Princess Clarysa?"

Her breath caught in her throat at the sight of him. He looked dark and dangerous despite the bright sun shining down upon them. "Very wonderful to see you again," she said. She extended her hand, hoping

Stellan would kiss it. But he only nodded, and a tight, quick nod at that. Her smile faltered as he looked away. Clarysa frowned. *Did I say something wrong?*

Lionel appeared confused himself, but covered it with a reassuring smile. "Off you go then, cousin," he said, turning her around and giving her a light pat on her bottom. The men laughed. "It's time for the hunt." He lowered his voice as he escorted her a short distance away. "Get him alone at lunch. You'll probably have better luck then."

Clarysa nodded, fighting a lump in her throat. She hoped Lionel's assessment was correct. She kept glancing over her shoulder as she walked toward the meadow's edge, watching the men--well, watching Stellan, really--as they mounted and trotted off. His greeting left much to be desired, but she chalked it up to shyness. He lived an isolated life, after all.

Clarysa watched them leave. She strolled to and fro, practically wearing a rut into the hard earth while awaiting his return. Thoughts raced through her mind. What would be the best way to get a conversation going with him? What would he care to discuss? Should she pick a serious topic or light? Serious would show she had brains, but considering the stories she'd heard about his dismal living conditions, perhaps it would be better to start off with something frivolous. But then he might mistake that approach for the way she was all the time! Serious or light? Light or serious?

Finally she decided. Clarysa would start with a topic that was *lightly* serious. It would have to do. Unless, of course, a seriously light one would be better.

* * * *

Hours passed. The servants laid out a variety of side dishes on several long tables. Two large pits had been dug for the roasts. Meanwhile, the cooks were busy checking the fire's temperature and adding spices to marinades in their usual persnickety manner.

"Here they come," said one.

Clarysa hovered excitedly nearby. For once she didn't care about the size of the game captured.

Shouts and laughter permeated the air as the hunters neared. They dismounted, and some walked into the forest to relieve themselves. Others tended to the horses, and five or six delivered the game to the cooks. Thirsty riders opened jugs of wine and passed them around freely. It had been a good hunt.

Clarysa spotted Stellan tending to his horse. She snagged some carrots from a tray, her heart pounding as she neared his steed. The stallion eyed her but did not protest her presence, especially after she raised one of the carrots to its mouth. Stellan was lost somewhere on the other side of the great beast. The horse's noisy chewing caught his attention, however, and he suddenly appeared opposite her.

"Your horse is beautiful," she said, stroking its neck after it had hungrily devoured the food. "What's his name?"

Stellan rolled his eyes. "What do you think?"

Clarysa shrugged. "I couldn't possibly guess. What is it?"

Stellan chuckled derisively. "Horse."

Clarysa admonished him with a look. "Oh, stop teasing!" She narrowed her eyes. "And why the patronizing face?"

"Because I have more important things to do than sit around thinking up silly names for my animals, that's why."

His words stung. They *really* stung. Clarysa paused mid-stroke. She'd only been making conversation. *Is this how it is, then? Our dance meant nothing to you?* Attempting to quell hurt feelings and suppress the growing knot in her stomach, she forced a polite smile. "Then I won't bother you further. Everyone who knows me will tell you I can be very silly." Clarysa spun around, picked up her skirt so as not to trip and look even sillier, and stormed off.

Hastily wiping tears, she dodged horses and servants and other assorted obstacles. *Over two months of waiting for his cold shoulder? Isn't it obvious? He doesn't care about you. You're nothing but a foolish little nuisance.* Clarysa was beginning to have some insight into how her family viewed her behavior. It was not a pleasant feeling.

Someone called her name, but she refused to acknowledge whoever it was. She kept barreling ahead. But then a shadow passed across her vision, and she had to stop, for Stellan blocked her path.

"Clarysa, please wait," he said, holding out an arm to prevent her escape.

She pressed her hands against her stomach in an attempt to manage her anxious state. "It was a stupid question, Stellan. I'm so sorry."

"No, it wasn't. My answer… It was my answer that was stupid. I…" He paused, absentmindedly rubbing the back of his head and avoiding her gaze.

There he goes again. Clarysa glanced away as well, but his tall, striking figure, emanating warmth and a pleasing masculine scent, was too tempting. Therefore she summoned the courage to look up. When she did, it was straight into his deep green eyes.

"Let's start over." He took a deep breath, and this time his voice sounded genuinely friendly. "It's wonderful to see you again."

Clarysa curtseyed. "The feeling is mutual." The ambient noise faded to a murmur as she lost herself in the handsome features before her. His skin appeared very pale, even in the bright sunshine, but it was intriguingly offset by his dark and lustrous hair. He was like an imperious, cold statue waiting for her warm embrace and gentle kisses to awaken him. Those thoughts led to more mischievous ones, and soon Clarysa was breathing much more deeply than usual.

Stellan's gaze abruptly snapped up and away. The blush spreading across his cheeks hinted at the hills and valley upon which he had just feasted.

Clarysa smiled knowingly, but he was in danger of retreating back into his shell. Perhaps a diversion was in order. She cocked her head toward the buffet. "Shall we find something to eat?"

Stellan nodded. "I'm starving."

They began to walk, and then Stellan cleared his throat. "So, what do you think is a suitable name?"

"A name for what?"

"My horse."

"Oh! Well, umm… Let's see…uh… Yes, that'll do nicely. How about 'Midnight'?"

Stellan inclined his head. "It's…very acceptable."

Clarysa clapped and grinned. "You know he's going to sleep much better at night from now on, since he's got a name."

Stellan's eyebrows shot up. "You don't say?"

Clarysa nodded vigorously. "Oh, yes!"

"And if someone should ask my whereabouts while I am grooming him, should that person be told I will be available 'after Midnight'?"

Clarysa snorted, and then gave him a friendly nudge. "You might want to rethink any career as a traveling jester, in case such a thought had crossed your mind."

A trace of red heated Stellan's usually cold face again. "Consider it rethought."

The two walked on to the camp.

* * * *

Stellan and Clarysa sat on her blanket apart from the camp proper and under the shade of a great oak. Servants kept them supplied with appetizers until the main course was ready. Occasionally, their hands brushed as they reached for the food, prompting exchanges of shy smiles. Clarysa coaxed him into a steady conversation as they ate, asking him about the hunt and gossiping about various escapades of Lionel and the others.

After they were sated on the last of the wine and dessert, Stellan leaned back against the tree. Clarysa sat by his long, outstretched legs, fingering tufts of grass and thick roots. She used her sudden interest in all things botanical as an excuse to occasionally graze his thigh or knee with an errant hand. Stolen glances informed her the prince didn't seem to mind. Truth be told, she wanted to dance again, or have some other excuse to be in his arms. The compelling shape of his lips made her wonder about any other talents he possessed, aside from magick. She understood his reticence in kissing her hand before their comrades, but perhaps here, in the bucolic, private setting, he'd feel more comfortable.

Clarysa intended to make him feel as comfortable as possible.

So she chattered on, making lighthearted jokes even as she edged closer, and then closer still. At one point, she leaned forward with a smile, knowing her arms pushed her breasts together and hoping the view pleased him. *What a gentleman--he's not even looking!* Clarysa brazenly toyed with the gilded fabric along her neckline, shivering in anticipation as she waited for the searing path his gaze would surely make once he noticed.

Despite the obvious interest he had displayed a few hours before, he still didn't glance down. Even though they sat so close one of her thighs pressed against his, he seemed distant. Preoccupied. The mystery of him only made her want to know him more.

His clean, earthy scent of sandalwood made her frantic with need. How could she reach him? Naughty ideas filled her mind, like straddling his lap and planting wet kisses all over his face and neck. Though sexually innocent, Clarysa had learned everything she needed to know about pleasing men from conversations with Lionel. Meeting Stellan increased her eagerness to experiment.

In a fit of impulsiveness, she rested a hand on his thigh. It felt muscular and firm. She gave the hard flesh the barest of squeezes.

He grabbed her hand. "What are you doing?" Suspicion laced his tone.

His response flummoxed her. Stellan wasn't reacting the way most men did to a young maiden's charms. "Just...I don't know...exploring?"

Gently, he removed her hand. "This isn't the time."

Staring into his troubled, yet mesmerizing eyes, Clarysa searched for any flicker of mutual attraction that would contradict his words. Nothing surfaced--no emotion at all. Had she misjudged? In the garden at the wedding, when they first met, his expression had been so gentle and yearning. It was as though he had wanted to kiss her.

Perhaps she had misremembered. Maybe there wasn't any attraction on his part. Was she too mundane--too unexceptional--for this dashing sorcerer? Probably.

He glanced away. Clarysa noticed a flush inching up his neck.

Idiot! You're making him uncomfortable. No wonder he's not interested. Chagrined, she left his side and poured them both wine. It seemed she would have to settle for conversation, but even that promised intrigue. She posed a question that had burned in her ever since she learned his identity. "Stellan, why is it always snowing in your land?"

The sorcerer looked at her, relief chasing away any lingering discomfort. He folded his hands on his lap. "Ah, the age-old favorite query. It's an ancient curse, if the rumors are to be believed. I don't know if it's entirely true, but I can tell you what I know."

Clarysa nodded, glad her question had eased the tension.

"As you're probably aware, snowstorms have plagued the area for several hundred years, almost since the castle first appeared. From what I've been told, a powerful king built Vandeborg. I couldn't tell you his name, however, because there were no records to be found. Stern but fair, he ruled over a fair number of subjects and commanded a moderate army."

"Was he married?"

"Yes, but he fell in love with a commoner. She was a servant, or a serving girl in a tavern... Something like that. They carried on a torrid affair. Naturally, the Queen discovered the betrayal."

Clarysa gasped. "What did she do?"

"According to the tale, she sought out a sorcerer--probably one of my ancestors--and ordered a curse put on the King and his lover. I don't know how the curse affected the woman, but the King was cast into a deep sleep and placed in an unbreakable glass casket. It was placed in the middle of the throne room."

"How eerie," she whispered.

"Hmm, yes, I suppose. However, the sorcerer took pity on the King, and included a loophole in the incantation." Stellan paused and took a draught of wine. "At each full moon, the King's doppelganger could walk the land for an entire night. It's rumored he spends the time searching for his lost love, for only her kiss can break the cruel magick."

"But why is there so much snow?"

Stellan grinned. "The sorcerer's personal touch. It's a way to protect the King as he lays in the casket."

"Oh," she said, and fell silent for a few moments. "Then how did you know about the casket?"

"I found it."

Clarysa perked up. "Truly? When?"

"The day I first arrived there."

She stared at him, openmouthed. "Is it still in the throne room?"

"No. I moved it to a chamber deep within the castle."

"What do you think happened to his love?"

Stellan shrugged. "The Queen ordered her execution, most likely. If this king does rise up as the legends say, it would be highly unlikely he knows. His spirit will wander the lands forever, searching for someone who is no longer alive."

"Oh, how awful."

A slight chill by way of a breeze brought with it a moment of silence.

Clarysa gave him a sympathetic look. "What a desolate and sad place your kingdom is. Why don't you leave?"

"And go where? I...can't return to my homeland."

His sharp tone startled her. She bit her lip. "My apologies. I didn't know."

Stellan shook his head. "It doesn't matter. Besides, the location is very strategic for hunting down Pestilence."

Clarysa tapped Stellan's boot to get his attention, for he was staring off into space. "I should like to visit your kingdom some time. With your permission, of course!"

"I don't think it'll be much to your liking."

"Is that a yes or a no?"

Stellan eyed her for a moment. "You have my permission, but it's a moot point. Your father would never allow it."

"Oh dear, you're right." Clarysa cocked her head. "I'll think of something!"

Stellan leaned forward, his expression serious. "Well, if you ever do travel there, you must never take the path through Dungeon Forest. Do you understand me? Never!"

A shiver ran through her. *He's awfully intense about it.* "Why not?"

"I know it was originally the quickest route between Aldebaran and Vandeborg, but now it's dangerously enchanted. There are sabrewolves and other deadly creatures. Few people have passed through that forest and lived."

"But you have! You've made it through."

Stellan shrugged noncommittally. "Just promise me you'll never go there."

Clarysa nodded. "I promise." Then an idea occurred to her. "I know! Why don't you come on the next hunt? I'll...I'll be hunting, too."

"That can be arranged," he murmured.

"Wonderful," Clarysa breathed.

"Are you two having fun yet? Or should I be asking if you're both decent?"

They turned to see Lionel strolling toward them. Clarysa jumped up to greet him, only to be met with his arm wrapping loosely about her neck. She shrieked in mock fear.

Lionel easily kept her wriggling form at bay. "Stellan, if this wench gives you any trouble, any at all, you inform me immediately so proper consequences can be meted out!"

Clarysa giggled and squirmed madly. Stellan looked on with a polite smile. After a few more tortured moments, Lionel released her.

"Anyway, I've come to let you know we're heading back."

"So soon?" Clarysa asked, staring up in dismay from her glass of wine.

"What do you mean, 'so soon'? We've been here all day."

"One more hour," she pleaded.

Lionel rolled his eyes. "Are we back in the nursery now? We'll be riding home in the dark if we don't depart in the next half hour."

Clarysa scowled, and then masked her irritation for fear of appearing unseemly. She cast Stellan a hopeful glance. "So I'll see you at the next hunt?"

Lionel laughed. "And so you're inviting yourself along on the rest of them, eh?"

Clarysa crossed her arms. "I can if I want to."

Stellan stood and donned his cape. "I'll be there, as long as I'm not needed elsewhere."

Clarysa could barely contain her squeal. Escorted by Lionel and Stellan, she walked back to the main group as the servants tidied up and loaded the horses. Her heart pounded hard with excitement.

She would see Stellan again, but not for another month! However could she wait that long?

Chapter 8

The sun splashed warm, golden rays over the traveling hunting party. Clarysa sighed contentedly. Everything about the day had been so perfect. She listened as cheerful voices rose in song, servants and royalty alike. The strength of camaraderie coursed strong through the group as it traveled a main road into the heart of Aldebaran. The Belleressort estate lay roughly an hour away.

Lagging on her steed near the tail end of the procession, she pulled her cloak tight against the cool late-afternoon air. Apple, her horse, ambled forward at a casual pace. Occasionally she would glance behind her, hoping Stellan had changed his mind and would appear. Such was not the case, but at least she'd had several precious hours with him.

Clarysa thought him simply extraordinary. She had never met anyone like him, either. Though gruff in manner, he possessed an intriguing vulnerability. The day's events replayed themselves constantly in her mind. Every time he had spoken, a bracing thrill had run down her spine. Then there was his haunting, handsome face. He could use some fattening up, but his tall frame and piercing green eyes more than made up for it. He also possessed enough mystery for a thousand men! That quality alone was enough to make her melt in rapture.

Based on the legend surrounding him, Clarysa speculated life must have been horrible for him. Everyone in Aldebaran despised and feared him. She herself was guilty of judging him based on nothing but hearsay. Now, however, she knew the truth, and would act accordingly.

Though fantasies about altering the destiny of his life ran through her head, the more realistic option might be found in simple gestures. Welcoming him into her family was one. Then there were the advantages only wealth could bring. She had already decided she would buy him a gift, perhaps a few new tunics or the latest fashionable cape. Lionel would help her pick out something. Or maybe a--

"Something's heading this way!" shouted one of the cooks.

Edward issued a formal halt. The procession came to an immediate stop.

Clarysa looked left. A group of villagers were racing across the plain. A massive herd of feet and dust, they seemed to run at an impossibly fast pace. The town of Arcadia was about a mile beyond the hill. *Is there a fire?*

The riders ahead skewed sharply right. Then desperate cries and shouts of "Run!" and "Watch out!" and "Make for the woods!" ripped through the air.

"What's wrong?" Clarysa cried.

"I think we're under attack," said the same cook as before.

"By whom?" Clarysa's voice grew shrill. "What are they after? Do they know who we are?"

But before she could receive an answer, the villagers were upon them. Scores of belligerent men and women dove into their flank, scattering the royal hunting party. A wild, frenzied look accompanied each person's unnatural, bestial gait. Horses and their riders drifted about everywhere leaving nothing more than a jumbled panorama. Dumbfounded, Clarysa could only stare as some of the guards and servants formed a protective barrier around her.

"What's wrong with them?" she asked.

"Difficult to say," one of the guards speculated. "But we'll get to the bottom of it."

Craning her neck, she sought Edward and Lionel. After a moment she spotted them, swords raised and teeth bared, valiantly fending off the rabid attackers. Clarysa watched in horror as one of the villagers leaped into the air, hammering one of the riders from his horse. The pair fell onto the ground with a sickening thud, and began wrestling in a cloud of dust. *These people...they're acting like animals--so crazed and berserk!*

More villagers appeared. They wielded chunky weapons of axes, stones and wooden clubs. They swung clumsily but fast, grunting and howling their wrath. Several of the King's guards lay dead on the ground, their gory remains splattered in thick, random blankets.

Clarysa shuddered. But it wasn't only the violent exchange of blows scaring her. It was their eyes--she had caught a glimpse of the man's eyes as he hurtled toward the rider.

Blood red. The orbs had been suffused with crimson, obscuring even the pupils.

A chilling thought quickly enveloped her. *No, it can't be. How is it possible?* But the truth could not be denied. "Pestilence," she croaked out, her throat now coated with dust. "It's Pestilence!"

No one seemed to heed her warning. Instead, her companions shouted at her to reverse direction. Clarysa glanced wildly left and right. Five or six villagers were closing in on her group. She was weaponless, but she dare not abandon her kin. Yet what could she do? Nothing. Nothing but sit there and stare into the glazed expressions of her attackers.

Lionel and Edward sped forth, apparently intending to join her. More villagers surged across their path, effectively blocking their advance. Anxious voices buzzed all around her. A cloud of dust. A blanket of blood. A cacophony of shrieks. Then she lost sight of her brother and cousin.

She didn't know where to turn, but then a guard directed her horse for her. "I'll escort you away from here, Your Highness!" Following his lead, Clarysa spurred her horse into a gallop.

Within seconds, they became separated from the rest. Clarysa looked back, gasping as a one-armed villager gave chase. He gained on them unnaturally fast. One soaring leap and he landed on her guard's horse. Man and monster exchanged a round of blows.

"Keep going!" the guard ordered, even as the villager bit off his ear.

The guard and villager crashed to the ground in a tangle of bloody limbs.

There's nothing you can do here. Go! Clarysa whipped her head forward and rode on. Tears streamed down her cheeks. Soon the sounds of the skirmish faded entirely. Before long, only the rhythmic beat of Apple's hooves trampling the ground remained. Her heart rate began to slow; her breathing began to stabilize. She gingerly pulled on the reins to slow the frightened beast. They both desperately needed to catch their second wind. Attempting to regain her calm as well as the horse's, she cooed into its ear. She had control over her own behavior, at least.

There. Her overworked lungs ceased their lament.

Clarysa looked cautiously behind her. She hadn't realized the contagion was so widespread. *Those poor people. They're nothing more than savage maniacs.* The Aldebaran citizenry had to be warned. But which return path would be safest?

She contemplated turning back to help her brother and cousin, only to squash the idea. She had no weapons on her. But so many of her people were at risk. She frowned, feeling useless and stupid for running off. Yet she couldn't stay here in the middle of nowhere and do nothing.

Apple pawed the ground, turning her head anxiously from side to side. Clarysa leaned forward, stroking her mane for comfort. "There, there," she said in dulcet tones. "I'll figure out something, don't worry."

Clarysa sighed, a long, slow sigh that seemed to go on for years. Others were depending upon her, and she wasn't about to let them down. But what were her options? More importantly, whose aid could she enlist?

Stellan!

Perhaps it wasn't too late. If she rode hard, as hard as her mare could muster, she might catch up with him. With a fierce cry, she swiftly changed direction, and spurred her steed west toward the cold, unrelenting darkness of the Snowflake Kingdom.

Chapter 9

At first, the roads Clarysa took were familiar, well worn. As a youth, she had explored these woods and fields many times in the company of Lionel and other relatives. Memories of gathering mushrooms and wild berries sprang to mind. On this side of Dungeon Forest, Eastender's Road was landscaped and well maintained. Clarysa even passed a few startled travelers. They stared in surprise as she galloped past, shouting warnings.

As she traveled on, the road before her narrowed and took on a rougher form. Large craters appeared, threatening to devour them whole. On the horizon, the sun had gone to rest, replaced with a gloomy dusk. Trees pressed up against the road, crouched amid thick bushes and other wild, scraggly undergrowth.

While Clarysa stopped at a small stream so Apple could drink, owls hooted.

Back on the road, the forest's nocturnal citizens began their routines. Unseen creatures skittered alongside the road. Night eyes followed her progress from the shadows. She scanned the darkened path before her, alert for obstacles. Regardless of the danger, she forged ahead.

At a crossroads she pulled tightly on the reins, urging Apple to stop. In the inky sea now surrounding her, she couldn't quite remember which road jutted from Eastender's toward Vandeborg. She only knew that one angled north…somewhere. Was this particular path the correct way or not?

The journey seemed to be taking longer than it should. The murky surroundings did little to inspire confidence, let alone a clear view. Without a torch, her horse could very well collide with something. But if she didn't remember the correct route soon, she would have to consider turning back.

No, failure wasn't an acceptable option. Her people were counting on her to press onward for help.

Oh, but wait! Clarysa noticed a wide opening in the forest wall. How had she not seen it before? She peered into the clearing. True, it didn't appear to be much more than a path for errant pigs, but it was a path nonetheless. Squinting, she even spied something white on the ground farther in. It emitted a soft, luminous glow in the burgeoning moonlight. Was it snow? With renewed vigor, Clarysa guided Apple onto the trail.

Once through the narrow opening, the path seemed a straight shot. The horse galloped away. Snow crunched underfoot. The air felt markedly cooler, prompting Clarysa to pull up her hood.

Apple swerved suddenly to avoid a large tree. Heavens! Where had it come from? Clarysa flicked the reins. "No, silly, don't slow down!"

But the mare had no choice. The path--if it still was one--became glutted with gnarled, blackened trunks. Branches swayed overhead as a chill wind teased her. Apple slowed to a trot, then merely a walk. Tentacle-like roots necessitated careful navigating. Clarysa groaned. This was taking forever. She eased her horse slightly right, as it seemed the path resumed in that direction.

They wandered for many long minutes. Slivers of moonlight poked through the canopy above and then night reared its stark head with a vengeance. The snow here lay thick and deep. Apple's ears pricked up. Clarysa glanced around. It appeared they were not alone.

Chittering sounds rose from the darkness, first from one side, then the other. Clarysa yanked on the reins, forcing Apple to a stop. The mare snorted her protest. This most definitely did not seem like a proper place to stay, but Clarysa needed to find her bearings. She leaned forward to stroke Apple's mane and ease some of its fear before continuing.

All at once, the surrounding forest fell silent. It was as if the giant hand of death had clamped down on everything surrounding them. Clarysa's loud heartbeat was the only sign of life.

She tried to detect any lights, any movement in the area ahead. Unidentifiable animals scampered among the low-lying bracken. *Henceforth, you carry flint with you.* Chilly air seeped past the folds of her dress. She rubbed her hands together for warmth. *Am I lost? Where in blazes* is *his castle?*

More chittering arose. This time surrounding her; this time laden with grunts. Clarysa whipped her head around. What was that snapping noise? Small, inky-black shapes seemed to be drifting alongside the horse, but it was difficult to see anything clearly in the oppressive darkness. She rubbed her eyes. It was only bushes, a trick of the scant moonlight and its many shadows.

Apple reared high into the air, throwing Clarysa to the side. She slammed against a trunk. Pain exploded throughout her body as she tumbled to the ground. Strange noises erupted around her, sounding like gleeful titters. No wonder her horse had spooked; these were no ordinary nocturnal animals.

Dazed, Clarysa rose on shaky knees. "Apple?"

A soft neigh broke the silence, followed by the horse's terrified shriek. "Apple!"

Clarysa sprinted toward the sound. The horse lay a few yards distant. Something had brought her crashing to the ground. Dropping to her knees, Clarysa crawled forward. "Apple?"

The horse was still, but something else moved. Clarysa heard a squelching sound. A warm, metallic smell filled her nose. She inched closer. After reaching her horse, she slowly peered over Apple's back.

An imp squatted between its legs, feasting on the horse's innards. At least, that's what she thought it was. No larger than a small dog, its dark hide resembled those she'd seen in illustrations. But she wasn't surrounded by warm candlelight and soft blankets, nor could she simply close a book to ward off the ghoulish image. Her current predicament was far more perilous.

The realization hit her like a rock: she had stumbled into Dungeon Forest.

She had difficulty catching her breath. Stellan had warned her about avoiding this place. Now she understood why. But she hadn't meant to ignore his advice. Where had she gone wrong?

Noise interrupted her thoughts. The macabre scene before her wasn't over yet. Blood gushed forth from Apple's body, the surrounding snow soaking it up like a sponge. The imp, seemingly unaware of her, chomped mercilessly, at one point pulling hard at a resistant tendril of flesh. Clarysa gagged, then quickly covered her mouth.

It was too late. The creature turned. Blood dripped in torrents down its tiny chin. As their eyes met, its fangs spread wide in a vicious leer.

Scrambling to her feet, Clarysa ran. She ran like she had never run before.

Branches scratched her face as she pushed past them. "Stellan!" she shouted, then increased the volume. "Stellan!" It was pointless--he would never come. "*Stellan!*"

Clarysa cried his name until her voice grew hoarse. She darted about the forest for what seemed like an eternity. Fear drove her without mercy. Her straining lungs thirsted for air.

Farther and farther she ran, blindly, until an outstretched root sent her crashing earthward. "Oh no!" Pain shot through her ankle. Clarysa slumped to the ground, tearful and shaking. *Keep going. If you stay here they'll come and tear you apart!*

But her legs refused to cooperate. Clarysa moaned. Why oh why had she taken the path? It had seemed the right choice at the time. The scolding voice of her eldest sister echoed in her head. *"Why don't you ever think before you act?"* Then Stellan's words came back to haunt her. *"You must never take the path through the forest... It's dangerously enchanted... Few people have passed through that forest and lived."*

Clarysa whimpered at the thought of being trapped in Dungeon Forest forever. But memories from the recent attack flashed into her mind. If she could find Stellan, there was a good chance lives could be saved--many, *many* lives. Resolve to stand filled her. She would find a way out of this hellish forest and complete her mission.

Reaching out an arm, she used a tree to prop herself up. Glancing up at the thin slice of moon visible through the trees, she charted a path roughly west. Gingerly, she tested some weight on her ankle. It felt swollen, but perhaps it was not broken. She could walk on it if she was careful.

Clarysa limped forward, but was forced to a stop. Her cloak had stuck on something. She turned around and gave it a tug.

A miniature two-legged creature sat on the edge, preventing her escape. Other than its wide, pale-lit blue eyes, Clarysa couldn't make out any of its other features. With two tiny, but extremely strong hands, it tugged at her cloak in deliberate mockery.

First imps, now goblins? Clarysa attempted to steady her panicked breathing. Perhaps it was only her overactive imagination. She gave her cloak another tug. But the creature had an unnatural heaviness to it. It seemed to enjoy sitting right where it was. To struggle against it appeared futile.

Slowly, she eased the cloak from her shoulders. A quiet titter issued from the goblin's mouth. *Carefully... Almost there... Now run!* Clarysa dropped the cloak, leaving it far behind as she stumbled away. A chorus of angry voices arose from the darkness around her.

The cold air stiffened her limbs, and the injured ankle only further impeded her progress. Onward and onward she ran, tears flowing freely down her cheeks. At a particularly crooked oak tree, she heard thumping noises from all around. A multitude of creatures suddenly dropped from the trees and dove toward her through the undergrowth.

Clarysa was surrounded.

All manner of nightmarish fiends closed in with glowing eyes and bared teeth. They snapped their jaws and slurped and smacked their lips. She avoided looking directly at them and ran. Given their small size, perhaps she had a chance of breaking through their ranks. Not so. Multiple hands latched on to her legs. Down she went once again. Death began to whisper in her ear.

Is this my fate? I simply wanted to help, to be useful. Oh, Stellan!

One of the creatures landed on her back. She tried to dislodge it, but collapsed under its weight. The rough ground scraped her cheek. Tiny paws tore at her dress. Then something hard, pointy and cold pierced her, like an icicle plunging into her shoulder blade.

Clarysa groaned, writhing with pain so sharp it threatened unconsciousness. Wetness coated her back--blood! Acute dread filled her. She would never see her family--or Prince Stellan--again. *I failed you all. Please forgive me!*

A canine growl pierced the air. Was she to be torn apart by demons and finished off by wolves? The malevolent snarls grew alarmingly closer. Paralyzed by fear, Clarysa squeezed her eyes shut and waited for the end.

Chapter 10

As the wolf neared, Clarysa braced herself. The fangs would sink into her flesh any moment now. *No, no, no! Have mercy!*

Then she heard an unmistakably human voice, though the words sounded incoherent. *Is someone really there, or am I hallucinating?* A wave of demonic squeals pierced the night air and faded abruptly away. The weight lifted from her back.

Strong hands gripped her waist. Someone had found her. A man. Clarysa was too weak to resist as the stranger lifted her onto a nearby horse. He mounted behind her. Once astride, he flicked the reins sharply and the horse galloped away.

The man covered her with his cloak. The heat of his body did little to mitigate her frigid state. Her teeth chattered uncontrollably. Exhausted and dizzy, she leaned back against her rescuer.

On and on they rode. Eventually, they emerged from the dark canopy of the forest. Moonlight shimmered across large hills of snow. The night was clear and the air brisk. The horse's strong muscles rippled up and down as it plowed through the wintry mix with seemingly little effort. Beside them, a great white wolf kept pace.

After they cleared the last hill, a castle broke into view. Clarysa studied it from beneath heavy eyelids. The nighttime dressed most of the fortress in shadow, but it was moderate in size and had seven or eight pointed towers. The horse and wolf raced across a bridge that led to the front gate. As they approached, someone opened it from within.

As soon as the doors clanged shut, the horse stopped. Her rescuer dismounted. Clarysa looked down. A rush of relief coursed through her upon discovering Stellan's face. She smiled weakly as he eased her from the saddle. *Put the weight on your good foot!* came the bleary thought. Once on solid ground, she gazed up at him.

Stellan gripped her shoulders with pincer like hands. "Foolish woman!" he barked. "That was incredibly stupid of you! *Incredibly* stupid! I told you never to take that road, and I meant it!"

Clarysa clutched a fistful of his cloak to steady herself. It seemed a monumental effort to speak. "I...I came to warn you. Villagers attacked us as we returned. They were... Their eyes...so bloody. I think they're infected! We need your help."

Stellan's furious gaze thawed, but only a touch.

"There was no one else to spare...only I escaped." She tried to squelch the odd discomfort building in her chest and lowered her gaze. Her voice dropped to a whisper. "Please...forgive me. I remembered your warning too late. I meant no disrespect." Loosening her grip, she stepped back. Her hand reached behind, seeking out a wall to lean against. Finding none, she slumped against Midnight. "What...what other choice did I have?"

Stellan turned aside. "Patrulha!" he bellowed. In the dimly lit entry hall, Clarysa spotted a number of dark-clad figures approaching. One of them took the lead.

"Right here," said a woman. She stepped into the light of the nearest torch.

Clarysa gazed at her with intense curiosity. For one thing, the newcomer towered above her. Patrulha had dark features and unkempt hair. Thigh-high boots along with a thick leather tunic adorned her body--a warrior's garb. A black patch was slung across her right eye. Her left one lingered, giving Clarysa a brief appraisal before locking onto Stellan.

Stellan began to issue orders. "Assemble twenty of our men and saddle up. We ride to Aldebaran."

Patrulha cocked a brow.

"Pestilence attack," Stellan responded. "Humans, this time."

Patrulha nodded and darted off.

Clarysa's breathing became more labored. Nevertheless, she forced out her question. "Who is she?"

"Captain of my guard--such as it is." He turned away to consult with one of the men.

Clarysa didn't want to bother him, but then her chest constricted in an alarming manner. Gasping and wheezing, she collapsed on the floor. She heard an older woman's voice cry out.

"Heavens above! The Lady!"

Stellan rushed to her side. "Clarysa? What's wrong?"

Groans of pain spilled from her lips. "I feel so cold."

He picked her up effortlessly. "Quickly," Stellan shouted. "Draw her a bath by the fire!"

He carried her sluggish form across the entry hall. A cool draft made her shiver. Her gazed fixated on a piece of her torn and tattered dress as it dragged along the stone floor.

Next to a roaring hearth, he placed her in a big wooden tub. Warm water flooded into it, reviving her slightly. Clarysa opened her eyes.

A woman with an expression of unabashed curiosity stared at her. She wore a smudged apron over a patterned red frock. Clearly a servant. A rat's nest of curly, brown hair streaked with gray crowned blunt features. Creases lined her mouth and eyes; here was a woman in her late forties, at least.

Clarysa wet her cracked lips. "Hello. I'm Clarysa."

The woman propped a hand on her hip. "And I'm Gretchen." Her warm, earthy voice was infused with a heavy accent. She smiled, the act revealing a wide gap between her two top teeth. "Very pleased to make your acquaintance."

Stellan appeared at her side with a fresh bucket. "And I'll be pleased if you'll stop talking. Keep the water coming."

"Yes, Your Highness." Gretchen winked before slipping from Clarysa's view.

Stellan dumped the water into the tub. Clarysa could see the steam rising from it, but it didn't feel as hot as it should.

Stellan gripped her shoulders and pulled her forward. She gasped as he yanked her dress halfway down her back. His fingers probed her skin, searching for what, she didn't know. One spot in particular ached horribly. "What do you see?"

"Exactly as I thought," he muttered, releasing the material and gently coaxing her back into the water.

"What's wrong with me?" she asked, her voice sounding like an ugly croak to her ears.

"Imp's Kiss," he responded. "One of them was on your back. It bit you."

Clarysa struggled to speak through chattering teeth. "W-what's Imp's K-k-kiss?"

Stellan knelt beside the tub. He pulled one of her arms from beneath the water. The healthy glow of her skin had dissolved into an unnatural pallor marked by dark blue veins. "You'll freeze to death if we don't keep you warm," he said grimly, lowering her arm gently back under the water. "I'll be right back."

Stellan disappeared from view. After Gretchen had filled the tub with two more buckets of water, he returned. He raised a small vial to her lips. "Here. Drink this antidote. It will destroy the poison."

Clarysa gagged; the concoction he had hurriedly tossed down her throat tasted horrid. It smelled of rotten meat and had a slimy, viscous feel as it slowly slid down her throat. *Is this some kind of sorcerer's trap?* For the first time, she wondered if she had made a mistake in coming. Was that Edward's gloating face staring up at her from the water?

By reflex, she tried to spit it back up, but Stellan clamped a hand roughly over her mouth. "Swallow it," came his command. "Now!"

Tears sprung to her eyes, but she complied. No strength remained for any other response. Only when he was sure she had drunk the entire concoction did he release his hand.

Stellan grabbed a bucket from Gretchen's hand as she approached the tub. He dumped it in quickly and tested the water. "It's getting cold already. Have Ghyslain help you."

Gretchen nodded and hurried away.

Stellan looked thoughtful. "The potion's full effect will take time. You will stay here and recover. I'll prepare a follow-up treatment for Gretchen to administer, and you won't give her any trouble about drinking it. That *is* understood, is it not?"

Clarysa nodded slowly to indicate her obedience. Though firm to the point of being draconian, clearly Stellan was only trying to help her. *I was wrong to have doubted you.* "Where are you g-going?"

"My men and I will ride to Aldebaran to deal with the infestation. You are not given leave from my castle until I return. That is also understood."

Clarysa reached out and grabbed his hand. There was so much she wanted to learn about him. Labored breathing impaired her ability to speak, and pains shot through her chest. She could only stare at him, his face unreadable. She wondered if he cared about her, or if he was simply performing his princely duty.

Stellan eased her hand back into the water. "Just rest," he said, his voice echoing faintly in her head, "rest." His face began to melt away and soon vanished altogether from her consciousness.

Chapter 11

A candle stump tried valiantly to pierce the darkness of the cascading stairwell as Stellan descended to his workshop. As he opened the door, a kaleidoscope of deep red and green hues splashed over him, emanating from the luminous contents of the glass jars stored inside. They contained potent mixtures he had fashioned over the years.

He placed the candle on the room's rough-hewn table and gathered a number of jars from the shelves. Scratching sounds eked out from behind the walls, but Stellan paid them no heed. He had to work quickly if he was going to stop the Pestilence outbreak in time.

He unrolled a padded bundle of empty vials. He lined them up on the table along with bowls, funnels, measuring spoons, tubing, and stirring rods. Some of the potions required little more than precise measurement and mixing; others would only activate with heat, a task Stellan accomplished using a specially modified burner.

Occasionally, he flipped through a well-worn bundle of papers--his book of potions. He knew most of them by heart, but where Pestilence was concerned certainty was crucial.

Would his small arsenal be enough? Stellan had developed them through extensive trial and error over the years, and he was still learning. Other than an apothecary he'd once known, he had only his memory of childhood studies to guide him in the magickal arts. Now he regretted not seeking out sympathetic sorcerers for consultation--if they even existed. The Black Mage ruled by instilling fear rather than respect. During his fifty-plus-year reign, only Stellan had dared oppose him.

His gaze followed a path up to the topmost shelf in the back of the room. There, a grayish glow oozed forth, easily drowning the rainbow-colored hues around it.

It was still there. Despite its obvious danger, its capricious results, Stellan was loath to part with it. Even now, its power called to him.

Memories inundated him as he stood there quietly regarding the pulsing orb.

He had been fifteen when he'd stumbled onto that leafy path within Dungeon Forest. Even though he'd previously explored the area many times, he had never seen its inviting entrance. Curious.

* * * *

Horseless at the time, he'd crept along on foot. Rounding a bend, he'd encountered an impossibly tall man draped in a long, flowing robe. The stranger's cowled, hidden face should have sent Stellan scurrying, but his desperate need for human contact had kept him rooted to the spot.

A slender, bony hand urged Stellan closer. He joined the cowled man beneath the shadow of a large oak tree. "What are you doing here," inquired the stranger, "in this land so far from home?"

"I am searching for herbs with which to mix my potions. My name is Stellan. May I ask for yours?"

The man leaned on his staff and chuckled. "Of course you may ask, but do not expect a quick and honest reply. After all, a name represents that which makes a person. When one simply gives it away, he gives away a bit of his soul as well."

Stellan had only nodded at the cryptic remark, not truly understanding its implications. "Well," he'd said, "I'm going to leave now."

"Wait!" cried the robed man. "I have something for you." He produced an old earthen pot from his capacious robe, a pot spotted with age. "You said you needed herbs. This, I assure you, is far more potent than any plant."

Confused, Stellan had frowned. "Why are you offering it to me, sir? I don't know you and have nothing to offer in return."

"Consider it a gift then," the man said, "one to aid you in your magick. My bones are tired and old. I have need of it no more."

Stellan was intrigued, so he stepped closer. "What is it?" he asked, bending over to study the mottled pot. He still hadn't committed to accepting it. "Raven's root? *Calillon* leaves?"

The stranger shook his cowled head. "The power to breach the walls of life and death."

Now Stellan was *definitely* interested, for power was one possession he lacked. He reached for the container. The pot was smooth and warm in his hands. A thin slit of pulsing grayish light was visible where the lid met the body, but Stellan didn't dare open it until he was back home. His heart rate sped up. This was a true find indeed!

Stellan looked up to thank the stranger, only to discover he was gone. He should have questioned the disappearance, but he was too excited about his new acquisition. Container in tow, Stellan turned and began the long journey back to icy Vandeborg.

* * * *

The memory faded. Stellan gasped at the sight of the jar in his hand. A shudder ran through him. He didn't remember picking it up. As if it burned, he hastily returned it to the shelf.

Little had he known what unspeakable power dwelled within the dread container, but he'd been too eager to find out. Upon returning to Vandeborg, opening the lid was all he'd needed to do in order to unleash the power within. The result had been both magnificent and terrifying.

Yet the experience had nearly cost him his one true asset--his mind. No one could expect to survive such an encounter with their wits intact. Somehow, he'd managed to replace the lid and end the macabre parade before any more damage had been done. If it hadn't been for Gretchen and her family, he would have succumbed to madness.

In retrospect, he should have questioned the stranger harder about his identity. Was he a rogue sorcerer? A demon? A spy sent by the Black Mage? Who knew what devil's bargain he had unwittingly agreed to that day. Years passed before he'd realized such a "gift" came with a price. What price Stellan would yet pay remained to be seen.

Stellan bundled up his full vials. It was time to depart for Aldebaran. At the door of his workshop, he cast a rueful look toward the ominous glow on the topmost shelf.

"That's not a mistake I'll make twice," he muttered, slamming the door behind him.

Chapter 12

Clarysa awoke and discovered she was in a cocoon of thick blankets. Only her face was exposed. She opened her bleary eyes and stared into the flames of a robust fire. Where was she? Then it all came rushing back--Stellan's castle!

She crawled from the makeshift womb of brightly colored blankets. Looking down, she fingered the rough cloth of the nightgown she wore. It was a far cry from the silk and fine linen filling her wardrobes back home.

Clarysa shivered in the brisk air. She wrapped herself in a blanket. At the foot of the hearth, she discovered thick woolen socks and a pair of slippers. Guessing their worth in the frigid castle, she donned them quickly. She raked her fingers through her disheveled hair. *I must look a fright.*

There. Now it was time to find someone, anyone. She had no idea how long she had lain there, but she remembered Gretchen coming to wake her periodically to take more of the potion. Clarysa put a hand to her lips, her stomach churning at the memory. Stellan! Had he returned? What about the Pestilence threat? She had to find answers.

Clarysa grasped the door's large iron handle. Opening it took all of her strength. A cool draft of air rushed in and sipped quietly at the room's warmth. After a few moments' rest, Clarysa stepped into the hallway.

Yawning, she crept down the murky passageway. A light shone at the far end, drawing her like a moth. She shivered despite the blanket. *I can't believe how cold it is here.* Even in the dead of winter, her father would never allow his castle to be so uncomfortable. This would take some getting used to.

Winded, she stopped to rest against the base of a pillar. Clarysa braved a look around and upward. The vaulted ceilings disappeared into fathomless shadow. Statues lined the walls, their visages appearing ominous. Most were of men clad in ancient armor. Hideous beasts of stone reached outward with coiled tails and dangerous-looking claws. A scratching noise mysteriously emanated from behind one of them. Though faint, it sounded purposeful. Clarysa shuddered, and continued her search.

As she neared the source of the light, Clarysa heard voices. She hoped one of them belonged to Gretchen. Shuffling up to the doorway, she peered slowly around the frame.

Ahead of her lay the kitchen. While expansive and well lit, it was also smoky and cluttered. Mismatched tables and chairs centered around the large hearth. Pots and pans of all sizes hung from rusty hooks. Everything seemed to bear the stain of careworn age.

Garlic and onions hung in sacs along the walls, and potatoes spilled from a huge bin in one grimy nook. Liquid bubbled from the iron pot atop the fire. The air felt toasty and smelled like slow-cooked soup.

Clarysa then gazed in wonder at the sight of a covered, brightly painted wagon in the opposite corner. It sat there like a plump, bulbous flower at the height of its bloom. Large wheels ran outside the body of the van, which sloped outward considerably toward the eaves. Deep blue curtains embellished the opening. Clothes hung drying on various ropes that stretched from wagon to walls. Clarysa thought it magnificent. Even with her avid reading of the history books, she had never seen anything like it.

"Well, come in, come in! Don't be a stranger, my dear."

Clarysa focused on the voice's owner. It was indeed Gretchen. Her appearance resembled a brightly colored butterfly, accented by coin necklaces and bracelets that jingled as she expertly navigated the room's obstacles. She wiped her hand on a towel and then used the same to reach for Clarysa's elbow and assist her down the steps.

"How are you feeling?" The older woman took a moment to study Clarysa's face, rubbing and pinching her cheeks with strong, calloused hands. "Aye, I think you've recovered for the most part. Come and sit. I was just getting us some lunch." Gretchen nodded toward a young man seated at the main table. "This is Ghyslain, my son."

Clarysa barely remembered him from the night of her rescue, but was glad of the chance to meet him properly. Brown hair tied in a ponytail and one large hoop earring accented Ghyslain's appearance. He had the gangly bearing of a teenager but none of the awkwardness. He grinned and waved hello, then stood to offer her a seat.

Clarysa curtsied. But her weak legs rebelled, and she toppled over into a stack of carefully arranged baskets. Gretchen and her son rushed to her aid. They guided her into a sturdy chair by the wooden table.

"I'm so sorry! Please forgive me."

Gretchen chuckled. "That's what you get for using such fancy manners around this place. Ghyslain, the cups, please." Gretchen busied herself at the hearth, ladling soup into three large bowls.

Metal silverware landed in the steaming bowls. It was dull and scratched, yet betraying skilled craftsmanship. Gretchen placed the bowls deftly on the table as the boy filled three earthenware mugs with water. She retreated to the pantry, returning with thick slices of dark, crusty bread. "Old family recipe," she said, lifting her mug in cheer.

Clarysa smiled and turned to her meal. It was a thin potato soup with garlic and onion, speckled with carrot. She ate steadily for a few moments. "This is wonderful, thank you, Gretchen. How long have I been asleep?"

"Three days," came Gretchen's nonchalant answer. She slurped hard, some of the soup running down her chin.

Clarysa straightened up. "Thr…three days?"

"That's right." Gretchen regarded her, slowly wiping her mouth with the back of a hand. "Why? Was there somewhere you needed to be?"

"No, I…" Clarysa nervously fingered her spoon. "It seems like I nearly died!"

"I'll not lie. You had a serious brush with death." Gretchen took their bowls for a refill.

Clarysa chewed thoughtfully on a piece of the tough bread. It was mostly tasteless and she didn't care for it, old family recipe or not. "Any word from Stellan?" she asked.

Gretchen shook her head. "Don't expect him back for a week, at least. He hasn't got the men to spare for messengers."

Clarysa nodded her understanding and resumed eating. But her stomach already felt full, so she pushed the bowl away after only a few more bites. She sipped her water. The food had given her energy, and she was bursting with questions. The first flew from her mouth before she could stop it. "I thought Stellan lived alone. Does he… I mean, is he, uh, is he with anyone?"

Gretchen looked up sharply.

Clarysa winced. *Idiot! You were rubbing shoulders with death and that's all you can think about?*

Mirth made Gretchen's eyes sparkle. "You mean like a…a companion? A lady friend, perhaps? Is that what you'd like to know?"

"Yes," she said softly.

Gretchen stroked her chin. "Well, no, unless you count..." A thoughtful look passed briefly across her face. "No, he doesn't." Her lips broke into a wide smile. "Why? Do you have someone in mind for him?"

Clarysa looked down, blushing furiously. "Just wondering," she muttered.

Gretchen snorted. "Well then, are you finished eating?"

Clarysa nodded. Gretchen and Ghyslain gathered the dishes.

As they worked, Clarysa noticed how carefully Gretchen conserved the remaining food. Even her own uneaten soup went back into the pot. Clarysa recalled the vegetable pastry she had so carelessly wasted during the hunt and felt ashamed. Was Stellan *that* poor? She recalled other clues, such as his patched clothing, lean appearance and voracious appetite. At the time, she had thought nothing of it. Surely a prince could not be so destitute that every scrap of food had to be saved!

But perhaps so. Here she was, in a castle so drab and dreary and bare. She *had* to help somehow. Looking down, she tugged off two rings from her fingers and placed them on the table. When Gretchen returned with a rag to wipe the table's surface, Clarysa gestured for her to take them. "They should be several weeks' worth of food, I would think."

Gretchen looked horrified. "Oh, no, milady, oh no oh no! If the master finds out, he'll have my head! He's got a horrible temper, you know!" She pushed them back across the table.

"Oh, but you must accept them! Especially after all you've done. Think of it as my gift to you."

Gretchen eyed them wistfully. "I do miss my spices! I know how to cook, and cook well, but it's been so hard these past years. More and more he sits in his tower playing that infernal...here, Ghyslain!" She scooped up the rings and handed them to her son. "Go with Froll to the village. You know what to get!"

Ghyslain, his calm composure now flushed with excitement, bowed deeply toward Clarysa before bounding from the room.

Clarysa stared after him, beaming. Her donation wouldn't solve all of Stellan's problems, but at least it was something. Then she turned to Gretchen. "There's a village nearby?"

"Gods of fortune, no! It couldn't possibly survive here." She gestured toward the doorway. "They're going to one across the southern border of the kingdom."

"Oh." Clarysa studied her hands, but soon abandoned them in favor of more interesting quarry. "I feel so much better now. I was wondering, if you don't think me rude, who exactly *are* you? How long have you worked for Stellan?"

Gretchen grunted. "Aye, that's a tale in and of itself. If you have the time," she said with a wink, "and I know you do, I'll make us some tea and tell you the account of how my family came to live in this wretched wreck of a castle."

Chapter 13

Two mugs of strong, hot tea lit upon the table. Clarysa wrapped her hands around hers for warmth as Gretchen settled in her seat. The gypsy woman cleared her throat and began.

"A long time ago, my husband and I decided to return to his father's home by the sea after many years of wandering among the Hemling Mountains. They're on the northern edge of Falcon Heights. Ever been there?"

"No, I haven't."

"You should go sometime. Beautiful area. Anyway, it felt right to make a visit as I was heavy with Ghyslain at the time. This was about oh, fourteen years ago. Our group included myself, my husband Besnik, his brother Froll and our daughter Patrulha."

Clarysa's eyes widened at this revelation. *The Captain of the Guard!*

"The journey started out with smooth riding and only the most beautiful of weather to grace our way. We couldn't have been happier." Gretchen's eyes glossed over at some distant memory. "But my husband, fortune bless him, had a singular idea to take a shortcut, mainly to avoid entering the Wastes. He swore he knew it like the back of his hand." Gretchen clucked. "Well, that couldn't have been further from the truth as it turned out. Something must have changed long before we arrived, for the roads were confusing and poorly marked. We became lost. Set adrift without a thought of where to turn. More tea?"

Clarysa nodded, and Gretchen paused as she filled both their mugs.

"A vicious snowstorm waylaid us--a real howler. There was something odd about it. The change of weather was as night and day, being sunny and warm one minute, and freezing cold the next. Needless to say, we were ill-prepared. The storm toyed with us, driving us deeper and deeper into its belly." Gretchen shivered. "It lasted for days. Our food supply dwindled down to crumbs, and you could forget about any kind of a fire.

We were wet to the bone, constantly. Thought the reaper was upon us for sure then!"

"How awful!" said Clarysa. "What did you do?"

"What else could we do? We traveled on. And of course, that was the perfect time for me to go into labor. The storm and all must have induced it, for the contractions began something fierce!" Gretchen rubbed her middle-aged belly with a wry smile. "It was high time we found shelter, for I knew the baby weren't holding back none!

"We went on, blind as bats. As luck would have it--and to this day I thank the gods of fortune for their kindness--we stumbled upon this very castle. Whether it was night or day, I can't recall, for it always seems dark as pitch in this land." Gretchen let out a low sigh before continuing.

"Now imagine Stellan's surprise at this point. Here he is, a young boy, scared and all alone in this awful place. And you can right believe me when I say it looked a hundred times worse than what you see now." Gretchen took a sip of tea. "So we ride up to the front gate, and we're knocking and shouting like a crazed mob. My water had just broken. It seemed an eternity before he finally opened the door, and then only a crack. Besnik practically forced his way in. We entered, soaked and shivering, dripping like drowned rats."

Clarysa was spellbound by the tale. She held her breath as Gretchen leaned closer.

"And what did you think happened next?"

She shook her head. She couldn't imagine.

"Why, I gave birth to Ghyslain right inside the door. I plopped down nice as you please and out he came."

"How terrible!" Clarysa gave her a sympathetic look. "What did Stellan do?"

Gretchen snorted. "Didn't have much choice to do anything but watch. You should have seen him back then, all skin and bones. Paler than a corpse and dressed in rags. He must have been about fifteen. Never said a word during those first few days, just stared and pointed whenever we asked for anything. Not that he had anything to give other than a roof over our heads."

She wrinkled her nose. "The place smelled like death, and with good reason. I'm telling you, no lie, there were dead bodies all over the place! Rotting, maggot-loving corpses everywhere we turned. All twisted in strange positions." Gretchen pointed behind her. "One right here, too, face down in the hearth!" She shook her head. "God only knows what the boy did. Something devilish to be sure, for a dark cloud seemed to hang over him, sapping his will and confusing his senses. The horse was having trouble pulling the wagon, if you know what I mean."

Clarysa shook her head.

The old woman tapped her forehead. "Sick in the noggin, he was. Let me tell you, a few days after our arrival, a wild look seized his eyes, one like a crazed beast."

"What did it mean?"

"He had 'the grip' for sure. It was something fearful to behold. In all my born days I've never seen anything like it. That look, and the awful laugh! The poor dear began eating dirt right off of the floor. We knew we had to help him."

Clarysa winced at the unexpected news. This was far worse than what she had anticipated. "What did you do?"

"My husband and Froll caught him, bound him up tight and left him alone in a room to see if it would leave his mind." Gretchen's features darkened. "It took over three and a half moons for it to pass! I fed and bathed him as best I could, like a newborn babe--but one with the occasional bite my way!" She leaned back, her face appearing more relaxed. "In time, it passed. All's the better!"

Clarysa couldn't believe her ears. Stellan seemed so rational and calm. "Still, what a terrible ordeal."

Gretchen placed a comforting hand on Clarysa's. "The important thing now is he's back with us and sworn off that wicked magick for good, aside from a few medicinal herbs here and there. After all, who knows what the gods extract from a man's soul every time a mortal defies them?" She sipped her tea, looking thoughtful.

Clarysa nodded, her stomach fluttering anxiously. *Yes, who knows? And there I was asking him to perform simple tricks like a child would.* Memories of the conjured rose flooded her mind. *What price will he pay for that, I wonder?* The thought chilled her bones.

Clarysa cleared her throat. "How did you survive after that? I mean, with the snow and all."

"Well, we shared what little we had with Stellan, stretching our provisions for days and days our first month. Eventually, Besnik was forced to leave to find supplies. He returned just in time, too, for we'd had nothing but water for the two days prior. It was rougher than you'd ever believe."

"Where is your husband, if I may ask? Did he go with Stellan and the others?"

A melancholic expression passed over Gretchen's face. "He passed on many years ago. Bad heart."

Clarysa's voice grew hoarse. "Oh, I'm so sorry. After all you've been through."

Gretchen patted her hand briefly. "Don't be, child. I've been blessed. Besides, he lives on through our two beautiful children." She swallowed more tea. "Now where was I? Oh, yes, how we survived. Months passed before the young prince ever said a word. But one day, as I sat alone nursing Ghyslain by this hearth, Stellan appeared at the doorway. He tried to act all formal and haughty, but I knew there was a needy boy underneath his bluster.

"So I invited him in and we drank tea--much like we're doing now. I asked him if there were something on his mind. Let me tell you, his words came tumbling out so fast it was like a dam had burst! Would we please stay and live here and help take care of the castle, he said. He would protect us. Truth be told, I nearly laughed in his face. How was this skinny pole of a boy going to protect us, let alone a flea? Then he told me about his powers, slight as they were. I don't know if you're aware, but a sorcerer's abilities grow stronger once he reaches manhood. Or womanhood, if she's female."

Clarysa shook her head. "The only things I know about the people of the Western Wastes are what I've heard through tales."

"Well, consider yourself informed. To this day, I wonder if Stellan was disastrously naive, for the boy had nothing, like I said. Then, before I could answer, he asked for our allegiance. 'You must never leave me,' he demanded. 'You will belong to me, and I to you.'" Gretchen sighed. "Serious words from one so young. To stay would mean a whole lifestyle change, and for nomads like us, that idea was hard to swallow. But we owed him much. I found it difficult to turn aside such generosity. With Ghyslain so young, it made sense for us to stay put for a while. So I discussed it with Besnik, and we agreed to remain for a year." Gretchen smiled grimly. "That year stretched into fourteen more."

The fire spit and crackled during the subsequent silence, sending an amber cascade up the chimney. After a few minutes, Clarysa ventured to speak. "So you became like…like his family."

Gretchen nodded. "So we did. Besnik and Froll helped Stellan make repairs as best they could. But the castle seemed to have a mind of its own. They would fix one part and another would disintegrate before your very eyes. Nevertheless, Patrulha and I spent our days making the living quarters as comfortable as possible. But we always ended up back in the kitchen!

"Eventually, Stellan's guard dropped, and he spent most of his time with us. I'm sure he wouldn't admit it to you yet, but I remember countless hours he spent tending to our son. Ghyslain adores him. Though he may appear cold and distant, the prince is not arrogant. He cooks and cleans and mends along with the best of us." Gretchen laughed. "Not exactly the picture that comes to mind when you think of your usual royal, is it?"

Clarysa smiled. No. Stellan was unlike any man she'd ever met.

"Now," Gretchen continued, "even as a teenager, Patrulha was already an imposing figure of a female. Over the next several years, Besnik trained both her and Stellan in the art of swordsmanship and fighting."

"And so he made her Captain?"

"Uh-huh. They're very close. Same age, in fact. In those days they were downright inseparable. Used to ride off together to heaven knows where. And when Besnik died, Patrulha took it awfully hard. Stellan guided her through a difficult time."

"And what of Froll? I remember you mentioning him a few moments ago."

"Oh, he's been wonderful! Took up Besnik's place without a single complaint. Though I don't mind saying I feel a wee bit guilty, for I never had feelings for him like I did Besnik. But I think he's found himself a lovely woman in the village. He's been our connection to the outside world all these years. I don't know what we'd've done if he hadn't encouraged Stellan to market his special potions and such. He sells them to the merchants and travelers in the village, along with what little knickknacks and jewelry I can cobble together."

"And *that's* your only income?"

"Aye. We've searched the castle many times. Everything of value here had already been plundered by thieves long ago."

"I see." *So he really is poor. I'll talk with Father as soon as I return. These people can't go on like this.*

"So, the years passed. Between Besnik and Froll, they coaxed Stellan out of his shell, and helped him build the modest kingdom he has today. Stellan even managed to recruit a small group of men loyal only to him. You'll meet them after they return, I'm sure."

Clarysa nodded. "I'd like to."

Gretchen stood. "But I've talked your ear off. Come, I'll walk you back to your room. I'm sure you'd like a bath and some fresh clothes."

Clarysa agreed. On the way, she digested what she had learned. She and Stellan came from such different worlds. Would they be able to find any common ground between them?

Chapter 14

Clarysa recovered completely a few days later. Her first intention was to explore the castle. Gretchen didn't seem to care what she did as long as she didn't go outside.

One morning, she encountered a room she had never visited before. She peeked inside, slowly swinging her lantern from left to right. There wasn't much there--only some rusty armor, a few chests and another doorway, painted green. The door's surface appeared smooth and clean, unlike anything else belonging to the drab, gray castle.

Clarysa bit her lip. Did the room beyond hide the former king's resting place? She recalled the story of the mysterious coffin Stellan had found. Her curiosity hungered as if a starved beast, and demanded to be satisfied immediately. With one quick look about her, she stepped into the musty chamber.

Three long strides later she was at the viridian door. *It's probably secured,* she thought. But when she took a chance on the iron handle and pushed, the door swung silently open. *Well, this is a shock. Now I have to enter!*

Grasping the lantern tightly, she entered. The area before her was extremely dark and dank, like a tomb. She could only see a few inches ahead. Lowering the light, she noticed wooden steps disappearing into a lightless abyss. A slight draft slinked up from the depths, sharing its fetid air. Cautiously, Clarysa tried the first step. It seemed solid enough, so she tried the second, then the third. Downward she went into the unknown.

The air grew increasingly colder as she descended. Even as she tightened the thick layers of wrapping she wore, exposed skin voided her body heat like a hemorrhage. Soon, she lost track of how far down she had traveled. Clarysa was thinking about retreating when she arrived at another door. She held up her light. This door was completely black, instantly swallowing up the light, reflecting none of it. *How odd.* Her breaths sounded alarmingly pronounced in the dead air.

Clarysa ran her other hand along the door's frigid surface, half expecting to be sucked into a hellish otherworld. She felt indentations. The curious markings were only millimeters in depth, but appeared to cover the entire surface.

Shaking slightly, both from fear and excitement, she jiggled the door handle. The sharp, pointed knob turned easily and the dark slab of wood moved inward. Rays of deep blues and greens spilled out, slicing through the oppressive dark sea surrounding her. Warily, she crept into the room.

Clarysa stared about her in slack-jawed amazement. Hundreds of luminescent containers lined dozens of wooden shelves and emitted a collective spectral glow.

In the center sat a battered wooden table. Several metal instruments, molded to bizarre shapes, were strewn across it. An open book took up one corner. Clarysa didn't recognize any of the words. The creased, worn pages spoke of frequent use.

What a strange and wondrous place, she thought, drinking in the room's preternatural delights. *What glorious magick does he perform here?* A smile spread across her lips at the thought. But this lighthearted elation plummeted when a distinct scratching sound came from beyond the walls. Slight at first, and soft. It must have been a rat, but what in the world could it possibly find to eat in this place?

The sound grew harsher. Now it seemed like nails raking across the walls, accompanied by a low, rhythmic thump. The air turned bitingly cold. A sudden draft blew out the lantern.

In the darkness, something touched her hair.

Clarysa yelped and ran for the exit. She stumbled through the door and shut it quickly, but not before catching a glimpse of an apparition filling the room. A hideous, pulsating entity that defied description. If ever a nightmare were personified in the flesh, it lay beyond that door now.

Wide-eyed in terror, Clarysa bolted up the stairs. The ethereal thump-thumping sound faded with each hurried step. Up and out the green door she flew. Wasting no time, she slammed it closed. Chilly sweat ran in rivers down her skin as she attempted to gather her scattered wits. *That is the last time I let my curiosity get the better of me in this place.* She headed for the warm, safe kitchen, attempting to purge the noxious terror from her mind. *Heaven only knows what kind of horrors Stellan has faced here. Heaven only knows!*

* * * *

Much later, after Clarysa had regained some feeling of normalcy and a healthy respect for all things ethereal, she asked Gretchen to show her the throne room. Like her father's castle, this room had vast murals splayed out across the walls. But these were far different from those back home. These depicted only dark and dangerous images.

Stellan, Gretchen explained, used to spend days creating them, often having nothing more than charcoal and a blank wall. Clarysa absorbed the vistas of giant gargoyles, imps, goblins, and other demonic creatures. Scattered among the sinister illustrations were beautiful, willowy nudes, women with long, flowing hair and dark eyes. They stared at the viewer no matter where one stood.

Next, Gretchen showed her the library, one overrun with heavy, cobwebbed tomes and ornate woodwork. Some of it had rotted away or fallen into disrepair. Many of the books were so fragile they were entirely unreadable, or worse, consumed with worms. Nevertheless, Clarysa transported a good number of them into the kitchen to read while Gretchen tended to her duties. Many contained delightful illustrations, some of them in color. The stories they contained transported her into worlds the likes of which she hadn't known existed. Reading helped mitigate the long wait for Stellan's return.

When night clothed the castle in its ebony cloak, Clarysa joined Gretchen and her son in the kitchen. The two younger folk played cards or sang. Ghyslain, as it turned out, was an accomplished guitarist. Gretchen frequently sewed, humming along with his tunes.

Froll, a cheerful, laid-back fellow with dark, straight hair and squinty eyes, joined them for a day in between trips for supplies. Clarysa liked the bright bandanas he wore, and the way his belly shook as he laughed. Sometimes, he would smoke a pipe and tell her gypsy tales from far away.

More days passed, and still no sign of Stellan.

One afternoon, Clarysa realized she had been wearing the same dress a few times too many. It had belonged to Patrulha in her younger years. The others probably didn't care how she looked, but she wanted something nice to wear when Stellan returned. She approached Gretchen about the matter.

"I saw some old clothing in the royal suite," Gretchen told her. "Patrulha never wanted any of it, but they might suit you. Let's go see if any of them still hold together."

They sauntered up a level, and entered a chamber as wide as a field. "Is this where Stellan sleeps?" Clarysa asked, eyeing the once-luxurious mahogany bed. Somehow it had split in two, and was draped in nothing but silky cobwebs.

"Oh, no. He uses one of the servant's rooms by the kitchen. It's much warmer there, y'know."

Gretchen used her candle to light some of the torches ensconced in the walls. "Here we go!"

A huge wardrobe stood to Clarysa's right. Gretchen pulled the doors open wide. They creaked so loudly Clarysa feared the whole wardrobe might collapse.

Gretchen poked her head inside, nudging aside a rat with her foot as she did so. Clarysa joined her, giddy with anticipation. But rifling through the dusty material only gave her a fierce sneezing fit.

Gretchen chuckled. "I see you're in quite a rush there."

After an hour of searching, they finally struck gold--a lacy, off-white gown with wide sleeves. It had been stored more carefully than some of the others, and thus retained its luster. Clarysa tried it on. Much to her delight, it fit perfectly. She wrinkled her nose. "I should clean it first!"

"I'll help you," offered Gretchen.

They headed back downstairs.

Clarysa hugged the dress to her chest. "You know, I should like to learn how to cook."

"Oh, I see! Is that so, hmm?" Gretchen's voice echoed loudly as they descended the stone staircase.

Clarysa offered a supplicant look. "If it wouldn't be too much trouble, of course."

Gretchen shook her head. "No, of course not!"

And so once her new--old!--dress had been washed and hung up to dry, Clarysa joined Gretchen at the hearth for her first cooking lesson. Her days in the wintry wilderness brightened considerably as she began to feel like a more productive and vital member of the eccentric household. If only Lionel could see her now, what would he say? And Edward--keeper of the royal decorum? The blood vessels in his neck would surely explode!

As for Stellan, what thoughts would he have upon encountering a member of the Aldebaran royalty scrubbing a century's worth of scum from the walls? Clarysa could scarcely wait to find out!

Chapter 15

"They're coming!" Gretchen announced in the predawn darkness as soon as Clarysa opened her bedroom door. The woman fingered a handful of gold pieces in the light of her torch. "Stellan sent a messenger ahead, courtesy of your cousin."

"Lionel!"

Gretchen glowed with excitement. "I'll be able to cook something decent for once."

"We can have a feast!" Clarysa clapped her hands and smiled.

Gretchen chuckled. "Hurry and get ready."

They spent the day preparing a cornucopia of dishes based on ingredients brought by Froll and Ghyslain from the village market. Meat roasted on spits over the fire. Platters overflowed with breads and assorted cheeses. Three kinds of soup warmed in large clay pots and jugs of wine sat on a cart, ready to be rolled out.

Froll set up four long tables in the throne room. The hall blazed with scores of candles.

Clarysa couldn't resist the urge to keep peeking out the front gate. Stellan had saved her life and helped her people all without hope of reward or political gain. She would do anything for him. *Maybe I can be his reward*, she thought with a devilish grin.

Come late afternoon, the party was expected any minute. Clarysa wanted to help serve, so the gypsy insisted she wear an apron over her dress while she readied appetizers. Clarysa fingered the coarse material. This was certainly a first.

Gretchen faced the hearth, basting the meat. Clarysa sat at the table cutting oranges. As she reached for the seventh piece, a man with a wild mane of red hair appeared at the doorway. Grinning, he put a finger to his lips for silence. He tiptoed across the room to the hearth. Then he grabbed Gretchen from behind and gave her a loud, rambunctious bear hug.

Gretchen shrieked, arms flailing. As she turned around, Clarysa could see a fierce blush on her cheeks.

"Keep your loutish hands off me, you scurvy rat!" Gretchen beat on him with a large wooden spoon. "Out! Out of my kitchen this instant!"

Clarysa laughed until tears streamed from her eyes. The hefty soldier passed by her table and helped himself to a handful of grapes. "They call me Hunter Red. Nice to meet you, miss! Having a lovely day, are we?"

He threw up an arm in defense as Gretchen drove him on, wielding her spoon like a battle-axe. "Don't bother her, mister. We know your kind, oh yes we do!"

With a parting wave, Hunter disappeared through the door. Gretchen stood looking after him, breathless and chest heaving. She grinned upon meeting Clarysa's inquisitive gaze, but would say no more. Tucking her hair behind her ear, she turned back to her cooking. She was humming.

After Clarysa finished making the appetizers, she peeked into the great hall. As the men arrived, they piled their cloaks in one corner. They stood around shaking wet hair and warming themselves by the grate's blazing fire. Conversation and laughter filled the air. To look at them, one would never think they had returned from a dangerous mission. Chairs scraped against stone as they sat at the tables, eagerly awaiting the most anticipated guest--the main course. Gretchen and Ghyslain appeared by her side, laden with trays of food.

"You wait here," Gretchen instructed her. "Let the food and wine calm them down first."

Clarysa reluctantly returned to the kitchen. She couldn't wait to hear about the heroics Stellan had performed against the Pestilence horde.

After the main course had been delivered, Gretchen handed Clarysa a wide platter full of rolls to pass around. She carried it carefully into the hall. The air felt toasty warm and smelled strongly of spiced meat.

She slowly made her way down the long table, offering rolls. Most of the rough-looking men were engrossed in their meals, but a few noticed her. Some stared with frank curiosity. Others nodded politely.

Clarysa's heart skipped a beat as she spotted Stellan at the far end. A few days' growth of beard and soiled clothing couldn't obscure his handsomeness. It seemed like they'd been apart for months instead of a few weeks. She had daydreamed about their reunion hundreds of times during his absence.

Holding her breath, Clarysa stepped forward and held out the platter. But the dream didn't come true. He didn't even turn his head while grabbing a roll. Clarysa was crestfallen. *Am I that invisible to him?* For someone who never lacked for words, she suddenly couldn't think of anything to say.

She'd seen him display the same cold, impersonal manner at the hunt. *He isn't interested, so why do you persist? Fool.* Lower lip trembling, Clarysa quietly moved on to the next diner.

"Wait!"

She instantly spun back around at the sound of Stellan's commanding voice. "Yes?"

"I'll have another," he said as he reached for the platter--this time catching sight of its server.

Clarysa smiled. His look of surprise indicated he hadn't even recognized her. With a borrowed bandanna covering her hair and the new dress, she must have looked like a hired servant. She pushed the tray before him and awaited his response.

Stellan's furrowed brow pronounced itself as his face darkened. Leaping to his feet, he tore the platter from her grasp and slammed it down upon the table. "Gretchen!" He searched the hall. Some of the men glanced up at his shout, but most kept their heads bent down over their plates. "*Gretchen!* Woman, I command you to attend me *at once!*"

Gretchen rushed over, necklaces clinking. "What is it? The soup cold? What's wrong?"

"This!" he said through clenched teeth, gesturing sharply to Clarysa. "Dishing up to the men like a common wench. You know who she is. What's wrong with you?"

Gretchen wrung her hands. She opened her mouth to reply when Clarysa laid a hand on Stellan's arm. "No, wait! It's not her fault. I *wanted* to help. I asked her to let me! Stellan, it's all right. I wanted to do my part. Really, it's all right!"

He turned and glared, his eyes burning holes into hers.

Undaunted, Clarysa picked up the scattered rolls. She held out the platter, practically shoving it under his nose. "I made them myself. Try one--please!"

After cutting one more heated glance at Gretchen, Stellan scooped up a roll and bit into it. His eyes were cast downward as he chewed, and Clarysa found herself admiring his face. If she hadn't been studying him so intently, she might have missed the slight relaxation of his shoulders. "Well, what do you think?"

After swallowing, he tore off a fresh piece. "Needs more salt," he murmured. "Taste for yourself." He gently pushed the morsel against her lips and into her mouth.

He grazed her tongue with his fingertip, and the pressure he exerted told her it was no accident. Clarysa almost forgot to chew. Well, she wanted to start sucking on his finger, but given the public arena that would have been very unseemly. Instead, she let her tongue drag upon the long, firm digit as he withdrew.

His widening eyes and parting lips gave her hope. His heart was not as cold as he would have her believe. His blood certainly ran hot, judging from the heat of his finger.

The hall became abruptly quiet. By this time, Clarysa was so happy she didn't care what kind of spectacle she created. After what seemed like an eternally blissful moment, Stellan resumed his seat. She moved to pick up the platter, but the sorcerer stayed her with a tenacious hand on her arm.

"Cervantes," he said to the man on his left, "give her your seat."

The burly man in question gave a quick, knowing smile to his neighbors and chuckled.

"Cervantes," Stellan continued, his voice deepening, "perhaps I wasn't clear."

"Oh aye…aye," said Cervantes, who immediately stood to find another spot. "You was most certainly clear, all right!"

"Oy, Cervy!" shouted Hunter from down the table. "While yer up, could you pass me some of her buns? I hear they're delicious!"

A round of laughter erupted. Clarysa blushed. Cervantes picked up two rolls from the platter and threw them none too gently toward Hunter. Hunter caught one, but the other hit him on the forehead and bounced off. The men laughed harder still. Eventually, their tales from the recent battle resumed.

Clarysa studied Stellan's reaction. He was ignoring them. He pointed to the chair next to him. She sat. Wordlessly, he fixed her a plate before resuming his own meal.

Clarysa's stomach was all aflutter. She could only pick at the food. So she used the time to observe Stellan's people.

The stalwart form of Patrulha sat across from the prince. Clarysa noticed the captain kept stealing glances at him. Clarysa studied her in between bites, noting her chiseled bare arms and broad shoulders. Black leather bands circled both wrists. Her hair was the same color as Gretchen's, though tamer, and still damp from the falling snow. She, too, bore the spectral pallor of one who languished far beyond the sun's rays. Clarysa wanted to ask how she had lost her eye but ultimately thought it best to hold her tongue.

"Didn't your mother ever tell you it's not polite to stare?" Patrulha turned on her sharply and pounded the table. The boisterous group fell silent.

Clarysa blushed again, mumbling an apology.

Patrulha's eye narrowed. With a final, quick glance toward Stellan, she abruptly stormed off in a huff. For a few awkward moments, no one spoke.

"Eh, don't mind her," said Hunter. "She's had a chip on her shoulder long as I can remember."

Clarysa dared not look up. Surely everyone at the table could feel the waves of heat emanating from her flushed cheeks. Alienating Stellan's captain of the guard was hardly a way to make a good first impression. She finished the rest of her meal in silence.

An hour later, the last bite was consumed and the last of the table wine drained. Clarysa looked around with surprise as the men helped clean up. They carried plates into the kitchen, wiped down the table and mopped the floor.

A hand cupped her elbow. "Come with me," Stellan said.

He led her to a private study, away from the noise and smoke. A comforting fire burned in the grate. The intimate chamber had better furnishings than the other rooms Clarysa had seen. Antique decorations lined the shelves, and tapestries hung on each wall. A plush crimson rug with silver embroidery drew the eye to the center of the room.

Stellan carried a jug of wine and two goblets. He filled one and gave it to her before pouring another for himself. Then he stretched out on the room's red settee, one knee raised while the other dangled off the side. Clarysa watched his languid, sensuous movement with prurient interest. Stellan's body lay open before her, like a book. Was it an invitation, or the alcohol speaking for him? She settled into a stuffed velvet chair to calm the butterflies in her stomach, sipping sparingly.

Neither one spoke at first. Clarysa remembered her apron and took it off. Stellan was staring at her from beneath drowsy eyelids. "Is something wrong?"

"Where did you get the dress?" His voice sounded dulcet, low--and slurred.

"Upstairs. From the royal suite. Is…that all right?"

Stellan nodded, staring at her. But he wasn't looking at her face. As a vigorous heat spread across the exposed skin of her chest, she ached for the cool touch of his strong, graceful fingers to follow. But his attention shifted back to his wine.

Clarysa heard a yip, and then a large white wolf appeared from behind the settee. It bypassed Stellan and sniffed around Clarysa's feet.

"How lovely!" she cried, reaching out to stroke its fur. She rubbed its cheeks and gazed closely into its light gray eyes. "There are some tasty bones for you in the kitchen. Have you tried them yet?" The animal licked her hand. Clarysa looked up and smiled. "What's its name?"

Stellan smirked. "Wolf."

Clarysa winked. "With an 'e,' of course!"

"I'm only going to say yes because I haven't the energy to go running after you again." A brief smile graced his lips. "Anyway, I suppose you'd like to hear about what happened."

Clarysa raised a hand to her face. "Oh, yes, of course! Did you find Edward and Lionel? Was anyone hurt?"

Stellan shook his head. "To answer your questions, yes, and no, not in great numbers. We tracked down and destroyed as many of the infected as we could find. I advised Edward to increase security and alert healers across the kingdom. I'll do what I can in the way of future patrols."

"Thank you, Stellan. I'm indebted to you."

Stellan absentmindedly scratched Wolfe behind his ears. "No thanks needed. By the way, Lionel sends his greetings. He said you're very brave."

"Really?"

"Really. He also said after the King is through punishing you, he's got a few consequences of his own to administer."

Clarysa laughed nervously. "He's joking."

Stellan shook his head. "No, I don't think so. They were sick with worry, Clarysa."

Anxiety tightened her throat. "But I was only trying to help! What else could I have done?"

"You were right to contact me. But you chose the most dangerous way possible." Stellan put down his goblet. He knelt before her, studying her face by the light of the fire.

Fingertips pressed at her cheeks and neck, the gentlest of massages. So close to him, Clarysa saw details she hadn't noticed before. A pale scar across his left cheekbone. Flecks of gold in his emerald eyes. The sharp slant of his nose. She tasted the wine on his breath as it purred between slightly parted lips. Lips she desperately wanted pressed against hers.

After a few moments, he murmured a hoarse, "How are you feeling?"

Clarysa swallowed, feeling nervous and excited at the same time. His innocent, nurturing touches shouldn't have caused pulsing swirls of heat between her thighs, but they did. "All better, thanks to you. I did everything you said."

Stellan nodded his approval. His hands lingered against her skin. Their faces seemed only a hairsbreadth apart. She heard his breath quicken, or was it hers? Then his head angled to the right. Moisture exploded in her mouth. This was it. He was going to kiss her.

A flicker of desire ignited Stellan's eyes, though he fought to keep them open.

Clarysa pulled back with a start and gazed at him sympathetically. *He's exhausted.* Alas, it was time for more practical action. "You should get some sleep," she said firmly, trying to mask her disappointment. "You can tell me the rest tomorrow."

Stellan sighed, and some of the paleness returned to his cheeks. "That reminds me--I told Edward I'd escort you back immediately. We leave at dawn."

"But--"

"Dawn."

Now it was Clarysa's turn to sigh. "All right." She reached for his hand and crushed it against her chest. "I'm so glad you're safe."

Stellan's hand felt hot. Clarysa was tempted to keep him near, but he needed rest. She guided him back onto the settee. It wasn't difficult. The man was practically asleep on his feet. "You should sleep. I'll see you in the morning."

Stellan stared upward. Reluctantly, it seemed, he let go of her hand. "In the morning," he echoed.

At the door, Clarysa looked back with a wistful expression, but Stellan's eyes were already closed. "Good night, my handsome prince," she whispered, and shut the door.

* * * *

The next day, as promised, Stellan rose early to escort her home. Clarysa shared a heartfelt goodbye with Gretchen. Froll, Ghyslain, Hunter and the others saw them off at the gate. Clarysa made many promises to return, feeling certain her visit had opened a much-needed door between Aldebaran and the Snowflake Kingdom.

As she and Stellan rode, snow fell heavily upon them. At least the air was calm. And Gretchen had lent her a cloak to shield her. A few of Stellan's men provided additional security at the rear, but remained at a respectful distance.

The journey was over far too soon. As they approached the Aldebaran border on the southern edge of Dungeon Forest, the sun broke into view as though a theater curtain had parted. The bright, warm air welcomed Clarysa and her escorts with amber splashed kisses.

She had hoped to spend more time alone with Stellan, but movement down the road dictated otherwise. A company of the King's guards were riding toward them. Stellan stopped and dismounted. Clarysa did the same, albeit reluctantly.

She placed a hand on his forearm. "When will I see you again?"

Stellan merely looked at her.

She withdrew her hand, taken aback by his morose expression. "Am I that horrid? You look as if somebody just died."

"No, of course not."

Clarysa looked over her shoulder. The soldiers were nearing. "Then what's wrong? You know you can visit me any time."

"I...think not. Despite my efforts, your brother Edward loathes me. No doubt he's poisoned the King against me."

Clarysa scowled. "That...that can't be true!"

Stellan regarded her solemnly. "Are you sure? Then why have I been barred from Aldebaran? Those were Edward's parting words, apparently speaking on behalf of your father."

Clarysa gasped. A vision sprang into her head. A vision of her hands around a certain brother's neck. But first she had to find a way to see Stellan again--soon. "Then you should invite our family to your castle to discuss an alliance. Send an invitation and I'll bring it to the King myself. Compose the most urgent and diplomatic message possible regarding Pestilence. I'll have a talk with Father--a very, very long talk. Lionel will help me. We simply need to get you an audience with him. Oh, Stellan, we've got to try *something*."

But her plea was cut ruefully short as the King's men arrived. The lead guard saluted her and brought forth an extra steed. "Our orders are to bring you back, Princess--immediately," he said.

Stellan gripped her shoulders. "Clarysa," he said, holding her gaze steady with a resolute stare, "go home. You'll be safe there. I promise."

"But--"

His grip tightened. "It's not meant to be. You have to accept it."

A chill went through her. Clarysa shook her head vigorously. "I don't have to accept anything! Why do you give up so easily? Stellan, I--wait!"

She reached for him, but before she could make contact, he had mounted Midnight and was guiding the horse around. He glanced at her a final time, stern and remote. Soon, he and his men disappeared down the road.

Just like that, he was gone from her life. Her temples throbbed as she stared hard into the distant gloom of his kingdom, trying to will him back through sheer mind force alone. Unfortunately, he never came galloping forth to sweep her away. *It's over, then.* She had to face the sorry fact that their brief encounters hadn't been enough to win his heart.

Being a princess in a golden noose, she had neither the support nor the freedom to pursue him even if he *had* harbored feelings for her. *Oh, who are you trying to fool? Obviously he doesn't think you're suited to him.* Her eyes watered. Stellan probably preferred women like Patrulha, strong and fierce. Clarysa was nothing like her. She was nothing but an idealistic weakling.

Ignoring the guard's proffered hand, Clarysa dropped to the ground. Dust soaked up her tears as she refused to move from the spot for a very long time.

Chapter 16

One month later

"The answer, dear daughter, is no," rumbled King Leopold.

Clarysa stood at the foot of his throne, waving the invitation in the air. It had arrived that morning. Luck was with her, at least she had thought, for she had intercepted Stellan's messenger while stepping out for a morning stroll. Subsequently, she had slipped into the royal study and helped herself to the King's seal while he held court. There she had scripted a most kingly reply. Stellan's messenger left with it before the seal had even dried.

Excitement coursed through her blood like a river swollen with spring's melting snow. The feeling was in sharp contrast to her mood over the last few weeks, ever since Stellan had rejected her so soundly. Clarysa had agonized endlessly over his curt farewell. Edward had refused to discuss the matter of his exclusion from Aldebaran, upon which Clarysa had unleashed a torrent of tears. The only person who'd been able to calm her was Lionel. They secretly commiserated about the separation from their friend.

As evening fell, Clarysa stood before her father, begging for his cooperation. Like a common courtier requesting an audience, she had presented the invitation with high hopes. His response shocked her, for she had felt certain, *certain* he would agree to at least a simple dinner affair. But no.

"How can you refuse?" she argued. "How can you even entertain the very idea? After all he's done for you…for Aldebaran!"

"'*All* he's done'? Nonsense. We could have easily handled that minor situation ourselves. Examine the facts, daughter. He only came because you sent him."

"Minor?" The words sputtered from her throat. "Father, I was there. I can't fathom calling that rampaging mob a 'minor situation.' Besides, I've already told him we'd attend!"

The King's glare manifested like a roiling storm cloud. "You did *what*? Accepted it on my behalf?"

"I had to do what was right."

"It wasn't right at all. You *lied*, Clarysa--not just to me, but to him. He may be one of those detestable warlocks, but he is still a prince. Have you no respect for protocol? Or for *me* and how your action would reflect upon my court?" Leopold slammed a fist upon his armrest. "How many times have I warned you about that brash impulsiveness of yours? *How many times, child?*"

Clarysa opened her mouth to speak, then thought better of it. He only addressed her as "child" when he was livid, as he definitely was now. During these moments, it was best to simply bite her tongue.

"I cannot just strike up an agreement with that man. There are political ramifications, most of them deleterious." The King raised a quick hand to block her protests. "No, no, don't say anything. Nothing! I know exactly what's running through your naive little head." Her father sighed. "I appreciate what he's done for us in the name of safety, Clarysa, and I'm not ruling out future alliances when the time is right. But heaven help me, he comes from a family full of rogues, charlatans and murderers! Is this the type you would have us associate our good name with? I might as well abdicate the throne."

"But if you took the risk you'd save the lives of countless citizens. You'd be a hero!"

"Don't bother with flattery. This conversation is over."

Clarysa crossed her arms. "I've seen what those Pestilence victims can do. You're making a serious mistake, Father."

"Then so be it," he responded in a tired voice. "There are matters your King--as well as your father--knows better than you. Now go to your quarters."

His entrenched denial stunned her. When tears failed to move him, she spun about on her heel and stomped off to her sleeping chamber. The bed frame shook with the force of her landing. There she cried and pouted and cried some more. Beneath her anger, embarrassment reared its ugly head. *She* had encouraged Stellan to take the risk, after all. Now, because of her miscalculation, the King would appear as though he had reneged. Stellan would be furious and hurt--and it would be all her fault.

Father, how could you be so cold? There really must have been a royal order barring Stellan from the kingdom--or was someone trying to bar Stellan from *her*? She hadn't exactly made a secret of her attraction to the elusive sorcerer prince. However, her father had never directly informed her of this edict. Why tell Edward but not her? Did he mean to leave open a back door? Clarysa massaged her aching forehead. Why did it always come down to politics, even in the King's own family?

She poured herself a goblet of water and stepped out onto her private balcony. The stars twinkled merrily. Clarysa reclined on her divan. A warm breeze caressed her skin. As she sipped, her thoughts drifted to the sorcerer. Stellan's wealth was not in jewels, gold or fine clothing. It lay embedded in magic and mystery and charismatic friends. Clarysa sighed, aching to explore every last dark and enchanted corner of his world. *But he's a sorcerer*, sprouted a warning voice in her head. *He's dangerous*.

"But he's a very handsome sorcerer," she whispered. "And so what if I like danger?"

There were other qualities in him she admired. For one thing, her boundless energy didn't seem to ruffle him. In fact, nothing seemed to ruffle him very much. *We suit each other perfectly.*

Clarysa frowned. There she went again, making plans where none should form. But Stellan's fragile trust of her would turn to hatred her if her father didn't accept the invitation. She couldn't bear the thought of being one more person who had let him down. She had to avoid it at all costs. Trust, love--those two things bound together everything in life worth having.

Clarysa rose slowly, her thirst a distant memory. Perhaps…perhaps all could be salvaged if *she* responded to the invitation. If her father couldn't see reason where Pestilence was concerned, then it was up to his youngest daughter to ensure something effective was being done about it. And Stellan had more answers than all of Aldebaran combined.

That night, thoughts erupting like a volcano, Clarysa composed an urgent letter to her cousin Mirabelle.

The very survival of Aldebaran depends on your courage, she began.

Chapter 17

Stellan sat upon his throne, his chin resting uncomfortably in his right hand. He maintained this position for exactly two hundred heartbeats before switching off to his left hand, which, oddly, was even more uncomfortable. Thoughts raced helter-skelter through his mind. How would the King react to his proposal? Would he fully understand the ramifications of Pestilence spreading to his populace? Could he possibly put aside his bigotry against practitioners of magick--read: himself--and rally his army against the threat?

Stellan had witnessed first hand the rapid degeneration Pestilence wrought on a living being. Within hours of the initial contact, the body and mind were lost. The recent infection of humans proved the plague had become much more virulent. Stellan sighed as he slid his left hand up over his forehead. *Excellent work, Alucard, excellent work. How long did it take you to configure the devil's brew this time, I wonder? What unspeakable forces have you conspired with?* If Pestilence had indeed spread as far as the outreaches of Aldebaran, as he suspected from the mysterious deaths there recently, then King Leopold had only months to respond.

Stellan had sought Gretchen's advice, as well as Froll's, and they'd counseled him extensively. All of the inhabitants of Castle Vandeborg were in agreement--Leopold *must* be made to understand the threat.

To accomplish that task, Stellan had decided he would do anything--including washing several hundred years' worth of grime from the castle walls. If forging an alliance with Aldebaran was simply a matter of following royal protocol, as ridiculous as its rules may be, then he would do it. There was too much at stake, too many lives at risk. So, pail of water and rag in hand, he had set to work.

Several weeks of backbreaking work passed.

Gretchen cleaned a set of porcelain dinnerware, one Froll had purchased at an emporium located a five day's march away with money left over from Clarysa's forfeited rings. Perhaps it was ostentatious, but visiting royalty expected to be surrounded with ostentatious finery. Such attention to detail could only further Stellan's cause.

Besides, the dishes did much to lift the spirits of a tired cook accustomed to the brittle earthenware she had been using for years. Stellan could hardly begrudge her the change.

Finally, the castle began to take on the appearance of something "less than detestable," as Gretchen remarked. It would have to do. All that really mattered was King Leopold understanding the gravity of the situation.

The hour of the King's visit arrived. Stellan ended his rumination and joined the others in the entrance hall. By necessity the gate remained closed, but Ghyslain faithfully kept watch along the wintry ramparts for the Aldebaran procession. The other inhabitants of Vandeborg waited anxiously.

"How does the weather look?" asked Gretchen.

Hunter cracked open the front door. "Not bad," he told her. "Almost clear, for this place."

They waited.

After an hour, Stellan stopped pacing the entrance hall and retreated to the throne room. He fiddled with the various decorations. He adjusted and readjusted the lighting. Then he sat at the head of the long dining table. The entire area was redolent of sweet sauces and meats. He fought to control his growling stomach.

Three hours later, Gretchen entered. She, too, made a number of unnecessary corrections, this time to the silverware. Turning to Stellan, she pursed her lips. "I can keep the food warm, but it won't be as good."

"Do it," Stellan muttered.

They waited more.

An hour later, she sauntered up to him again. "I should feed Ghyslain on the tower. The poor boy's probably half-frozen to death, but he was determined to keep watch. Let alone how hard it is for everyone to be around this much food and not eat."

Stellan tried not to groan. "Fine."

After the others had shared a meal in the kitchen, Froll tried to entice Stellan with a game of cards, but he was in a dangerously foul mood and waved him off. He continued his vigil at the head of the table.

Froll played cards with Hunter in one corner. Patrulha appeared and leaned against a wall with arms crossed. The Captain of the Guard looked at him, but didn't say anything. She didn't have to. Stellan knew what she was trying to tell him with her measured, one-eyed stare. He glanced away. Now was not the time to provoke him. After a while, she took the hint and left.

The hour of midnight approached. Gretchen wandered in and encouraged Stellan to eat. He waved her back to the kitchen. After she left, he frowned. The Aldebarans should have arrived by now, even if a storm had delayed them.

He stared into the fire. The candlelight--staged to properly welcome the expected visitors--was dying down. Shadows lurched across the walls. Wolfe slinked around his master's chair, sensing a dark change in his master's mood. He howled mournfully.

"Silence!" Stellan shouted. His voice echoed wildly around the chamber as the animal dutifully complied.

Gretchen appeared carrying a plate laden with fine victuals. "Well, eat something, at least. Be a shame to let all this food go to waste."

"*I told you I wasn't hungry!*" Stellan lashed out. The delicate porcelain smashed into a hundred pieces against the floor, leaving a soiled path of food in its wake. Gretchen cried out in surprise. But Stellan was beyond the ability to care anymore. He pushed away from the table and stormed out of the room.

"Fine!" he heard Gretchen shout after him. "Be that way! You think I'm going to clean up after you? Some prince you are--behaving like a spoiled brat. How about a little spell to make your shitty attitude disappear?"

She screeched like a banshee, the sound following him up the stairs even to the next floor. *Damn that woman and her foul mouth.* Stellan rushed through the corridors, melting into the darkness like a ghost. He grabbed an old iron bar and clubbed randomly at the walls as he strode. An old suit of armor crumpled under his wrath. *This is how all the kingdoms will fall, by refusing to stand together under a threat. Those stupid fools!*

Stellan hammered away at the armor until his arms burned with pain. When violence failed to sate him, he tore open one of the tower doors and buried himself in a great snowdrift on the balcony. He sat there for countless hours, all the while being pelted by the hail and wind of a newly arisen storm. *Go on, you bastard. Attack me with everything you've got!*

He mentally worked through the situation at hand, turning every piece of the puzzle over and over from every possible angle. Perhaps he should saddle Midnight--*Why do you insist on using that infernal name?*--and search the countryside. After all, it was possible the King's party had become lost. The thought rebounded about in his head for a few moments, only to be immediately nixed. No. The King traveled with an entourage of guards and attendants. The King's procession did not get lost.

A more distressing thought occurred. Maybe Clarysa had changed her mind. What if some other man had caught her fancy in the meantime? Stellan wouldn't doubt it. What would she want with a man known as "the Dark Prince" anyway? She was the stunning princess of a wealthy king. She could have any man she desired. Why trudge through blizzards and hail and biting cold to see a temperamental loser with nothing but a ragtag bunch of servants? He was a fool for having trusted her.

Never again.

He trudged indoors. Dripping and wet, Stellan retreated to his quarters. Shivering violently, he lay down, denying himself the comfort of blankets. Flashbacks lodged in his mind of his first few nights in Vandeborg. They struck with the speed of lightning, forceful and unpredictable. Strokes of rejection and abandonment saturated the canvas of his memories.

This is the way it will always be for me, and I accept my fate. I do not need the aid of others. I don't need the love of others. I never have, and I never will. Shutting his eyes, he fell into a fitful, haunted sleep.

Chapter 18

After five hours of an exhausting ride, Clarysa rode up to the front gate of Vandeborg castle at midday. She was laden with a heavy coat of snow as well as relief. This time, she had wisely avoided the path through Dungeon Forest and had located Vandeborg by way of the main roads, posts and other markings with relatively little trouble.

Thanks to her cousin Mirabelle and a cleverly planned visit, Clarysa had a cover story that would give her at least two days in which to execute her plan. Before her time ran out, she had to convince Stellan her father was worth the effort it would require to form an alliance.

The sun slid behind a veil of portentous mists. The blinding white of the Snowflake Kingdom made for a stark and lonely place. Despite the ominous surroundings, Clarysa dismounted and yanked on a lonely bell rope, the only object left to greet her out front.

The gate creaked open slowly, splashing wan torch light onto the snowy ground. A calloused, milky white hand thrust a lantern forward. "Who's there?"

"Ghyslain, it's me!" Clarysa pushed back her hood and tried to smile past her chattering teeth. "May I enter?"

"Yeah! I mean, please come in." He hurried to raise the rusty portcullis.

Clarysa guided the horse behind her and stepped inside. She shivered. The air felt like an oven compared to outside.

"Let me get Mum, and then I'll see to your horse."

Clarysa nodded, shaking the snow from her hair. A moment later she heard Gretchen's voice.

"Is it truly the lady there?" The gypsy woman strode forward, extending her hands. "Oh, how wonderful to see you!" They embraced. Gretchen observed Clarysa at arm's length, a concerned stare etched across her face. "What are you doing? Don't tell me you rode out here all alone?"

Clarysa withdrew the invitation from her cloak pocket. "Gretchen, I know I'm late, but I've come. My father…sends his regrets. Is Stellan here?" She held out the invitation.

"What's this?" Gretchen read the parchment, and then bit her lip. "Oh. Well, he's in his tower, but… I don't know if he's up to receiving any visitors."

"Please, you must tell him I'm here."

"Of course, but as to what'll happen then only the gods know. But enough chatter out in the cold! Go to the kitchen and warm yourself. I'll be right back."

"Thank you." Clarysa strode into the now-familiar setting and settled onto a chair by the kitchen hearth. She held her frozen hands out to the blazing fire and focused expectantly on the doorway.

Several anxious paces around the kitchen later, an ashen-faced gypsy appeared. Clarysa rushed toward her. Gretchen walked forward with feet of lead. Clarysa frowned. "What's wrong?"

Gretchen held out cupped hands. Coarse shreds of the invitation filled them.

Clarysa gasped. Icicles stabbed at her heart.

"You have to understand, Princess, he took it very hard."

Clarysa fingered the pile, her gaze softening. "I knew he would. That's why I'm here. I *must* see him, Gretchen."

"He won't budge. Around here, his stubbornness is legendary."

"Then I'll have to convince him." Clarysa donned her cloak. "Please tell the prince I'll be waiting for him. Outside."

Gretchen's chin dropped. "What?"

"You heard me." Clarysa bustled from the room.

"But that's insane. You'll freeze to death!"

Clarysa turned with a wry smile. "Perhaps, perhaps not. My fate is in Stellan's hands, now, isn't it?" She exited the castle through the postern gate and stepped out into the subzero environment.

The wind had picked up. If Stellan didn't come soon it was going to be a very, *very* frigid wait. But wait she would. She had to prove herself to Stellan. Aldebaran's future depended on her perseverance.

Clarysa pulled her hood down low over her eyes and covered the lower half of her face with a scarf. Giant snowdrifts towered above, leaving little room to maneuver. Very well. She had planned on standing there anyway.

After a few moments of fretful hovering, Gretchen disappeared inside.

An hour or two passed. Maybe three. Abstract concepts such as time began to muddy. Clarysa had difficulty concentrating in the white hell surrounding her. The air's frigid fingers had sapped all of her warmth some time ago. After her feet had given out, she hunched down in a groove of densely packed snow. A thick coating of flakes devoured her in a suffocating blanket of white. But she didn't move. *He'll come. I'll wait as long as it takes.*

Faith in her strategy, however, began to wane ever so slightly. Lest she forget, Stellan was a sorcerer born of the Western Wastes. They were demons in human guise, all of them--or so she'd been taught. Only the might of Aldebaran had kept them from taking over the Five Lands. Was Stellan as civilized as he seemed? Or would his true nature call him back into the abyss?

It was now perilously dark. Her body was numb from the cold. Finding her way home now, in this condition, would be nigh impossible. Failure loomed heavily. And fear--she could die out here. What if Stellan meant for her to die, to teach her father that only fools would dare incur the Dark Prince's wrath?

The gate sprang wide open. Footsteps crunched loudly in the snow and then stopped. Clarysa strained to gather her wits. Had she really heard those sounds or only imagined them? With stiff fingers, she rubbed the coating of ice from her eyes.

Black boots, black cape. Definitely Stellan. He said not a word, only motioned for her to stand. She lurched to her feet. With a wobbly gait, she followed him back through the entrance.

The prince led her to his study. Pointing to the fire, he said, "Warm and dry yourself here. Dinner will be served in half an hour. After eating, you will leave." He turned sharply on a heel and left.

She stared after him in dismay, ignoring the fierce needles of pain as her limbs began to thaw. Nothing in this kingdom came even close to matching Stellan's icy demeanor.

Gretchen appeared bearing hot towels. She busied herself by warming Clarysa back to life.

* * * *

White linen draped a hastily prepared table in the throne room. Candles glittered upon gnarled bases. A fire blazed in an imposing hearth. Stellan slumped in his chair, exuding an air of guarded sullenness. He refused to meet anyone's gaze.

Next to him, Clarysa sat straight with folded hands while Gretchen ladled soup into porcelain bowls. The gypsy attended to them like a skittish cat. Silence held the room firmly in its unyielding grasp.

"I like what you've done with the place," Clarysa said after Gretchen left.

Stellan crouched low over his bowl, shoveling the vegetable medley into his mouth. No answer came.

Clarysa gazed at him undaunted. She began to eat. Every so often she would speak, complimenting the dishes or posing idle talk, but Stellan ignored her each and every time. It was as if she were nothing more than a pesky spirit.

Gretchen served the main course. Large platters crowded with hearty slabs of pork, roasted garlic mashed potatoes, savory greens and other root vegetables landed on the table. It was truly a feast fit for a king, as this was the same type of food so painstakingly prepared for her father. Clarysa thanked Gretchen effusively, prompting her to prattle on at length about her recipes. A warning grunt from Stellan quieted her, his face now masked in a constant scowl.

Time passed slowly. Clarysa became bored with carrying on a one-sided conversation. Craving Stellan's interest more than refreshment, she started playing with her food. The only explanation possible was that the snow and ice must have addled her mind. As she pushed the food around on her plate, she giggled under her breath. She couldn't help it. The tension filling the room threatened to suffocate her.

After this went on for some time, Stellan pounded the table so hard a few plates crashed to the floor. "*What* is so infernally funny?"

Clarysa showed him her plate. "Remind you of anyone?" Laughing, she pointed at her plate. By now, she didn't care how powerful a sorcerer he was--the man was acting like a sullen twit. And he had a thing or two to learn about how to properly receive a guest.

Stellan shot her an astonished look and then glanced down. His brow furrowed. He looked at her again. Then back to the plate. "You dared... I can't believe you did that."

"It's my best work yet, don't you think?" She collapsed into giggles and snorts.

His lips twitched. Then they spread into a wide smile, for Clarysa had shaped her vegetables and mashed potatoes into a face bearing an exaggerated grimace boldly rivaling his own.

She looked into his eyes, and soon they were both wiping away tears of mirth.

Taking a deep breath, Stellan spoke in a resigned voice. "My deepest apologies, Clarysa. I've been a terrible host." He met her gaze, and his words came aloft like a warm summer breeze. "I'm glad you came."

Clarysa placed her hand over his. His skin felt warmer than she expected. "Me, too."

The meal progressed much better after that.

* * * *

They finished dessert an hour later. Immediately, Clarysa stood. As was her kingdom's custom, she offered Stellan poetic thanks for his hospitality. After her speech ended, she gave her leave.

Stellan set down his wine goblet. "Wait, where are you going?"

Halfway across the room, Clarysa stopped. She spoke over her shoulder. "Your instructions were to leave once I ate." She shrugged nonchalantly even though her heart was breaking. "Dinner is over. Now I'm leaving per your order. Good night."

Clarysa had barely reached the doorway when Stellan rushed over and blocked her way. "You're not going anywhere right now. There's a storm. Naturally, you must stay. End of discussion."

"But you said--"

"Forget what I said. I was acting like a fool." He smiled, his cheeks bearing a hint of warmth. "Come with me," he said with a proffered arm. "There's something I want to show you."

Clarysa gladly accepted. Her heart thumped hard as she grasped his elbow. "What is it?"

"A surprise." He began escorting her upstairs.

Clarysa held a hand to her chest. She was being taken--alone--deep into the lair of a mysterious, unpredictable warlock. Much as she craved adventure, this encounter was propelling her into new territory. Was she ready for whatever surprise Stellan meant to show her?

Chapter 19

"Oh, how beautiful!" Clarysa gazed in wonder at the ancient pipe organ before her. So *this* was his surprise. He was a musician, too?

She sat on the organ's bench, running her fingers lightly over the keys while Stellan tended to the fire across the room. *I wonder what it sounds like?* A sidelong glance revealed Stellan's back was to her. She pressed a key.

A pipe shrieked in protest. Clarysa covered her ears and screwed her eyes shut as the noise continued to reverberate again and again in her head.

Stellan turned around, chuckling. "I guess I should have warned you."

Clarysa cracked open an eye. "Now you tell me!"

Stellan joined her on the bench. It hadn't been built for two, which forced their thighs to meet. Clarysa shivered.

"Are you warm enough? That's about as high as I can get the flames, unfortunately." He gestured to the diminutive fire struggling to stay alive.

Concern tinged his green eyes. For a moment, she was lost in them. His desire for her comfort more than made up for the drafty room. "I'm fine, thank you."

Stellan aligned his hands atop the keys. "Well then, what would you like to hear?"

"I don't know anything about this type of music. Play your favorite piece."

Stellan thought for a moment and then began to play. Booming power chords filled the room.

Clarysa listened and watched, entranced not only by the melancholic tune, but also by Stellan's virile features. *He's an expert musician, a sorcerer, a skilled hunter and a prince. What more could I possibly wish for?* His thigh flexed against hers as he worked the pedals. The harmony of his movements made her wonder if he would play her body in the same way. Then Clarysa's neck and cheeks became warmer, for Stellan had chosen that moment to turn and look at her.

After a moment he grinned. Clarysa shot him a questioning look. The man was up to something. "Look at the keys," he urged.

Clarysa glanced down. His hands were dancing on air above the keyboards, and yet the music still played!

She gasped, the blood quickly draining from her face.

Stellan laughed, and the transformation made him seem a man unacquainted with the meaning of sorrow. He rose and motioned for her to join him by the fire.

Clarysa hesitated. She peered intently at the moving keys, tossing a mystified glance in his direction. "Is this magic, or some kind of mechanical devilry?"

"Does it matter?"

She moved cautiously toward the hearth, half-worrying the organ might rise and follow her. "I suppose not." She nudged Stellan playfully on the shoulder as they sat on the floor, but the Prince seemed deep in thought. For a long time, they both stared into the flames.

Quiet moments like this propelled her thoughts into directions that were perhaps better left alone. This time, however, was one she could hardly let be, especially since she didn't know when they'd have another rendezvous. "Stellan," she said, "there's something I've been meaning to ask you..." She paused for a moment, gathering the words. "I don't want this to come out wrong or upset you, but I can't help but wonder."

Stellan glanced up. The intensity of his gaze made her breath catch.

"Will I have to read your mind or are you going to tell me what it is?" His voice sounded grim and mildly sinister.

She smiled nervously. "You can read minds?"

He shrugged noncommittally.

"Oh, I see. Well, continue playing Sir Mysterious if you like. Anyway, Lionel and I... Well, we've heard stories about you for so long I must admit it's strange to think about how I'm standing here with the real flesh-and-blood legend. It's quite surreal."

Stellan rose to lean against the wall. He folded his arms. He smiled devilishly. "Go on. I think I like the sound of this."

"Well, with all I recall hearing about you, I can't help but wonder, where are your parents? Should we be thinking about arranging a meeting between them and my father?"

Stellan's grin quickly faded. "No."

"But why not? I think..."

"I said no, and that's all I have to say about it."

Such harsh words. His sudden change unnerved her, but she decided to press onward. Her kingdom's safety depended on her ability to break through Stellan's carefully constructed defenses. "I understand what it's like to have your family members against you."

Stellan lifted his head, his eyes two smoldering coals threatening to wither everything in sight. "Do you? Well let me ask you this, Princess. As you and daddy dearest squabble over important matters like what kind of pheasant to feast upon or which gowns to wear, have you ever had to wonder when your next meal might be? Better yet, as a child, were you ever awakened in the dead of night by the cold steel of your father's blade against your throat? Have you ever..." His voice faltered.

A moment of uneasy silence passed. Clarysa held her breath, not daring to speak.

Stellan made a fist. "Were you ever forced to watch your own mother waste away before you...flesh dripping off her bones?" His jaw muscles bulged. "Answer me, Clarysa! Have you? Because I have!" His voice fell to a whisper. "My father killed my mother before my very eyes. An early test of the damnable magick I came to call Pestilence. This is the sight I have been condemned to live with all of my life, burned into my memory. It's the first thing I think of as I wake, and the last thing I see before I sleep."

Tears welled up in her eyes. No wonder the man seemed so tortured! "My deepest condolences, Stellan. I had no idea."

He shook his head. "Your sympathy is wasted. I deserve my hateful existence. I saw how my father and uncle were, but I did nothing to stop them. I saw again and again how the Black Arts perverted their minds. Not all of us think only of evil gains, you see. Only my mother and I..." His voice wavered. "I should have saved her."

Clarysa rushed forward and wrapped her arms about him. He clearly needed support more than anything in the world.

"Hush. You don't have to speak of it anymore. Forget I said anything."

"No," came the strained answer. "I *should* remember. I should increase my pain and suffering, for if anyone deserves such a fate, it's this loathsome man you see here before you."

"I don't believe that and neither should you."

He disengaged from her embrace. "I know you mean well, but hear the truth, Clarysa. Remember your history lessons? The 'normal' people of Aldebaran were glad to be rid of us. They massively outnumbered those with magickal talent and took full advantage. In fact, their plan succeeded far better than they knew. When they exiled my ancestors long ago, few survived the journey. Fewer still survived the harsh environment of the Western Wastes." Stellan looked at her bitterly. "No, I suppose those particular tidbits of information never made the rounds in your nighttime fairy tales, did they?"

Clarysa wrapped her arms about her middle. "I know about the banishing, but naturally our teachings told a different account. To my people, they were ridding a plague of evil from the lands."

Stellan smirked. "Naturally. And I suppose all the children who died on that torturous journey were also part of this 'plague.'" He blew out a breath. "Your forbearers never gave a moment's thought to the consequences, did they? Not to mention the unyielding resentment their actions would foster among my people."

Clarysa hung her head. "No. No they didn't. Our tapestries..." Her voice failed her.

"Yes, I can imagine. They must paint a decidedly biased picture." He stared at his right hand. It began to glow with magickal power, then immediately waned. "After being driven out into the Wastes, dissent grew among those who survived. The oldest clan leader tried to maintain control, but he was ill and his magick was severely weakened. One night, a young man seething with vengeance saw the opportunity. He staged a coup." Stellan's gaze locked with Clarysa's. "If I were to tell you the manner of the deaths that followed, it would give you nightmares for years."

Clarysa could only nod slowly. Was her father aware of this information? And if so, why risk ignoring the lessons of history?

Stellan crossed his arms. "Of course, all of this occurred long before my birth. But it's the world my mother and I were born into...a world where the first words a child is taught are a call for death to the outsiders. Magick took on a whole new form--and purpose. My people explored dimensions that had once been forbidden. Talents that had once been nascent and elementary were cultivated into much more powerful skills. They reasoned that if the outsiders' bigotry had made them fear our ways, then we would give them sound cause to tremble in the night."

"Is that why Pestilence was created? Revenge against Aldebaran for something that happened decades ago?"

"Many sorcerers believe we survived the Wastes for one reason and one reason only--to witness the souls of the outsiders torn to shreds and cast before us into oblivion."

Stellan's expression turned distant. What was he thinking? Clarysa finally dared to break the silence. "But…why do you torture yourself so? I'm sure your mother wouldn't blame you. You were only a child. What could you possibly have done?"

"I was twelve at the time. Father brought me before him. Said he had something he wanted to show me. Said I should remember it well if I wanted to become a true sorcerer. You see, I had a litter of wolf pups. They were orphans I'd found on the edge of the Wastes. Every day I rose early to nurse them. Every day I watched them frolic in the courtyard." Sorrow contorted his face.

"What happened?"

"My father slaughtered them all. Said this is what the outsiders had done to us, and what we would soon wreak upon them."

"How awful!"

"It gets worse. Like an idiot, I just stood there. I hadn't come into my full power yet, so I didn't dare cross him. This hesitation to act would later come back to haunt me, for it prevented me from opposing my father when I knew he was wrong." His head dropped; his words tumbled to the floor. "Perhaps I could have saved Mother if I had just done something. *Anything.*"

The Dark Prince smashed his fist into the stone wall beside him. "Well, no more!" He hit the wall again, stripping the flesh from his bare knuckles. "Now I'm stronger. I am no longer the timid boy with a soft heart for animals and his mother. Experience has changed me, hardened me with fresh purpose. I know this--and soon, so shall they."

By "they" Clarysa guessed he meant his father and uncle. She reached out and cradled his bloody hand in the folds of her skirt. "I don't believe that."

Stellan cut her a look and tried to withdraw his hand.

But she maintained a firm grasp. "Well, stand there and glare if you like, but the boy with the soft heart is still in there. I can feel it! He may have built a mighty wall to protect himself, and he has every right to feel angry with the world, but a part of him still cares about the good in it."

Stellan snorted. "What makes you think so?"

"Because he's here with me right now."

He glanced away.

She studied his scraped hand and then began lightly stroking it. "Such lovely hands," she whispered.

Something like a warning growl issued from his mouth, but he didn't pull away.

She shouldn't breach his protective shell too fast or too soon, or she risked alienating him altogether. After all, she now understood what she represented to him. "Stellan, change has to begin somewhere, with someone willing to take up the mantle." She swallowed hard. "If I haven't made it clear before, I'm doing it now. I want to help you." Her gaze poured deeply into his. "For what it's worth, you've converted me to your cause. Please believe me!"

The prince nodded, a sly grin tugging at his lips. "There is a way you can help," he murmured.

Her heart pounded, hoping his definition of "help" included a hug, or maybe even a kiss. "Yes?"

"Clarysa, would you care to explain how you came here without an escort? Or, for that matter, without the King?"

She winced. "Who says I did?"

His stern gaze warned her against any mischief.

"All right. The truth is very few people are brave enough to visit this spooky, old castle of yours."

"Spooky? Who told you that? And you haven't answered my question." He ran his fingers across her belly.

Clarysa shrieked with laughter. She liked this other Stellan, so funny and playful. Nothing like the beast others made him out to be. "How can I answer anything when you're tickling me without mercy?" She spun away and darted across the room.

"If that's the case, I have other techniques at my disposal." Grinning wickedly, Stellan sidestepped in an attempt to corner her.

Clarysa scooted along the wall just out of his reach. "You'll have to catch me first!"

Stellan chased her around the room. By the third pass, Clarysa's heart raced uncontrollably. She wanted him to catch her, but at the same time craved the thrill of being hunted.

A second door caught her eye. "What's through here?" she asked breathlessly. She tugged at the iron catch and opened the door. She made it through the opening just as Stellan dove for her.

Clarysa stumbled onto a freezing catwalk lined with a stone parapet.

"Oh, my!" She stopped to survey the nighttime view of the castle below, buried in ice and frost and shadow. A canopy of stars glittered brightly above. "I didn't realize we were up so high!"

Stellan's steadying hand clamped against her elbow. Clarysa shivered. The predator had caught his prey. "This is the highest tower," he murmured into her ear.

His breath made her skin tingle. She stepped forward carefully, letting her palms rest on the waist-high parapet. "It's beautiful. I can see why you come up here to play."

They stood still for a moment. Save for a light sprinkling of snow, nothing moved below. The organ music simmered quietly in the background. Clarysa stared about her, transfixed. *I could become accustomed to this view.*

An icy blast swooped in and she shuddered violently. The edges of Stellan's cape flew up, snapping high into the air. As the material settled down, it wrapped her body against Stellan's in a warm embrace. Clarysa hadn't seen his arms move. More of his magick? *Delightful!* She rested her cheek against his chest. It felt so firm and broad she wanted to stay there forever.

"And what about you?" he whispered after the wind died down.

"What about me?"

"Do *you* think I'm 'spooky'?"

Startled, Clarysa looked at him. His anguished gaze captured hers, searching for an answer. She moistened her lips. "Not at all. I think you're wonderful."

She became aware of a new sensation as his hands hungrily explored her waist and hips. *Why am I breathing so hard?* She clung to him, feeling giddy. In fact, she wanted to say, I love you! But words would only sound harsh and awkward in this gloriously ethereal moment, high above his beautiful and enchanted kingdom.

All across the land below snowflakes drifted down--lightly at first, then with renewed vigor. Stellan gazed at her now through half-lidded eyes, his lashes tinged with wetness. Clarysa's excitement mounted as he pulled her hips closer, drawing her upward. As he bent his head down, she rose on tiptoes to reach him. Their lips met in a warm, vibrant kiss. Clarysa trembled, but not from the cold. She encircled his neck and stroked the glossy, uneven locks she had yearned to touch for so long.

As the kiss deepened, he began exploring more than her waist and hips. Thighs, back, neck, hair... He caressed every inch with deft, eager strokes. Clarysa gasped as he swept her hard against him, leaving her feet dangling. Still, he kissed her, even as her bottom pressed alarmingly against the parapet. Excited, spellbound, impassioned, she clutched him tightly. Her girlish daydreams hadn't come close to the actual thrill of Stellan's embrace and hot, raw affection. Giddy thoughts raced through her mind about their future. *He is the one!*

Stellan's kisses grew frenzied, more demanding. Clarysa wondered at how heavy her breasts felt, crushed as they were against his solid chest. Where their hips met, she could feel Stellan's hard length. It inflamed her desire to slip her hand between their bodies and stroke him there. But the Dark Prince held her tightly in his embrace, his questing tongue gaining intimate knowledge of her mouth. With a happy sigh, Clarysa parted her lips wide so he could know it completely.

She clamped his waist with her legs. Moaning, Stellan gripped her hard and ravaged her mouth as the bloodthirsty snowstorm howled around them. Wind lashed at their clothing while snow and hail accosted them without mercy. Clarysa paid the weather no heed. All she could think about was finding relief from the pulsing heat between her thighs. She was wound so tightly with need.

Clarysa bucked against him. Intense pleasure spiraled deep within her. If Stellan could slip his hardness inside her right now, she would be complete.

"Oh yes," she gasped as he feasted upon her neck. She rolled her hips in a way she hoped would entice him. How else could she signal her readiness?

Stellan growled. "I'm going to lose control if you keep doing that." He grazed her ear with his teeth, prompting a cascade of tingles across her skin.

"I don't mind," she panted. "It will feel so good!" She dragged her tongue, slick and hot, along his stubble-roughened cheek. He shuddered violently. She put her lips to his ear. "I'll do that again anywhere you want."

For a moment, he closed his hands dangerously tight around her waist. He thrust his tongue so far into her mouth she couldn't breathe. Clarysa absorbed every inch, hanging onto him for dear life.

Then he broke the kiss, his snarl of frustration echoing across the snow-laden countryside.

"Damn it, Clarysa! We must stop before this goes too far."

Swinging her away from the parapet he deposited her in a large snowdrift. Reluctantly, she dropped her legs from his waist. He plunged a hand into the snow by her shoulder and paused to catch his breath.

Clarysa groaned in protest. "But, Stellan, it feels so right!" She gently touched his lips. "I ache for you so much."

He caught her hand in his. "The feeling is mutual," he said, his breath ragged. "But we risk too much throwing caution to the wind. Our situation is too complicated."

Stellan was right. She sighed. "And politically fragile."

He gently wiped a fresh coating of snow from her forehead. "Yes. I'm glad you understand."

Clarysa frowned, fighting back tears of disappointment. "What are we going to do?"

"Well, we should start by going inside. You're shivering." He extended a hand and helped her stand. "Come. It's time for rest."

* * * *

The midnight hour had come and gone when they retreated inside. Wine had never made Clarysa as drunk as Stellan's kisses. She wanted to stay up and talk, but he insisted she rest for a few hours before he escorted her back to Aldebaran.

Hands entwined, they descended to the main floor. At the door of her guest room, Stellan slipped an arm around her waist and pulled her close. He gave her a passionate kiss goodnight. Breathless, Clarysa watched him leave for his quarters. The deep shadows of the passageway quickly swallowed him.

As soon as he was gone, the hairs along the back of her nape rose. Cautiously, Clarysa stepped forward, peering into the gloom. There it was--an open door a few rooms down. Candlelight spilled through the narrow opening. Clarysa detected the face of a woman.

Patrulha.

Clarysa waved, but the Captain of the Guard swiftly shut the door. Clarysa put a finger to her swollen lips. How much of her intimate exchange with Stellan had Patrulha seen? Did it bother her in some way? Feeling uneasy, Clarysa shut her door and went to bed.

* * * *

After a refreshing sleep, Clarysa rose, made herself presentable, and went to the kitchen. Gretchen was already up preparing breakfast. Ghyslain was setting the table. Stellan sat there cutting bread.

"Good morning, all," Clarysa said from the doorway.

"Good morning, Princess," Gretchen said merrily. She winked as Clarysa headed for the table. "Did you have a lovely dinner?"

"I did, thank you."

Gretchen slowly stirred the large kettle of porridge. "I heard the entertainment portion of the evening lasted far into the night. Now *that* must have been something to see."

Clarysa blushed. "I, ah... The pipe organ made beautiful music." *Heavens, how much does she know?*

Ghyslain snorted out his laughter, dropping a piece of silverware in the process.

"Enough," growled Stellan.

Clarysa looked at him in alarm. But he appeared more contemplative than angry. The tension drained from her shoulders.

"You can sit here," he told her, pointing to the space on his left.

Clarysa sat. Gretchen ladled out porridge and drizzled a generous dollop of honey over each bowl. The way Stellan and Ghyslain attacked their food, she guessed they considered honey an indulgence.

A series of knowing looks passed between the gypsy woman and her son as the four of them sat eating. Clarysa didn't mind. If her association with Stellan brought them comfort and happiness, then it was a good sign of things to come.

Stellan still maintained his guard, but he didn't scowl nearly as much as the previous night. When Clarysa pressed her thigh against his, he didn't move away.

A half hour later, she and Stellan were astride their horses, ready to depart. Gretchen, Ghyslain, and Froll saw them off.

"Come back soon," Gretchen called as she and the prince rode off.

Clarysa smiled and waved at the gypsy family, but her heart was sinking. *If I even can.*

Snow fell at a steady pace. Clarysa coaxed him into conversation by telling jokes and plying him with more questions about his habits and pastimes. Along the way, they made a few stops to rest or kiss, but mostly to kiss. At the edge of the Snowflake Kingdom, warm sunshine replaced the chilly precipitation and so they removed their heavy cloaks and scarves.

After they crossed the Aldebaran border, Clarysa gasped. She motioned for Stellan's silence, and quickly led him off the road. They hid behind a group of oak trees.

"Did you see them?" she asked.

Stellan nodded.

Clarysa frowned. "My father's men."

Stellan leaned forward on crossed arms. "Let me guess. You left without permission."

Clarysa hung her head. "I-I couldn't possibly stay away. My father is wrong about you, and I'm going to prove it."

Stellan frowned. "By losing his trust? By placing yourself in a position where he will likely *never* be open to the encroaching Pestilence threat- -or us?"

Clarysa bit her lip. "I know. I'm sorry. I wasn't thinking." Her eyes burned. "I'm stupid that way." Scalding tears ran down her cheeks.

The prince nudged his horse alongside hers. He coaxed her chin upward with his fingertips. "Look at me."

As she did, he smiled. "I fear you're going to be in dire straits, but I'm glad you risked it." Cupping her cheek, he leaned forward and gently brushed her lips with his.

Clarysa sighed and pulled back. "I'd better go before I make matters even worse." She brushed his cheek with her fingers. "Come to the next hunt--but don't let Edward see you! I'll send word to Lionel. He'll help us arrange a meeting."

Stellan nodded, his expression turning stony.

Clarysa stared resolutely ahead as she guided her horse from the forest. If she looked back upon Stellan's face again she might never return home. She spurred the horse down the road. Within minutes, the company of Aldebaran royal guards surrounded her. Despite the warm sun shining upon her, Clarysa shivered. She knew what was to come only too well.

* * * *

The King berated Clarysa long and loudly. Blustery words castigated her for hours. All of her family gathered to watch, their faces congested with disapproval. Clarysa stood with arms crossed. Let them stew in their righteous indignation. She may not have made the safest decision, but at least she'd tried to do the right thing. Why couldn't her father understand the stakes?

Edward in particular looked as if plagued by a constantly foul smell. Clarysa groaned inwardly as her brother waxed ad infinitum about her "deceitful," "irresponsible," and "delinquent" behavior. He even offered to ride immediately to Vandeborg to strike a verbal reprisal against Stellan. Edward and her father argued over the proposal for some time, with the King eventually ruling it would be quite unnecessary.

"Now, Clarysa," her father said, "Before I declare my final thoughts on the matter, do you have anything to say for yourself?"

"I love him," was all she would say.

Sharp intakes of breath echoed about the court.

"So be it. My decision is this: you will never leave the Kingdom of Aldebaran or see Prince Stellan again."

* * * *

"I don't know." Lionel sifted through a pile of tunics in his bedroom. "It sounds too risky, even for one who thrives on the edge such as myself."

He and Clarysa had recently returned from a local bazaar. The room lay buried under an assortment of shirts, pants, and hats--a veritable rainbow of accessories. Presently he stood before a full-length mirror evaluating different combinations of colors and fabrics. "What do you think of this? Too outré, perhaps?"

Clarysa groaned, languishing away on his bed among a number of his purchases. It was the first time in three months that the King had let her out of the castle. Three long *torturous* months, according to his cousin. No letters. No verbal communications to be passed on or received. No anything. In fact, she had been allowed to visit Lionel only under the stipulation that he would maintain constant supervision. She was forbidden to leave his sight, except to sleep or bathe.

"But I *have* to see him! We won't get caught, I promise. You're too smart for that."

"Perhaps," Lionel said with a grin. He tossed a shirt aside purposefully so it fell on her head. "But I'm afraid flattery will get you nowhere in this particular instance. Besides, I'm keen to avoid any kind of royal punishment right now. Nothing must come between me and my bazaars."

Clarysa threw the garment aside. "Lionel, be serious. I love him. Haven't you ever been in love before, truly and deeply?"

Lionel mulled the question over for a moment. Looking at her through the mirror, he noted her pale face and grieved expression. It pained him to watch her deteriorate like this. Hair that had once outshined the sun now appeared listless and dull. Her appearance was sickly and thin from lack of appetite. Tears welled constantly in her eyes, especially when she thought no one was looking. *I know the King's been hard on you, but, well, he's the King, as well as your father. What would you have me do? I can hardly fault him for trying to protect you, especially from yourself!*

He gestured at her plain gown. "Well, if this is what it does to a person, you're welcome to it." He held up two pairs of pants. "Blue or magenta?"

Clarysa eyed him tiredly. "Blue."

Lionel tossed the rejected pair onto a corner chair. "Be gone magenta, thou art cast aside by the command of her royal highness, Princess Clarysa."

How he adored the bazaar! It had been a delightful morning, except when Clarysa would sniffle or lose her focus and stay endlessly rooted to one spot, staring off into space. Her morose display wouldn't have been so bad if it she hadn't repeated the show every five feet. Not so delightful. Even her favorite strawberry pastry puffs hadn't been enough to lift her spirits.

"I'll take all the blame if something goes wrong, I swear." Clarysa changed to a kneeling position. Her voice trembled. *"Please*, Lionel! I've no one else to turn to."

Lionel slowed as he tried on another shirt. Should he tell her he saw Stellan at all of the last three hunts? He had caught glimpses of the Dark Prince among the trees, but had not acknowledged him for fear Edward would find out--and possibly kill him.

Clarysa wiped away yet more tears. He couldn't imagine what she was experiencing because this kind of heartbreak was so foreign to them, privileged as they were. But if she were anything like him--and she was--her emotions ran deep and strong. Clarysa may have had the disposition of a silly little foal more often than not, but she knew a good person when she saw one.

And she was attempting to protect Aldebaran by aligning herself with a sorcerer in a position to do something about it, even if her choice was an unpopular one.

The clothes and shiny trinkets lost their appeal for the moment. Lionel began to fold and put everything away. "Even if I arranged a meeting, Clarysa, what then? What about the future?"

She leaped off the bed and embraced him, leaning hard into his chest. "One meeting would be enough. I'll figure out the rest later."

"Yes, well," he said, extricating himself from her grasp, "it's still not going to happen overnight." Hands resting on her shoulders, he regarded her solemnly. "Return home for now. Mope about as you have been. I'll send word after everything is ready." He paused for a moment, then added, "I hope you realize the position you're placing me in, cousin--and the danger."

Clarysa lowered her gaze and gave a quick nod.

Lionel continued softly, "Good. Because I'm not quite sure I fully understand the ramifications myself, although I don't imagine they will be pleasant at all!"

Chapter 20

Stellan waited in a grove thick with birch trees, his obsidian cape billowing softly in the breeze. Nearby, a low-slung stone fence sloped toward the ground and disappeared beneath it, a remnant, perhaps, of a dwelling long ago. He stood in the shadows while Midnight grazed a few feet away. Wolfe paced in the woods around him, the only bodyguard he'd ever needed.

Glossy leaves covered the ground, still damp from a recent rainfall. In the horizon, fog crept across the hills of northern Aldebaran, effectively covering them in syrupy blankets.

Over three hours had passed while he waited, hoping Clarysa would come. Lionel had brokered the meeting weeks ago. Perhaps he had forgotten? Worse still, had Clarysa placed Stellan entirely out of her mind? She'd been absent from the hunts. Either she was being kept under lock and key, or she'd found a more interesting suitor. No doubt, a "normal" prince from one of the other kingdoms would be far easier to put up with than him. Stellan gritted his teeth, once again wondering why he'd placed such an unprecedented amount of trust in her.

Still, he wanted to believe. He risked his life by lurking in Aldebaran's woods, but he didn't care. Clarysa was all he thought about, even at the expense of the growing Pestilence threat.

His companions had noticed. Patrulha, for one, had been intensely vocal about her displeasure regarding his…preoccupation of late. "You had better focus your mind on what's needed soon, oh lordly prince, or everyone around here will wind up dead--or worse!"

She only used her favorite reproach, "oh lordly prince" when something deeply upset her. She might have had a point, he conceded. Perhaps Stellan would best serve everyone if he forgot about Clarysa and concentrated on the issue at hand--eliminating Pestilence. He had to be ready for whatever his father planned to throw at him.

But a hunger he struggled to understand propelled him to gain his fill of the youngest Aldebaran princess. What if he never saw her again? Could he continue on as he had been, a bitter hermit with a heart rotting from disuse? When he probed inwardly for an answer to resolve his confusion, none came.

A snapping twig yanked Stellan from his reverie. He turned his head in the direction of the noise. Two riders approached. Lionel was one. The other was some kind of servant, cloaked and hooded.

Stellan revealed himself. They exchanged hushed greetings.

"Wait here," Lionel instructed. He turned his horse around. "My squire will wait on you until the time of your meeting."

Stellan grabbed Lionel's arm and lowered his voice. "Are you sure he can be trusted?"

Lionel glanced over his shoulder, smiling faintly. "Oh, most certainly. Been with me for years."

They clasped hands. "Thank you," Stellan said.

He watched Lionel ride off. Turning back around, Stellan found himself in the tight grip of the squire, the servant's arms locked around his torso. Cold dread invaded his chest. *Squire...or soldier? What deceit is this?* Stellan broke the hold and pushed against his chest with a powerful thrust of his hand. The squire flew through the air and landed on the ground with a loud cry.

Stellan glanced down at his hand. Something hadn't felt right. He looked up. Or sounded right.

Whimpering softly, the figure struggled to sit up. The hood fell back, revealing a head of wavy, golden hair.

Stellan rushed over, his heart in his mouth. "Clarysa! Why didn't you say something?" He kneeled down, slipping an arm behind her back.

Slightly dazed, she stared at him, her eyes moistening. "I couldn't help myself. I wanted to surprise you."

"I understand, but you shouldn't startle me like that."

Clarysa moaned, clinging to his neck. "You can't begin to imagine how much I've missed you."

Stellan pressed his cheek to hers, delighting in the touch of her soft, dewy skin. Then he kissed her, hard, feeling breathless and consumed with hunger. She eagerly returned the gesture, her mouth cleaving to his so yearningly it was all he could do to not tear off the rough-spun clothing she wore. It was a long time before either of them used their lips to speak.

* * * *

Next to the remains of a meal, Clarysa nestled against Stellan beneath a makeshift canopy. She described the long confrontation with her father and resulting punishment. Stellan listened attentively, his furrowed brow darkening his roguish features. She feared he thought the worst of her, but what could she have done differently? Her every move was watched; truly she was a bird in a gilded cage.

"Our time is running out," Stellan said. Sighing, he stroked her arm. "I want to see you again, but how we can arrange it without discovery eludes me. And we shouldn't have to sneak around like wayward children."

"You could see me every day if we were married." Clarysa gasped and covered her lips. "I'm sorry. I didn't mean to say it out loud."

Stellan dropped his gaze.

Clarysa looked askance. *Now look at what you've done. You've either angered or embarrassed him. Probably both.*

An awkward silence ticked by. A warm breeze ruffled the damp grass. Then a light rain began to fall.

"Clarysa, are you sure that's what you'd want?"

Clarysa stared at him in shock. "What do you mean?"

He jabbed at his chest. "This--me! This life of mine. There's not much I can offer you. I have no wealth to speak of. No royal treasury."

"There are more important things than wealth."

"I have no friends. You're accustomed to--"

"Lionel's your friend. He adores you. And, uh--" Her gaze flicked to the canine snoozing nearby. "--and Wolfe."

"My castle is frigid, even in the summer."

"Well, then, I'll put on a cloak!"

"I hate crowds."

"People are overrated."

"My family despises me. I'm surprised they even let me live this long."

Clarysa knelt and faced him squarely, her nose less than an inch from his. "*I'd* be your family," she whispered. "And if all this is some attempt to scare me away, Mr. Big Bad Dark Prince, you've failed miserably."

"Clarysa!" Stellan caressed her cheek. "Such fearlessness!" He dropped his hand and grasped hers. A wistful expression softened his features. "You're the best person who's ever come into my life."

"And you're the most exciting person who's ever come into *mine*."

They kissed again, knocking the canopy to the ground with their wild frolicking.

Clarysa sucked in a breath as Stellan lay atop her. He covered her face with urgent kisses and pushed his hips between her thighs. "Stellan, I don't want to stop, but we haven't much time. We must think of something before Lionel returns."

Undeterred, Stellan gently squeezed her right breast. "Think of what?" His hot breath washed over her ear.

Clarysa arched into his heavenly touch despite the risk. "How we can be together and give you unrestricted access to Aldebaran. Oh yes, keep your hand there--that's lovely." Clarysa sighed happily as Stellan placed a searing kiss on her neck. She grasped the back of his head and pulled him closer. "Pestilence...Pestilence uprisings have been reported more times than I can count. I don't think the campaigns against it have been very successful, either."

The way Stellan moved his pelvis against hers caused a rush of pulsing warmth between her legs. One of his hands tunneled under her shirt. His fingers skimmed the underside of a bare breast. *What was I saying?*

No matter how seductive his touch, she had to stay focused. "Not only that, but Lionel said he heard the King was considering canceling future hunts because of the outbreaks."

Stellan pulled abruptly away and sat up, cursing under his breath.

Clarysa scrambled into a sitting position. She understood his frustration--she hadn't wanted to stop either. But time was running out. "And I have a guard now at all times. I can't help you properly with so much scrutiny." When he didn't respond, Clarysa tugged at his collar. "Do you know any magick that will help?"

Stellan scowled. "You don't understand what you're asking."

"Oh there must be some kind of potion or something that will change my parents' minds. I could slip it into their wine. Isn't that how it's done?"

"Oh, *gods!*" With a vehement shake of his head, Stellan stood. Gazing downward, his face reminded her of his castle, icy and rigid. "Just as I'm beginning to think you understand my predicament, you go and spout something completely ignorant! 'Slip it into their wine', she says." His voice mocked without restraint. "Damn it, Clarysa, your parents aren't puppets. I can't just pull their strings when it's convenient for *you.*"

Anger flared as if he had slapped her. "Convenient for *me?* That's uncalled for! I'm only trying to figure out a way to achieve this alliance."

He threw up his hands. "So manipulating the King and Queen is your brilliant strategy? Which will last for exactly how long, Princess? Well, I'll tell you--for as long as the potion lasts, which is no time at all, because nothing like it exists! What kind of sorcerer do you think I am, that I can possess people? Or do you believe I can control the sun and the moon as well?"

Who was this man spitting such vitriol? Didn't he appreciate anything she had done? "Perhaps I misspoke about your abilities, but at least I'm not giving up!"

Stellan scowled. "Is that what you think of me, Clarysa?" His voice sounded low and dangerous. "That I'm a coward?" He continued before she could respond. "You don't have to say it. I know that suspicion has been lurking in your spoiled little head for some time." His features contorted, grew more cold and hard. He slammed a fist against the nearest tree. A handful of leaves fluttered to the ground. Then he turned away, clenched fists by his sides.

Spoiled little head? Was that how she came across to him, a spoiled princess? Tears pricked her eyes as she stood. "Your life has been awful. Living through that kind of horror must make it difficult to face the day. That's what I meant. I know you're not afraid."

Despite her attempt to regain a civilized exchange, no comforting words came from the guarded man before her. The rain had stopped, but clouds hid the sun. She shivered in the cool breeze as it sifted through the trees. How could she have been so stupid? Or rather, so idealistic. Part of her didn't want to believe the astronomical obstacles between her and a life of bliss with Stellan. But she couldn't be as cynical as he appeared to be. It wasn't in her nature.

Clarysa couldn't stand the dreadful silence. Wanting to reach him but not knowing how, her frustration only grew. "I apologize for offending you. Why don't you say something?" Stepping closer, she placed a hand on his shoulder. "Don't you care about what happens to us?"

He stiffened under her touch. "Should I? We've spent what--all of five days together? Hardly enough time to build a proper foundation."

"But Stellan, I…I *love* you."

He turned and glared. "Don't confuse infatuation with love. You're in love with my reputation, not me."

Clarysa stared at him in shock. Tears coursed down her cheeks. "Then I must mean nothing to you. Is that what you're trying to say?"

"We're too different. Our families are in complete opposition to one another." He rubbed a hand through his hair. "Why are we even sneaking around like this?" He spread his arms wide, gesturing to their surroundings. "Is this love? We're *adults*, Clarysa."

She buried her face in her hands. Her temples ached as though she'd been kicked by a mule. "If you think it's so bad, then why did you even come? Everyone talks about how horrible the warlocks of the Wastes are. I thought you were different!"

"Well, perhaps you thought wrong."

She heard Stellan's cape snap as he whirled and strode toward away. *Away?* She spun around. His black form skulked among the trees, now a good stone's throw beyond her. "Stellan...Stellan, wait!" Clarysa ran forward, breathless from the daggers of fear slashing at her heart. "Why are you leaving? Stellan, please don't go!"

But he had mounted his horse. Clarysa threw herself forward and grabbed his leg. "Don't leave like this! Stellan, we're meant for each other--I feel it in my heart of hearts. We *will* find a solution. Let's talk and cast aside our doubts this time. Darling, *please!*"

An iron hand reached down and pushed her roughly away. Not so hard that she fell, but enough to make his emotion clear. Emerald eyes burned with an infernal glow, prompting her to take a step back. "The only thing I'm going to cast aside is my stupidity for having thought we could make this work. Hear this, and understand--I'll do my utmost to destroy Pestilence, but that's *all* I'm going to do."

A hard knot lodged in her throat. Her next words came out a hoarse whisper. "What about *us*?"

"I'm going to forget 'we' ever happened." His scowl deepened. "I'd advise you to do the same."

Stellan muttered a curt order, prompting Midnight to canter away. In a matter of seconds, rider and horse disappeared among the trees.

Clarysa dropped to her knees, the pain in her chest so great she feared heart failure was imminent. Only gasps escaped her. *What am I going to do? Oh, Stellan...I love you. Don't leave me!*

But, he *had* left her. What recourse remained for her now, she didn't know. The silken noose had accomplished its task--there would be no more stolen moments or exciting ventures into his mysterious kingdom of eternal winter. There would be no more Stellan.

Collapsing upon the ground, she wept.

Some moments later, a strong hand descended upon her shoulder. She scrambled to her feet from fright...and hope. But it was only Lionel. Had he witnessed the terrible fight? Clarysa wondered how long he had been there.

"Come," said the Duke, drawing her close against his warm, familiar body, "it's time to go. You can tell me all about it on the way home."

Chapter 21

Marcus wiped the sweat from his moist, blond locks. Exactly five hundred and twenty-two paces he marched before turning. Five hundred and twenty-two was the breadth of his surveillance area before he spun on one heel and commenced marching five hundred and twenty-two paces back. He knew the exact number. It was burned into his memory forever, for he had counted each pace time and time again to pass the long, lonely hours.

The day was shaping up to be hot enough to squeeze water from his sweat-soaked clothes. He stopped marching at three hundred thirty-four steps and sighed. This was his lot day after day, parading up and down around the kingdom's western perimeter as…well, as a lookout for cows, apparently. He glanced over to the contented beasts lying in the shade, slowly chewing their morning cud. *That's the life,* he thought. *Not out here traipsing up and down for twelve hours a day in this stifling garb.*

But his commander had doubled the border patrols a week ago. Apparently, the order had come directly from the King himself. What they were supposed to be on the lookout for, he wasn't sure. Foot soldiers were never consulted about these matters.

Marcus fingered the rough material of his uniform, standard issue for all Aldebaran military. With little education under his belt, and no money to his family name, it had been either join the army or something along the line of stable hand. Marcus grimaced. Better to be a cow's guard rather than a horse's butler. Step number three hundred and thirty-five it was then…

An expansive shadow loomed across the sky. Marcus glanced up. A large flock of ravens flew by, large enough to momentarily blot out the sun. *Never seen anything like it before. Wonder what's got them all spooked?*

Heather Massey

Marcus heard footfalls. Turning around, he discovered the cause. Hundreds of people were pouring out of the forest. He frowned. They had the appearance of men, but…weren't. For one thing, their flesh was covered in boils, and--in some cases--hung down, swaying in the wind like rags. For another, they all shared a unique trait--a pair of blood red orbs for eyes.

These were not men and women, but the walking dead--and they were rapidly advancing across the clearing straight toward him! Marcus turned and blew his horn in warning. Onward he ran, channeling every spare breath into the horn. But the creatures were moving distressingly fast. He risked a glance over his shoulder to see how close they were.

Marcus never made it beyond step number three hundred and seventy-six.

Chapter 22

Stellan's broadsword shimmered in the air as it came down with the force of thunder. The ancient blade had long since seen better days and cracked upon finding its target. However, the blade's last act was still true as a mottled, hairless head was separated from its skeletal frame.

"Strike for the heads, and do not let them touch you!" he boomed to the men around him. He drew two swords from their scabbards, then jumped from Midnight straight into a massive throng of Pestilence victims. Whirling about like a one-man army, he hewed hands from arms, and arms from bodies. He breathed hard through the bandana affixed tightly across his face; only his eyes were visible. When fighting Pestilence, the less exposed he was to contamination, the better.

"Clear!" Patrulha's voice sliced through the air, prompting Stellan to leap out of the fray. A downpour of arrows rushed toward the Pestilence horde.

"Reload!" Patrulha called.

Stellan remounted Midnight and stormed across the field to her.

"Loose arrows!" she ordered.

Again, a fresh volley sang and found their targets. The division of Aldebaran soldiers--what was left of them--stood back from the battle, confused. As Stellan reached Patrulha's position, a bloody, heavily bandaged officer joined them.

"You have no right to interfere, sorcerer," barked the officer. "This is our territory and ours to defend."

Stellan reigned in his stallion alongside Patrulha, ignoring the soldier. "Any of ours injured?" he asked.

"Two, but minor. As for Leopold's men, the numbers are much worse. I estimate twenty fatalities, at least."

Stellan loosened his bandana. "I see. Burn the bodies."

Patrulha nodded and gave the order. Stellan looked across the battlefield. Word of the attack had come while he had been investigating a reported sighting near a bustling Aldebaran village. An old codger and his wife had tipped him off. They cared not in which guise the help was cloaked, only that it was forthcoming.

If only he had arrived here earlier, he could have saved more lives. The people of Aldebaran had no idea what they were up against. *That proud fool of a king's son should have listened to me.* Another thought came, unbidden. *At least I know* she *is safe, for the present.* If enough time went by when Stellan refused to acknowledge even her name, then there might be a chance he could forget.

He made a fist. It would take an eternity, at least.

The officer cleared his throat. "Listen to me! This land is under the protection of His Majesty Leopold. Seeing as how the first attack wave caught us unawares, I am now the highest-ranking officer on the field. Because of this, I must…"

Patrulha cut him a dour look. "Be silent, little man. You're dealing with forces beyond your understanding."

The officer sputtered a protest.

Stellan shielded his eyes from the sun. Something moved at the forest's edge. "Looks like they're amassing another wave. How are we doing on the formula?"

"The last assault depleted it, and we're low on arrows."

"Damn it." He slammed a tightened fist into his opposing hand. "Prepare to light the fields. We'll torch it with our remaining arsenal."

Patrulha turned to give the orders, but the Aldebaran officer accosted her. "Now see here, *woman.*" This last word he spat into the heavy dust surrounding them. "I must first clear this through the proper channels, as I…"

Stellan rolled his eyes. "Shut him up, will you?"

"Consider it done!" Patrulha slipped a hand into her side pouch and withdrew an item. The man's mouth opened wide to protest, but a blow dart entering his neck spoke for him. He fell to the ground, unconscious. Without a second glance, Patrulha turned and rallied the men. "Prepare for Scorched Earth!"

Stellan rode across the field, checking for survivors among the tall grass. He turned to see his rag-tag troops lining up under Patrulha's command whence he came, then he turned again to see a mob of Pestilence victims streaming out of the forest. They were only several hundred yards away. An upraised hand to his troops gave the signal to prepare for firing.

"No!" squeaked a girl's mouse-like voice from the grass. "You can't kill them! You can't."

Stellan gestured wildly, effectively belaying his order. "Who said that?"

"I did," said a girl of about ten. She ran up to him. "My mama and papa are with them. Don't hurt them. Please don't hurt them!"

Stellan glanced toward the advancing man-beasts. Their eyes gleamed and bounced like crimson fireflies. With one powerful movement, he scooped up the girl and spurred Midnight into action. The horse streaked across the field. Once Stellan had placed her on the ground at a safe distance, he looked on her grimly. "Your parents, are they infected?"

Tears streaked the girl's dirty face. "They...they didn't mean to hurt me! They..."

Stellan roughly grabbed her shoulders and shook her. "Do they have the eyes, child? Poisoned red with blood? Answer me!"

"Yes! But they aren't like the others, I promise! They can be cured. I know it. Don't kill them!"

Stellan turned away. He raised his right hand and then dropped it. A storm of flaming arrows soared over the field and hit the open area in time to meet the advancing horde. The girl beat her tiny fists at Stellan's torso as her plaintive cries rang on. "No! You can't do this! We've got to save them! We've got to save them!"

Easily fending off her blows, he picked up the child once again and mounted his steed. He frowned deeply as they rode on. "They're too far gone, little one. They're already dead."

Chapter 23

Since dawn, Clarysa had kept a vigilant watch from the west tower. The majestic structure overlooked the main road leading to her father's castle. Realistically, she shouldn't have been nursing any kind of hope. But for the past day the news had been on everyone's lips from palace advisors to farmers--the sorcerer who had saved the King's regiment from sure annihilation was heading straight to the heart of Aldebaran. Clarysa shivered for the hundredth time that morning, for soon she would once again lay her eyes upon the Dark Prince of the legendary Snowflake Kingdom himself.

She wondered at the change she had undergone even at the mere mention of his name. Her mood had lifted; her energy level soared. Up until then, she had spent the past month in a haze of despair and inactivity. As the days of her separation from Stellan wore on, she had chosen a self-imposed exile, emerging only when family business absolutely demanded her presence. What was there for her to do, anyway? Not only was there an edict forbidding her to go to him, but Stellan had established his own--against *her*. She cringed every time she recollected their argument. Yet memories of the enigmatic sorcerer consumed her. She could still feel his strong arms about her and his hot breath on her neck.

Was there anything she should have done differently? Clarysa had ruminated countless times over her behavior during their last encounter. No matter how she analyzed it, all the threads trailed back to her thoughtless comment. It was horrid enough Stellan's people suffered extreme prejudice from the other kingdoms; it was quite another matter for him to experience faithlessness from the woman claiming to adore him with all of her heart. For shame! Why hadn't she chosen her words more carefully?

Now, though, he had come to Aldebaran in complete disregard of the edict against him. Clarysa knew there were three reasons the King hadn't ordered him killed on sight. One, he had saved countless lives; two, because of her; and three, because he had sent word via messenger insisting on an audience with her parents. Despite a strong suspicion that once at the castle he wouldn't even acknowledge her, speculations ran wild in her mind. What could his presence mean?

A trumpet sounded, heralding the arrival of a visitor. Clarysa gazed into the distance. At first, only billowing dust was visible. The dust became a dark speck. Then the speck transformed into a fully formed rider and horse racing toward the castle.

Clarysa wasted no time. She flew down the tower stairs and ran to the court as fast as she dared.

Once there, she chose a spot on the balcony with a wide view of the thrones. It was strategic for another reason--to hide from Stellan. She had to avoid the agony of a second rejection. At least this way she could admire him from afar.

Various attendants and advisors filed inside. The King and Queen entered, followed by their usual entourage. Each took his or her respective place. The court was so quiet she could have heard a feather drop.

The large gilded doors to the throne room slowly swung open. A man in full Aldebaran regalia stepped through. "His Royal Highness, Prince Stellan of Vandeborg," announced the herald with all due pomp.

Clarysa's breath hitched. The Dark Prince strode forward wearing a stern expression. With his pale face and black cape, he looked like a specter risen from the underworld. He dragged a large sack beset with stains. Thud. Thud. Thud. His boots echoed about the room as if thunder. A row of anxious guards fingered their weapons.

Upon reaching the foot of the throne dais, Stellan stopped. Gloved hands loosened the ropes of the sack. In one fell motion, he dumped the stinking, infested carcass of some anonymous villager onto the floor of the royal court.

The smell was abominable. Clarysa lost count of how many people averted their faces. Many gagged, others coughed. The Queen placed a delicate hand against her mouth.

"What in the name of the Five Lands is this?" said the King, pointing at the body. Veins bulged in his neck, feeding the fire of his flushed, angry face. "Don't you have any idea where you are? Is this...*crudeness* of yours so necessary?" The remark gave Stellan pause, but only for a moment. He held out his right hand and dropped something onto the corpse. It burst into bright flames. Clarysa wondered if it were magick or a simple incendiary device.

Stellan watched the corpse burn for several minutes, his emerald eyes amplified by the greenish glare. Eventually the flesh blackened and began to disintegrate. Then, and only then, did he turn his attention to the King and Queen.

"Fifteen years ago, King Renaudas of the Western Wastes sanctioned the creation of a magickal plague, a disease of the mind that spreads like a fungus and infects the blood. It proliferates quickly and without warning. All it requires is access to an open wound. That's it. No more, no less."

Stellan's hawkish gaze bored into each person before him. "Over time, this contagion will drive a person mad, stoking his or her capacity for violence and aggression. The victim is driven to fight even past the point of death. There is no cure, and it must be stamped out. Period." Stellan leaned forward, effectively staring down the King. "Either Pestilence will overcome your people, or they will die from the rampaging onslaught of its victims." He pointed at the pile of ashes on the floor. "On your present course, this is your future--and believe me when I say it does not make exceptions for those of royal blood."

"But why?" demanded her father. "Why has that demon beast of a king done this?"

"Isn't it obvious? Pestilence is intended as an agent of control. Infect enough people or animals, and you have an invincible army--soldiers who fear nothing and want nothing but death in their wake. A legion without need for food or shelter. They require neither sleep nor rest, nor reward, nor payment." Stellan scowled. "Tell me, Your Highness, who would win against such an unstoppable force? You? Your army? No."

The King stared at him, aghast. Her mother looked pale, switching her gaze back and forth like a frightened bird. Clarysa nearly forgot to breathe as she listened. She clutched the balcony rail tightly. She had heard Stellan speak of the dangers, but this news was too much to fully absorb at once.

"Why come to me now, at this late hour? Why come at all, you damned warlock?" her father made no attempt to hide his ire. "If you knew about this evil fifteen years ago, why didn't you warn us? What are you trying to hide?"

A wry smile passed across Stellan's lips. "So you would have trusted me more at age fifteen than you do now, hmm? What about ten years ago? Or five? Would the answer have been any different then?"

The King frowned in concession to Stellan's point.

"No," Stellan continued, "I and I alone had to find a way to combat this. My efforts involved many failed experiments. The Arts are not for the faint of heart, or the impatient. Besides, for a while it seemed Pestilence might prove too unpredictable to use as a weapon. Its results were random at best. Time appeared to be on my side."

"Then what happened?" demanded Leopold. "These recent attacks hardly feel random. And why haven't we seen this before if it has truly been in our midst as long as you say?"

Muscles bulged in Stellan's jaw. "You might ask instead why it was so long in coming. Let's just say you would have tasted its wrath long ago if not for my efforts."

Clarysa drew her hands to her chest as pride swelled within. Stellan had protected them for nearly all of his life. *My darling, why didn't you say something sooner?* She chafed at the impenetrable wall surrounding his heart. She wanted to fling herself at him and beg forgiveness. She wanted to do it right now! But the debate below continued, and she dare not sabotage Stellan's efforts. Though dramatic and forceful, they were obviously sincere.

Her father was peering at the stalwart sorcerer with obvious misgiving. "How is it that you, and only you, have the knowledge to fight this so-called 'Pestilence'?"

Stellan's eyes narrowed. "Unfortunately, I am quite intimate with its origins."

Edward sneered. "Why, because you had your devil's hand in its creation?"

The accusation cut deeply. Clarysa pulled at her hair in distress. She should have known Edward would cause strife.

Stellan stepped forward, furrowing his dark brow. "No, I did not," he said, "but my father, King Renaudas of the Western Wastes, did."

Clarysa recoiled in shock as a collective gasp arose from the people below. This was certainly news to all of them, and it was quite possible the worst news they could have received. When Stellan had told her his father had been involved with Pestilence, she should have insisted on more information. *How could one man possess so many secrets?*

Since birth, every Aldebaran citizen had been taught to despise and distrust the sorcerers of the Wastes. Tales told to little ones often recounted how they had the heads of serpents and frequently devoured their young. Adults whispered among themselves how they brokered deals with the Devil himself, and deserved to be put to a miserable death. Clarysa had heard the stories too, but believed little of it, much to the chagrin of her instructors--and her family. Lionel had been the only other exception.

But now she realized the depth of Stellan's "predicament," as he had called it. Her falling in love with the heir to the throne of the Western Wastes spun dizzying ramifications, none of them good. In fact, they were downright awful. Regardless of Stellan's origins, her love remained true--even if he despised her. However, there was still the daunting issue of her father.

"*You*," her father spat out, "*you* are the spawn of the maniacal demon of the Wastes."

"Yes," Stellan replied calmly. "I am the son of the Black Mage and a descendent of the people your kind pushed out into the wastes to die a dog's death all those years ago. I am also the only hope you have of survival *if* we act together."

The King gripped his armrests. "Why would you do this?" he said. "Why break with your brother warlocks?"

"Because, Your Majesty, contrary to what you and your people may believe, we are not all alike. I have no intention to stand idly by while thousands of your people are slaughtered, even if that is what you believe of me."

Silence fell over the room as the King stared at him intently. A number of his advisors dove forward, clamoring for his ear. Hushed whispering echoed throughout the court. Clarysa strained her ears but couldn't hear anything.

The King waved them away. "So what, exactly, do you propose?"

"An alliance."

Again came the excited gasps as everyone began talking earnestly among themselves. Clarysa bit back a squeal of excitement. Had her brief friendship with Stellan truly helped make a difference?

The King held up a hand for silence, but before he could speak, Edward leaped down from the dais.

"An alliance for what, pray tell? So you can spy for the Black Mage and the rest of those necromancers?" Edward squared off, facing him. "I find it highly curious you always seem to make an appearance whenever there's an attack." He turned and smiled coldly at the King. "A mere coincidence?"

Clarysa groaned. *You idiot! That's not true and you know it!*

Edward spun around pointed a finger at Stellan. "Why not answer, warlock? After all, it was *you* who chased those monstrosities here. *You* planted them so you could turn around and play the hero." Edward's voice turned menacingly low. "I know what you've really come for, pauper, and you shan't have her."

"Edward!" her father bellowed. Next to him, her mother frowned. But he ignored them. "We don't require your tedious superstitions or childish parlor tricks. Leave here at once!"

Stellan stayed rooted to the spot, looking sardonically amused. "I came to offer the *King* my aid, and the *King* has yet to answer. Do you seek to supplant his rule so soon?"

Edward bared his teeth at the cutting remark, one that perhaps hit entirely too close to home. "You dare defy me in my father's court?"

"Yes, I do, for the sake of those who aren't such fools."

In a flash, Edward drew his sword. Stellan did the same. A face-off erupted between the two. The crowd turned restless.

The pair began encircling each other, mongoose and cobra. Guards looked urgently to the King for instruction, waiting for his command to intervene, but he merely watched the men with a torn expression.

Edward thrust forward, a move Stellan airily deflected. Faster and faster their swords clashed, a blur of clinking metal and arcing limbs. Each a master of swordplay, each intent on defeating his opponent. Other audience members rushed forward, forming a circle about the two. Soon, the number of onlookers swelled to fill the room.

Oh, no! Clarysa ran from her post. Once on the first floor, she bounded into the court from a side entrance. Pushing aside bodies, she shouted at the top of her lungs. "Stop it, Edward. *Don't!*" But they seemed not to hear her. She had to find a way to stop them before either was seriously injured. But how?

A sword? No. A shield? Clarysa quickly dismissed the idea, for she had never been allowed to train and would be hopeless at wielding one. *But there must be something I can do!* Fear seized her heart as Edward became more and more vicious in his attacks, his features twisted into pure bloodlust. If Stellan's blood were spilled…

Clarysa couldn't bear to finish the thought. She headed for the fray. A guard grabbed her arm, but she shook him off and charged ahead. She dove between the dueling pair as Edward angled forward with another thrust.

Cursing, he compensated with a side step, but his sword tip tore her right sleeve in two. Clarysa grunted as the resulting injury burned a streak of painful fire up her arm.

Edward glared. "Get out of the way, you fool!"

Clarysa raised a fist. "Not until I've knocked some sense into your head!"

Her brother hesitated but briefly. "Very well. Side with the devil warlock then!" Edward drew back his sword for an imminent death stroke.

"*That is enough!*" The King's voice boomed. "Edward, Clarysa, you will stand down *at once!*"

A contingent of guards flew between them. Edward backed off but not without hurling a scowl toward Stellan. Clarysa glared at her brother, arm still raised, her chest heaving. "You may be firstborn, but you had *no right* to threaten him. I am so sick of your judgmental, arrogant--"

Something tightened about her wrist. Ironclad. It was a hand. Stellan's hand. His intense green eyes poured into hers, and her anger melted away. Clarysa opened her clenched fist slowly and lowered her arm.

She stared at him, oblivious to the guards surging around them like a restless tide. "Prince Stellan, on behalf of the Aldebaran royal court, I apologize deeply for the threat to your life. Are you all right?"

Stellan nodded, wiping sweat from his brow. Then he gasped, and seized her right arm. "You're hurt!"

Clarysa glanced down. A trickle of blood seeped from the torn slit of her sleeve. She had barely noticed it. "I'm fine," she said hoarsely. It was a small price to pay for Stellan's life. Clearing her throat, she turned to face the King.

"Father, I must protest Edward's madness. Prince Stellan comes to offer protection, and *this* is his welcome? A ridiculous display of arrogance and stupidity?" She motioned angrily toward her brother, now sulking in a dark corner. "How shall we greet the enemy when they are crawling up onto our door? By flinging the gates open and welcoming them inside? Because that's what we'll be doing if we ignore the Pestilence threat. Stellan saved my life, and Lionel's, and countless others! How many more times does he have to risk his own before you'll trust him even an ounce?"

Leopold stared at her for what seemed an eternity. Then he raised a hand for his advisors to circle round.

Clarysa inched closer to Stellan while they deliberated. "I never thought I'd see you again," she whispered.

Stellan only gazed at her, his expression unreadable. At least he was looking at her, but for how long? Clarysa wondered with a sinking feeling if he was simply being polite.

The King spoke. "Prince Stellan, I will grant you this temporary alliance, but only until this 'Pestilence,' as you call it, is eradicated from Aldebaran. Once the task is complete, the alliance shall be dissolved! Now come with me to the war chamber."

Clarysa smiled triumphantly and held Stellan's arm, intending to lead the way. Here was her chance to make amends!

But he refused to budge. "In a moment, Your Highness. With all due respect, there is one other matter I wish to discuss."

The King sighed, but resumed his seat. He listlessly motioned for Stellan to continue.

The sorcerer's black-gloved hand pushed Clarysa aside as he fixed his gaze on her parents. He did so without even a smile or a bow of the head. The act made her feel very small. Alone. No matter that the court overflowed with people, she might as well have existed in a void. Biting her lip, she backed slowly away as insight dawned. Stellan wanted nothing more to do with her--and he had made a public point of doing so.

Of course he intended to speak with her parents further. He would need financial support for his crusade against Pestilence. What folly to believe he had come for her as well. *No, you've ruined everything,* admonished the voice in her head. *Edward was right, you're nothing but a deceitful interloper.* She remembered her spiteful plan soliciting Stellan to drug her parents, and the rush of shame prompted tears. Trapped within a cocoon of guilt, she couldn't escape the damming thoughts. *No wonder he left, you spoiled, immature brat!*

Clarysa didn't dare cause Stellan any more pain. She turned toward the court entrance. As she did so, her peripheral vision caught Stellan as he dropped to one knee. *Yes, well, I suppose a healthy dose of humility will open our coffers wide for you. Farewell, dark sorcerer, and may the gods of fortune smile upon your quest.* But her heart didn't share in the diplomatic thought. No. Her heart was dying a slow, sure death, and she deserved every bit of it.

Tears ran down her cheeks, splashing over her trembling lips. As she reached the entryway, Stellan spoke. Clear and sonorous, his voice rang out. "I've also come to ask for Princess Clarysa's hand in marriage."

The onlookers' response sounded three times more shocked than before. Clarysa halted, pressing a hand against her chest. Surely she had misheard.

She took a step forward and then paused. Hadn't she? Because if not… She risked a glance over her shoulder.

"Never!" Edward shouted as he started for his sword again. "We'll never admit the demon child of Renaudas into our family!"

Clarysa spun around. *Damn you, Edward!*

One of her sisters fainted. Meanwhile, Clarysa felt as if she were leaving her own body. Her breath all but vanished and she grew lightheaded. She stared ahead at the man in black, his head bowed in supplication. It took every last drop of self-control to prevent herself from careening about the royal court in excitement. She *hadn't* heard wrong. Edward's reaction was proof enough. In fact, things couldn't have been more right. *He wants to marry me!* Joy slammed into her like an avalanche.

Her father, however, sputtered and choked like a dying torch. He passed a ring-studded hand over his face. "Young prince, you...you ask far too much of me. Far, far too much."

Clarysa immediately snapped to and fastened her gaze on her father. *Oh no!* Moving stiffly, Stellan resumed a standing position.

"How could I *possibly* allow such a union? Do you have any idea, any at all, how a marriage to a necromancer such as yourself would impact our royal line? Our ancestors would rise from their tombs in protest!"

"Let me split this cur in half, Father," said Edward, holding his fully drawn sword before him, "for his appalling affront to your good name."

"She will not bring some devil dog into our family! Think of my reputation, Father!" said another sister.

"Father!" cried Clarysa. She rushed forward to stand by Stellan's side. "This is *my* life we're discussing, not some mere political transaction. I love him, Father! And I wish...I *need* to be with him...always! Do you hear me? *Always!*" She reached out her hand, seeking his. To her great amazement, he clasped it tightly.

The crowd spit forth a new round of reprimands. The most vociferous were from the nameless advisors grouped all about the King as if hungry pigs at the trough, each vying for attention.

As the verbal melee continued unabated, Stellan remained silent, his expression unmoved. He stood as if a statue. Nary a muscle twitched in his face. Clarysa couldn't blame him. The Aldebaran royal court was a formidable foe, and he had taken a monumental risk in declaring his desire for her--mind, body and soul. His vulnerable appeal wrought fresh tears from her eyes. All she wanted to do was throw her arms about him in a never-ending embrace.

Her mother rose and bade all to silence. She placed a gentle hand on her husband's arm. "Aren't you forgetting something?"

Perplexed, her father stared at her.

Clarysa watched with bated breath. *What are you going to say?* Her mother met Clarysa's gaze briefly before turning back to her husband.

"Our daughter has chosen Prince Stellan whether we approve or not. So I must ask you this--does not your impassioned blood flow in her veins? Great ambition marks your sovereignty, yet you express surprise that similar ambition marks her love." She turned to Stellan. "And he," she said, indicating the sorcerer, "he has maintained the royal decorum by making his proclamation in public before the King. By his very right, he deserves fair consideration. Tell me, young prince, is her hand worth so much that you will renounce your family and the corruption for which they stand?"

Clarysa stared at him expectantly.

Stellan bravely met the Queen's gaze. "It is."

"Will you promise that no harm will befall her by the hand of you or any other warlock?"

"I will."

"There, Leopold, my husband and king, you have your answer." Looking satisfied, her mother resumed her seat.

Clarysa noted with wonder the persuasive look that passed from her mother to her father. The Queen noticed her gaze and flashed a brief smile in her direction. She then leaned toward her husband and added a few final words. "Her mind is made up. Tell me, would you have us lose a daughter or gain a son?"

Her father sat with a brooding expression. Several uneasy minutes passed. A deep silence permeated the room as he contemplated his decision. After a long time, he finally spoke.

"So be it...Stellan. You and Clarysa may marry. And now to the war chamber, if you please."

The words were low, unenthused, but they came--oh, they came! Clarysa feared she would faint from excitement. She gave Stellan an exuberant smile. He stared back, appearing flush with relief.

Then Clarysa remembered all was not reconciled. Her words came out in a mad rush. "Stellan, I'm so sorry for my inconsiderate statements. I never meant to imply you're a coward. You're the bravest man I've ever known. And I'm sorry I suggested--"

"Clarysa," he interjected with a squeeze of her hand. "It's all right. Don't torture yourself." His emerald eyes swam with tenderness.

She sobbed sharply, even as her parents' entourage moved past them. "You're being so kind, when I've been so horrid."

"That's not true." The prince glanced briefly toward the doors. "I must go, but I wanted to tell you something. Look at me, Clarysa."

Wiping her face, she glanced up.

"It took some time, but I realized you were right. Old fears were holding me back, and it prevented me from being the man you deserve. Could you have confronted me about it using a little more tact?" His lips curved in a half smile. "It would have been easier, but the truth is I might not have taken your words to heart as strongly. You'll have to forgive me--I've never done anything like this before. But from now on, whatever happens, we'll find a way through it. I wanted you to know."

He drew her to him in a tight embrace and delivered a kiss so intense the act knocked the breath from her. Relief and happiness tore through her entire body, followed by an unparalleled surge of arousal. It was unrealistic to think the kiss could go further right here in the court, but she parted her lips anyway. Stellan slipped his tongue into her mouth for a warm, shivery, glorious moment.

All too quickly, he pulled away. "I'll see you later," he said before turning about sharply to follow the King.

Clarysa stared after him, nursing the hand he had squeezed the entire time in his earnestness.

While Stellan sat huddled with her father and his top commanders in the war chamber, Clarysa wasted no time making wedding preparations. After bandaging her arm, she set a date for three months hence. Messengers sped off in every direction. The first, of course, was dispatched promptly to Lionel in Belleressort.

Happiness filled her every fiber. She paused by a window, gazing out onto the grounds below. Pestilence was still out there. With such a threat looming over the Five Lands, a wedding seemed like a trivial matter. But the event would bring hope, as well.

Clarysa shuddered. She would stand by Stellan regardless of the outcome--even if Pestilence struck at the height of their wedding day.

Chapter 24

Stellan arrived home late after his meeting with Leopold, so late even the moon slept. Feeling confident and enthusiastic--for once--he wanted to share his good news. Gretchen and the others were already in bed, however, so it would have to wait until morning.

The decision to approach Leopold had been a sound one, fraught with intriguing possibilities. Pestilence's infiltration of Aldebaran was regrettable. Stellan could only hope his resources would be sufficient to eradicate it. They *had* to be, for Clarysa's sake. Nothing must happen to her. Nothing!

He brewed a pot of tea in the kitchen. After filling his mug, he reclined in a chair by the hearth. The fire was modest this time of night but it provided sufficient warmth.

Reality caught up to him in the form of a wedding. Being a married man was one thing; the whole idea of a wedding *ceremony* both amused and terrified him. He would have to learn some more dances, for he could scarcely expect Wind in the Willow to satisfy their guests.

He sipped the tea, catching his reflection in the liquid. Hmm. *Him*. Married. He had almost given up on the idea. Actually, it was more like he had never thought about it. Marriage was an exclusive fellowship from which he had been summarily blacklisted. A destitute prince with inadequate social skills and a despised pedigree. Who would want him? And now a parvenu by way of marriage. How a man's fortune could change in a moment!

And what about children? Stellan chuckled. He knew nothing about parenting. Nothing good, anyway. But the thought of Clarysa's belly filled with his child warmed his heart. She would know what to do.

Other thoughts swirled in his mind. Would their offspring bear magickal talent? Would he prefer a boy or girl? Which was easier? Or were both equally difficult? Stellan shook his head. *I have stared into the mysteries of life and death and yet I cannot answer a simple question.*

As he daydreamed, the tendrils of the fire reminded him of Clarysa's hair. A vision of her face stared back at him, laughing and filling with love. Relief lingered inside him, a reminder his gamble to ask for her hand had been successful. Still, he wondered--what did she see in him? She could have anyone she wanted but had chosen him. Had forgiven him after his appalling behavior. Loved him, unconditionally. The resulting emotion caught him unaware. Stellan blinked hard a number of times as he finished his tea.

Carrying a torch, he ambled through the halls, intending at first to retire but excitement made him restless. Though his breath still fogged the air, the castle seemed warmer somehow, and less sterile. Speaking of which, Clarysa should have her dream castle. Stellan made plans to brew as many potions and powders as possible to sell in the village, maybe even as far as Falcon Heights. There were some exquisite spells he could bottle, for a good price too, if he worked hard enough. Maybe he should even begin tonight. Industrious thoughts flooded his head.

Which was why, perhaps, he had barely noticed someone was following him.

At first he thought a ghost teased him; the south wing was full of them. Stellan slowed his pace and strained his ears. There was definitely a presence. Far too light to be Froll or Patrulha, and much too stealthy for the likes of Gretchen or Ghyslain.

He scanned the darkened hallway before him. Then, in one deft move, he plunged his free hand into the shadows, bringing forth a human form. "Who are you?"

"Rather jumpy tonight, aren't we?" came the velvety voice of his sister. "You're getting sloppy in your old age. Or are you being domesticated like some beast brought in from the wilds and forced to sit at his new master's side? I wonder." Sada's green orbs glittered by the torchlight. A dark, luxurious cloak swathed her statuesque form.

Stellan released her, but held the torch between them like a barrier. "What are you doing here?"

"Oh, dear brother, I've come to congratulate you!" She held up a box wrapped in purple silk and tied with gold threads. "You're to be married. How delicious!" The cordiality lay only in her words; her eyes stood empty, like a tomb.

He blanched. *How did you know?* "News travels fast."

Sada extended the gift, but his fist precluded the acceptance of her offering.

"I don't want your congratulations. Get out." He turned on a heel and stormed away.

Sada shared the same long legs; she easily kept pace. "Stellan, please stop and talk with me. This is a momentous occasion."

"I have nothing to say to you."

She grabbed his arm. "A few words is all I ask."

Stellan veered off in the direction of the study. He probably shouldn't have granted her an audience, but if he were able to glean any information about his father's plans then it might be worth the trouble. When they reached the study, Stellan motioned for Sada to precede him. He shut the door and locked it.

"Make it quick," he said, standing before the fire. He did not invite her to sit.

"I must admit to tremendous envy," Sada began. "I thought I could persuade you to return to the Wastes with me, to rule jointly. We'd be so strong together." The sorceress sighed. "But you have a compassionate heart. You always have, though I fear it could mean your downfall." She cocked her head. "Clarysa... What a darling little buttercup."

Stellan clenched his jaw. There was something...unsavory about the sound of her name on Sada's lips. "Sada, I'm only going to say this once. Take over the Wastes if that's your desire, but I want no part of it. You're not welcome here. Not in Vandeborg, not in my kingdom, not in my life."

"Surely you don't mean that."

"Surely I do." Crossing his arms, he glowered at her.

Sada placed her gift on a nearby table. "My, you're the epitome of gratitude. I came to wish you great happiness and fortune."

"Consider it done. Now get out."

Her eyes flashed with preternatural power. "Not 'til I've said my piece."

Stellan made a fist. "I knew you had other motives."

"How astute of you." Sada braced her hands upon the back of a chair. "I've come to warn you. Father wants you dead. In fact, he sent me here to carry out his order."

Stellan tensed. It was no idle threat. He and Sada may have been twins, but in terms of sheer magickal ability she outmatched him tenfold. "That could be true, or it could just be another one of your head games."

Sada arched a shapely brow. "Believe what you want, but it's the truth. You've been interfering with his plan for too long and he's had enough. Taking up with Aldebaran was the final straw."

"So why haven't you killed me already?"

Her eyes glittered in the firelight. "Because I'm your flesh-and-blood sister. We have a bond--"

"*Had.*"

Sada frowned. "We have a unique bond, the power of which Father has yet to grasp. I'm not as cold as you think. Ambitious, yes, but where you're concerned I still have a heart. Therefore, I'll make you an offer. Reform now and return to the Wastes with me. I'll persuade Father to grant you a reprieve. Of course, you'd have to renounce this kingdom. And Clarysa."

"And if I refuse?"

"I haven't decided yet. There are many factors to consider. Father has his ideas about how to expand our reign. I have mine."

"In other words, you want me around for as long as I'm useful."

Sada smiled coldly. "Something like that."

Stellan walked past her and opened the door. "I officially refuse your offer. Now leave."

Sada headed toward the opening. "Very well," she said, the chill in her voice echoing the icy glint in her eyes. "You had your chance." Then she glided through the door like a wisp of smoke and was gone.

Stellan grabbed her "gift" and bolted to the pipe-organ tower. He stepped out onto the balcony. On the horizon, dawn crept across a milky, overcast sky. He watched Sada depart on her steed, the snow descending like a curtain as the wind advanced from the north. Only after the murky whiteness had swallowed her entirely did he relax his guard. Yet he remained against the parapet a few moments more, lost in anxious thought.

Mixed feelings about his sister abounded within him, fear and loathing and admiration all wrapped up together like one of Gretchen's balls of yarn. Father had always favored Sada; his preference had been clear to Stellan from childhood. For one, she possessed the lion's share of magickal talent and ambition. But it wasn't enough to make her happy.

Stellan knew the patriarchal chains of control frustrated Sada to no end. Years before, she had solicited Stellan's promise to rule with her jointly when the throne became his. Not as husband and wife, but as equal partners. At the time, the plan had seemed workable. Shrewd and indomitable, witty and ravishing, she would make a far better king than he.

As far as Stellan had been concerned, she was welcome to the monarchy. He would have been content to engage in more creative pursuits. But that was before Pestilence entered the picture.

Though she would undoubtedly deny it, he was sure Sada had disclosed his plan to betray their father all those long years ago. The moment she learned his intentions threatened her quest for power, she'd retaliated in anger.

At the time, his actions must have seemed like treason. How dare he oppose the Black Mage! How dare he destroy a room's worth of plague serum, not to mention "valuable" records kept on its development! Renaudas's wrath that day had been terrible, catastrophic. He was apoplectic with rage and an unstoppable force.

Stellan pushed up a sleeve and fingered the long scars on his right arm, evidence of his father's eldritch power and fury. Yet if Sada had stayed quiet, he might have escaped punishment. Regardless, he wouldn't have done anything differently. Pestilence had been a misguided plot. There had certainly been no reason for his father to test it on his own people.

A twinge of deep-seated sadness passed through him. Or their beloved pets--or Mother.

Since then, emptiness had filled his heart. Whatever brotherly love he'd felt had vanished. Stellan found it difficult to forgive Sada's betrayal, especially since she'd once meant the world to him. As a result, "trust" became a foreign concept.

As if her betrayal hadn't been bad enough, his father had recreated the serum, as evidenced by all of the victims Stellan had encountered during his exile. In the beginning, he had accomplished all he could with the means available. Now he only wanted to be rid of Pestilence completely.

Stellan stared down at Sada's gift. Snow speckled its graceful folds. Mistrust filled his mind. It could be a trap with some sort of magickal danger enclosed. He would have to remain ever vigilant.

Memories flooded back of his early adolescent years, when he had thought Sada and he would be together forever. They had shared everything, told each other everything. Given their past emotional bond, no wonder Sada thought she could convince him to join her planned coup. She hadn't the slightest inkling how much he had changed. *Either she believes I'm a fool, or a poor desperate fool, but I am neither!*

With a heave, Stellan threw the tiny box into the great, swirling snowstorm that had sprung up around him.

Chapter 25

Drifting along on the edge of sleep, Clarysa tossed and turned in the satin sheets of her bed. The official wedding date was only days away. Each night she reviewed mental lists of all the various tasks she needed to accomplish. Each night she wondered if the wedding would even happen since Stellan was constantly battling Pestilence outbreaks. No matter. She would wait as long as required. The safety of the Five Lands came first.

This particular night, her anxiety about it all must have tormented her more than she'd realized, for visions of a peculiar dream roiled about in her subconscious mind, coming and going like waves on a shore.

Sleep came at last with visions of Stellan beckoning her into slumber--and other nighttime delights. But this was not to last, for her sensuous fiance was soon replaced by lissome specters that slid silently along her bedroom walls. Try as she might, she couldn't see them clearly. Their presence unsettled her. Who were they? What was their intent?

A sensation followed. Her body became airy, light as a feather. Clarysa was floating and twirling among the demonic shapes, a bizarre dance macabre against the prismatic vistas of the horizon. Was she flying? Impossible. But it felt so real!

The vision blurred and disappeared. Clarysa exhaled--and she was awake. Or was it more dream-state trickery?

Her head ached so much it was like a blacksmith was splitting it open upon his anvil. She tried to rise from the nest of coarse blankets. Yet no matter how much effort she put forth, her body refused to cooperate. Opening her eyes, she saw the woven pattern of a thatched roof above her. This wasn't her room!

Clarysa screamed, but panic reduced the sound to a mere whimper. Grogginess muddled her mind. Time seemed to both contract and expand simultaneously. *Where am I?*

She became aware of a pinching sensation in her right arm.

Her stomach twisted at the pain. It hurt. A great deal. Such a vivid dream! But the pain helped Clarysa gather her wits. She turned her head. A thin translucent tube protruded from her wrist. It pulsed with a soft, incandescent glow. Clear fluid flecked with bubbles traveled through it. The other end looped around the arm of a beautiful woman with raven-black hair and frosty skin who sat next to the bed. The other end of the glowing tube was embedded in her forearm. Was this truly happening, or was it a dream? Again, it seemed impossible to tell.

Clarysa tried to form words, but no sound emerged. *Who are you? What's happening to me?* The woman across from her smiled icily, but did not speak. *How bizarre. How very...* The vision faded. Clarysa fell into a black sea of unconsciousness.

Chapter 26

Stellan gazed over the parapets of Vandeborg onto the wintry landscape of the grounds below. The wind caused his red-lined cape to swoop up and fold about him as if it had a mind of its own. He held open the palm of his hand, watching the falling snowflakes melt one by one as they struck his warm flesh. The wedding was only days away. Would his happiness with Clarysa be just as fleeting? He clenched his hand into a tight fist.

Three months had passed since the establishment of the alliance, and he was taking a rare break to recoup and prepare more potions. Like a man possessed, he'd been working day and night to eradicate Pestilence from Aldebaran. Tirelessly, he followed every lead--tracking, studying and destroying any infected. In time, he might be able to develop a cure, but for now, well, he did what he thought best in the interest of safety.

Unrestricted access, as well as Leopold's endorsement, had made an astonishing difference. Education appeared to be the key, for most people, understandably, knew little of the dark magick that threatened to transform them. Village by village, Stellan had been teaching the citizens about the early symptoms. He told them what to watch for, and most importantly, what to do. No contact must be risked, no further communication with the infected attempted.

Stellan leaned onto the frozen stone wall before him. His efforts were paying off, for there hadn't been a confirmed sighting of a victim in over a fortnight. Was it too much to ask for this nightmare to end? Could he and Clarysa finally proceed with the wedding? It appeared so, but his life had a way of unexpectedly taking a sharp turn whenever things seemed to be leveling off for the better. Dare he hope this pattern had finally been broken by meeting Clarysa? A sudden updraft of snow blasted his questioning face as if to answer him with mockery.

Several times while out in the wilderness patrolling, he'd thought he had caught a glimpse of a spy from the Western Wastes. Were his father and Alucard aware of his latest betrayal? It seemed certain. Little could escape the eyes of the Black Mage, for he could command many mysteries, dark and terrible. No wonder Pestilence was so virulent, for its very essence had been culled from his father's blood.

He brushed away the snow sticking to his face. Unbidden, his thoughts drifted to his sister. *Sada, if only you could see beyond the blind hatred that clouds Father's thinking. But then, you always were his favorite and like him in so many ways.*

Hail began to pelt him. Stellan turned. It was time to head back inside and momentarily forget the past that forever haunted him.

* * * *

Back inside the castle, Froll, Hunter and Ghyslain were busy scrubbing away at the walls. Stellan had communicated his need for the castle to look its best. After all, it would soon be Clarysa's home as well. Not being one to think himself above such manual labor, Stellan grabbed the nearest pail and brush and set to work.

Gretchen sauntered about, clucking and nodding her approval of the men's work.

"Froll, you'll be wanting to clean that spot over there again." She pointed to a stained corner. "This time put more muscle behind it!"

Froll looked up, his haggard face betraying exhaustion. "I've been at this bloody work for more than five hours now, woman! Who do you think I am?"

Gretchen pursed her lips. "A lazy dog who'll be glad to put in *another* five hours if he wants to see any supper tonight. Now get to it!"

Froll smirked. "If I'm a lazy dog, that must make you the queen bitch!"

The men's laughter splashed out against the dank walls. Even Stellan chuckled with amusement. Gretchen came over and whispered an aside to him. "Stellan, a quick word, please, if you don't mind."

He nodded and put down his cleaning tools. Gretchen led him to his bedroom. She was silent the entire way, save for the clinking of her jewelry.

"Is something wrong?" he asked.

"No, not at all."

At the doorway, she cocked her head. "Go in and tell me what you think."

Stellan pushed aside the door, and then abruptly stopped short. Bright colors of every hue sprang forth, bewitching his eyes with their heavenly splendor. Slowly, he stepped forward.

There, in the middle of the room stood Gretchen's rudimentary sewing dummy, which she often used to create new clothes or patch and repair old ones. This was not the case today, however, for upon it hung the most elegant outfit Stellan had ever seen inside his castle. The material was woven of a cobalt blue, one so dark it appeared black. The tailoring reflected influences both gypsy and the classic style he usually preferred, dating back to clothing he had raided from Vandeborg's previous occupants. Colorful threads lined the edge of the matching cape. Shiny new boots stood beneath it.

Stellan fingered the expensive cloth and then glanced shyly back toward Gretchen. "Is this…?"

"For the wedding, yes." Gretchen chuckled softly as she leaned against the door frame. "Thought you were going to wear that ratty, old thing?" she asked, gesturing to his usual outfit. "Even the rats wouldn't be caught dead in it."

Stellan glanced down at his frayed clothing and grinned. "I was so busy with everything else I hadn't given it much thought." His cheeks grew warm and his throat tightened. "Mama, it's… I don't know what to say."

Eyes shining, Gretchen walked forward and embraced him. "You said enough just then."

He was about to propose a fitting, but footsteps thudding down the passageway made him pause. Ghyslain popped into view, flushed and breathless, a daffy grin on his face. "Lady Clarysa is here."

Stellan frowned. "What? But how could she…?"

"I let her in a few moments ago. She asked to see you."

A jab of excitement punctured Stellan's chest. He motioned for Ghyslain to lead the way. Gretchen followed, smoothing her hair. "I'll make some refreshments!"

Stellan hurried to the front hall. The wedding was only three days away. He hoped nothing was wrong. His stomach jumped with anticipation. It had been a long few weeks since they'd seen each other.

Clarysa was waiting for him in the throne room. She appeared resplendent in a white cloak lined with fur. A flowing pink dress peeked out from underneath. Her smiling face shone brighter than the sun. Stellan swept her up in his arms.

"Why didn't you send word? I would have met you halfway at least!"

Instead of waiting for her answer, he feasted upon her lips for a few dizzying moments. Odd. Something felt different, something…ineffable. Drawing back, he studied her. "Have you changed your hair?"

Clarysa giggled. "No, nothing like that. I'm just so happy to see you!"

"Me, too." He embraced her once more, pressing himself hard against her with an almost bestial urgency. *Gods of fortune, how much longer until the wedding night?*

"Gretchen's preparing something to eat. Let's wait in the study so you can warm up."

Clarysa nodded. She adjusted the strap of the leather satchel hanging from one shoulder as they walked.

"Here, let me." Stellan reached out a hand and she passed it to him.

Once in the study, he deposited it on a chair, then turned to help her remove her cloak. As he hung it up, Clarysa opened the satchel.

"What's in it?" he asked.

"Something to help us celebrate!"

She revealed its contents--a jug of wine. "My father sends it with his blessing and congratulations. It's one of the most valuable vintages in the entire kingdom."

Stellan dutifully studied the container and then turned to his betrothed. He languidly stroked her cheek. "Interesting. I wouldn't have thought he'd waste it on a 'damnable warlock' such as myself. Maybe it's his way of accepting me." Slipping his hands around her waist, he avidly kissed her cheeks and neck. He wondered at the change in her. There was definitely something unusual. She must have sprinkled her skin with a new fragrance. Or maybe it was the glow experienced only by brides-to-be. "You didn't ride all the way here simply to give me this, did you?"

Clarysa wriggled from his grasp. "Let's have a toast!"

"All right," he said, though the scent of her had already made him drunk.

He rummaged about for a pair of goblets. They stood across from each other, the wine resting on a high-legged table between them. Clarysa made a great hoopla about opening the bottle, waxing poetic about its symbolism and such. Stellan listened attentively, basking in her presence with delight.

Clarysa poured the wine. The dark red liquid gurgled into the wide-rimmed glasses, giving off a dense, fruity smell.

She handed one goblet to Stellan, and daintily picked up the other. "To us," she said simply.

He grinned. "To us!" Though the rich wine beckoned, he couldn't take his eyes off her. Nor, apparently, could she, for her gaze studied him eagerly over the rim as she drank.

The wine tasted delectable and sweet. Still unaccustomed to such rich libation, Stellan inadvertently drained the glass in one swallow.

Wiping his lips, he reached for the bottle. "Excellent," he murmured. "It's certainly superior to any I've had before." As he lifted the next round to his mouth, his hand suddenly lost its strength. The room swirled as the floor rippled in waves. The goblet left his grip, exploding into hundreds of crimson fragments on the stone floor below. Stellan looked down in confusion. *What's happening?*

He shifted his gaze toward Clarysa. A hard glint flashed from her eye. She retreated to one corner of the room. "What…is this?" he croaked.

She didn't answer.

Vision blurring, he reached for the table to steady himself. But he missed and went crashing down on his knees. Blood coursed through his veins like a tidal wave. A roaring sound pummeled his eardrums while strange pinching sensations and cramps tore through his abdomen.

Something was in the wine. Poison? "Clarysa?" he ground out. "What have you done to me? Why have you…"

Stellan blinked hard and rapidly. It was difficult to concentrate. He only saw a blur of pink standing some feet away. Then a prickly sensation rippled beneath his skin from head to foot. The cramps in his roiling stomach intensified. His blood felt as if it were on fire. Perspiration ran in torrents from his body.

Nearly prostrate, he grunted at the sensation of his stomach being turned inside out. His clothes constricted, biting into his skin as if they were five or six times too small. But it was nothing compared to the pain of Clarysa's betrayal. Her actions didn't make any sense.

The pain became a thousand knives slicing away at his chest. Was he dying? His thoughts suddenly scattered. World enfolding upon itself… gravity overbearing…torn apart… Then, all light faded as a deluge of shadows overcame him.

Minutes--or perhaps hours--later, Stellan regained consciousness.

He looked up, his vision a watery sea of shifting shapes. For a terrifying moment he couldn't even breathe. When air once again filled his lungs, it felt as though he had to learn how to breathe all over again. He tried to stand but immediately fell forward with a sickening thud. Strangely, he had the strength, but somehow lacked the knowledge to use it.

Derisive laughter rang out in the room, unmistakably female. Stellan lay there, eyes shut against residual aches. Slowly, fire again began to flow in his veins. He mercilessly beat his head against the floor, a feeble attempt to organize the chaos in his throbbing head.

Sada, he thought. *Magick!*

He opened his eyes. The crowing form of Sada stood before him, adorned by Clarysa's flowing pink dress. No--not Clarysa. Clarysa had never been there. Sada's icy green eyes stared back amid a face frozen with hatred. His sister had come seeking vengeance.

Stellan groped for words that would not--could not!--come. Only raspy growls managed to claw their way through his raw throat.

Sada withdrew one lone object and held it aloft before him--a mirror. For the first time, Stellan saw what he had become--a slobbering animal with thick dark fur and the snout of a wolf. A thing. A beast.

What have you done? Fear pumped through his heart, and then a deafening, mournful howl escaped him. Though his limbs still felt tender and unsure, Stellan maneuvered his bulky form into a standing position. *Kill you*, he thought, and made ready to plunge his newly formed fangs into Sada's throat.

Seemingly from out of nowhere, a multitude of chains shot forth, effectively ensnaring him. They coiled about his arms and legs and bit into his fur-covered flesh. Several stout men faded in from ethereal mists and held him at bay. Stellan thrashed about, overturning furniture and slashing at them with ungainly paws. He had to escape. Now. *Find Clarysa.* If Sada had harmed her…

Fear for her safety fed him strength. A rage overtook him. In an instant, Sada's minions lay crushed on the floor, drowning in pools of blood.

He turned to face his sister, but she was nowhere to be found.

Stellan let loose a howl of fury so loud and fierce it shook the castle's foundation. He bolted from the room and tore through the corridors. Then he bounded toward the front gate and freedom, hunting for his beloved.

Chapter 27

King Leopold sat upon his golden throne a humbled man. It appeared the warlock his daughter had so ill advisedly brought into their midst was perhaps correct in some of his mad assertions. Strange attacks had been occurring all over his kingdom. Ordinary weapons were minimally effective against these noxious mutants. Only Prince Stellan's mysterious potions successfully destroyed them. Leopold's people were growing restless in their fear. His military commanders were advocating a preemptive attack against the sorcerers of the Wastes.

And now they inform me my daughter is missing.

Leopold rubbed his temple in an attempt to stop the aching. Although his crown grew heavier with each passing day, it was the mantle of fatherhood that stole most of his thoughts. Clarysa had been right here in the castle--under her father's protection--and somehow she'd been abducted. Leopold knew he must find her. While tempted to initiate a search himself, the strategy would be unwise. Therefore, he had ordered Edward to report to him. But over two hours had since passed. Tardiness was atypical for his firstborn and could not bode well.

He waved a messenger over.

"Yes, Your Highness?"

"Ride to the Southern Marshes and look for--never mind." Leopold discovered Edward striding toward him. The King dismissed the messenger.

Edward bowed. "My liege," he stated officiously, "I must apologize for my inexcusable tardiness. I fear the mounting attacks have made it most difficult--"

Leopold shook his head. "You have new orders. Find Clarysa. Take as many men as you need."

Edward nodded. "I'll recover her. I'll start with the castle of that warlock fiend." The prince scowled. "If only I had broken the degenerate's neck when I had him here before me!"

Leopold stayed him with a large, bejeweled hand. "Caution, Edward. We do not know if he's involved. His words of warning rang sincere, and he's been instrumental in stopping the Pestilence attacks. Besides, why kidnap someone who is your betrothed and longs to be with you?"

"I still say it's a trick."

"Do not be so rash. You will soon find that once you wear the crown, the world is a much more complicated place than you ever imagined."

"But why else was she taken, then? Who else could possibly be responsible?"

Leopold shook his head. "The motives are political, that's all we can be sure of." He stood and placed his hand upon Edward's shoulder. "Begin with Vandeborg if you must, but I fear you're allowing hatred to blind you. You still have much to learn before you assume the crown of our forebears."

Edward tore away from his father's touch, a taut grimace besmirching his face. "And I tell you that this devil has bewitched Clarysa! He probably ordered one of his minions to do his dirty kidnapping work for him. In return, I intend to lay siege upon his castle and tear it down stone by stone if need be!"

"Come now, cousin! I should one day introduce you to the mightiest weapon I know--the fine art of confabulation."

Leopold looked over at the entrance. Duke Lionel stood there, armed with nothing more than an arched brow and wry grin.

"That is, 'conversation.'" Lionel quickly strode across the chamber and joined them. "If you had spoken more than two sentences to Stellan, you would know--as I am thoroughly convinced--he had nothing to do with Clarysa's abduction."

Edward turned his angry countenance onto his cousin. "Am I the only who has not fallen under the spell of his devilry? I shall order our forces to raze the entirety of his 'magickal kingdom' to the ground. Then we shall have time for talk!"

Lionel stepped up in defiance, right hand encircling the hilt of his sword. "But only if I allow it, which I will not!"

"Enough!" said the King.

Both men immediately snapped to attention.

"Edward, you and Lionel will lead a garrison to Vandeborg. If Prince Stellan is guilty of any crimes then he shall be punished as is my right as a King and father to mete out. Until then, your mission is to find Clarysa."

"But, my lord!"

"That is my final word. Now go."

Leopold watched as Edward and Lionel left the hall. He passed a hand across his face, praying for Clarysa's safe return.

* * * *

Lionel, Edward and seventy of the finest soldiers in the Aldebaran military marched rapidly to the Snowflake Kingdom. They crouched low together in a deep trench of snow within sight of Vandeborg. The sky was overcast, but only a light snow was falling.

Although Lionel had tried to remind Edward that the land there was eternally held in winter's grasp, he'd refused to believe it. Thus, to allow for more weapons, the Prince had refused to carry more than a basic cloak for the arctic environs.

Lionel, however, had listened closely to Clarysa's firsthand accounts of the icy kingdom and took them to heart. He was dressed smartly in a hooded, fur-lined coat, sleek yet oh-so warm. "Don't blame me for your own arrogance, cousin," he said to the shivering Edward. "After all, I did warn you!"

"Yes, you did, didn't you," Edward said, voice dripping with frozen sarcasm. "And this will also be the last time you remind me of said warning, dear cousin."

Lionel gave him a jaunty salute. "Message received and understood. Now shall I walk up to the front gate and announce us?"

"No. We'll wait here until nightfall and then infiltrate the castle under cover of darkness."

Lionel glanced over the shivering troops. Their military apparel was only suitable for the temperate climes of Aldebaran. "Well, that's fine with me. But do you really think the men can endure the wait?"

"Sir," said Edward's second-in-command, "the gate's opening!"

Lionel and Edward followed the line of the man's pointed finger. A large, wolfish brute burst from the castle gate. They watched as it streaked across the snow. Lionel stared at it in shock. He'd never heard of such a creature. Had it attacked Stellan in his own castle? The implications were sobering.

"Where's it headed?" Edward demanded.

Lionel scanned the landscape. A dark shape was approaching the castle. "Look there," he said. "That might be its target."

A wagon emerged from among the snowy hills. Lionel narrowed his eyes. Strangely garbed men and deformed creatures grouped about it in a mad procession. *How odd.* There was a figure on the wagon. As the wagon's bulky wheels turned, drawing it closer, a distinctly female shape emerged.

Lionel sucked in a breath. "Clarysa!" He swiveled his head left. The beast was heading straight for her.

Edward gauged the predicament at the same time. He ordered their best bowmen to position themselves for attack. Lionel and Edward led twenty soldiers forward, trudging as quickly as they could through the sea of snow.

But not quickly enough. The beast gained the wagon with preternatural speed. Lionel watched in horror as it leaped onto the wagon.

Edward ordered an immediate halt. He raised his arm. "Aim for the beast!" he ordered. "Loose arrows!"

A swarm of death screamed through the air.

Chapter 28

Clarysa opened her eyes, jarred awake by the quaking underneath her feet. Blinding whiteness stung her pupils. Something cold and soft trickled across her cheeks.

Snow.

As her vision acclimated, she absorbed other sensory details. Stiff limbs. Soreness in her back. Extreme cold. Her hands and feet had gone numb. Damp hair flicked with ice hung about her face.

This was no dream. *Where am I?*

Clarysa glanced down and noticed she wore her nightgown. But she'd been dreaming! Or had she?

She quailed. This predicament was no dream. Coarse ropes lashed her to a pole atop a rickety wagon. All manner of peculiar creatures surrounded her. Short, squalid men taunted her in some bizarre tongue as they stomped about the wagon. Some reminded her of the goblins she'd encountered in Dungeon Forest. They waved banners with grotesque animal shapes and indecipherable runic scripts scrawled upon them. One of them spit at her.

Clarysa turned away in horror, only to discover that some of the creatures pulled at thick chains attached to the wagon. They were dragging it toward a dark fortress--Stellan's castle.

She scanned the towers. Backlit by a yellow glow, a figure stood at a second floor window. Patrulha? No, it wasn't her. Clarysa squinted, and then cried out in recognition. The figure bore a strong resemblance to the woman from her dream.

Where is Stellan? Why doesn't he come? Clarysa's insides coiled with fear. *Maybe these horrid things captured him--or worse!*

She fought to loosen her bonds, but her deadened limbs simply wouldn't cooperate. Clearing her throat, she tried to scream, but only feeble whimpers escaped. The garish voices of her captors savagely mimicked her.

What's going to happen to me?

As if to answer her thought, a dark haired beast towering seven feet tall burst through the castle gate. Muscles bunching, it bolted across the snow-packed earth. Once in range of the wagon, it immediately launched itself toward her.

Chapter 29

Stellan burst through the castle gate.

He spotted the wagon approaching. Nostrils flaring, he caught the scent of the figure upon it. Clarysa! She was tied to a pole, looking battered and dazed. What had Sada done to her? Clarysa would freeze to death if he didn't reach her in time.

Roaring, he jumped onto the wagon. It creaked in protest under his tremendous weight. Stellan gazed at the pale, fragile woman he loved. Bruises plastered the exposed skin of her arms and neck. Grit smudged her nightdress. Distraught, he tried to call her name, but only the harsh sound of snapping jaws came. With his heightened senses, he could smell the fear in her. Clarysa stood frozen, staring up at him in abject terror.

Don't be afraid! It's me! He reared up on his hind legs, batting away at the spears and fists of the creatures surrounding the wagon. Stellan became aware of shouts ringing through the air. A commanding voice spoke.

"Aim for the beast. Loose arrows!"

The hiss of angry spikes tore through the air. Stellan ignored the incoming volley. One thought dominated all others--save Clarysa.

He shielded her with his body and then shredded the ropes trapping her. Several arrows pierced his back, halting his progress. Stellan roared out his pain. His blood poured in torrents down his back, filling the air with a coppery odor.

Lionel ran toward him, leading a contingent of soldiers all bent on rescuing Clarysa. Already they had notched a fresh set of arrows and were taking aim.

Again he tried to speak, but could utter nothing. Out of options, he swept Clarysa up onto his shoulder and leaped off the wagon. Lionel's name burst from her mouth in a desperate shriek.

A flare of jealousy made him growl. Lionel wasn't her true savior--Stellan was. Clarysa wouldn't have feared him if it weren't for Sada's interference. He curled his free hand--now a formidable claw--into a massive fist. The beast side of him craved a bloody fight with his oppressors while the human side urged caution.

One of the henchmen blocked his way and thrust a spear toward him. Stellan grabbed the weapon, spun it, and jammed the sharp end into the man's neck. The attacker slumped to the blood-spattered ground.

Stellan bared his fangs in heady vindication. With his enhanced form he could take them--he could defeat all of them!

Clarysa screamed again. Logic broke through his beast-hazed brain. *Soldiers advancing... Want to kill me... Must protect her!*

He barreled across the snow with incredible speed. Despite his wounds, Clarysa felt no heavier than a leaf resting on his shoulder. The sounds of the King's men giving chase faded into the background as he carried Clarysa toward the dark depths of Dungeon Forest.

Chapter 30

Clarysa hung over the beast's massive shoulder, one covered by bloody, coarse fur. What manner of creature *was* this thing? It seemed neither wolf nor human, but rather a hideous blend of both. She bobbed up and down like a village girl's rag doll as the beast raced through the dense blanket of foliage. Each step thrust the creature's collarbone painfully into her stomach.

Clarysa pounded the beast with all her might. After her arms tired, she kicked it as hard as she could. But her efforts were useless. Striking the brute had about as much effect as punching a stone floor covered with a thin rug.

The creature sped on. Where was he taking her? As the gray light about them faded, fears about Stellan's fate flashed through her mind. What if this monster had devoured him and his broken body now lay deep within its bowels? What if it had torn her beloved limb from limb, splattering blood and bone across the castle floor? What if Stellan lay slowly dying from a thousand vicious bites? What if, what if…?

For perhaps the hundredth time, Clarysa cried hoarsely for the beast to release her. Each time, menacing snarls were her only answer. They traveled for what seemed like hours, far into the late afternoon.

Whenever she regained an ounce of strength, she resumed her resistance.

"Let me go, you horrid brute!" She twisted and pinched at its fur--all to no avail. Rough hide and hands numbed with cold conspired against her. As if it could understand spoken language, she continued her verbal assault. "You're disgusting and I hate you!"

Clarysa tried to batter its chest with her knees, but it held her tightly. Her ire grew hot again. Blasphemous words spouted from her mouth. She would fight the monster until the end, if necessary.

While hurling more insults, she discovered a small amount of slack. A brash plan seized her tired mind. She kicked the beast hard and slid forward, down its back. Then she snatched one of the arrow shafts and ground it deeper into the creature's flesh. Thick rivers of blood oozed forth.

The wolf-thing slammed Clarysa to the ground and pinned her tight. Her breath whooshed out as the impact jarred her from head to toe.

Mistake! She threw up her hands in a measly defense as the beast unleashed its howling fury mere inches from her face. She squeezed her eyes shut, expecting at any moment for its glistening fangs to rip into her tender flesh.

But nothing happened.

Ever so slowly, ever so carefully, Clarysa opened her eyes.

The beast stared back, snarling and frothing at the mouth. Its breathing was labored, its eyes bloodshot. Saliva dripped from its tongue in copious amounts. But it did *not* attack!

What did the beast want from her? Fear and confusion manifested in hot, frequent tears. The sound of her ragged breaths mixed with those of the beast's. "Have mercy. Kill me now or let me go!"

Clarysa's pleas faded as she sagged in defeat. The beast then hoisted her onto its back once again and sprinted ahead.

Many more hours seemed to pass. Clarysa no longer struggled. The last of her strength had ebbed away.

Finally, they stopped in a copse of trees. A thin layer of snow covered the ground. All around them flakes trickled down from the sky, throwing a blanket of silence over the landscape. Clarysa knew their pursuers would be hard pressed to find them. Was she now the beast's prisoner forever? She listened to its heavy panting. Several arrows still extended from its back. Was it resting? It seemed to be. Clouds of warm, moist breath gushed from its mouth.

The beast eased her down. Clarysa's heart pumped madly. Now was her chance. She had saved her strength for this moment. The instant her feet touched the ground she turned and ran. Her legs felt like fire, solid as porridge, but she hurtled away nonetheless.

But she was no match for the beast. Thick, powerful claws grasped her gown, tearing the material as it drew her back. It whipped her around and with one arm at her waist easily pinned her against a nearby tree. All the air left her lungs. The rough bark chafed her bare skin. She pushed and slapped at the claw pinching her stomach. When she hurled insults at the beast, it snarled. When she yelled her protests, it howled.

After several minutes of this, Clarysa tired and grew still. *This...is getting me nowhere.* Perhaps a more civilized approach would yield better results. She eyed the monster with the steeliest gaze she could muster. "What exactly do you want from me?"

They stared at one another in silence. Then the beast's gaze dropped, first to her neck and then lower. A husky, bestial moan issued from its throat. Clarysa glanced down and blanched at the generous way her breasts spilt from the loose confines of her gown. Her stomach curdled. "Not that!" she cried. "Let me go, I beg you!"

The beast grew calmer, quietly observing her. *I think it understands me!* If the beast meant to ravish her, it would have done so by now.

Huge, vivid green eyes met hers. Curiosity overcame her. "What... who are you? What have you done with Stellan?" Angry desperation infused her voice. "If you harmed him, so help me *I will kill you.*"

It pulled her close again, tucking her tightly beneath a solid, muscular arm. Bending down, with her body squashed against his side, it reached out a claw and began to form something in the snow.

And after it finished, Clarysa gasped. For there, nestled among the crisp and crunchy flakes, it had etched a name, and the name was *Stellan*, with a crooked arrow pointed toward the beast.

He slowly released her. This time, she did not run. Instead, she slumped to the ground, clasping her hands to her mouth to stifle a scream. She stared at him. *I can hardly believe it, but it must be! The eyes. This beast has Stellan's eyes.*

He crouched low to the ground and avoided her gaze. A hush fell over everything. All about them, the falling snow intensified its rate. A lone bird in the distance broke the silence, calling out to its own kind.

Gingerly, Clarysa reached out and fingered a tuft of fur on the beast's--on Stellan's arm. It gleamed a dark metallic blue. "Who was the woman I saw at the castle?"

A guttural bark met her ears.

Oh, no, he can't even speak! Clarysa crawled forward and motioned for him to look at her. She rubbed a day-old laceration on her right forearm. "Stellan, she did something to me. I thought it was a dream, but then I woke up, and...and I was on the cart." Her eyes burned. "And she did something to you, didn't she? Was she...someone you loved?" She held her breath, awaiting the answer.

Stellan shook his head violently and scratched out another word in the snow. He pointed for emphasis.

Clarysa stared. The word, rudimentarily drawn out, read Sister.

Her jaw dropped open. "I didn't know you had a...but that's right, you never told me much about your family." Clarysa wiped away a fresh set of tears. "They obviously don't want us to be married. Oh, my love, how awful that she did this to you...to us!"

She reached out her hands. At first, he turned away. But she persisted, gently stroking his face and snout. He felt strange beneath her touch, but only his shape had changed, not his personality.

Leaning forward, she pressed her cheek to his and slipped her arms around his neck. "At least we're together now."

Something warm and wet touched her cheek. It seemed he was trying to kiss her, but his form made the effort clumsy and awkward and he ended up just licking her face. With the tip of his tongue, he brushed away each of her tears as they fell.

Something cold and wet coated her hands as she held him. Clarysa drew up her outstretched arms before her--blood. She turned to him in alarm. "Darling, we have to get these arrows out."

Stellan growled his assent. Clarysa took a deep breath and steeled herself as she studied the deep wounds before her. "Brace yourself!" She plucked out the first one, yielding an intense wail of pain from both nurse and patient. He had gripped one of her thighs in the process, and as she yanked the arrow out, he had squeezed her hard. Clarysa collapsed on her side, nursing a rapidly bruising leg. When the pain reached a tolerable level, she searched around for a thick tree branch for him to bite. "Here," she said, "I think both of us are going to need it if we're to get through this."

The other arrows were buried more deeply and took more time to free. After she finished the gruesome task, she ripped off a piece of her gown and created a makeshift bandage. Unfortunately, the blood quickly soaked through the flimsy material. Both woman and beast fell back in exhaustion against the snowy ground.

All around them, the snow continued to silently fall.

They rested for a while, Clarysa pressed against him for warmth. Then Stellan rose on his hind legs, signaling that they needed to keep moving. Extending a massive paw riled with sharp claws, he helped her stand.

"I hope it's not far, wherever we're going." Clarysa stumbled forth. Her feet kept slipping out of the ill-fitting shoes someone had put on her. She hugged her body tightly in a feeble attempt to retain warmth. Her body temperature seemed to be lowering with each step she took.

Flashes of light-headedness threatened to strike her down. But she persevered. Love alone drove her on, and she trudged behind her prince.

I can hardly complain. At least I'm not injured. Or a beast. She looked at Stellan's bloody back. Her heart ached for him.

They trudged on.

After another hour of walking, Clarysa stopped and hunched near the base of a tree. "I...I'm sorry. I need to rest," she said weakly. She stuffed some snow into her parched mouth.

Stellan swiveled his head around, sniffing the air. Apparently not satisfied, he bent down and scooped Clarysa into his arms. She wrapped her legs around his waist and slipped her arms around his shoulders. She tucked her face into the warm crook of his thick neck. They continued onward for many more miles.

As night drained the last remaining vestiges of light from the surrounding countryside, they reached the entrance to a cave. Panting, Stellan carefully lowered her to the packed-dirt floor.

In the darkness, Clarysa lost all sense of direction. She stumbled about until Stellan took her hand into his, leading the way. She heard the *clink* of a metal latch and felt an out rush of stale air. Stellan led her through an even darker passageway.

This was no ordinary cave. It had all the earmarks of a secret hideout.

Stellan dropped her hand. Clarysa sat down, hugged her knees to her chest, and shivered. Rustling sounds met her ears. He was rummaging about in the dark. If her teeth weren't chattering so hard, she would have inquired about his purpose.

Soft amber illumination filled the room as Stellan ignited a large fire in the hearth. Clarysa rushed to its warmth and nearly singed her hair as she huddled next to it. Pain seared her hands and feet, but the sensation comforted her. It was a sure sign they were thawing and not a victim of frostbite. Though she had thought all her tears spent, she cried with relief.

As Clarysa warmed by the fire, Stellan lumbered into the room with a snow-packed bucket. He emptied it into the cauldron hanging over the fire. After repeating the act four more times, the cauldron was soon full of hot water.

He then brought forth strips of cloth and several dark-colored bottles. Some were filled with oddly colored liquid and others with a thick, sweet-smelling salve. Clarysa guessed them to be magickal potions and ointments. Stellan fumbled around with several of the jars, but his oversize hands were far too clumsy for the delicate containers. He grunted in frustration.

Clarysa placed her hands over his paws. "Let me help you." Using gestures, he showed her how to clean and dress his wounds.

Next, he revealed a store of tea and dried meats. All of it seemed stale, but it was certainly better than a diet of melted snow and tree bark. Clarysa soaked part of the meat in her tea to soften it. Stellan, on the other hand, found its condition to be entirely suitable, for he gulped down a portion big enough for at least five men. He lapped tea noisily from a large bowl.

Her appetite sated, Clarysa grew drowsy by the warmth of the fire. It had been a long, arduous day. She found some musty-smelling blankets and created a makeshift bed by the hearth. After Stellan finished eating, she motioned for him to join her. He padded toward her on all fours, nostrils flaring. She drew back the coarse blanket, her expression tender.

Stellan lay and curled up his great form. Clarysa crawled into the warm space between him and the fire. As she molded her body to his, a massive swath of coarse fur tickle her back. Beneath his coat lay a solid wall of corrugated muscle. *No wonder he carried me so easily. Such brute strength!*

With each rise and fall of his chest, a surge of warm, feral breath coated her neck and shoulders. Clarysa reveled in the comfort of the sweltering hollow, shifting her hips back to close the remaining space between them. Very little clothing separated fur from skin, she belatedly realized. Before going to bed, intense summer heat had prompted her to discard all her undergarments. At the thought, her cheeks warmed while a distinct coil of arousal tightened deeply within her.

Had Stellan noticed her near nakedness?

She shifted closer. Now her back was flush against his chest and abdomen. Regardless of her determination to be brave, tears threatened. Would this be their fate, woman and savage beast? Did any part of Stellan the man exist in this form? Clarysa worried that the cure for his transformation was far from reach. Ultimately, she decided it didn't matter. Her love for him knew no limits. She absentmindedly rubbed her cold feet against his legs for warmth.

Would there be a wedding anymore? How would they even communicate? Her heart would break if she never heard his voice again. She stroked his fur and drummed it with little pats spurred by anxious need. She wanted so much to be a part of Stellan, to join with him in everything. No matter what happened, she would be with him--even if he remained a beast forever.

Soon, she writhed against him, seeking reassurance that despite his strange body, he still cared. With a whimper, she tried to draw his massive form as close as possible. Stretching, she searched for his face behind her. She held her hand there, against his muzzle.

Then she sensed movement.

Clarysa thought nothing of her bare legs that now intertwined with Stellan's broad hind ones, but apparently he did, for one of them suddenly jutted between her thighs, splitting them wide apart. Or was it something else? The shadows thrown by the fire threw her senses into chaos.

Flexing her thighs, she pressed against him harder. Need drove her-- this was still Stellan, her love, and she wanted to comfort him. A slow, rhythmic dance evolved as she rocked gently against him. Warmth spread within her, and then a telltale dampness.

The beast's rough fur slid against the bare skin of her legs. The thrilling contact made her feel reckless and she squirmed even more. Behind her, the beast inhaled and then exhaled, harmonious with her own deep breaths. In time, a singular hardness protruded into her back. She froze. Was it a claw? A muscle? Or something emanating from regions dark and forbidden?

Clarysa closed her eyes and swallowed. A faint whisper of apprehension made her shiver. Would she? *Could* she?

Fixated on the hard, muscular weight between her thighs, she was only dimly aware of a massive, clawed extremity that stretched, swelled, and fanned apart above her. Then in a wicked rush it clinched her waist, encasing her in a firm grip. It was not so tight she couldn't breathe but she couldn't easily escape, either. The razor-sharp claws brushed the underside of her breasts, but did little more than graze her skin through the fabric.

Stellan's embrace amplified her growing excitement. It was as if they were one, difficult to know where beast ended and woman began. Perspiration trickled from her brow. When had it grown so hot? Clarysa pushed hair back from her face even as she continued to wiggle and rub against him wherever freedom permitted. All the wanton grinding suddenly caused her gown to slip from her shoulders. A breast spilled forth. Brazenly, the rosy tip transformed into a hard, aching nub. She didn't bother to cover it up.

Low, otherworldly rumblings from the beast echoed repeatedly throughout the cave. Clarysa's vision swam as her desire mixed with confusion. What was about to happen here? Could she really surrender herself in this manner? *He has to know you don't fear him. Otherwise you'll drive him away.* To what extent she could prove her loyalty in this dank, cold hollow, with his unnatural form, she wasn't entirely sure.

But Stellan was so close and everything else so far away. The fire roared on, logs crackling and tongues of flame licking and sucking at the air as though in a state of constant thirst. Perspiration beaded Clarysa's face and chest. Wild fantasies raced through her mind. She wanted the beast...wanted Stellan to lap at her skin until she was drenched. By now, his breath fell across her like waves of desert heat. Occasionally, his muzzle rubbed against her head, revealing the hardness of his fangs. It made her wonder about other things, other parts of him. What they felt like. Looked like. Tasted like. The thoughts made her feel utterly wicked.

Stellan shifted his weight. He heaved upward and rolled, bringing Clarysa with him. At first, the room seemed to turn in on itself, but then she fell gently onto her hands and knees. Somewhere in the dark behind her was the beast. Heat radiated from his body along with an earthy, masculine scent. It washed over and through her. Coupled with the warmth blasting from the fire, she was positively drunk with rapture. Mercurial shadows danced along the curved, pockmarked walls, an exaggerated relief of their entwined bodies. But the beast's next move wrested her attention abruptly away.

He pressed his midsection hard against her bottom. For a long moment, he held himself there. *What is he going to do?* Was he testing her devotion, or was his mind clouded by bestial instincts? The question danced on her tongue, but she held it. He couldn't answer her anyway. In fact, the less she knew, the more exciting the situation became.

He grasped her thighs with his cold, pinching claws. Then he spread her legs wide apart.

Clarysa gasped. Heat was gathering in her core as if she had bottled the very fire before her. An unstoppable quickening electrified her body. *Is this some kind of enchantment he's working upon me? Was there an unusual ingredient in the tea?*

Something warm and moist touched her bare left shoulder. As the wetness spread, she glanced over. Stellan was laving it, his tongue surprisingly soft, the caress gentle. Arching her back, she responded with a low, yearning purr. The thrill she was experiencing had nothing to do with potions or spells. Clarysa pushed back, sealing her bottom against his rugged, compact pelvis. No, this was animal attraction, pure and simple.

She froze as a long, impossibly hard shaft of flesh slid between her thighs. Smooth as silk, it pulsed with a vigorous, decadent heat. With a quick, final thrust, the beast wedged it firmly against her sex. It was, Clarysa realized with a sudden start, the great beast's wide cock.

Blood thundered in her veins as she sought to master new feelings and exotic sensations. The solid shaft now lay smothered beneath her sex, thighs and belly. The bulbous tip reached all the way to her belly button.

A brief silence followed, and then from out of the darkness, the beast released a deep groan of pleasure.

Her breath came in short, rapid bursts. Her breasts felt heavy, as if swollen with blood. Both nipples brushed lightly against the blanket. She trembled with the intensity of her arousal. But a more urgent matter demanded her attention--the plump, aching skin of her sex. The rampant stimulation had created unbearable engorgement. The only way to assuage the itch was to press down upon the beast's cock. So, Clarysa did exactly that.

Oh, sweet heaven! Squeezing with her thighs, tightening her inner walls, rubbing up and down his length, Clarysa writhed against him with abandon. Her mound swelled further, gripped in a web of raw lust. A fresh burst of secretion filled her mouth, echoed by moisture seeping between her legs. With every pass of her sex, she coated his rigid member. *Harder. Squeeze harder. It feels so good! Oh, Stellan!*

Where her bottom met his pelvis, the fur felt sticky and matted. Faster and faster she moved, her breasts bouncing freely. Eventually, the beast caught one in a paw, hoarding it like a rare jewel. No matter how jerky or wild her movement, Stellan accommodated her, letting loose the occasional snort or growl or sharp exhalation of breath. Sometimes he lowered his head to sniff her hair. Occasionally, he stroked her back with long, slow licks of his massive tongue.

His responses prompted Clarysa to work harder at showing her devotion. She badly wanted to show him his appearance didn't matter.

Mounted upon a shaft of adamantine flesh, with nothing but a whisper of a nightgown shoved up around her shoulders, Clarysa rolled and rocked her sweaty hips, stoking the flames of an explosive climax. All senses alight, she was reborn into a slick, twisting mass of pleasure. Shuddering and moaning as she lay in Stellan's grip, Clarysa experienced a pure, sudden ecstasy as all the fear and anxious thoughts left her mind. Gone were all the recent aches and pains and chills, replaced by a coma of intense relaxation. In that freeing, transcendent state of heightened arousal, she was ready to submit to anything the beast wanted.

As her surging blood began to ebb, she greedily sought a second climax. This time, Stellan moved. With her, but also against her. His turgid flesh seemed to concentrate with increasing precision on the flooded folds of her sex. A scorching surge of lust was her only choice, and this time she rode out her pleasure with a series of short, high-pitched cries.

Stellan's embrace grew tighter, more insistent. The paw clutching her breast now returned to her hips. As he spread her thighs wider, the inner muscles strained to the point of discomfort. Her legs shook as she struggled to maintain her position. Now her belly and breasts lay flat against the blanket, while her bottom reared upward at an impossibly high angle.

The beast's ragged moans shattered the confined air of the cave. Clarysa raised her head to speak, wanting to ask if they could change positions. But a formidable paw lowered it back down. Stellan's grinding movement indicated he wanted something more. A ball of firm, warm flesh kept bumping into her sex. It felt good, and so she closed her eyes and relished in this new touch.

But then he began to push harder.

The beast held her fast. She was so wet he kept slipping, but he renewed his efforts with increasing vigor. As the pace increased, the delicious ache transformed into soreness. She grabbed the blanket for leverage, beginning to suspect Stellan had lost all perspective on his own strength. As a beast, he had at least twice the power of an ordinary man.

The manner in which he thrust his pelvis against her, panting and bucking relentlessly, revealed his desire to possess her. Claim her. But this was not Stellan, her wounded, mysterious prince. This creature was a nightmare of macabre realms and vicious appetites.

They didn't fit together quite right; either he was too large, or she was too small. The claws gripping her tender skin somehow felt longer--and sharper. *Oh, why couldn't it stay like before?* Lost in her selfish pleasure, she hadn't anticipated such raw hunger in response. How much of a price was she about to pay? Panicked, Clarysa strained and heaved, trying to escape his grasp. Then she heard the sound of his jaws snapping.

A howl of triumph--

Tearing, unbelievable pain--

Clarysa screamed.

Not only did she scream, but she pummeled the ground with balled fists. "Stop, Stellan--it's too much--stop it *now!*"

At first, nothing changed. The beast pressed down upon her with incredible force. Clarysa's abdominal area felt distended and uncomfortably full. A cold, deadly chill coursed down her spine. Regret chased her fear. The unwanted advances made her question all her silly, girlhood dreams of wild adventures. The poor insight she had exhibited was both terrifying and sobering. Clarysa uttered a final, pleading cry, lost, she feared, in the beast's wild grunting. But he released her with a roar of anguish as loud as a thunderclap.

The beast growled as it abruptly withdrew and reinstated a wide pocket of air between their bodies. The cool drafts rushing in around her seemed to clear her mind. Exhaustion and cold must have sapped all of her judgment. Stellan's mammoth size and bestial strength had evolved into something beyond either of their abilities to control, a temptation best left alone.

Tears streaming down her face, Clarysa watched miserably as he retreated toward the back of the cave, away from the fire, away from her. No more could they find solace in a warm embrace, or even lay within several feet of each other. The kind of lust they had just experienced promised a great and terrible punishment.

Clarysa collapsed upon the blanket, clutching her cramped, aching middle. Stellan seemed to be feeling infinitely worse, judging by the low keening emanating from the murky corner in which he crouched. The sound broke her heart. Despondent and guilt ridden, a tear slipped down her cheek. *What have I done?*

For now, her exhausted limbs and drowsy mind insisted on rest. Tomorrow they would have to find a counter-enchantment. Clarysa drew the blankets up to her chin, staring morosely into the fire. Even the flames seemed subdued now. *I love you, dearest, whatever happens.* She closed her eyes and sleep overtook her for the remainder of the night.

Chapter 31

Clarysa awoke with a start. The old blanket wrapped tightly about her offered its morning greeting by way of a noxious, musty scent. Pushing it aside, she stared absently into the crackling fire before her. Murkiness surrounded her, and it took her a moment to orient herself. Where was she? Then she registered deep muscle aches throbbing in her legs. Her back felt as if were splitting in two...and memory came rushing back in an instant.

Stellan! She whirled around to reach for her beloved--but no one was there. There was only an indentation in the makeshift bed, nothing more.

"He's gone," said a woman. Gretchen approached from the darkness, a worried look on her face. "Are you all right?" She held a hand to Clarysa's forehead.

She was back at Vandeborg, in the kitchen. She sat up slowly, trying to shake off the cobwebs and ignore the pain. "What time is it?"

"Nearly six."

Gretchen placed a bowl of watery gruel in her lap. Clarysa lifted it to her mouth and slurped it down. The liquid scalded her throat, but the frugal meal returned some much-needed energy. After she finished, she looked at Gretchen with a vengeful expression. "Did you see what that witch did to Stellan? I'm going to kill her!"

Gretchen perched on a short stool with her back to the fire, casting a dark silhouette. "You may have to wait in line," she said with a grim chuckle. "Besides, you'll never get past your own Aldebaran soldiers. A band of 'em have been roving the grounds for hours. But I...well, let's just say I refuse to let any of those scoundrels in here."

Clarysa frowned. *Edward! I refuse to believe you're my own brother.* She grabbed the gypsy's knee. "Where is he?"

"Where's who?"

"Stellan!"

Gretchen cleared her throat. "I don't know. He showed up with you a few hours ago. Gave me a nasty fright! Poor Ghyslain, he went mad with fury trying to fight him, thinking you needed rescuing. But then we solved the puzzle." She sighed, and then let loose a sob. "Oh, my poor son!"

Clarysa bit her lip. She didn't know what to do or where to begin; she only knew she had to do something and quickly! "But where did he go? You must have *some* idea where he went. He wouldn't just leave us like this!" Her heart beat with a steady panic.

Boots suddenly scraped the floor behind them. "But he did leave you, *Princess*." The last word was spat out, full of venom. "Perhaps you should get used to it."

Gretchen and Clarysa turned as Patrulha entered the kitchen, dressed in full battle gear. She assembled some food and stuffed it into a number of sacks.

Clarysa stood, the blanket hanging askew from her shoulders. "Where is she... Patrulha, where are you going? I want to find Stellan. Will you help me?"

Patrulha ignored her.

"Leave her alone, child!"

"But where is she going?" Clarysa stared at Gretchen expectantly.

"Eh, for a patrol, I think."

"What do you mean, 'I think'?"

Gretchen turned and busied herself with a pot over the fire. Ignored on both fronts, Clarysa marched up to the Captain. "You're going to look for Stellan, aren't you?" She laid a firm hand on Patrulha's arm. "You know where he's headed, don't you?"

Patrulha turned, her one good eye firmly set on Clayrsa's hand. The warrior woman slowly picked Clarsya's fingers off one by one. She turned abruptly and strode from the kitchen.

"I'm not stupid, you know!" Clarysa cried after her. She spun around and headed for the clotheslines. "Tell Ghyslain I'm borrowing some of his clothes," she told Gretchen. Clarysa snatched pants, a shirt and a furred cloak. She began to change where she stood.

Gretchen stared at her, seemingly at a loss. "Gods of fortune, missy, what do you think you're doing?"

"Finding Stellan. Patrulha knows where he is, and I'm going with her." Clarysa shoved her feet into a pair of boots and paused to glare at the gypsy. "Why are you trying to keep him from me?"

Gretchen stomped a foot. "Because we don't know where he went! Sure, my daughter has an idea, but she isn't certain." The gypsy woman turned her attention back to her pot. "We've sent word for more of our men, so stay put. They'll find Stellan one way or another."

Clarysa pursed her lips. "So Patrulha's heading a search party? Then that's where I belong too!" She grabbed the cloak and threw it over herself. The material nearly swallowed her whole, for it was at least two sizes too large for her petite frame.

Gretchen grabbed her by the shoulders. "Listen, Clarysa! He brought you back because he wants you to be safe."

Clarysa gritted her teeth, feeling rage swell as her gaze bored into the other woman. *"But he needs me."*

"He needs you to be safe! Now think for a moment. What if he returns and you're not here? Or worse yet, this folly of yours leads to your death? Do his wishes mean nothing to you?" Gretchen scowled, and her voice dropped to a grumble. "Begging my lady's pardon, but you're being selfish. Very selfish indeed."

Wrenching out of her grasp, Clarysa covered her ears and stormed out the door.

* * * *

She strode purposefully through the castle halls on her way to the stable. Why couldn't others see past her royal person? Did they think of her as some helpless girl, unable to fight or help in the search? Hadn't she braved the dangerous journey to this castle twice by herself? Clarysa shook her head and increased her pace.

Approaching the west wing, she heard whistling emanating from the stables. There, she found Ghyslain brushing down a stout Palomino. The boy ceased his tune and looked at her with concern. "My Lady! You should be resting. What are you doing here?"

"I need your assistance. I should be out trying to find Stellan."

Ghyslain frowned. "But it's not safe for you out there."

She stepped forward and laid her hand on his. "Ghyslain, please! I can't stay here and pace in circles like your mother wants me to do."

"Mum will have my head if I let you go."

Clarysa suppressed a sigh of frustration and went to stand by the opening. Dawn had broken, but here in the Snowflake Kingdom it merely meant the overcast sky became a lighter shade of gray.

"Ghyslain, Stellan is my life. I'll go on foot if I have to. At least on horseback I'll have a fighting chance." She looked back over her shoulder. "I love him. Please help me."

Ghyslain expelled a breath. He pushed a hand through his hair and paced the stable. At a wooden hutch he paused, and then withdrew a bulging sack of feed. Returning to the middle of the stable, he proceeded to saddle the Palomino. "I'm only doing this because you've helped us in so many ways," he said. Sighing, he muttered, "Gods of fortune have mercy on me when Mum finds out."

"Patrulha's party, when did they leave?" Clarysa asked, mounting in a rush.

"A short while ago, heading north." The young man placed a hand on her arm. "Don't do anything stupid."

"I won't." Clarysa turned the horse toward the gate and called over her shoulder. "We'll bring him back, I promise. And thank you!" With a final wave, she rode away, leaving a maelstrom of snow in her wake.

Chapter 32

Stellan's massive jaw tore at the young hare's raw flesh. Blood spilled over the sides of his mouth and dripped down onto the snow-white ground beneath him. The meal took the edge off of his ravenous appetite, but he needed more.

As he sniffed the air, he struggled to remember his mission. What was it? Another rabbit, perhaps?

No! He had to find the man who could reverse his deadly condition.

He leaned against a tree to get his bearings. How long had he been running? He couldn't remember. In fact, with every passing hour, it seemed more and more difficult to think. He cupped his head with two massive paws and tried to concentrate, to remember the task at hand.

Clarysa! Memories of her flooded into his mind. Sweet memories, but also painful ones. The way she had kicked, cursed and battered at him went far beyond the physical discomfort. Of course, she couldn't have known it was him, but still… She had nearly killed him.

He slid to the ground. The arrow wounds still hadn't fully healed. The pain cut into him like a mace gouging out his spine. Perhaps he should have handled her with more gentleness, but he had only wanted to get her to safety and away from Sada. She who had once been his beloved sister. The person who had made him a monster.

Stellan's thoughts drifted to Clarysa's agonized cries in the cave when his hunger had spiraled out of control. He'd been nothing more than a slavering wolf demon.

That's what you are.

The cold air seeped into his soul. He missed the warmth of the fire, the warmth of Clarysa cradled by his side. He especially missed the feel of her soft, curvaceous body. They'd been pressed so close together, only separated by the gossamer fabric of her gown. And her smell! He had perceived the musky scent of her arousal a hundred times stronger than a human ever would, and it had sparked in him a fierce and primitive lust. She had seemed to enjoy the intimacy they shared.

At first.

But he had gone too far.

The memory caused his huge wolfish eyes to moisten. Stellan deeply regretted having caused her pain. This prompted recollection of his promise to Queen Arietta. He had since given Clarysa reason to fear him. Their relationship had caused her harm as a result of Sada's anger. Now the King and Queen would think him untrustworthy. They'd probably take Clarysa far away, to a place where he'd never be able to find her.

A sharp ache formed in the pit of his chest. He shouldn't have allowed the intimate contact no matter how much they loved each other. His control had been absolute... Hadn't it? It was difficult to recall everything clearly. But that must be the answer. Had he succumbed to his darkest desire, his sharp claws and unnatural size would have quickly rended her delicate form into bloody shreds. Stellan pushed the grisly thought out of his mind.

On the horizon, a lone wolf's cry seemed to herald his uncertain future. What if he remained trapped in this body? As much as his departure would devastate them both, the honorable choice would be to disappear from Clarysa's life entirely. At the thought, Stellan let loose a booming, sorrowful howl, causing a flock of birds to scatter above him. *Gods of fortune, don't desert me now!*

The thought of living a cursed existence filled his mind with fire. He leaped up and smashed his fist into the trunk. The tree buckled and shook violently. All its limbs sent their share of accumulated snow earthward. Stellan's knuckles throbbed with pain, but it helped him concentrate. He *had* to continue his journey. This magick was beyond his scope.

He pressed onward, attempting to resist the call of his wolf brother's forlorn wail. There was only one person who could help, and Stellan had to reach him quickly. If his suspicion was correct, transformations of this magnitude became more and more difficult to reverse with every passing hour.

He reached Ravenwood Pass and made his way swiftly through the Hemling Mountains, traveling north into Falcon Heights. Many months had elapsed since his last visit. A single memory spurred him forth, to the Valley of the Clouds, where the unknown sorcerer dwelled.

Even in his bestial mind, he knew what he found there would seal his fate forever, for either good or ill.

Stellan raised his snout. It was well past noon, and the sun was beginning to drift into the western skies. Good. He was on the right path. Perhaps he still had time.

Exhausted though he was, he sprinted ahead toward his destiny, whatever it might be.

Chapter 33

"These tracks continue to run westward," Lionel noted. "And by the size of them, along with this fresh blood, I'd say we have our beast." He rose from his knee and turned to the officer standing next to him. "Do you concur?"

The man snapped to attention. "I do, sir. It's fortunate you picked them up again. I thought we'd lost 'em a while back."

Lionel lightly slapped his gloves against the strident young man's chest. "Luck had nothing to do with it. I know how the beast thinks."

"Sir, I must point out that we are rapidly losing light. Shall we set up camp here for the night?"

Lionel glowered. "And let that beast have my cousin? What are you thinking, man? Every moment we stand here delaying allows him to put more space between us! No, we press onward."

The officer stiffened. "Understood, sir." He turned and relayed the order.

Lionel scanned the countryside. *Oh mighty Prince Stellan, where are you and your expert tracking skills when we need them? When Clarysa needs them?* To make things worse, Edward had only given him a skeleton crew for the search and rescue, and this was for the protection of his own sister! Was his grudge against Stellan that strong?

His thoughts switched to the threat facing Aldebaran. Strange fires had been sighted around the perimeter of Vandeborg upon his departure. Was this the beginning of the massive invasion Stellan had warned of? Lionel made a fist. *Where the devil are you, man?* Stellan's disappearance was a perplexing mystery.

"Sir! Sir!" A young soldier ran up to him, gasping and wheezing as though he were ready to vomit forth his own insides.

"Take it easy, lad! You're going to burst your head in half running about like that! Now what do you have to report?"

The soldier pointed to a ridge about a quarter mile away. "There's a cave. Tracks are all over the place."

Lionel flexed his hands. "Gather the men."

"Yes, sir." He raced off.

Lionel peered into the distance. He could just make out a darkened entrance on the rocky wall. The young and gangly crew assembled before him, arms at the ready.

"Prepare you weapons and brace yourselves for battle. Our quarry lies there," he said while pointing to the cave. "Princess Clarysa is to be protected at all costs! And I want the fiend who took her lying dead before me by morning. Am I clear?"

A resounding answer of "Yes, sir!" made it evident his order was highly understandable.

Lionel drew his sword and led the troop forward. *Very well, devil. You had best pray Clarysa is unharmed, or I shall personally see that your death is the most excruciating in the history of the Five Lands!*

* * * *

Clarysa exited the stable and guided her steed up a hill. The air was clear except for an occasional flurry. She easily picked up the Captain's trail as the sun climbed higher behind a haze-filled sky. Frigid morning air seeped into the gaps of the thick scarf around her head. If nothing else, at least her feet felt comfortable, buried in fur-lined boots. She glanced back. Vandeborg loomed, dark and gloomy, behind her.

She continued ahead. Then she spied movement.

Patrulha, Hunter, and three other men were riding steadily across the snow. Clarysa was about a half mile behind them. The blurred edge of Dungeon Forest lined the horizon on the east, while rolling, snow-covered hills filled the scene to the west. Clarysa had only a vague sense of the direction in which they headed. Vandeborg soon faded behind her in a sea of gray and mist.

She began to wonder if the Captain was trying to lose her, for it seemed every time she caught up to the party, they sprinted ahead even faster. A cruel trick, if that were the case. But the obstacle only made her more determined. Clarysa plodded on.

Hours passed. The blinding white fields grew precipitously darker. Clarysa glanced up at the dour-faced clouds. They foretold a long and terrible storm.

Snow began falling at a furious rate. She pulled her wrappings about her tightly, but the action did little to mitigate the bitter cold. Clarysa strained to see Patrulha's rescue party amid the gloom. She urged the brave Palomino on. *I hope I'm not leading us both to a frozen death on this lonely plain.*

Waves of icy precipitation washed over her as she traveled. A biting wind kicked up, making her eyes smart with needlelike precision. She gritted her teeth. This had to be Nature's version of a wintry torture chamber. Clarysa prayed the horse would not drop from coldness and exhaustion, as she herself felt dangerously close to doing.

Gathering her wits, Clarysa called out to the riders before her. But the wind snatched her words away. The distant shapes of riders and horses began to blur. She fought to keep her eyes open. Were they traveling to a location within the Snowflake Kingdom, or somewhere beyond? Would she catch up to them in time?

The search party finally halted. Clarysa spurred her horse forward. Patrulha and Hunter exchanged glances at her approach. They had seen her, no doubt. Their adversarial posturing hinted at an argument. Clarysa inched closer until she was near enough to hear them.

"I'll take full responsibility. You won't have to worry about a thing."

"I said no! She'll slow us down."

"But she's kept up this far. That counts for something, doesn't it?"

"Hardly."

"Patrulha, don't be an ass. She's only trying to help."

"No one asked her to come."

"Well, she's here now. We can't spare anyone to go back with her. And I for one won't be the one to deal with Stellan if we don't. Will you?"

Patrulha glared at him with her good eye. Silence appeared to be her answer.

Hunter smiled. "Then it's settled."

Scowling, Patrulha pulled her scarf back against her face. Her brows furrowed as she stared at Clarysa. "Staring, spying, eavesdropping--will you be gracing us with any of your other bad manners, dear Princess?"

Clarysa's heart sank. "I only want to help Stellan," she mumbled. How was it she managed to offend Patrulha at every turn? As the Captain turned away and rode on, she risked a glance at Hunter, seeking assurance. He motioned her forward.

"Best keep up before she changes her mind!"

He gave her horse's rump a firm slap as she rode past him. Clarysa sighed with relief. A fresh burst of adrenaline revived her. Heading due north, they were soon swallowed by the wintry might.

* * * *

Night fell. Clarysa and her companions made camp just past the Snowflake Kingdom's border. The weather change had been so marked it had been like walking through a waterfall. The countryside here splashed with abundant greenery; about them, a cacophony of tree frogs sang the night away. The horses munched on a well-earned meal.

She was relieved to be beyond the snow and mind-numbing cold. How had Stellan and his people coped with it all these years?

The weary party gathered firewood and soon had a roaring flame going. Each collapsed beside it with outstretched fingers and toes. Hunter leaned over to offer Clarysa a metal flask, which she readily accepted. Ill-tasting liquor rushed into her mouth and she coughed. But then a warm, tingly sensation spread throughout her body. She smiled demurely in thanks.

The motley crew cobbled together a sparse meal of nuts, dried meats and raw greens plucked from the edge of a nearby meadow. Strong tea brewed in a heavy pot washed everything down. Hunter explained they would only rest for a few hours. He encouraged Clarysa to sleep, and offered her a spot close by the fire.

For the first time in days, Clarysa could see the stars twinkling in a silent rhythm above her. Despite the long, hard ride, her thoughts were restless. She worried about Stellan, wondering if he was safe and if he had found help. She feared the wayward hunter who might cross his path. He wouldn't know Stellan had been human; he would only attack. Visions of his stuffed corpse on display at the local fair flashed in her mind--the largest and most rare saberwolf. Her darling prince, reduced to nothing more than a grand prize. Clarysa shuddered.

Gretchen's parting words echoed in her mind. "Selfish," she had called Clarysa. Was she? After a great deal of brooding, Clarysa came to the conclusion that perhaps she *had* been self-centered in her decision, but only to an extent. For if death were to befall Stellan in some far off land, she would never forgive herself for not even trying to locate him. Surely he would understand! If she had made a reckless choice to follow Patrulha, it had only been because Stellan's life was at stake.

Patrulha.

What did Stellan's transformation and disappearance mean to her? Why did Gretchen say nothing of her daughter's decision to leave, especially at a time when the castle needed her protection the most? Clarysa raised her head and glanced around. Hunter and the other men sat huddled together, talking quietly. A dark figure sat separate, amid a group of large boulders many yards away.

Patrulha.

Clarysa rolled over. Thoughts continued to flood her brain as sleep eluded her. There were too many questions without answers. She and Patrulha both had Stellan's best interests at heart, yet they were unnecessarily at odds with each other. Clarysa had to at least attempt to clear the air between them.

She walked to the boulders. She said nothing at first, only watched Patrulha through sidelong glances. The Captain of the Guard sat on a flat rock. She had lit a small, separate fire for herself. A naked sword blade lay across her knees, and she sharpened it with measured force. Occasionally, she swallowed something from a nearby flask. Clarysa could smell the alcohol in the air.

She inched closer. Against the fire's light, Patrulha looked like one of the legendary warriors in the tapestries back home, a fierce, noble creature from some exotic land. The flame danced off the blade's surface, yielding a prismatic glow about the giantess before her. Attempting to appear nonchalant, Clarysa ambled forward.

Patrulha abruptly paused in her task and looked up. "Can I help you with something?" Her voice was as cold as the wastes behind them. "Or would that interfere with your spying?"

Clarysa winced at the surly tone. "I…couldn't sleep."

No reaction came aside from the quiet crackling of the fire.

Clarysa found the silence disconcerting. "Lots of thoughts were going through my head. Questions, you know?"

"Like?"

"Well, I was wondering…what happened to your eye, for one thing?"

There it was, hanging in the air--a question asked that could not be brought back, a thought that could not be undone. *Ugh. Could you have been any less subtle?*

Patrulha resumed her sharpening. "Ask Stellan when we find him."

"But I'm asking you!"

The Captain snorted. "Well, I guess you are, then." She pursed her lips. "Very well."

Clarysa sat on a nearby rock, hands folded in her lap.

Patrulha stared at the ground, utterly silent. Then she slowly raised her head and began her tale. "Once upon a time, there were two warriors, a man and a woman, who were exploring the local countryside. After much ground had been covered with nothing extraordinary to report, they happened to come upon a rather odd man in his shop. He was furiously banging away and bending metal before a roaring fire. This man, with a fat, red face all covered in sweat and a shiny bald head, ceased his work upon their entrance. He demanded to know what business the pair had with him."

She took another swig from her flask. "Well, the man and woman didn't know the proper response except to comment on how they admired the man's handiwork--with one sword in particular standing out from the many displayed on a back wall. The man took it down and swung it about in the air to test its balance. This was all it took to confirm the pair's suspicions--it was a magick sword, one with the power to deflect and shatter all manner of spells. 'This is an extremely rare weapon,' said the man to the woman, which of course caused the woman to desire it by her side. 'How much?' she inquired to the queer man before her. But the man laughed and shook his head.

"This only caused the woman to desire it even more, so she asked again, 'How much do you want for this fine blade of yours?" Once again, he rebuffed her. 'More than you can afford, young ragamuffin.' Well, this put the woman beside herself. Now she *had* to have the weapon at all costs, despite the man's insistence that she forget it.

"The swordsmith then pointed to many other fine blades he would willingly sell, 'for a fair bargain,' he said. But even this would not do." Patrulha paused for another swig.

"'No,' said the woman, 'I want this sword--no other!' Well, the man with the red face and balding head stared at her for a long time. 'All right,' he finally declared, 'I'll tell you what I'll do. I'll sell you this sword then, but not for coin.'

'Excellent,' said the woman in her arrogance. Inwardly she was laughing, thinking he would want her body in trade for a few nights, or maybe a week. The sword was easily worth the price, probably more so. Her companion wouldn't have been pleased, but he had made no claim on her, so she stuck out her chin and planted her hands proudly on her hips. 'Name your price,' she said.

'Your right eye,' he stated.

The woman snorted in disbelief. 'You jest.'

'No,' he said quietly, turning his back on the pair. 'Now be out of here! I told you, you couldn't afford it.'

"Well, what do you think the woman did? For pride flowed through her veins, and lust for a sword she would surely never see the likes of again. But there was one other prize to win, or so the woman thought. She believed her companion would reject her cowardice if she backed down and reward her with his undying devotion if she did not."

Patrulha stopped sharpening the sword and hurled it into the earth near Clarysa's feet. "So, I got my sword. End of story."

Clarysa sat before her in astonished silence. She didn't know what to say, but knew she had to come up with something. "I…I don't understand. Why did he want your eye?"

Patrulha shrugged. "He didn't. He only wanted to see if the person who possessed the sword also had the fortitude to own it. Besides, I knew we needed it to fight Pestilence. This was about the time of the first outbreaks and Stellan had said it was likely to worsen. Obviously, his predictions were correct."

"But…your eye! What kind of a trade was that? I mean, couldn't Stellan have conjured up some kind of payment?"

Patrulha shook her head. "A sorcerer's power doesn't work so easily. Magick--well, true magick at any rate--requires time and preparation. It isn't just a flick of the wand and there it is, as some might have you believe." She chuckled. "This purchase was a spontaneous one anyway. The merchant took me to a back room. I sat down, he plucked out my eye, and I walked away with an enchanted sword."

Clarysa held a hand to her mouth in an effort to suppress her rising nausea. "How barbaric!"

"Well, at least he threw in the patch for free!" Patrulha threw back her head and laughed.

The sound was unnerving, more like the squawk of a desperate vulture. "Didn't he give you something for the pain? It must have been horrible."

Patrulha's laughter quickly faded. She regarded Clarysa solemnly, speaking in a low voice. "You have no idea."

Clarysa regarded the gleaming weapon before her with a renewed respect.

They sat together for a while, heads bent so closely they almost touched, studying the weapon together. Clarysa wondered if she and Patrulha could overcome their differences enough to become friends. She hoped so.

Eventually, Patrulha brought the moment of intimacy to an end. "Go back to sleep, Clarysa. Eight more hours of riding lie ahead of us and we rise before dawn."

But Clarysa stayed rooted to her seat. Another question nagged her, one swaddled in sympathy for the lonely woman next to her. She probably risked offending the Captain, but she was a close friend of Stellan's. Clarysa wanted to understand her better.

"Patrulha, you said you wanted two things from losing your eye. One was the sword, the other 'undying devotion.'"

Patrulha frowned. "What of it?"

Clarysa's countenance softened. "One would have to be daft not to guess how you feel about Stellan."

Patrulha stared into the fire, silent.

"Haven't you told him?" asked Clarysa.

Patrulha stood. "That was a long time ago. Besides, he's the happiest I've ever known him to be. You two should be together."

"But, Patrulha--"

The Captain glared down at her. "I'm here to rescue him because he deserves a better life, and obviously that means one with you. I've accepted the inevitable. Now I'm asking you to do the same."

"I... As you wish." Before Clarysa could say another word, Patrulha turned and stalked away into the night.

Chapter 34

Clarysa rose with the others in the dark hours of the morning. They consumed a cold, meager meal in near silence. Afterward, they packed the saddlebags and resumed their trek. Clarysa held back, taking up the rear. Her position gave her the freedom to observe Patrulha, who rode point.

Clarysa reflected upon the information she had candidly given up the night before. Logic didn't seem to apply to her--but perhaps that was the mystery of Patrulha. Clarysa wasn't so sure the warrior woman no longer harbored certain feelings for Stellan. It would certainly explain her icy attitude toward Clarysa all this time. A twinge of guilt made her sigh. *Patrulha deserves happiness, too.* Unfortunately, she had no idea what would give her satisfaction.

The sun climbed higher in the sky as they traveled. Warm air carried aloft scents of honeysuckle and pine. Had Stellan lumbered through here in his bestial form? Clarysa searched about her as they continued, desperate for a glimpse of him. But only sprinting rabbits and butterflies appeared.

As the day edged past the noon hour, Patrulha held up a silent hand.

Everyone halted. She dropped from her mount and crouched low to the ground. She appeared to be searching for something.

"What are you looking for?" Clarysa asked.

"Patience, Princess," Hunter murmured.

Whatever Patrulha was searching for, she found it. She motioned for everyone to continue down the serpentine path before them. The captain pulled Hunter aside for a few private words, words Clarysa could not determine despite her best efforts. Why wouldn't these people tell her anything?

The road descended into a shallow valley, one with a sprawling stone-and-mortar building in its belly. It was buttressed by fenced lots of various plants and greenery. Dollops of every color exploded from fragrant blooms. Clarysa stared about her in wonder as they rode along a neatly lined path. Upon reaching a wooden gate, everyone dismounted. Clarysa followed their lead, securing her horse to a nearby wooden rail. An intricately lettered sign hung from the entrance's red awning. Highlighted with complicated symbols, it swayed back and forth in the light breeze. Apothecary, it read. What did the symbols mean?

Clarysa stepped forward to unlatch the gate, only to be stopped by Hunter's burly arm. "You don't want to do that," he said.

She huffed. "Why not? Will somebody please explain where we are and how this is helping Stellan?"

Patrulha turned to her with a wry look. "Think I'm the rash one, do you?" She scooped up some pebbles from the path. "Well, think again." She tossed the stones against the gate. They faded into spots of reddish gas that quickly blew away in the breeze. Clarysa took a step back in horror. Without a sound, each of the rocks had simply ceased to be.

Hunter nodded down to Clarysa's hand. "That could just as well have been you, lass." Clarysa swallowed hard, her gaze transfixed upon the venomous gate.

Patrulha unsheathed her sword. She proceeded to carve several intricate patterns on the gate's surface. They glowed a bright green before quickly disappearing. After Patrulha carved the sixth glyph, however, the gate opened and beckoned them inside.

Patrulha instantly strode through. Hunter turned with a reassuring smile, his outstretched hand bidding Clarysa to precede him, which she did--cautiously. The rest of the group followed close behind.

Clarysa studied the humble abode as she approached it on the crunchy gravel path. A combination of gray stone and wood, it appeared roomy and well-maintained. *What a curious place. But where are we?*

The first to reach the door, Patrulha pounded on it mercilessly. A few minutes later, an elderly man with a wiry frame opened it.

"Where is he, old man?" She pushed past him to get inside.

Clarysa accepted Hunter's invitation to precede him, although she felt like an intruder. Still, the apothecary's shop was a fascinating place. Hundreds of small, brightly colored bottles surrounded her. Each rested neatly on dark walnut shelves, interspersed with leather-bound books of all sizes. The wooden floor creaked noisily under her feet. Its polished surface reflected the golden light of oil-burning lamps. Medicinal odors and perfumed scents weaved together in the air.

The old man inclined his head as Clarysa and her companions grouped about him. "I'm doing quite well, my dear. Thanks for inquiring." One corner of his thin mouth curved up. "What can I do for you, Patrulha?"

"Don't waste my time. Where's Stellan?"

"Why, I haven't seen him in over a year."

"We found the tracks outside, Hans. Don't ever mistake me for a fool."

The apothecary sighed, stroking his silver goatee. "Of course not. I've heard the tales of those unfortunates who have." He gestured toward a red doorway in the back. "He's here, but is *not* to be disturbed under any circumstances. You'll never guess the fright he gave me, bursting through my door in that guise!"

He's alive! Thank heaven! Clarysa pushed herself between them. "Is he all right? I need to see him!"

Hans regarded her curiously over the rim of his glasses. "And who might you be?"

"I'm his wife...I mean, I *will* be. We were to be married. His witch of a sister interfered. I was abducted, and she... Oh, where *is* he? Please take me to him. Stellan!" Clarysa called out. She stepped toward the red door, only to be halted by the apothecary's iron-hard grip around her upper arm.

"You'll do nothing of the sort," he said firmly.

"But, sir, you don't understand--"

"Sit!"

Hans maneuvered her into a chair. Clarysa landed with such force it nearly tipped over. The apothecary pulled up another one, and motioned for the others to gather 'round. "Your Stellan came to me a short time ago. His shape... Well, let's just say he was in an extremely bad way. If he had delayed any longer, you might have never seen him again--at least not as you knew him." Hans paused to wipe his glasses with a corner of his shirt. "Together we're edging closer to an antidote. Been up forty hours straight. Very challenging when your partner can't even speak." He pointed a finger at Clarysa. "At any rate, he must *not* be disturbed. The potion has to be exact. The slightest movement in the room could affect the measurements. Trust me, that's an outcome you don't want."

The echo of a snarl reverberated from the back room.

Clarysa put a hand to her temple, fearing the worst. "What will happen if you can't get the potion right?"

Hans glanced behind him, then faced Clarysa again. "You must understand that time is against us. The curse corrupted not only his body, but also his mind. Every hour, every minute, his intellect wanes. His blood grows more feral with each passing moment."

"What do you mean?" Clarysa whispered. "What's happening to him?"

"If he does not ingest the correct antidote soon--and I mean within the next hour--there will be no reversing the spell. In mind and body, he will remain a beast forever."

Patrulha reached down and grabbed a knot of the apothecary's shirt in a fist. "Then you'd best be getting back to work!" she ordered, and half pushed him in the direction of his workroom. "I'll ensure there are no further interruptions." This last remark she directed with great obviousness toward Clarysa.

Hans retreated to the back room. Patrulha assumed a wide stance before it with arms crossed. Nothing short of a battering ram would get past her, that much was clear.

Clarysa wilted in her chair, feeling utterly useless. There was nothing she could do but wait.

Chapter 35

Clarysa sat pensively, her arms wrapped tightly about herself. The wooden floor creaked periodically whenever someone shifted or walked about the room. No one spoke.

Hunter raided the pantry. He passed around jars of pickled vegetables and a crusty loaf of rye bread. Clarysa shook her head as he approached. In her jittery state, she wouldn't be able to keep any food down. Hunter shrugged and moved on.

With food consumed and appetites tamed, the men reclined or sat on the floor to rest. The air grew still and quiet.

A soft *thump* broke the silence. Alarmed, Clarysa looked at the door. The sound had come from outside. Patrulha gestured for continued silence and then motioned for one of the men to investigate. She and the others took up strategic positions inside.

Hunter escorted Clarysa to a hiding place behind a high counter. After he left to join the others, she immediately peeked around the corner, giving her a wide view of the expansive room.

Sounds of violence filtered through the walls. Metal grated against metal. Muffled shouts and curses burst forth. Patrulha sent out a second man. Wasting no time, she drew her sword.

A large boulder smashed through the north side window. In quick succession, another penetrated the adjacent wall. When a third hurtled straight toward her head, Patrulha dove into a forward roll and sprang to her feet. More shouts filled the air. Clarysa looked up to see dark figures streaking back and forth past the remaining windows. *Who are they?* Had someone followed them here? Once again, Clarysa was bereft of any weapons. She crept out onto the floor to grab a large shard of glass. *This will have to do.* She returned to her hiding place.

The door burst open. Clarysa gaped at the sight of the callous-looking soldier who appeared. His armor was devoid of any light or reflection.

His demeanor was one of death. Her paltry shard held no chance against this being.

He charged into the room, only to have his head depart his shoulders as Patrulha deftly struck him down. Her sword severed the armor as if it were passing through smoke. Other strange soldiers poured forth. Some wore ebony uniforms and wielded gleaming swords. Others looked more like ill-tempered mercenaries. They were clearly after something. But what? Were they here to capture Stellan?

Patrulha whirled about, a demon of combat. Her sword clashed with those of the enemy, sometimes battling two or three at a time. Entranced, Clarysa watched as Patrulha effortlessly dispatched all who attempted to breach the door. Armored bodies began to pile up near the entrance, a testament to her prowess.

More enemy soldiers came. The fighting intensified. Blood coated the floor, creating hazardous footing. The number of angry voices outside seemed to increase a hundredfold. The fighting seemed like it would never end. Should she seek out Stellan? No. She would only become a liability if found.

Maybe she should have given up her royal status long ago. If she were more like Patrulha, she could have contributed something meaningful to this quest. Now she was only a burden, like a gangrenous limb. A gangrenous limb who had insisted on tagging along with no clear plan. *Idiot.*

By the entrance, the Captain was locked in mortal combat with a soldier who had forsworn head armor for a menacing facial tattoo. The enemy's meaty hand tightened about Patrulha's neck as he held her against the wall. His sword arm poised dangerously at her midsection.

Patrulha's face grew red. Sweat-dampened hair plastered her cheeks. She struggled violently and then bared her teeth in a snarl. A well-timed kick to the man's midsection loosened his death grip. Patrulha then delivered a series of punches that sent him to his knees, followed by a powerful blow from her sword. Clarysa glanced away as the man's severed head dropped to the floor.

Panting hard, Patrulha wiped her blade clean on the soldier's clothing. Then she looked toward the open doorway and froze. Clarysa followed the line of her gaze, then clamped a hand to her mouth.

The woman from her dream stood in the doorway.

A lavender cloak draped the woman's supple figure. She regarded Patrulha with green eyes as vivid as Stellan's. Her onyx hair had been trussed into a sleek bun.

Stellan's sister! Clarysa found the resemblance troublesome and eerie. What was she doing here?

A flowing purple flame appeared to hover about her form, yet never touched her. The air reeked as if sulfur and flesh had been ignited together in one awful melange. From her vantage point, Clarysa could only see Patrulha's back, but she had an unobstructed view of the sorceress in all her preternatural power. No wonder the soldiers had been able to breach the magickal barrier. This sorceress must have destroyed it.

Stellan's sister took a nimble step forward, but stopped as Patrulha blocked her path, sword upraised. The sorceress sighed, her expression one of grace and malice combined. "I might choose a different strategy if I were you."

Patrulha flexed her hands, tightening her grip. "You have no business here, Sada."

"Come now, Captain. Are all gypsies as arrogant and stupid as you?" Faster than the human eye could follow, she flicked her wrist in a circular pattern, leaving the air about her boiling in shadow and thunder.

But except for the slight vibration of Patrulha's sword, nothing happened. The Captain uttered a low and confident laugh. "Now I remember why I had to have this blade--to cleave snotty bitches like you in half!"

Sada laughed merrily, as though they were two friends gossiping. "Well, I see the kitten brought her own toys!"

The sorceress advanced. Patrulha glanced quickly in the direction of Clarysa's hiding place and then leaped over the ruined wall. Sada followed her outside, gliding over the rubble on some kind of magickal force. Clarysa changed position to see them better.

The sorceress's eyes flashed a brighter green. The air about them darkened. Unearthly sounds shrieked from their hateful realms, as Sada's visage contorted into impossible forms. Multicolored shards of death rained down upon Patrulha, but her sword drew them from harm's way. The Captain of the Guard grunted. The acrid air about her continued to pop and sputter as the two combatants locked horns again.

Sada waved an arm. A black, shapeless mass rose from the ground. Bizarre creatures swam within it--a cluster of scaly tentacles with barbed ends, creatures with snapping claws, soul-sucking ghouls. Sada flicked a finger. The roiling mass enveloped Patrulha, spinning around her like a vortex.

Grimacing, Patrulha slowly rotated her sword. The enchanted weapon began to absorb the mass.

Clarysa was distracted by a figure appearing at the gap in the wall. She choked back a cry of relief and waved for Lionel's attention. He jumped over the rubble and ran to her side. "Clarysa! You don't know how overjoyed I am to see you! Are you all right?"

Clarysa nodded as she clung to him.

"We arrived a short time ago," he whispered in her ear. "Rainier and I and a few others tracked the saberwolf creature to this place. During our approach, we spotted these intruders skulking about the building." Lionel wrinkled his nose. "Men from the Wastes, most likely. Beastly lot, if you ask me." He smiled reassuringly. "We took care of the ones outside." He pointed to Sada. "Except for her. Stay here. I'm going to offer my assistance." Lionel rose in the direction of the dueling pair.

Clarysa held him back. "No, you mustn't! That woman is a sorceress. You'll have absolutely no defense against her. She'll kill you before you could even draw your sword!"

Lionel's facial muscles twitched as he considered her warning. The air continued to crackle about the two. Then he crouched back down. "I daresay you're right."

They resumed watching, for it was the only action they could take.

Outside, Patrulha closed in on Sada, still with her back to Clarysa and Lionel. Sada's eyes filled with venom. Her body glowed with otherworldly power.

Patrulha bolted forward, deftly changing sword hands as she did. Her sword now rested squarely in Sada's abdomen. Clarysa gasped and started to rise, only to be stopped by a cautious Lionel. "I don't think it's over just yet," he whispered. "Look!"

Clarysa strained to see. Before them all lingered the mortally wounded Sada, still standing defiantly on her feet. Blood trickled from the corner of her mouth, yet her lips curved upward in a cruel smile.

Clarysa frowned. *Why is she looking so smug?*

Sada backed away, ever so slowly. Her face paled as the sword left her body, but the smile--her ever-devilish grin--did not falter. A dark stain ballooned on her side, a reminder that steel could still harm those of the Arts. Then, with a knowing look to the shop, she glided away and out of sight.

Lionel stood and shouted for his men, but Hunter waylaid him, having re-entered from the rear of the store. "Leave Sada to me. Guard Clarysa." He stormed off.

Clarysa stared intently at Patrulha, who hadn't moved. "Patrulha?" She approached the Captain with Lionel close behind. "Patrulha?" Clarysa stepped around to face her.

A jeweled dagger protruded from Patrulha's good eye. She was still on her feet, but stone dead.

Lionel caught her body as it fell. He laid her gently on the ground. Clarysa knelt beside him, cradling Patrulha's head. Blood was everywhere. "Oh no. Don't die. Please don't die!" Tears ran down her face in torrents.

Hunter ran up to them. "Couldn't find her." He blanched upon noticing Patrulha. "Damn that infernal sorceress!" He sank to his knees beside the fallen warrior in grief.

Clarysa cried harder. Then a shadow passed over her.

She looked up. Right into Stellan's eyes--a now fully human Stellan.

He knelt opposite her, naked but for a strip of cloth wrapped around his hips. He looked upon Patrulha's bloody face. A tic in his clenched jaw was the only hint of life in his stony expression.

A fresh wave of tears overcame Clarysa as she remembered her conversation with the Captain by the previous night's fire. She grabbed Stellan's arm. "She loved you!"

He stared at her in shock.

"She...loved you. Not like a sister, but as a woman." She drew the warrior's blood-soaked head closer to her chest. "I don't think she ever had the courage to tell you. And now, she'll never be able to!" Clarysa pressed her cheek against Patrulha's forehead and sobbed. *I'm sorry. I'm so sorry!*

For a long time Stellan was silent. No tears. No emotion. He turned to Hunter. "You are now the Captain. Report."

And so Hunter filled him in on the details of their journey, Edward's army, and the recent battle on the apothecary's doorstep. He ended it with one chilling comment. "Vandeborg remains under siege."

At this Stellan pulled Lionel aside. Clarysa only half listened as they discussed plans to return to the castle for a counterattack. The Duke informed them that a contingent of the King's men had since been dispatched from Aldebaran to provide reinforcement.

"And there's the matter of your sister as well," added Hunter. "She's wounded, but I couldn't find a trace of her."

Stellan nodded curtly. "Hans will need help cleaning up. Let's restore order here and begin preparations for the return journey. I have to find some clothes."

The men dispersed to fulfill his orders. Stellan paused to look upon Clarysa and the deceased Patrulha. A shiver passed through her. She had never seen his green eyes so dark and cold.

He walked away without another word.

Clarysa stared after him. There could be only one reason he was ignoring her. *He thinks it's my fault. He blames me for her death!*

And he would be right. Patrulha's words came back to haunt her: *I'm here to rescue him because he deserves a better life, and obviously that means one with you.* She had chosen to fight Sada, drawing the sorceress away so Clarysa would be safe. But at what cost? Anguish crushed her heart like a steel vise. She had lost a potential new friend, but Stellan had lost a member of his family.

Clarysa bowed her head, certain her relationship with Stellan was no more.

Chapter 36

The scorching noon sun blazed mercilessly down upon Clarysa as she and her companions departed from the apothecary's shop. With Lionel and his group, their number had swelled to seventeen. Some of the men nursed injuries from the recent fight. Patrulha was the only casualty. Her horse dragged her body on a makeshift litter. It carved deep ruts into the earth as they headed back to Vandeborg.

Clarysa stared longingly at the back of Stellan's head. He had yet to utter a single word to her since resuming human form. She had never seen him look so sullen and heartsick--each emotion appeared to permeate his very soul. Perhaps Patrulha's death had altered his feelings about her, feelings he might never recover. Was this possible?

"Rubbish," Lionel had told her after she'd confided in him about her fears. "Let him be," he cautioned. "The man obviously needs time to be alone with his thoughts. Give it to him."

And this she did. But it was difficult. The ache in her chest only grew more pronounced with every passing minute.

It's your fault. If you had respected his wishes by staying at Vandeborg, Patrulha might still be alive.

They traveled late into the night and then broke for camp at the edge of the Snowflake Kingdom. Clarysa busied herself by helping Hunter make supper. While passing around food, she noticed Stellan wasn't by the fire. When her own meal sat upon her lap, she could barely swallow the food. Concern for Stellan overwhelmed her. She could stand the separation no more. Abandoning her meal, she searched for him.

She needn't look far. She discovered him sitting forlornly by Patrulha's body.

Clarysa approached quietly and sat beside him at a polite distance. He didn't acknowledge her presence, but neither had she expected him to. Head bowed, he held the dead woman's hand. Clarysa watched the sorrowful scene for several minutes. Then, compelled by sympathy, she placed a comforting hand on his arm.

Stellan choked out a sob. He looked up at her, tears streaming from his eyes. "Clarysa, help me."

"Anything. What do you need?"

His face twisted in anguish. "What am I going to tell her mother?"

The strain in his voice betrayed the depth of his sorrow. Clarysa opened her arms. Stellan dove forward and let her cradle him. He wrapped his arms tightly around her waist and buried his face in her lap. His whole body shook.

She stroked her fingers tenderly through his hair. "Tell her the truth--she was a brave and beautiful warrior who was loyal to her prince until the end."

She gazed at Patrulha's shrouded form, willing herself to hold back tears. He needed her to be strong. Stellan shuddered with the force of a monsoon as he emptied his grief. It felt as though he would never release her.

"Clarysa, forgive me," he said, his voice muffled. "I know I've ignored you. That was cruel of me. It's just…I didn't expect to lose her so suddenly. I always assumed she would die in battle someday, but not this, not so soon."

"I know how much she meant to you," she whispered. A tear rolled down her cheek. "It's all my fault. I'm so sorry."

He raised his head. "No," he said forcefully. "That's not true."

"But she was protecting me--us--so we could be together. If I hadn't been in the shop, distracting her, the battle might have ended differently. She might have lived."

His cool hand cupped her cheek. "Don't torture yourself. Patrulha knew the stakes. The choice to help us was hers, and hers alone."

"But, Stellan, she was in love with you. Her eyes…her eyes followed you everywhere." Hot, salty tears burned her cheeks. "But my presence made it difficult for her to declare her feelings. I knew how she felt, and *I said nothing!*" Clarysa choked back a sob. "I was so selfish!"

Stellan lifted her chin. Though wrought with exhaustion, his expression was tender. "Clarysa," he began, "a love between Patrulha and I would have been nothing more than shared misery. That's all." His lips grazed hers. His warm breath filled her mouth as he spoke. "But with you I feel as if I can actually find happiness, *true* happiness. It means so much you've accepted me for who I am--especially considering I wasn't my true self for a time. Few women, if any, would have stood by me as you did."

"That's because I want to spend the rest of my life with you no matter what your appearance."

"That's a relief." He pulled her into his embrace. "And guess what?"

"What?"

"I like that you're silly."

Despite her tears, Clarysa grinned at the unexpected compliment.

His hands tightened around her waist. "And I love how you're so... uninhibited."

As Stellan pressed his lips to hers, she surrendered to his urgent, demanding kiss. Arousal flared in her core, though she dare not display any kind of wanton behavior in the presence of their companions. She molded her body to his, reveling in his heat and maleness. Oh, how she had missed him! If only she could stop the hands of time to preserve this one moment.

But Pestilence still threatened the Five Lands. Until they defeated that menace, there would be no happiness for them anywhere.

Chapter 37

The darkening sky echoed Clarysa's somber mood as she and the others prepared to travel through the Snowflake Kingdom. Despite the recent fight, the real battle had yet to begin.

In near silence, they donned heavy shirts, cloaks and scarves in preparation for the pending climate change. As Clarysa rode with the group into the outlying plain, the weather greeted her with long, frigid fingers. The icy wind blew fresh snow into her face. The abrupt change in temperature once again tested her mettle.

The sky opened up and the snow fell in buckets. A blinding snowstorm unleashed its fury, slowing their procession to a crawl.

Stellan looked to the sky, then turned back, his face filled with ominous portent. "I've seen dangerous weather here, but never like this," he shouted. "It cannot be a good sign. Stay close together!"

He signaled to Hunter. The two men dismounted. Using coils of rope from the saddlebags, they linked all of the riders together. Stellan took the lead. Clarysa was in the middle, preceded by Lionel. Would Stellan be able to lead them safely through, or would the storm overwhelm even his expert tracking abilities?

They rode for hours. Periodically, Stellan would stop and reach out a hand. Ethereal fire came from it in spurts. It must have been some kind of magickal compass, for he altered direction each time he used it. Once, Clarysa caught sight of his haggard expression. The exertion was taking its toll.

Hours later, the storm weakened, having spent the entirety of its might. As the sheets of snow retreated, Stellan led the group behind an outcropping of boulders near Vandeborg's perimeter. They could now discern the enemy encampment. It stretched, snakelike, around the stone fortress.

Hunter removed the linked ropes while Stellan, Clarysa and Lionel studied the scene.

"Edward is responsible for this, isn't he?" Clarysa whispered.

Lionel nodded. "He's consumed with bringing Stellan to his knees. I see the reinforcements have arrived. Expect him to attempt a breach of the castle at any moment."

Hunter joined them. "What are your orders, Stellan? I'm ready to smash some sense into their heads, but the men could use some rest after the journey."

Stellan nodded in tacit agreement. He pointed to an outlying stretch of rocks near the northeast wall. "See that? It conceals an entrance I discovered by accident one day. Never thought I'd have to use it."

Hunter's eyes widened at the revelation. "An emergency *exit* is more likely, but it'll serve our purposes all the same."

Clarysa cast a worried glance toward the Aldebaran troops. "But how are we going to slip past them?"

Stellan's deep green gaze locked with hers. "Leave that to me."

* * * *

Thirty minutes later, Clarysa watched in awe as thousands of bats descended on the Aldebaran troops. Blindly, the soldiers swatted at the creatures in an attempt to drive them off. Slashes of their gleaming blades accomplished nothing, for they were overwhelmed in number.

Stellan's rough hand closed about hers. He drew her into the long, winding passageway that tunneled deep into the blackened earth. The horses barely squeezed through, and only then by lowering their heads. A dank underworld poisoned with the smell of rot greeted them as they descended. Frozen stalactites jutted toward them, jagged and hungry for their weak human flesh.

Gretchen and her son met them as they emerged onto one of the castle's lower levels. She reached first for Stellan. Standing on her toes, she patted his cheek and briefly tousled his hair. "I knew it was you the moment I saw those bats."

Stellan shook his head wearily. "No easy feat, but it did the trick."

Clarysa glanced shyly at the gypsy. "I apologize for being so rude to you."

Gretchen turned to her with a welcoming embrace. "Not to worry. I'm just relieved to see all of you back!"

But the sea of long faces did not share in her joy. Gretchen shot Stellan a questioning look. A solemn Hunter Red dragged the litter forward and revealed its secret. The gypsy woman took in the sight, and then her alarmed gaze latched onto Stellan.

Stone-faced, Stellan muttered a single, curt reply. "I'm sorry."

Gretchen wailed, a baleful keen that blanketed them all with its misery. She rushed forward, but Stellan halted her with an arm. She clung to him, her face a sea of anguish. Grief devoured her remaining strength and she collapsed into a fetal position by his feet.

Ghyslain stood nearby. His haunted, empty expression betrayed his refusal to believe his sister was truly dead.

Clarysa could hardly bear to watch. She wondered why Stellan didn't offer her comfort. Gretchen needed him. But then Clarysa remembered his words from the night before. He must have felt responsible for Patrulha's death. After all, it was his sister who had plunged that hateful blade. A rush of sympathy for him went through her. To feel extreme guilt on top of such an acute loss must have been more agony than most people could bear. *No wonder he tries to bury all his emotions.*

Clarysa bent down and wrapped her arms around the gypsy, now uncontrollably sobbing. She stroked her shoulders and uttered soothing words as best she knew how. Eventually, she coaxed Gretchen to her feet so they could follow the others to the main floor.

As they entered the great hall, the rest of the castle's inhabitants watched, shell-shocked, as the litter bearing Patrulha went past. Froll fought to hold back tears, but quickly lost the battle. Ghsylain took his mother from Clarysa and guided her toward the kitchen.

Thirty or so of Stellan's men now crowded the area, aimless and disorganized. No one appeared to know what to do. Clarysa stood idly by, feeling awkward and helpless.

Stellan strode into the center of the hall. "Gather 'round, men."

Clarysa hurried to a spot at the front of the group. What was he going to do?

Stellan stood on a dais and addressed his loyal followers. "My friends, Patrulha's loss was both unexpected and painful. But we cannot allow our grief to dissuade our cause, for the battle is not yet won. And you know as well as I that she would have wanted us to fight with everything we have.

"I have lived a lonely existence for many of my years. I've cursed the gods and circumstances that led me to this bewitched kingdom. But somehow each one of you found me. You trusted me and supported my efforts to keep Pestilence from the Five Lands."

He held up a hardened fist and regarded everyone in the room one by one. "Hope was restored in my broken spirit as well as body. Look about you. All of us are gathered here for a reason. For each of us in his own way bears an albatross. In one way or another, we have all gone against our peers and society's acceptance."

Stellan's head made a quarter turn, singling out Clarysa even as he addressed them all. "Each has a story to tell. Each of us has braved poisonous insinuations, and, in some cases, defied the razor-sharp blades of others to stand for what is right in this world!"

He stepped forward, his arms outstretched on either side. "Our fallen comrade, Patrulha, knew some causes were worth dying for. Are we to let her selfless sacrifice be in vain?"

A resounding chorus of "No!" thundered in the hall.

"I'm glad you agree." Stellan raised his voice with renewed vigor. "Even now my father schemes to conquer all of the Five Lands. His instrument is Pestilence, and of all the sorcerers in the Western Wastes, I alone stand in his way.

"Yet other, more immediate challenges await us. The misguided crown prince of Aldebaran seeks our downfall. The assembled troops outside await his order to attack. Also, my recent ordeal at the hands of my sister has demonstrated the lengths to which my family will go to sow seeds of conflict and pain. Transforming me into a beast was Sada's way of giving me a chance to repent my ways. My only chance. I've no doubt that the next time she and I meet, we will fight in a battle to the death.

Clarysa clamped both hands across her mouth. *A magickal duel? To the* death?

"The coming battle will shape the destiny of the Five Lands for years to come. Together, we are the future. So let it be remembered that on this day, we individuals, spurned by society, bound together and defeated those who would destroy us and what is right!"

A deafening roar of cheers went up, drowning out all of the war drums now beating incessantly outside. Clarysa gazed at Stellan with deep admiration.

A guard rushed forward and whispered in Stellan's ear. The Dark Prince nodded and turned to his warriors. "Aldebaran attacks! We must go to Vandeborg's defense. Are you with me?"

Again a deafening roar went up, one whose sound far belied its small numbers. The men leaped into action. Rusty armor was dispersed to those who were not already suited. Swords, maces, arrows--anything that could possibly be used as a weapon was passed out to ready hands.

While the men raced to their positions, Stellan turned to Clarysa. "If the sight of blood does not trouble you, I fear the men will need someone to tend to the injured." He stared at her expectantly.

Clarysa nodded. "I'll take care of them."

"Good. Go find Gretchen. She'll instruct you."

Clarysa struggled to speak calmly past her trembling lips. "My love, please return safely to me!"

"All the demons of the otherworld couldn't keep me away from you." He bent down and crushed her lips with his.

She welcomed Stellan's rough, bruising kiss with open arms. His hot, thrusting tongue laid waste to her mouth as he cupped her bottom with fingers of iron. Clarysa sensed his adrenaline and power flowing throughout his body.

All too soon he broke the kiss. "I must go." He strode away, quickly blending into the shadows.

As Clarysa headed to the kitchen, an uneasy fear grew inside her. Battle meant carnage, pain and death. How could hope ever survive against such odds?

Outside, apocalypse waited.

Chapter 38

Overcast skies had spent their abated supply of snow, which allowed Stellan a glimpse of Dungeon Forest on the horizon--a rare event in the Snowflake Kingdom. He surveyed the Aldebaran troops from atop Vandeborg's eastern tower. Wolfe maintained guard by his side, a place the animal had refused to leave since Stellan's return.

Stellan turned to Lionel and Hunter, who stood beside him. "How has it come to this? Before me is the brother of my betrothed. Edward and his army are determined to carry the head of this particular 'warlock' back to his bigoted people as a prize. The man is hungry for my death, blinded by his hatred."

A stone missile launched from the trebuchet under Edward's order. It tore through the wall above the three men.

Edward's voice followed, amplified by a speaking trumpet. "You cannot hide in there forever, demon! Surrender my sister and I shall grant you a fair trial before your hanging!"

As if Stellan didn't understand Edward's meaning, a boulder sailed over their heads and annihilated a nearby parapet.

Lionel sighed. "Stellan, let's negotiate with him on the fields below." He gestured to the derelict edifice about him. "I fear if we wait much longer all of this 'unique' decor of yours will be destroyed."

The duke moved to return inside, but Stellan held him back with a firm arm grip. "No," he said, "for that would be playing straight into our enemy's hands."

"Edward is not the enemy! He simply takes his position as heir apparent far too seriously. If you, Clarysa and I march out onto the field in solidarity--"

"I was not referring to your Aldebaran brethren, Lionel, but rather our mutual enemy who lurks below, waiting for your cousin to draw me out before attacking." Stellan scanned the horizon, then indicated the shadowy edge of Dungeon Forest. "We are not alone here, my friend.

See those darkened woods? Keep a close watch on the foliage and tell me what you see."

Lionel and Hunter exchanged looks and then both squinted at the area in question.

Lionel shrugged as another boulder crashed into the wall beside them. Glancing down in annoyance, he brushed a stray bit of dust from his cape. "I don't see anything other than the usual trees and bushes."

"Nor do I, m'lord," said Hunter.

Stellan pursed his lips. "Your eyes search for the obvious. Use your deductive reasoning."

Another boulder shook the castle, along with more of Edward's taunts.

Lionel grunted. "My dear friend, I hardly think this is the appropriate time for riddles."

Stellan directed their vision back to the forest. "You said you see nothing, correct? But where are the ravens that flock there every morning? Where are the squirrels? Or any other animal? None are there, for that's where our enemy--no doubt my sister--lies in wait." Stellan turned back to his friends. "She waits for me to come within range of her magick--and probably a legion of Father's finest soldiers."

"So what you're saying is we now have *twice* the problem we originally believed?"

Stellan nodded. "It's a great day for death, hmm?"

Neither of his companions responded. Another stone crashed into the castle wall next to them, shattering the silence.

Lionel leaned over the parapet. "Honestly, Edward, do you *mind?*" He tossed back his hair and turned to his companions. "Well, should we plan a preemptive attack or wait them out?"

Stellan frowned. "We're so few in number. I--"

"Stellan, look there!" Hunter pointed to the far edge of the battlefield.

Stellan exhaled sharply. Hundreds of misshapen Pestilence victims poured out onto the snow-covered land. Their number continued to swell. Behind them came the rank and file of his father's army.

"Surrender now, warlock, lest you suffer the same fate as the dead man you so gauchely dragged into the King's court!" Edward continued his harangue, unaware of the advancing horde.

"Edward," yelled Lionel. "Listen to me! Listen to reason! Clarysa is here, safe within the castle. Stellan is innocent of your charges and only wishes to protect us!"

But his voice failed to carry over the sounds of battle. The trebuchet continued to launch projectiles.

Lionel snarled in frustration. "Edward, you blind fool, open your eyes and look behind you!"

But Lionel's words fell short of their mark. Stellan sucked in a breath. The Aldebaran soldiers were about to be slaughtered by the Pestilence ranks clambering toward them. They were so focused on Vandeborg that the other looming threat escaped their notice.

Stellan spun around. "They've grown tired of waiting. Follow me!"

He ran to the castle's great hall. There, he kicked open a massive chest, one decrepit with rust and age. The chest was filled to the brim with arrows, arrows with an unearthly greenish hue about their tips. He turned to Hunter. "Take these and dispense them among our men," he commanded. "Do it quickly!"

"But the Aldebaran forces are in the way!"

"It's a risk we'll have to take. The entire field will lay thick with Aldebaran dead in a matter of minutes if we don't reach them in time!"

* * * *

Stellan led a charge of armed riders from the castle gate as the mob of attackers ran like slavering trolls toward the Aldebaran troops. Some came galloping on all fours and hissed like fiends; others ran with outstretched arms as rotten flesh swayed from their bodies. The advancing ghouls carried no weapons, but their pernicious blood was deadly enough.

"Don't touch them!" Stellan shouted. "Aim for the head but do not allow direct contact with your person!"

Edward turned, scowling, at the sound of Stellan's voice. Stellan and his men released a cloud of arrows from taut strings. Edward's expression lapsed into one of dread. Before Edward could rally his troops, the arrows rained down in sheets upon the Pestilence infected, crippling them into a writhing mass on the ground. Bloodcurdling cries pierced the air as the malformed creatures dropped in heaps, vomiting forth a sickening combination of blood and bile.

Stellan allowed himself a brief feeling of satisfaction at Edward's look of surprise.

He continued his assault against the Pestilence attackers. The once snow-white field now flowed a deep red, filled with the unholy sights and sounds of battle. The opposing armies met, and many a limb was hewn from its body. More arrows pierced the infected. But while many of the mutants fell, twice that appeared to spill forth from the forests.

"Reload and unleash!" shouted Stellan. Attracted by the sound, an emaciated, skinless Pestilence victim bounded toward him. He leaped into the air, a spindly projectile of bones and sinew. Stellan shot an arrow straight into the creature's eye socket. The attacker twisted about in midair for a few moments before dropping to the ground.

Again and again the embattled soldiers of Vandeborg fired upon the invaders as their replacements boiled over from the stygian forest. Stellan frowned as he assessed how outmatched they were. *We must prevail or the Five Lands will perish!*

The sky darkened. Stellan tensed, searching the field of combat for the cause. The hairs on the back of his neck rose as the new threat revealed itself.

Across from him on the field, a woman appeared, a haunting beauty dressed in a flowing gown of black and purple.

Sada!

Stellan narrowed his eyes. He wasn't surprised to learn she had survived Patrulha's final attack. There were plenty of ways for practitioners of the Dark Arts to outmaneuver Fate, depending on the price one was willing to pay.

Sada calmly drew closer amid the chaos. Her eyes were naught but black, her countenance, one of pure corruption. The battling troops parted in fear as she glided across the bloody battlefield.

"Prince Stellan of Vandeborg, hear me." she announced. "We pleaded with you to join our righteous cause, but you rebuked us. We ordered you to cease your aimless crusade, yet you defied us. I even offered you protection in a bestial form, but you have summarily rejected my strategy. Well, no more. We cannot allow these traitorous actions to continue. For your treachery, King Renaudas, the true sovereign of the Five Lands, has commanded your death. This is a sentence I am only too happy to deliver."

Led by Lionel, a sea of his men formed a protective ring, but Stellan ordered them back. Over Lionel's protests, he dismounted and approached his sister. He picked up an ominous change in her, as though a malicious entity shared her soul. "Sada, what have you done?"

Hideous laughter tore through the air, a harpy's cry mixed with thunder. "She who was once blind has been granted sight, brother, and power to command forces far beyond your comprehension!"

An unearthly glow formed about her. It grew brighter and brighter, a thousand times more intense than the burning sun above. An acrid smell filled the winds whirling about her. Then her impossibly high-pitched scream sent a great rain of fire streaming toward everything in its path.

The attack leveled scores of soldiers and Pestilence alike. Chaos reigned with weapons of smoke and fire.

Stellan glanced up to see a huge bolt descending upon him. A hard force knocked him aside. He fell fast, his cheek slamming into the slush-covered ground. The bolt hit the ground where he'd been standing only moments before. Static discharge crackled about him, but he was safe.

He felt a tug, a pull of magick. Turning his head, he discovered why. Sada stood within a large perimeter of melted snow. Her eyes were closed, her hands outstretched. Stellan sensed the momentum as she harnessed waves of invisible power from dimensions unknown.

How much time did he have for a counterattack? Cursing, he scrambled to his feet. Then he paused, shocked at the sight on the ground before him.

A scorched and dazed Lionel lay sprawled upon the ground. His hair and clothes were badly singed. Burn marks covered his exposed skin. Blood poured from myriad wounds.

"No!" An avalanche of distress hit him upon seeing Lionel's paralyzed form. With Hunter's help, Stellan snapped Lionel up on his horse and rode back to the castle. He yelled for the portcullis to be raised.

Lionel lifted his head and groaned, blood seeping from the corners of his mouth. "Oh, dear," he said, glancing down, "how inconvenient. This shirt is barely a fortnight old."

"Let's get you inside," Stellan told the cavalier Duke. As he rushed inside, his temples began to ache. Then he grimaced, for Sada's malignant laughter echoed mercilessly inside his head.

Chapter 39

The number of wounded soldiers escalated as Vandeborg Castle filled with the dread air of inevitability. The battle was not going well. Clarysa saw it in everyone's faces. She heard it in the men's frequent groans of pain.

She rushed to Gretchen's side with more makeshift bandages. They were strips of cloth soaked in a healing potion of Stellan's creation. Her glance fell on their patient, one young Aldebaran man, probably no more than seventeen at best. He had come in from the battle unable to feel his extremities. His chest was a sickening ripple of blackened soot, scorched by some unknown devilry.

Clarysa had soothed his wounds using cold water, which her patient then chased with several gulps of wine to numb the pain. She had asked him his name. "James, my lady," he had replied. He shared that before joining the King's army, he had worked with his father in the royal orchards, planting peach and apple trees.

Clarysa stared at him. His mouth lay open, his eyes opaque--and now he was dead. Peaches and apples. His father was so proud of the large, bountiful trees, he had said. Those were the last words his youthful frame would ever speak.

"Hurry, Clarysa. We need them now!"

Clarysa broke from her reverie to see Gretchen urgently beckoning her. She navigated the sea of broken bodies and ran forward, arms still filled with the dripping strips of cloth. Gretchen seized the material as well as Clarysa's right hand.

"Press down right here," she said.

Clarysa held her hand against a wailing soldier's side. It sank far deeper into the body than should have been possible.

"Keep the pressure on it. I'll be right back."

Blood oozed between Clarysa's fingers as the gypsy woman scooped a handful of healing flora from an earthenware pot. "Take your hand away, now." The man screamed in agony as Gretchen applied the herbs and several healing rags to impede the blood loss.

Clarysa stared aghast at the overflowing river of pain coursing through the great hall. *What dark sorcery are they defiling us with?* How much longer would Stellan and his men be able to hold out against it?

A familiar voice cut through the din of moans and cries of misery.

"Gretchen! Clear a table! We're going to need bandages and as much Hays Moss as we have," Stellan shouted.

Clarysa whipped around. Stellan burst through the archway carrying a prostrate form. Her brain registered a flash of blond hair along with a broken body draped in royal Aldebaran attire. She swayed in shock as recognition came.

"Lionel!" she cried.

"Move aside! Make a spot…yes, right there." Stellan laid Lionel down upon a table. Gretchen arrived bearing an armful of bandages. Stellan ripped apart Lionel's shredded clothing and worked furiously to staunch the flow of blood, which, sadly, seemed to be everywhere.

Clarysa rushed up and laid a hand on Lionel's cheek.

"Out of the way!" Stellan said, roughly pushing her aside. "No, wait," he reconsidered, grabbing her arm. He pointed to a nearby shelf with a blood-soaked hand. "See that large brown bottle? Bring it to me."

Clarysa nodded, eager to be of any help whatsoever. Clutching the bottle carefully, she brought it over. Gretchen and the prince worked diligently to slow the bleeding. Stellan injected Lionel with some of the liquid from the bottle. Gretchen threaded a wicked looking needle and began to stitch a wide, grisly gash in his side. Lionel's face paled. He gritted his teeth as the sutures entered and stretched his skin.

"Can't we give him something for the pain?" Clarysa asked.

"No time," Gretchen said.

"This might help." Stellan held a rag soaked with some kind of liquid against Lionel's nose and mouth. In a few minutes, he drifted into a state of unconsciousness.

Blinking back tears, Clarysa covered Lionel's burns in specially treated bandages. After the task was complete, she wiped his perspiring forehead with a cloth. She tried to avoid dwelling on the weak rise and fall of her cousin's chest.

Gretchen finished her stitching. She and Stellan joined Clarysa. All three watched over the Duke. The battle outside was momentarily forgotten.

"What happened?" Clarysa whispered.

Stellan's brow furrowed. "He saved my life."

"I'm sure he was glad of the opportunity to help you." Clarysa stroked Lionel's cheek. She wanted to be hopeful, but her cousin's injuries seemed grave. Tears spilled down her cheeks as she looked pleadingly at Stellan. "Is he going to…"

"I've done everything I can," he said, his expression grim. "Now he needs rest."

An angry voice cut through the air. "Where is Duke Lionel? I demand to see him!"

Clarysa sucked in a breath. *Edward!* To her right, Stellan made a discrete fist. She suppressed a groan. *Don't make a scene, Edward, not now!*

Her brother spotted her. His expression locked in a dirt-streaked scowl, he advanced.

Stellan bristled at Edward's approach. She laid a cautionary hand upon the Dark Prince's arm.

Edward pushed his way into their midst. After one glance at Lionel, he locked his angry gaze upon Stellan. Clarysa winced at the tension rising between them.

"Don't start with me," Stellan growled.

"I saw you put that cloth to his face. What have you done to him?" Edward pushed Stellan away.

Clarysa gasped. "Edward! You're being hasty!"

As Edward bent to inspect his unconscious cousin, Stellan grabbed his arms and shoved him against a nearby table. Edward drew back a fist, but Stellan leaped upon him before he could swing. The two men struggled against each other, rattling the table and overturning supplies. A glass bottle shattered against the stone floor.

Stellan pressed his forearm against Edward's throat. "I'm trying to save his life, as he did mine. Stop interfering or I'll throw you out of my castle!"

"It's true, Edward," Clarysa shouted. "Listen to him, *please!*"

Panting, Edward cut her a look. Then he took a deep breath. "My apologies. I was concerned for Lionel and spoke prematurely."

Stellan released him.

Edward neared the table. He looked remorseful as he studied Lionel's face. "Is he…"

Stellan shook his head. "Thankfully, not yet. But he needs rest. *Peaceful* rest."

Edward nodded. "I was…wrong. I shouldn't have mistrusted you. At any time." He leveled a gaze at Stellan. "Lionel's always been an excellent judge of character, but my stubbornness prevented me from recognizing the truth." His expression became one of determination. "I want to help you win this battle. Tell me what to do."

Stellan nodded. "Concentrate your men on Pestilence and the remaining enemy soldiers. I'll deal with the sorceress myself."

Clarysa bit her lip. Would her brother agree to the plan? He was accustomed to giving orders, not accepting them.

To her relief, Edward saluted him. After a quick nod to Clarysa, he left to carry out the orders.

She breathed a sigh of relief.

"Clarysa."

She looked up into Stellan's face. "Yes?"

"Find someone to help you move Lionel to my bedroom. Change his bandages as often as needed and keep him comfortable."

Clarysa nodded. "I'll take care of him. What are you going to do?"

Stellan clasped her hand and then turned sharply on a heel. He spoke over his shoulder. "I'm going to finish this."

Clarysa watched him depart through a veil of tears. Behind her, Lionel lay on the brink of death. Before her, Stellan was heading into battle. It could very well be this cruelly brief reunion would be the last time she ever saw either one of them alive.

Chapter 40

Stellan left the hall of wounded, his heart racing. He had to defeat Sada. She was now controlling Pestilence through unknown magickal means--no doubt a gift from their father. As for her newfound strength, Stellan could only guess what terrible door she had opened to acquire it. He smacked a fist against the wall. *I'm coming for you, bitch! One way or another, it ends now!*

He tore down to the depths of his workroom. He grabbed bottles left and right. Regarding them on the battered wooden table, he frowned. None of these would do; none were powerful enough. But what else could he use? He didn't have Sada's training or resources.

His gaze drifted to the topmost shelf. The stranger's gift still lay there, pulsing away as usual. The gift had nearly stolen his mind after he had dared to use its terrible power once before.

It's the only way, he thought. *Sada cannot succeed no matter what price I may pay.*

He shoved a chair against the shelves and used it as an ersatz ladder. Up he went and reached into the darkness--a darkness broken only by the awful grayish-white glow.

* * * *

Stellan stepped forth onto the bloody battlefield.

Before him, the remaining soldiers of Aldebaran were stretching the limits of their abilities to hold the forces of Pestilence at bay. They fared poorly. Several of the men had become infected themselves and had turned on their comrades within minutes. Edward never stopped fighting, never stopped issuing orders, but he now led a troop that was rapidly shrinking in number.

Sada stood apart from the chaos, her mad features glowing with satisfaction--or insanity? "So good of you to join us again," she said, projecting her voice with ease.

Stellan ignored her taunt. He set aside the sack he'd brought and drew a sword. The gleaming white hilt contrasted sharply with the black-as-pitch blade. He pointed the weapon toward his twin. "It ends now, Sada. It ends for fallen friends, for my beloved, and for Mother." He punctuated each word with a thrust of the sword. "It. Ends. Now!"

His breathing was steady, even, his concentration utmost. He angled the sword back over his head. The blade glowed white-hot. Stellan's entire frame shook as he channeled his magick. Perspiration ran in torrents down his face.

With a loud grunt, he aimed the sword toward Sada. The sword tip launched the luminous form of an ethereal woman, growing steadily in both size and power. She was transparent and beautiful, yet deadly in scope. She swept over the ranks of Pestilence, causing each to burst into flame.

But Sada had other plans. Her obsidian eyes flashed. The form of a ghostly wolf sprang from her body. This magickal familiar also grew in breadth and power until it reached the size of Stellan's.

They clashed above the battlefield. The "wolf" tore at the throat of the "woman," as strands of her long hair whipped around and attempted to strangle her opponent. Electricity ripped through the air, only for both forms to dissolve into nothingness--an effectual stalemate.

Stellan collapsed to the ground, mentally and physically drained. He had never attempted to manifest anything that size and scope before, and it had left him nearly depleted.

A broad smile stretched across Sada's face. Stellan cursed. She seemed able to recover much faster.

She extended her arms high above her head. Particles of light formed and swirled about her lithe frame, concentrating on her hands as its epicenter. Something there began to take shape. She conjured forth a small black-and-purple butterfly. Its diaphanous wings beat softly as it poised upon her index finger.

Sada's smile grew, radiant and warm. But Stellan knew the apparent sentiment was far, far from the truth.

Sada leaned forward and gently blew the gossamer creature forward with a kiss. It took to the air, flapping its wings as it grew larger and larger, finally reaching gargantuan proportions.

Stellan steeled himself. This was no simple sisterly kiss being blown his way. The lethal manifestation flapped through the air. As it neared, its head took on the appearance of the skull of Death.

He held his magickal sword out before him. The creature's earsplitting shriek assailed his ears. Stellan slashed away as the butterfly's mammoth wings enveloped him. He punctured one wing, then sought another opening. A second shriek sent a wave of agony through his head. He felt like tearing off his ears to make it stop.

Six powerful legs ripped into his flesh. Lavender flames engulfed his body. Stellan clenched his teeth against the stinging pain. He struggled to lift his sword, but two of the legs pinned his arms to his sides.

Hunter Red ran forward and attacked the butterfly with his sword, but to no effect. The mortal weapon passed right through the manifestation. The creature unfurled its proboscis and plunged the tip into Stellan's neck. It was feeding its ravenous appetite by draining his life force. Weakness forced him to his knees. He was dying right there on the battlefield, and his mocking sister knew it.

One hope remained. Hunter Red had seen his share of otherworldly spectacles. If only Stellan could guide him...

"Hunter, my sword. Take my sword!" Stellan had felt his lips move, but had he spoken loudly enough? Something was wrong with his hearing. He spoke again. Damn it! Were the words even leaving his mouth?

The butterfly glowed ever brighter as it absorbed his life force. Stellan could barely keep his eyes open.

Hunter threw down his useless sword and snatched Stellan's blade from his hand. The blade vibrated with power as Hunter hacked away.

The weapon easily sliced through the creature's body and wings. Rent beyond repair, its shredded pieces blew away into the wind. Bloody and decimated, Stellan crumpled to the ground.

As he fell, Sada held a hand to her head. Did he dare hope she had exhausted her powers? But no--she was already glowering in his direction. He didn't have much time.

Hunter stood over him, his brow wrinkled with concern. Stellan looked up at him, unable to move. The odds were terrible and both men knew it. Sada possessed more power than he'd thought possible. His own skills lay rusty in their crypt--years of inaction and lack of knowledge were the cause. Now he would pay dearly for his oversight, and his friends would pay right along with him.

He needed an army, but he had none--save for a loyal bunch of misfit paupers. Aldebaran's soldiers had acted valiantly, but they were poorly matched against the sheer number and power of Pestilence. Reinforcements at this point were unlikely. No, it was up to him and him alone--and he had failed.

Outmatched.

Outclassed.

Near death.

Hunter's lips moved but he couldn't hear what the man was saying. The butterfly's scream had knocked out his hearing. Was this condition temporary or permanent? It was impossible to say. An icy sensation crept into his bones. Darkness licked at the edges of his vision.

Stand up! Instead of his limbs cooperating, his life appeared before him in brief, melancholic flashes. He had wasted years retreating from the world; he understood that now. The safety of his isolated kingdom wasn't real. He had tried to convince himself that he didn't care or need anyone else, when in fact the opposite was true. Clarysa had shown him another path, where emotional risk taking would be rewarded, and in plenty. To retreat into death now would only be a sign he didn't trust her, didn't need her.

But he did. He *loved* her. He would move kingdoms for her. And there could be no safe place for her in the entire Five Lands if his father's mad scheme succeeded. Stellan could not--would not--die today.

Again the determined thought came--*this ends now.*

He clawed his way back from oblivion. The darkness receded. His clouded mind began to clear. Stellan rolled to his side, then maneuvered himself onto his knees. With a final heave, he rose to his full height.

One singular idea drove him. There was a final manifestation he could attempt. Though extremely dangerous, he had no other choice.

The Gift.

The gift bestowed upon him so long ago by the cowled man in the depths of Dungeon Forest. The gift that had almost destroyed his mind. But even if it succeeded this time, at least he could take Sada with him to a place of dark destruction where neither could escape.

The choice was made.

The winds whipped the snow into a frenzy about him. Stellan the Dark Prince of Vandeborg was now Stellan the Death-Bringer, defying even the gods' mighty will.

He reached into his sack and withdrew the large jar that had sat hidden in his workroom for so many years, a jar he'd never thought he would dare to open again. The outer surface pulsed, hinting at the terrible power it contained. With a deep breath, he threw the jar high into the air. The shimmering contents began to rain down about him. The power filled Stellan to the point of bursting. Sound surged back into his ears. Blood pounded in his veins.

The sky darkened. A swirling maelstrom of eldritch power shot forth and engulfed him, taking the form of brilliant shards of light. Stellan concentrated on a single vision: eradication of Pestilence.

Magickal energy waves radiated outward from him. They passed through everything and everyone on the battlefield--including Sada--but nothing happened.

Stellan clenched his fists. Nothing had come of the spectacular display. Nothing!

Sada smiled at him coldly from across the battlefield. Perplexed, Stellan remained frozen in his position, particles of light still swirling about him. Had the jar's contents been meant for a single use? If so, the stakes had now reached unfathomable proportions.

The remaining Pestilence army renewed its attack. Indecision tore at him. Should he engage Sada in physical combat or join the fight against Pestilence?

He was about to opt for the latter when the first cracks appeared in the earth. Small ones initially, but they lengthened quickly. Stellan cast a furious look at his sister. What terrible magick was she wreaking now? He had run out of options, short of strangling her.

But Sada's gaze was rooted to a crack on the field between them. There, a skeletal hand pushed its way up through the broken soil and grasped the leg of an advancing Pestilence-infected.

Similar developments began to happen everywhere. All across the battlefield, pockets of snow collapsed in on themselves as long-buried corpses scraped their way to the surface. They surged onto the battlefield like waves upon an ocean shore. From the skeletons of royalty to peasants to mummified soldiers, bodies in various stages of decomposition arose from the depths of the earth.

The dead walked.

Once free of the confining ground, the corpses advanced. With methodical vengeance, they ripped limb from limb. They targeted both the slaves of Pestilence as well as Sada's soldiers. The army of the dead was unstoppable. The fortunes of battle had turned against his twin, but at what terrible cost?

He had called upon their power once before. As an exiled youth driven by anger and grief, he'd used this magick to call forth the undead. He'd fancied creating a castle full of servants. He'd treated them like puppets, putting them through the motions of running a kingdom.

Then he'd decided he required an army to march to the Wastes and reclaim what was rightfully his. But being so immature, with his magickal talents vastly underdeveloped, he hadn't known how to control them. Instead, the power began to overwhelm him. Only the fear of being killed by his own undead minions had prompted him to redirect the magickal force back into the jar. The experience had left Stellan with a deranged mind and a castle full of rotten, frozen corpses.

Even now, he struggled to maintain control. His temples throbbed as he forced the corpses onward. Sharp stabs of pain threatened to split open his skull. He was a conduit for the magick's power, whatever its otherworldly source. He had to maintain his stance or risk breaking the incantation. But the effort was quickly draining his energy. The living-dead army wielded astonishing strength, but the Pestilence victims were more elusive than humans and harder to kill. If he continued for much longer, it might not be his mind that succumbed to the pressure, but his heart.

Stellan heard a familiar cry behind him. He turned to look. It was Gretchen. Her face pale and hair all askew, the gypsy woman kneeled in the snow. She was calling his name and pointing behind her.

Stellan followed the line of her finger. What he saw struck him with the force of a thousand blows. *What have I done?*

Patrulha.

She marched onto the battlefield. She wore her usual battle gear, her short green cape fluttering. Strands of unkempt hair obscured her face. Stellan stared as she approached. The sights and sounds of battle faded away as he absorbed this harrowing event.

How can it be? Was she still alive, or an illusion? Against all logic, hope flared in his heart. As she reached a spot a few feet from his position, he forced his lips apart. "Patrulha!"

She stopped and then stiffly turned her head to gaze at him.

Stellan recoiled, for she stared back with eyes unseeing. One was a bloody crater, the other was still hidden by her patch. Her skin looked ashen, ten times more so than when she was alive. She hovered at the fragile juncture between the living and the dead.

His invocation must have summoned her. Stellan frowned. He hadn't meant for Gretchen to see her daughter in such a macabre state. Or for Patrulha to become a pawn in his conflict with Sada. Her appearance gave him pause. What gave him the right to command the dead, anyway? Like a fool, he hadn't even questioned the matter.

The act reeked of something his father would do--or manipulate Stellan into doing. He sucked in a breath as a new suspicion arose. The cowled man in Dungeon Forest had probably been Renaudas. Stirring up the hostilities between his children would play right into his hands. Knowing Sada's abilities, he had ensured his son could compete with her. *Bastard!* Stellan made a fist. He should have anticipated this very situation. But in his haste he hadn't considered the possibility. Well, at least he was aware of the deception and could make less harmful choices. He would find another way to defeat Sada.

But first he had to figure out what to do about Patrulha. He swallowed hard, seeking the right words to address her. "What is your purpose here?"

Patrulha stalked forward. The rank odor of her decaying flesh flooded Stellan's nostrils as she neared. She closed the distance between them. Now they stood only a handbreadth apart.

Snow flecked Patrulha's hair and skin. She cupped the back of his neck, her touch ice cold even through her glove. Stellan braced himself as he gazed into her ravaged eye socket.

She stood still, and for a moment it was just the two of them. Memories flooded through him. He remembered the wariness with which they had first greeted each other after her family appeared out of the storm and landed on his doorstep. He remembered the training days with her father, the friendly competitions, the arguments, their travels, and the laughter, rare though it had been.

"Why are you here?" he whispered. Then he realized she probably couldn't speak. He opened his mind to her, acting on pure instinct.

And then it hit him. The force of Patrulha's memories punched through skin, bone and flesh to pierce the deepest core of his mind. Stellan gritted his teeth as her spirit filled him.

Her memories flashed by, many of them similar to his. The difference, however, was seeing himself through her eyes. The discovery was almost too much to bear, but he kept the link open. Stellan had never known the depth of Patrulha's capacity for tenderness and love. The experience left him humbled.

The perspective shifted. This time, Stellan felt Patrulha project a strong image of Clarysa. Then of Stellan and Clarysa together. As the picture filled his mind, emotions followed. Happiness. Loyalty. A fierce desire to protect them both.

Patrulha wanted to be their champion. "Are you sure?"

She didn't speak, but the hand about his neck tightened. Stellan was touched beyond words. His eyes burned hard with unshed tears.

Patrulha released her hand. She turned away from him. Toward Sada. With smooth precision, she drew her sword.

Stellan reached out an arm, desperate to keep her with him for a moment longer even in her undead state. "Patrulha, wait! You don't have to do this. I'll release you from the enchantment."

"Let her go, Stellan."

He looked to his right. Gretchen stood beside him, wrapped in a brown shawl. Her expression hollow, she stared after Patrulha with red-rimmed eyes. "You know as well as I that Patrulha is choosing this path. Dead or alive, her will remains her own."

Stellan nodded as understanding dawned. Only one force in the known world could overcome magick.

True love.

A shudder passed through him. Perhaps Patrulha wasn't being controlled by the jar's magick after all.

Gretchen pressed a hand to her heart as tears spilled from her eyes. "Farewell, dearest daughter," she said hoarsely. "May the gods of fortune enrich your soul for eternity."

Stellan considered Gretchen's words as an ache bloomed in his chest. Despite the horror of seeing Patrulha rise from the dead, she'd given the two of them her blessing. Gretchen was right. Patrulha was a warrior to the end--and beyond. She had shared as much during their mind link. Could he deny her the defining battle of her life?

"Patrulha, I..." Stellan clenched his teeth. No words could express the mixture of grief and gratitude surging through him like wildfire. "Thank you for this, sister. I'll never, ever forget you."

In response, Patrulha raised her enchanted sword with both hands, raised high to shoulder height. Then she began to run.

Ploddingly at first, for as a corpse her limbs still creaked with stiffness. Exhausted though he was, Stellan redoubled his concentration. He drew magickal power from every fiber of his body. As a result, Patrulha's speed increased as she headed straight for Sada.

Faster and faster she ran. Her feet became a blur as she practically glided across the snow. Shimmering with an iridescent glow, her spirit transcended her earthly form, expanding to over five times her normal size. Anything or anyone in her path was knocked to the side.

Almost there, thought Stellan. Sweat poured from his shaking limbs. *I've got to keep it going!*

Patrulha reached Sada's position. The dead warrior lifted her sword for a final attack.

Sada's last remaining knights rallied to protect her. Her stance indicated she was already initiating a counterspell. She raised a hand, one sparkling with blue fire.

Patrulha struck her with the force of a hurricane. Her sword arm arced in a swift, deadly maneuver, leaving a colorful rainbow in its wake. Electricity crackled and rent the air with a deafening tearing sound. Smoke exploded from the spot, obscuring the actual contact. Stellan dared not break his concentration yet, but looked with narrowed eyes to discern if Sada had been hit.

Nothing could be seen, save smoke and fire.

A bright flash mushroomed into the air. After several moments, the smoke began to dissipate.

All around Stellan, the corpses besieged what remained of the Pestilence army. Upon defeating the last mutant, they sank back into the earth.

Stellan collapsed, the white world before him growing black. The cold, hard embrace of Death rushed toward him.

Then there was only silence.

Chapter 41

As the fourth hour past midnight approached, Clarysa lugged her tenth bucket of water to the throne room. Sleep had eluded her the past two days, so while Stellan and Lionel lay unconscious in their respective rooms, she had dedicated herself to cleaning. Given the sacrifices so many others had made, it was the least she could do.

At the arched entrance, her arms trembled with the effort of holding the bucket. She set it down and paused to rest. The great hall contained four long rows of gravely injured soldiers. They lay on thin pallets and mounds of sheet-covered hay. Scores of candles lit the area and fires burned in all the grates. The air felt warm but stuffy. Pungent scents of medicinal ointments mixed with the odors of blood and unwashed bodies.

After the battle, Edward had sent for the top Aldebaran healers. While the women in red robes attended to the patients, Clarysa, Gretchen and a handful of uninjured soldiers cleaned the floors, clothes and bedding.

Clarysa had been shocked at the amount of blood and bits of human flesh she'd encountered, but braced herself nonetheless. It wouldn't do for Stellan to awake and discover his castle in shambles. So she had set to work.

She picked up her bucket and resumed her trek across the chamber. One last corner remained. Some of the patients were awake, talking quietly. Clarysa nodded and smiled to those she passed, trying not to flinch upon witnessing truncated limbs, swollen faces, and bruised skin.

She placed the bucket down and retrieved a worn brush from a cavernous skirt pocket. Gretchen had somehow found the time to adjust one of her skirts for Clarysa to wear during the cleaning phase. The baggy shirt she wore belonged to Ghyslain. But Stellan's family shared freely, no matter how little they possessed. It was simply their way.

Clarysa poured a splash of water onto the floor and began to scrub away dirt and stains of blood. Her sisters would probably faint at the sight of her laboring like a servant, but Clarysa welcomed the distraction. Keeping busy had helped her cope with the aftermath of the battle. And she wanted Stellan to know she considered no task beneath her. She would help him rebuild Vandeborg Castle until her hands fell off, if necessary. Tears rolled down her cheeks. He'd been unconscious for so long. Would she ever have a chance to tell him?

Clarysa scrubbed harder--and then harder still. As soon as she finished, she would check on Lionel and Stellan.

The hall was quiet save for her scrubbing. A half hour later, Hunter Red appeared, arms full of clean rags. No doubt Gretchen was responsible for his timely intervention. He helped Clarysa mop up the remaining grime.

Cleaning the rags in boiling water and hanging them up to dry in the kitchen stole away another hour. Needing respite, Clarysa quenched her thirst with a mug of icy water. Gretchen insisted she eat a thick slice of hot, buttered toast slathered with apricot jam. Clarysa knew better than to refuse her.

As soon as she swallowed the last bite, she rose. *I'd best check on Lionel now.* Her cousin's room was closer, so it made sense to go there first. Clarysa wrapped a shawl around her shoulders and left the kitchen. The trek through the corridor was as cold as ever. She shivered and quickened her step. At least Lionel's room would be warm.

Several yards ahead, soft amber light spilled through the partially open door. Clarysa eyed it with appreciation and hurried forward.

She slipped through the opening and closed it behind her. "Good morning, Lionel," she said softly, though she didn't expect a reply. Then she froze.

Lionel was not in his bed. Clarysa whipped her gaze around the room. In fact, he was nowhere to be seen at all.

Sheets covered the bed haphazardly, even trailing onto the floor. Sharp dread constricted her heart. The scene looked as though Lionel's body had been dragged from the bed. Which could only mean--

Her ragged sob pierced the air. Clarysa had trouble drawing her next breath. Her knees wobbled and she stumbled on her way to the bed. Kneeling before it, she fisted the sheets. They felt cold to the touch.

"Oh no. Oh no, oh no." It was horrible. *Unimaginable.* How could Lionel have died so suddenly? And why had no one told her? Or perhaps they were looking for her now. She should leave the room, find the person who had the unwelcome task of delivering the bitter news. But her grief paralyzed her. She couldn't move, couldn't think, couldn't speak. The Duke of Belleressort--dead. Was this the kind of macabre sacrifice true love demanded? Now she regretted having involved Lionel in her mad schemes. *Oh, my darling cousin, can you ever forgive me?*

Clarysa felt too numb even to cry. A nightmarish thought came--what if death befell Stellan as well?

An urge to be with him took over her body. Clarysa pushed herself to her feet. As she rose, she detected voices coming down the corridor. Two men were talking. Their footsteps slowed and she speculated they were heading toward the chamber in which she stood. Clarysa shut her eyes, as if blindness could stave off the next moment in time.

The door flew open. "And at the risk of sounding vain--which I admit is already a lost cause--if you could please send for my tailor. Keeping up appearances is important if we are too-- Clarysa! What are you doing up at this late hour?"

At the sound of her name, she opened her eyes. Ghyslain stood in the doorway, a concerned expression on his face.

A man stood next to him, dressed in a plain linen shirt and dark breeches.

Lionel.

Alive.

"My dear cousin, are you all right? You've gone dastardly pale." Lionel rushed forward.

Clarysa clutched his hand as he eased her into a sitting position on the bed. Her breath came in short, rapid gasps.

"Easy, now. It's all right. I'm here." Lionel glanced up. "My good man, would you kindly fetch her some water or tea?"

Ghyslain nodded and sprinted away.

Clarysa leaned hard against her cousin's chest as he draped his free arm across her shoulders. "I thought you were dead!" she cried. "I couldn't bear it!" She held his hand between hers, digging into his flesh for the reassurance it provided. Her flood of tears quickly soaked the front of his shirt.

"Clarysa, I didn't mean for you to enter and find me gone--I'm sorry to have frightened you so." His hold upon her shoulders tightened. "Stellan's medicine worked wonders. I awoke refreshed and with little pain."

"I'm so relieved," she whispered. "But where had you gone?"

"Ghyslain came by soon after I awoke. I insisted he take me to Stellan." Lionel's voice caught. "I can't believe the state he's in. Are you sure the healers have done all they can?"

Clarysa nodded. "They say we must wait, and be strong."

Ghyslain entered the room, bearing a tray filled with a pot of tea, mugs, bread, bowls of jam and dried meat. He set it down on a nearby table. "Tea for the Lady and Mum said you should have a bite or three to regain your strength, sir."

Lionel kissed her forehead. "Come join me. We're no use to Stellan if we starve to death."

Clarysa nodded. She joined Lionel at the table. Ghyslain served them despite her protestations, hovering like a mother hen. She sipped sparingly at her tea, her stomach in knots.

Lionel pestered her and Ghyslain with questions. He wanted to know every minute detail of the final battle. Clarysa let Ghyslain do most of the talking.

Halfway through Ghyslain's second recount of Patrulha's heroics, Clarysa heard a murmuring in the corridor. And it wasn't the sound of a wailing ghost. She sat up straighter. "Hush! Did you hear that?"

"Hear what?" Ghsylain asked.

"That sound. Listen."

She strained her ears. The muffled sound came again. A voice. Clarysa shot Lionel a look.

"Hurry," Lionel told her. "He might be in pain. Go to him!"

Her heart pounding, Clarysa raced from the room.

Chapter 42

Stellan awoke to the sound of a fire crackling. Turning, he saw a hearty fire burning in the hearth. Where was he? His bleary gaze registered only stone walls and shadows.

He tried to stand, but discovered his muscles lacked the required strength. Collapsing back, he rubbed his eyes. The sound of muffled voices drifted through the walls, which meant they were close.

"A-any…" The words caught in his dry, raw throat, but he forced them out regardless. "A-anyone…there?" He repeated his question two more times.

The clopping of running feet down the passageway was his answer. Clarysa burst into the room. A relieved expression lit up her face as her gaze met his. "Oh, thank heavens!" She ran forward and threw herself against him.

Stellan groaned in pain as she made contact, but he welcomed the feeling. It meant he was alive. Gazing into Clarysa's shining eyes, he gently stroked her hair back from her face. Her cheeks were smudged with dirt and she was dressed in rags, but she was still the most beautiful sight he'd ever seen. "What happened? Is everyone--"

Clarysa put her hand to his mouth. "Shhh. It's over. Sada…is no more. The Pestilence army is gone." Tears flowed down her cheeks. "It's over, it's truly over."

Stellan leaned back against the pillow. He wanted to believe those words, but they were premature. News of this battle would inevitably reach his father. But by defeating Sada, he'd created a significant dent in his father's plans. In time, he'd find a way to stop the threat for good.

He would cross that bridge later. Right now, he just wanted to drink in the moment of being alive and reunited with his one true love. "How long have I lain here?"

Clarysa wiped at her tears, and then held up five swollen fingers.

"Five hours?" But then why did he feel so exhausted?

Clarysa shook her head. "Not five hours, dearest, five *days*!"

Stellan was speechless, unable to fully absorb this information. He didn't try. Instead, he grasped her hand. "What's wrong with your fingers? Are they injured?"

Clarysa shook her head. "I've been helping with cleanup while the healers attended to the injured."

Stellan swallowed hard. Lionel! It all came back to him. Her cousin, his friend, now savagely injured. "How is Lionel?" Stellan asked, fearing the worst.

"He pulled through. And now you have as well--oh, I'm so happy you're both alive!" She leaned forward and soundly kissed his cheek.

Stellan relished the feel of her warm lips, but a wave of guilt chased it away all too quickly. "Clarysa, I apologize deeply about Lionel's ordeal, and everything you've suffered as a result." He paused to gather his thoughts. "If the recent events have been too stressful and you want to return home to the safety of your father's palace--well, I understand. You deserve so much better than a life of pain and grief." He gritted his teeth, bracing for her response.

Clarysa grasped his shoulders. Her fresh tears reflected the flickering of a nearby torch. "What are you saying? I *am* home!"

They gazed at each other, ignoring the sounds of footfalls and whispers as Lionel and Ghyslain peeked in to check on them. After they had gone, Clarysa stepped back and wiped her eyes. "You should eat something to regain your strength. I'll fetch you a meal from the kitchen."

"No." Stellan braced an arm against the bed frame. "I should move around. I'll come with you."

"If you're sure."

Leaning on her shoulder, he accompanied her to the kitchen. Gretchen was curled up on a chair before the roaring hearth, tucked beneath a colorful blanket and snoring.

Stellan sank his weary bones into a chair. Clarysa placed a bowl of steaming soup on the table before him. Hunger sparked fiercely in his gut, and he gulped the sustenance down as quickly. "Did you make this?" he asked.

Clarysa nodded.

He sighed. "I have reduced you to a common scullery maid." He grasped her hand tightly across the table. "But I'd like some more, please."

Clarysa smiled brightly at him, and the aches in his bones lessened. She served him again, and then thrice, and in that way, so passed the remainder of the night.

Chapter 43

Eight days after Stellan awoke, he, Clarysa, Lionel and Edward led a procession of their folk through the Snowflake Kingdom, past Dungeon Forest, and across the western border of Aldebaran. They brought with them the bodies of the deceased Aldebaran soldiers for burial.

Patrulha's remains had been recovered and now lay in a coffin deep under the snow beneath the great shadow of Vandeborg. A small, private funeral had been all he and Gretchen wanted. After a period of repair and cleanup, the survivors had turned to other matters.

Stellan had sent word ahead by messenger of their journey to Aldebaran, as well as to announce the coming nuptials. He and Clarysa wed in a morning ceremony under a canopy of cherry trees. Afterward, everyone celebrated the union as the bright sun shone overhead. The feasting and dancing lasted far into the afternoon.

Before Lionel returned to Belleressort, he took Stellan and Clarysa aside in a huddle. "Listen closely, because what I have to say is extremely important."

Stellan nodded solemnly. Clarysa stared at her cousin, an unreadable expression on her face.

Lionel's grip upon Stellan's shoulder tightened. "I want both of you to promise me something."

"Anything," Stellan responded.

Clarysa raised a delicate brow.

Lionel moistened his lips. "I want you to have many children, and you must promise to name at least three of them after me."

Lionel's earnest expression left Stellan dumbfounded. Was the request some kind of Aldebaran tradition? *What have I gotten myself into?*

Clarysa grinned and punched her cousin on the arm. "As full of yourself as ever, I see!"

Stellan chuckled. "Well played, my friend."

"Indeed. You should have seen the look on your face!"

As Lionel doubled over with laughter, Clarysa patted Stellan's back in a sympathetic fashion. "Welcome to the family."

* * * *

Clarysa had insisted that her and Stellan's first night together be spent at Vandeborg, so after a brief rest they prepared for the return journey. Servants packed several wagons' worth of goods and amenities, with more to be sent in the following days. As the couple made a final check, Stellan took note of the soldier guarding one of the wagons. He called Clarysa to his side.

"What's all this?" he asked, fingering the gold clasp of an ornate chest. Several more like it filled the wagon's interior.

"See for yourself." She withdrew a set of keys and opened one. It brimmed and sparkled with gold, jewels and all kinds of precious metals.

Stellan took a step back. "What is this? What's it for?"

Clarysa looked at him in amusement. "It's my dowry."

"What?"

She giggled. "Didn't you know?"

Stellan shook his head. "No. No, take it back. All of it." He shot her an anxious look. "I didn't marry you for your wealth. I'll not have them think that."

Clarysa smiled. "Stellan, it's all right! This is completely routine."

"But I can provide whatever you need. Make them take it back!"

"Here, now, listen." She bade him to sit on the wagon's edge so his face was level with hers. "Husband, let me make one point very clear." She kissed him, firmly and quite long, ignoring the attendants who tittered in the background.

After a minute or so, she paused to speak. "Stellan," she whispered, "you could be the wealthiest king in the Five Lands, and I'd still bring a dowry. It's tradition. Besides, even if you don't care about it for yourself, think about Gretchen. Think about Ghyslain and Froll and the others. They've sacrificed so much for you." She stroked his cheek. "Never again will they have to worry about where their next meal is coming from. Never again."

Stellan nodded, unsure of what to say. But even if he had known, his throat had choked up with a knot of eternal gratitude.

He and Clarysa departed. Their procession included Gretchen and her family and Stellan's modest entourage. The King and Queen, along with sundry attendants and citizens, waved farewell from the castle gate, but Edward rode with them as far as the border. Stellan thought he might actually learn to like this new Edward, less quick to judge and more humble. Along the way, they discussed plans for future visits and hunts. The journey passed by pleasantly under a blazing, late-summer sun. Song and laughter filled the air, as well as frequent prompts for the married couple to kiss. Stellan was more than happy to oblige.

A few miles from the peak of Eastender's Road, the party stopped to rest and eat in a verdant clearing scattered with birch trees and lichen. After the meal concluded, Edward bid them farewell and returned to Aldebaran. Stellan and Clarysa headed west, arriving at Vandeborg several hours later.

Once in the great hall, Stellan turned to his wife. "Close your eyes," he said.

She dutifully complied, and he led her up the wide central staircase. When he allowed her to see, she gasped, for the royal bedroom suite had been completely refurbished. The mahogany bed, now restored to its former glory, lay draped in swaths of rich red linen. Brightly colored pillows, throws and rugs accented the ornate furniture pieces scattered about the wide room.

Stellan built a fire in the hearth while Clarysa explored the room like mad. She squealed with joy upon discovering the myriad amenities of the washroom. Polished stones surrounded a large sunken tub. Stellan proudly demonstrated how to work the pipes. They were carved into a dragon's head motif and hot running water gushed out of them with the turn of a handle.

"Hot springs are under the castle," Stellan explained. "We discovered them during the renovation!"

Clarysa turned to him with arms outstretched. "It's incredible! You did all this work for me?"

He enfolded her with his cape, for the air would remain chilly until the fire's warmth spread. "I did it for us, if it pleases you, my beauty."

She stared up at him, eyes shining. "You've done nothing but please me," she whispered. "I love you, Stellan!"

"And I love you." Sighing contentedly, he kissed her. After a moment he pressed his lips to her ear. "I think we should try out the bath."

Clarysa's breathing quickened, resulting in a delicious tickle against his cheek. "You mean now?"

Stellan removed her cloak and shot her a wicked grin. "Yes, I do," he said, his gaze dipping southward as it drank in every one of her curves. He delivered another soft kiss before turning his attention to the bath. First he lit several thick, red candles, and then he manipulated the pipes until steaming water swirled into the basin below.

Satisfied, he turned around. Now it was Stellan's breath catching sharply in his throat, for Clarysa stood before him completely nude. She shivered, perhaps from the cold, perhaps from the desire glowing in her face. Her beauty overwhelmed him, especially as she didn't seem to know what to do with her hands. They fluttered like dainty hummingbirds against the hollow of her throat. Full lips parted with an urgent plea for him to hurry; the bath was ready.

Stellan realized with a start he'd been staring at her for quite some time. Blood rushed to his member, and primal urges--echoing from their tryst in the cave--coaxed it into a tight, thick erection. Finally, he could finish what he had started.

Crossing the short space between them, he set to work undressing. When had his clothes sprouted so many laces and knots? Clarysa smiled shyly while helping him to disrobe, and then, finally, they were skin to skin. Now she shivered steadily, clinging to him and feeling cold to the touch. He carried her into the tub. The water encased them in a warm embrace.

The liquid covered Clarysa up to her shoulders, teasing him. He could only see the faint outline of her body. In between fervent kisses they washed each other, sloughing away the dust from the journey using soft cloths and walnut-scented soap. Occasionally the hot water sloshed aside, revealing a tantalizing glimpse of a breast or knee. But underneath it was a different story. His hands learned the intimate language of her smooth back, dainty feet and the slight curve of her belly. Stellan could hardly believe his senses. How soft and supple was her skin!

Clarysa grabbed one of his hands and wrapped her lips around his forefinger. At the luxurious sensation, a memory flared--recollection of the time when he had fed her a piece of that roll before the curious eyes of his men. As she sucked his finger with slow, deliberate precision and sly glances, Stellan recalled how he had wanted to shove more than just a roll into her hot mouth.

"Would you...like to try out the bed?" he murmured. Rising from the water, he leaned against the basin's edge. Water cascaded down his chest and abdomen. Clarysa was intently watching the flow.

"Clarysa?"

"In a moment." She dove toward his midsection, sloshing water everywhere.

"What are you--gods of fortune, Clarysa!"

Stellan threw his head back. The way her mouth fondled his swollen shaft shocked him into happy delirium. She licked him from tip to base, her tongue sliding warmly against every hard inch. Her delicate hands closed around his erection, and she experimented with a few pumping motions. Closing his eyes and burying his hands deep into her golden tresses, Stellan envisioned the tub overflowing with his seed if he allowed her to continue unabated.

He was panting by the time she drew the whole length of him into her mouth. Hot. Wet. Tight. Rampant arousal made the contact almost painful. He fantasized about what could be accomplished with a well-aimed thrust. Or should he take her to the bed first? Stellan couldn't decide.

As if in response to his thoughts, Clarysa broke from him. "Didn't you want to try out the bed?"

She glided through the water to the stairs and left the bath. Glancing behind her every few steps, she ran to the bedchamber leaving a trail of wet footprints and giggles in her wake.

Grinning, Stellan quickly followed. Upon reaching the master chamber, he found her buried beneath the covers up to her eyes. In the dusky light from the fire, they glittered like gems. He was so heavy with need. Would he last long enough? *I must.* The woman before him deserved all the pleasure he could give her.

Stellan joined her beneath the bedding. First, he captured a breast in each hand. He devoured each taut peak in turn, eternally grateful he was ravishing the breasts of the naked woman from the Elysian River. He had never imagined such a compassionate and spirited woman could love a dark maverick like himself.

As he massaged her clean, fragrant skin with his hands and mouth, Stellan was grateful for Lionel's eternal wisdom. During a stolen conversation before the wedding, he had confided his inexperience to the worldly duke. Lionel had been most forthcoming, and so Stellan learned that if he touched Clarysa with a finger *thusly* and probed with his tongue *there* it would have a transformative effect.

Only he didn't think there would be a gush of moisture so quickly. Her musky essence coated his lips and tongue. Driven by curiosity, Stellan lifted his head. Clarysa's eyes were shut as her body convulsed. After the episode subsided, she gazed at him with a drowsy, happy expression. Then she reached for his hand and guided it back down between her legs. Stellan understood he should continue by pressing his hand to her *just so.* He lost count of how many times she arched her back in wanton delight.

The earthy, indescribable scent of her drove Stellan to the brink. It was time. He was ready to make her his own. A deep, delicious ache made him tremble. Despite the frigid clime, despite the snow and ice and chilly winds, he would not be alone. He was wanted.

His heart swelled with joy. From now on there would be only love and happiness in Clarysa.

Beautiful, sweet Clarysa.

* * * *

Clarysa stared lovingly at her Dark Prince. He parted her thighs with his strong arms and then anchored himself above her. A tickling sensation exhilarated her sex as he settled himself into position. She marveled at her aroused state. Traces of his delicious touch lingered in every hollow and crevice. He was such an attentive lover, and so patient.

So different from the beast.

But then again, Stellan's blood had been running through the beast's veins. It had shared Stellan's desires. Clarysa braced her hands against his shoulders, stroking them, squeezing them, giddy with anticipation.

How many times had she been lectured about how wicked the Dark Prince was? That she should shun and avoid his perilous kingdom and nefarious ways? Yes, he was so wicked that he had saved Aldebaran almost single-handedly. He deserved her trust and love more than anybody. She rubbed a tear away. *I'm the most fortunate woman in all of the Five Lands.*

He held himself so still above her, yet in the region occluded by shadow and mystery he pulsed hotly with life. Clarysa couldn't help but recall their wayward tryst in the cave. Gratitude filled her heart because they could now complete each other without the ravages of macabre sorcery. This was a moment long in coming, though they had known each other less than a year.

"Dearest, when will you...oh!" She arched her back and raised her hips in response as he joined with her. "Stellan," she whispered as he sank into her, "there's so much of you!"

He grinned wildly. "I'm not done yet." Holding her gaze, he pushed himself in even farther.

Clarysa moaned. "That's...oh..." Her swollen folds enveloped his hard, hot flesh. The feeling prompted a fresh wave of arousal.

Stellan swept his gaze over her bosom, apparently fascinated with the agitation spurred by his thrusts. But then he slowed. "Does it hurt?" Concern lined his sweat-dampened forehead.

"There's some tenderness, but mostly it feels wonderful!" Still, he hesitated. Clarysa slipped both legs and arms around his waist in a feverish grasp. "Harder, my love, as hard as you like!"

He thrust anew. His long, low moan filled her ear. As he pushed, she pulled, and the momentum built with a delicious rush of blood. As her pleasure swelled beyond all reason, Clarysa found it impossible to maintain any semblance of ladylike airs. She grunted lustily in response to his thrusts. When her foot slipped and dragged across the linen, she felt the thrill of her climax reverberate all the way to her toes. Shortly thereafter, Stellan bucked so hard it rather did hurt, but it was a pleasant kind of ache. Nothing was more thrilling than being this close to him.

"Clarysa!" he exclaimed, his voice constricted with urgency. "I'm going to release!"

"Oh yes! Anything you want!"

His hand enclosing her right breast tightened. Clarysa arched up against him as he slammed into her. As her pelvis met his, another orgasm ripped through her.

Stellan roared with such force the walls seemed to tumble down around them. Even the very air crackled with energy, as though they were in the midst of a lightning storm. Over his shoulder, Clarysa thought she saw streaks of ethereal fire leap across the room. *Ah, but it's just my excitement!* She writhed in pleasure as Stellan spread hotness in her so volcanic the linen below became sodden, warm and slick to the touch.

As his body slowed, she hungrily sought his lips and smothered them with her own. He returned the affection and stroked her breasts for a long time. By now, the fire had devoured its last smoldering embers and waned. Clarysa was glad of Stellan's thoughtfulness to wrap the blankets tightly around them, even though he hadn't pulled out of her yet. Then his lips were at her ear.

"I could... I mean, we could...have each other again." He swallowed. "If you'd like."

In the dark, in the master chamber of Vandeborg Castle, in the middle of the frozen wasteland that was the Snowflake Kingdom, Clarysa smiled the happiest smile of her entire life.

Chapter 44

"Stellan, wake up!"

Sprawled across the bed, Stellan turned over, pushing aside the blankets. Drowsiness lapped at him like a friendly kitten.

"Hurry, Stellan, come here! Come look!"

He passed a hand across the mattress. Where was his wife?

"Please, Stellan, *get up!*"

He cracked open an eye. For the first time in years, perhaps since his youth, he felt relaxed upon waking. And warm.

In fact, *very* warm--almost hot, even. Had Clarysa built the fire? How thoughtful!

Rubbing his face, he located Clarysa standing at a nearby window. She had wrapped the white, gauzy curtain around her naked body, inducing blissful memories from the night before. He became rock hard within moments. The woman had such appetites… Sleep suddenly eluded him. "Clarysa, what are you doing? You're much too far away. Come here." He smiled and reached out an arm.

Shaking her head, Clarysa shot him an urgent look. "No, you have to see this! *Please!*" She bounced up and down in her eagerness.

Stellan moaned at the sight and rolled out of bed. Standing behind her, he pushed aside the curtain and wrapped his arms around her waist.

"Look at the view," she cried.

He grinned as he looked down, devouring her neck and shoulders with his lips. "Breathtaking," he murmured. Reaching down, he parted her thighs, pressing his palm against the place that had given him so much enjoyment mere hours before. His hand came away moist. *Gods!* He would simply have to take her right there, right now.

Clarysa wriggled. "Not me, silly! Out the window!"

His gaze followed her pointing finger. The sight that met his eyes was enough to momentarily distract him.

The sun shone.

Water cascaded down the glass.

Patches of green spotted the castle grounds.

Stellan's heart skipped a beat. *The snow is melting.*

He barely had time to assimilate it all when a loud knock sounded at the door. Clarysa squealed and sprinted away to put on some clothes. The knocking continued, followed by a pair of excited voices.

"Have patience. We're coming," Stellan said.

As soon as they had dressed, Clarysa threw open the door. Gretchen and Ghyslain stood there, laughing and grinning like a pair of drunkards. They pulled Stellan and Clarysa with them, and all four ran down the passageway.

They arrived breathlessly at the main entrance. Froll stood there, rubbing his belly and beaming. He pointed to the floor, which lay buried under several inches of water. Wading through the miniature pond, Stellan led Clarysa outside. He shielded his eyes against the bright, yellow sun as it shone in a clear, deep blue sky. Water dripped and plopped all around them as the snow surrendered to the morning heat.

Gretchen dragged Clarysa and him to one part of the outer castle wall. "I think you should see this," she told them, and pointed to a small brass plaque embedded in the stone.

Stellan and Clarysa leaned forward to read the inscription it bore:

I found true love yet still I paid the price
And now this castle rests in snow and ice
When bravest love arrives at last to stay
At once the snow and ice will melt away
--King Darius the Seventh of Vandeborg

Meet the Author

Heather Massey is a lifelong fan of science fiction romance. She searches for sci-fi romance adventures aboard her blog, The Galaxy Express (www.thegalaxyexpress.net).

She's also an author. Indeed, she wrote a fairy tale romance in addition to her sci-fi romances. Why? Because, honestly, who can resist an opportunity to reinvent a classic tale like "Beauty and the Beast"? Certainly not Heather Massey!

Her stories will entertain you with fantastical settings, larger-than-life characters, timeless romance, and rollicking action. So sit back, relax, and pour yourself a cup of space java as the stories unfold. You deserve it.

When Heather's not reading or writing, she's watching cult films and enjoying the company of her husband and daughter. To learn more about her work, visit www.heathermassey.com